PENNY PLAIN

This is the story of how Jean Jardine finds riches and romance in the Scottish town of Priorsford. Her father was in the Indian Civil Service, but when Jean and her two younger brothers were orphaned they were brought up at The Rigs in Priorsford by Great-aunt Alison. To Jean eventually falls the lot of caring for her brothers and The Mhor, their young step-brother, who is a source of great amusement and delight to them all.

O. DOUGLAS

Penny Plain

Complete and Unabridged

ULVERSCROFT
Leicester

First published 1920

First Large Print Edition
published December 1974
SBN 85456 302 4

This special large print edition is
made and printed in England for
F. A. Thorpe, Glenfield, Leicestershire

to my brother
WALTER

1

"The actors are at hand
And by their show
You shall know all that you are like to know"
"MIDSUMMER NIGHT'S DREAM"

IT was tea-time in Priorsford: four-thirty by the clock on a chill October afternoon.

The hills circling the little town were shrouded with mist. The wide bridge that spanned the Tweed and divided the town proper — the Highgate, the Nethergate, the Eastgate — from the residential part was almost deserted. On the left bank of the river, Peel Tower looked ghostly in the gathering dusk. Round its grey walls still stood woods of larch and fir, and in front the links of Tweed moved through pleasant green pastures. But where once ladies on palfreys hung with bells hunted with their cavaliers there now stood the neat little dwellings of prosperous decent folk; and where the good King James wrote his rhymes, and listened to the singing of Mass

I

from the Virgin's Chapel, the Parish Kirk reared a sternly Presbyterian steeple. No need any longer for Peel to light the beacon telling of the coming of our troublesome English neighbours. Telegraph wires now carried the matter, and a large bus met them at the trains and conveyed them to that flamboyant pile in red stone, with its glorious views, its medicinal baths, and its band-enlivened meals, known as Priorsford Hydropathic.

As I have said, it was tea-time in Priorsford.

The schools had *skailed*, and the children, finding in the weather little encouragement to linger, had gone to their homes. In the little houses down by the riverside brown teapots stood on the hobs, and rosy-faced women cut bread and buttered scones, and slapped their children with a fine impartiality; while in the big houses on the Hill, servants, walking delicately, laid out tempting tea-tables, and the solacing smell of hot toast filled the air.

Most of the smaller houses in Priorsford were very much of one pattern and all fairly recently built, but there was one old house, an odd little rough stone cottage, standing

2

at the end of a row of villas, its back turned to its parvenu neighbours, its eyes lifted to the hills. A flagged path led up to the front door through a herbaceous border, which now only held a few chrysanthemums and Michaelmas daisies (Perdita would have scorned them as flowers for the old age), but in spring and in summer blazed in a sweet disorder of old-fashioned blossoms.

This little house was called The Rigs.

It was a queer little house, and a queer little family lived in it. Jardine was their name, and they sat together in their living room on this October evening. Generally they all talked at once and the loudest voice prevailed, but tonight there was not so much competition, and Jean frequently found herself holding the floor alone.

David, busy packing books into a wooden box, was the reason for the comparative quiet. He was nineteen, and in the morning he was going to Oxford to begin his first term there. He had so long looked forward to it that he felt dazed by the nearness of his goal. He was a good-looking boy, with honest eyes and a firm mouth.

His only sister, Jean, four years older

than himself, left the table and sat on the edge of the box watching him. She did not offer to help, for she knew that every man knows best how to pack his own books, but she hummed a gay tune to prove to herself how happy was the occasion, and once she patted David's grey tweed shoulder as he leant over her. Perhaps she felt that he needed encouragement this last night at home.

Jock, the other brother, a schoolboy of fourteen, with a rough head and a voice over which he had no control, was still at the tea-table. He was rather ashamed of his appetite, but ate doggedly. "It's not that I'm hungry just now," he would say, "but I so soon get hungry."

At the far end of the room, in a deep window, a small boy, with a dog and a cat, was playing at being on a raft. The boy's name was Gervase Taunton, but he was known to a large circle of acquaintances as "the Mhor", which, as Jean would have explained to you, is Gaelic for "the great one". Thus had greatness been thrust upon him. He was seven, and he had lived at The Rigs since he was two. He was a handsome child, with an almost uncanny charm of manner, and a gift of make-believe that made his days one long excitement.

He now stood like some "grave Tyrian trader" on the table turned upside down that was his raft, as serious and intent as if it had been the navy of Tarshish bringing Solomon gold and silver, ivory and apes and peacocks. With one arm he clutched the cat and assured that unwilling voyager, "You're on the dangerous sea, me old puss. You don't want to be drowned, do you?" The cat struggled and scratched. "Then go — to your doom!"

He clasped his hands behind him in a Napoleonic manner and stood gloomily watching the unembarrassed progress of the cat across the carpet, while Peter (a fox-terrier, and the wickedest dog in Priorsford) crushed against his legs to show how faithful he was compared to any kind of cat.

"Haven't you finished eating yet, Jock?" Jean asked. "Here is Mrs. M'Cosh for the tea-things."

The only servant The Rigs possessed was a middle-aged woman the widow of one Andrew M'Cosh, a Clyde riveter, who had drifted from her native city of Glasgow to Priorsford. She had a sweet, worn face, and a neat cap, with a black velvet bow in front.

Jock rose from the table reluctantly, and was at once hailed by the Mhor and invited on to the raft.

Jock hesitated, but he was the soul of good nature. "Well, only for five minutes, remember. I've a lot of lessons tonight."

He sat down on the upturned table, his legs sprawling on the carpet, and hummed "Tom Bowling", but the Mhor leaned from his post as steersman and said gravely, "Don't dangle your legs, Jock; there are sharks in these waters." So Jock obediently crumpled his legs until his chin rested on his knees.

Mrs. M'Cosh piled the tea-things on a tray and folded the cloth. "Ay, Peter," she said, catching sight of that notorious character, "ye look real good, but I wis hearin' ye were efter the sheep again the day."

Peter turned away his head as if deeply shocked at the accusation, and Mrs. M'Cosh, with the tea-cloth over her arm, regarded him with an indulgent smile. She had infinite tolerance for Peter's shortcomings.

"Peter was kinna later last night," she would say, as if referring to an erring husband, "an' I juist sat up for him." She had also infinite leisure. It was no use Jean trying to hurry the work forward by offering to do some task. Mrs. M'Cosh simply stood beside her and conversed until the job was done. Jean never knew whether to laugh or be cross, but she generally laughed.

Once when the house had been upset by illness, and trained nurses were in occupation, Jean had rung the bell repeatedly, and, receiving no answer, had gone to the kitchen. There she found the Mhor, then a very small boy, seated on a chair playing a mouth-organ; while Mrs. M'Cosh, her skirts held coquettishly aloft, danced a few steps to the music. Jean — being Jean — had withdrawn unnoticed and slipped upstairs to the sick-room much cheered by the sight of such detachment.

Mrs. M'Cosh had been eight years with the Jardines, and was in many ways such a treasure, and always such an amusement, that they would not have parted from her for much red gold.

"Bella Bathgate's expectin' her lodger the morn." The tea-tray was ready to be carried away, but Mrs. M'Cosh lingered.

"Oh, is she?" said Jean. "Who is it that's coming?"

"I canna mind the exact name, but she's ca'ed the Honourable an' she's bringin' a leddy's maid."

"Gosh, Maggie!" ejaculated Jock.

"I asked you not to say that, Jock," Jean reminded him.

"Ay." Mrs. M'Cosh continued, "Bella Bathgate's kinna pit oot aboot it. She disna ken how she's to cook for an Honourable — she niver saw yin."

"Have you seen one?" Jock asked.

"No' that I know of, but when I wis pew opener at St. George's I let in some verra braw folk. One Sunday there wis a lord, no less. A shaughly wee buddy he wis tae. Ma Andra wud hae been gled to see him sae oorit."

The eyes of the Jardines were turned inquiringly on their handmaid. It seemed a strange reason for joy on the part of the late Andrew M'Cosh.

"Weel," his widow explained, "ye see, Andra wis a Socialist an' thocht naething o' lords — naething. I used to show him pictures o' them in the *Heartsease Library* —

8

fine-lukin' fellays wi' black mustacheys —
but he juist aye said, 'It's easy to draw a
pictur,' and he wouldna own that they wis
onything but meeserable to look at. An',
mind you, he wis richt. When I saw the
lord in St. George's, I said to masel',
'Andra wis richt,' I says." She lifted up the
tray and prepared to depart. "Weel, he'll
not be muckle troubled wi' them whaur
he's gone, puir man. The Bible says, Not
many great, not many noble."

"D'you think," said Mhor in a pleasantly
interested voice, "that Mr. M'Cosh is in
heaven?" (Mhor never let slip an opportunity for theological discussions.) "I
wouldn't care much to go to heaven myself,
for all my friends are in" — he stopped and
cast a cautious glance at Jean, and, judging
by her expression that discretion was the
better of valour, and in spite of an en-
couraging twinkle in the eyes of Jock,
finished demurely — "the Other Place."

"Haw, haw," laughed Jock, who was
consistently amused by Mhor and his
antics. "I'm sorry for your friends, old
chap. Do I know them?"

"Well," said Mhor, "there's Napoleon
and Dick Turpin and Graham of Claver-

house and also Prince Charlie and — "

"Mhor — you're talking too much," said David, who was jotting down figures in a notebook.

"It's to be hoped," said Jean to Mrs. M'Cosh, "that the honourable lady will suit Bella Bathgate, for Bella, honest woman, won't put herself about to suit anybody. But she's been a good neighbour to us. I always feel so safe with her near; she's equal to anything from a burst pipe to a broken arm . . . I do hope that landlord of ours in London will never take it into his head to come back and live in Priorsford. If we had to leave The Rigs and Bella Bathgate I simply don't know what we'd do."

"We could easy get a hoose wi' mair conveniences," Mrs. M'Cosh reminded her. She had laid down the tray again and stood with her hands on her hips and her head on one side, deeply interested. "Thae wee new villas in the Langhope Road are a fair treat, wi' a pantry aff the dining-room an' hot and cold everywhere."

"*Villas*," said Jean — "hateful new villas! What are conveniences compared to old, thick walls and queer windows and little, funny stairs? Besides, The Rigs has a soul."

"Oh, mercy!" said Mrs. M'Cosh, picking up the tray and moving at last to the door; "that's fair heathenish!"

Jean laughed as the door shut on their retainer, and perched herself on the end of the big old-fashioned sofa drawn up at one side of the fire. She wore a loose stockinette brown dress and looked rather like a wood elf of sorts, with her golden-brown hair and eyes.

"If I were rich," she said, "I would buy an annuity for Mrs. M'Cosh of at least £200 a year. When you think that she once had a house and a husband, and a best room with an overmantel and a Brussels carpet, and lost them all, and is contented to be a servant to us, with no prospect of anything for her old age but the workhouse or the charity of relations, and keeps cheery and never makes a moan and never loses her interest in things . . ."

"But you're *not* rich," said Jock.

"No," said Jean, ruefully. "Isn't it odd than no one ever leaves us a legacy? But I needn't say that, for it would be much odder if anyone did. I don't think there is a single human being in the world entitled to leave us a penny piece. We are destitute of relations. . . . Oh, well, I daresay we'll get on without a legacy, but for your comfort I'll read to you about the sort of house we would have if some kind creature did leave us one."

She dived for a copy of *Country Life* that was lying on the sofa, and turned to the advertisements of houses to let and sell.

"It is good of Mrs. Jowett letting us have this every week. It's a great support to me. I wonder if anyone ever does buy these houses, or if they are merely there to tantalise poor folk? Will this do? "A finely timbered sporting estate — seventeen bed-rooms — ' "

"Too small," said Jock from his cramped position on the raft.

" 'A beautiful little property — ' No. Oh, listen. "A characteristic Cotswold Tudor House' — doesn't that sound de-licious? 'Mullioned windows. Fine suite of reception-rooms, ballroom. Lovely garden, with trout-stream intersecting' — heavenly! 'There are vineries, greenhouses, and pits' — what do you do with pits?"

"Keep bears in them, of course," said

Jock, and added vaguely — "bear baiting, you know."

"It isn't usual to keep bears," David pointed out.

"No; but if you *had* them," Jock insisted, "you would want pits to keep them in."

"Jock," said Jean, "you are like the White Knight when Alice told him it wasn't likely that there would be any mice on the horse's back. 'Not very likely, perhaps, but if they *do* come I don't choose to have them running all about.' But I agree with the White Knight, it's as well to be provided for everything, so we'll keep the pits in case of bears."

"They had pits in the Bible," said Mhor dreamily, as he screwed and unscrewed his steering-wheel, which was also the piano stool; "for Joseph was put in one."

Jean turned over the leaves of the magazine, studying each pictured house, gloating over details of beauty and of age, then she pushed it away with a "Heigh-ho, but I wish we had a Tudor residence."

"I'll buy you one," said David, "when I'm Lord Chancellor."

"Thank you, David," said Jean.

By this time the raft had been sunk by

a sudden storm, and Jock had grasped the opportunity to go to his books; while Mhor and Peter had laid themselves down on the rug before the fire, and were rolling on each other in great content.

Jean and David sat together on the sofa, their arms linked. They had very little to say, for as the time of departure approaches conversation dies at the fount.

Jean was trying to think what their mother would have said, on this last evening, to her boy who was going out into the world. Never had she felt so inadequate. Ought she to say things to him? Warn him against lurking evils? (Jean who knew about as much of evil as a "committed linnet"!) But David was such a wise boy and so careful. It always pinched Jean's heart to see him dole out his slender stock of money, for there never was a Jardine born who did not love to be generous.

She looked at him fondly, "I do hope you won't find it too much of a pinch, David. The worst of it is, you will be with people with heaps of money, and I'm afraid you'll hate to feel shabby."

"It's no crime to be poor," said David, stoutly. "I'll manage all right. Don't you worry. What I hate is thinking you are scrimping to give me every spare penny — but I'll work my hardest."

"I know you'll do that, but play too — every minute you can spare. I don't want you to shut yourself up among books. Try and get all the good of Oxford. Remember, Sonny, this is your youth, and whatever you may get later you can never get that back." She leaned back and gave a great sigh. "How I wish I could make this a splendid time for you, but I can't, my dear, I can't . . . Anyway, nobody will have better china. I've given you six of Aunt Alison's rosy ones; I hope the scout won't break them. And your tablecloths and sheets and towels are all right, thanks to our great-aunt's stores. . . . And you'll write as often as you can and tell us everything, if you get a nice scout, and all about your rooms, and if cushions would be any use, and oh, my dear, *eat* as much as you can — don't save on food."

"Of course not," said David. "But several nights a week I'll feed in my own room. You don't need to go to Hall to dinner."

He got up from the sofa and went and

stood before the fire, keeping his head very much in the air and his hands in his pockets. He was feeling that home was a singularly warm, kind place, and that the great world was cold and full of strangers; so he whistled "D'ye ken John Peel?" and squared his shoulders and did not in the least deceive his sister Jean.

"Peter, me faithful hound," said the Mhor, hugging the patient dog. "What would you like to play at?"

Peter looked supremely indifferent.

"Red Indians?"

Peter licked the earnest face so near his own.

The Mhor wiped his face with the back of his hand (his morning's handkerchief, which he alluded to as "me useful little hanky", being used for all manner of purposes not intended by the inventor of handkerchiefs, was quite unpresentable by evening) and said:

"I know. Let's play at 'Suppose'. Jean, let's play at 'Suppose'."

"Don't worry, darling," said Jean.

The Mhor turned to Jock, who was sitting at a table with his head bent over a book.

"Jock, let's play at 'Suppose'."

"Shut up," said Jock.

"David." The Mhor turned to his last hope. "*Seeing* it's your last night."

David never could resist the Mhor when he was beseeching.

"Well, only for ten minutes, remember."

Mhor looked fixedly at the clock, measuring with his eye the space of ten minutes, then nodded, murmuring to himself, "From there to there. You begin, Jean."

"I can't think of anything," said Jean. Then seeing Mhor's eager face cloud, she began: "Suppose when David was in the train tomorrow he heard a scuffling under the seat, and he looked and saw a grubby little boy and a fox-terrier, and he said, 'Come out, Mhor and Peter.' And suppose they went with him all the way to Oxford, and when they got to the college they crept upstairs without being seen and the scout was a kind scout and liked dogs and naughty boys, and he gave them a splendid supper — "

"What did he give them?" Mhor asked.

"Chicken and boiled ham and meringues and sugar biscuits and lemonade" (mentioning a few of Mhor's favourite articles of food), "and he tucked them up on the sofa and they slept till morning, and got into the train and came home, and that's all."

"Me next," said Mhor. "Suppose they didn't come home again. Suppose they started from Oxford and went all round the world. And I met a magician — in India that was — and he gave me an elephant with a gold howdah on its back and I wasn't frightened for it — such a meek, gentle, dirty animal — and Peter and me sat on it and pulled off coconuts with its trunk and handed them back to us, and we lived there always, and I had a Newfoundland pup, and Peter had a golden crown because he was king of all the dogs, and I never went to bed and nobody ever washed my ears and we made toffee every day, every single day . . ." His voice trailed away into silence as he contemplated this blissful vision, and Jock, wooed from his Greek verbs by the interest of the game, burst in with his unmanageable voice:

"Suppose a Russian man-of-war came up Tweed and started shelling Priorsford, and the Parish church was hit and the steeple fell into Thomson's shop, and scattered the haddocks and kippers and things all over the street, and — "

"Did you pick them up, Jock?" squealed Mhor, who regarded Jock as the greatest living humorist, and now at the thought of the scattered kippers wallowed on the floor with laughter.

Jock continued: "And another shell blew the turrety thing off The Towers and blew Mrs. Duff-Whalley right over the West Law and landed her in Caddon Burn — "

"Hurray!" yelled Mhor.

Jock was preparing for a further flight of fancy, when Mrs. M'Cosh, having finished washing the dishes, came in to say that Thomson had never sent the sausages for Mr. David's breakfast, and she could not see him depart for England unfortified by sausages and poached eggs.

"I'll just slip down and get them," she announced, being by no means averse to a stroll along the lighted Highgate. It was certainly neither Argyle Street nor the Paisley Road, but it bore a far-off resemblance to those gay places, and for that Mrs. M'Cosh was thankful. There was a cinema, too, and that was a touch of home. Talking over Priorsford with Glasgow friends she would say, "It's no' juist whit I wud ca' the deid country — no juist paraffin-ile and glaury roads, ye ken. We hev gas an' plain-stanes an' a pictur hoose."

When Mrs. M'Cosh left the room Jock returned to his books, and the thought of the Mhor, his imagination fermenting with the thought of bombs on Priorsford, retired to the window-seat to think out further damage.

Some hours later, when Jock and Mhor were fast asleep and David, his packing finished, was preparing to go to bed, Jean slipped into the room.

She stood looking at the open trunk on the floor, at the shelves from which the books had been taken, at the empty boot cupboard.

Two large tears rolled over her face, but she managed to say quite gaily, "December will soon be here."

"In no time at all," said David.

Jean was carrying a little book, which she now laid on the dressing table, and, giving it a push in her brother's direction, "It's a *Daily Light*," she explained.

David did not offer to look at the gift, which was the traditional Jardine gift to travellers, a custom descending from Great-aunt Alison. He stood a bit away and said, "All right."

And Jean understood, and said nothing of what was in her heart.

2

"They have their exits and their entrances"
"AS YOU LIKE IT"

THE ten o'clock express from Euston to Scotland was tearing along on its daily journey. It was that barren hour in the afternoon when luncheon is over and forgotten, and tea is yet far distant, and most of the passengers were either asleep or listlessly trying to read light literature.

Alone in a first-class carriage sat Bella Bathgate's lodger — Miss Pamela Reston. A dressing-bag and a fur-coat and a pile of books and magazines lay on the opposite seat, and the lodger sat writing busily. An envelope lay beside her addressed to

THE LORD BIDBOROUGH,
c/o KING, KING & CO.,
BOMBAY.

The letter ran:
"DEAR BIDDY — We have always agreed,

22

you and I (forgive the abruptness of this beginning), that we would each live our own life. Your idea of living was to range over the world in search of sport, mine to amuse myself well, to shine, to be admired. You, I imagine from your letters (what a faithful correspondent you have been, Biddy, all your wandering life), are still finding zest in it: mine has palled. You will jump naturally to the brotherly conclusion that *I* have palled — that I cease to amuse, that I find mysell taking a second or even a third place, I who was always first; that, in short, I am a soured and disappointed woman.

"Honestly I don't think that is so. I am still beautiful: I am more sympathetic than in my somewhat callous youth, therefore more popular: I am good company: I have the influence that money carries with it, and I could even now make what is known as a 'brilliant' marriage. Did you ever wonder — everybody else did, I know — why I never married? Simply, my dear, because the only man I cared for didn't ask me . . . and now I am forty. (How stark and almost indecent it looks written down like that!) At forty, one is supposed to have got over all youthful fancies and disappointments, and lately it has seemed to me reasonable to contemplate a common-sense marriage. A politician, wise, honoured, powerful — and sixty. What could be more suitable? So suitable that I ran away — an absurdly young thing to do at forty — and I am writing to you in the train on my way to Scotland . . . You see, Biddy, I quite suddenly saw myself growing old, saw all the arid years in front of me, and saw that it was a very dreadful thing to grow old caring only for the things of time. It frightened me badly. I don't want to go in bondage to the fear of age and death. I want to grow old decently, and I am sure one ought to begin quite early learning how.

" 'Clear eyes do dim at last
    And cheeks outlive their rose;
Time, heedless of the past,
    No loving kindness knows.'

Yes, and 'youth's a stuff will not endure,' and 'golden lads and girls all must like chimney-sweepers come to dust'. The poets aren't at all helpful, for youth — poor, brave youth — won't listen to their warn-

24

ings, and they seem to have no consolation to offer to middle age.

"The odd thing is that up to a week or two ago I greatly liked the life I led. You said it would kill you in a month. Was it only last May that you pranced in the drawing-room in Grosvenor Street inveighing against 'the whole beastly show', as you called it — the freak fashions, the ugly eccentric dances, the costly pageant balls, the shouldering, the striving, the worship of money, the gambling, the self-advertisement — all the abject vulgarity of it? And my set, the artistic, soulful, literary set, you said was the worst of all: you actually described the high-priestess as looking like a 'decomposing cod-fish', and added by way of a final insult that you thought the woman had a kind heart.

"And I laughed and thought the War had changed you. It didn't change me, to my shame be it said. I thought I was doing wonders posing about in a head-dress at Red Cross meetings, and getting up entertainments, and even my never-ceasing anxiety about you simply seemed to make me more keen about amusing myself.

"Do you remember a story we liked when

we were children, *The Gold of Fairnilee*? Do you remember how Randall, carried away by the fairies, lived contented until his eyes were touched with the truth-telling water, and when Fairyland lost its glamour and he longed for the old earth he had left, and the changes of summer and autumn, and the streams of Tweed and his friends?

"Is it, do you suppose, because we had a Scots mother that I find, deep down within me, that I am 'full of seriousness'? It is rather disconcerting to think oneself a butterfly and find out suddenly that one is a — what? A bread-and-butter fly, shall we say? Something quite solid, anyway.

"As I say, I suddenly became deadly sick of everything. I simply couldn't go on. And it was no use going burying myself at Bidborough or even dear Mintern Abbas; it would have been the same sort of trammelled, artificial existence. I wanted something utterly different. Scotland seemed to call to me — not the Scotland we know, not the shooting, yachting, West Island Scotland — but the Lowlands, the Borders, our mother's countryside.

"I remembered how Lewis Elliot (I

wonder where he is now — it is ages since I heard of him) used to tell us about a little town on the Tweed called Priorsford. It was his own little town, his birthplace, and I thought the name sung itself like a song. I made inquiries about rooms and found that in a little house called Hillview, owned by one Bella Bathgate, I might lodge. I liked the name of the house and its owner, and I hope to find in Priorsford peace and great content.

"Having been more or less of a fool for forty years, I am now going to try to get understanding. It won't be easy, for we are told that 'it cannot be gotten with gold, neither shall silver be weighed for the price thereof. . . . No mention shall be made of coral and pearls: for the price of wisdom is above rubies'.

"I am going to walk on the hills all day, and in the evening I shall read the Book of Job, and Shakespeare and Sir Walter .

"In one of the Jungle Books there was a man called Sir Purun Dass — do you remember ? Sir Purun Dass, K.C.I.E., who left all his honours and slipped out one day to the sun-baked highway with nothing but an ochre-coloured garment and a beggar's bowl. I always envied that man. Not that I could rise to such Oriental heights. The beggar's bowl wouldn't do for me. I cling to my comforts: also, I am sure Sir Purun Dass left himself no loophole whereby he might slip back to his official position, whereas I — Well, the Politician thinks I have gone for a three months' rest-cure, and at sixty, one is not impatient. You will say, 'How like Pam!' Yes; isn't it? I always was given to leaving myself loopholes; but, all the same, I am not going to face an old age bolstered up by bridge and cosmetics. There must be other props, and I mean to find them. I mean to possess my soul. I'm not all froth, but, if I am, Priorsford will reveal it. I feel that there will be something very revealing about Miss Bella Bathgate.

"Poor Biddy, to have such an effusion hurled at you!

"But you'll admit I don't often mention my soul.

"I doubt if you will be able to read this letter. If you can make it out, forgive it being so full of myself. The next will be full of quite other things. All my love, Biddy. — Yours,   PAM."

Three hours later the express stopped at the junction. The train was waiting on the branch line that terminated at Priorsford, and after a breathless rush over a high bridge in the dark, Pamela and her maid, Mawson, found themselves bestowed in an empty carriage by a fatherly porter.

Mawson was not a real lady's maid: one realised that at once. She had been a house-maid for some years in the house in Grosvenor Street, and Pamela, when her own most superior maid had flatly refused to accompany her on this expedition, had asked Mawson to be her maid, and Mawson had gladly accepted the offer. She was a middle-aged woman with a small brown face, an obvious *toupée*, and an adventurous spirit.

She now tidied the carriage violently, carefully hiding the book Pamela had been reading and putting the cushion on the rack. Finally, tucking the travelling-rug firmly round her mistress, she remarked pleasantly, "A h'eight hours journey without an 'itch!"

"Certainly without an aitch," thought Pamela, as she said, "You like travelling, Mawson?"

"Oh yes, m'm. I always 'ave 'ad a desire to travel. Specially, if I may say so, to see Scotland, Miss. But, oh, ain't it bleak? Before it was dark I 'ad me eyes glued to the window, lookin' out. Such miles of 'eather and big stones and torrents, Miss, and nothing to be seen but a lonely sheep — 'ardly an 'ouse on the 'orizon. It gave me quite a turn."

"And this is nothing to the Highlands, Mawson."

"Ain't it, Miss? Well, it's the bleakest I've seen yet, an' I've been to Brighton and Blackpool. Travelled quite a lot, I 'ave, Miss. The lydy who read me 'and said I would, for me teeth are so wide apart." Which cryptic saying puzzled Pamela until Priorsford was reached, when other things engaged her attention.

There was another passenger for Priorsford in the London express. He was called Peter Reid, and he was as short and plain as his name. Peter Reid was returning to his native town a very rich man. He had left it a youth of eighteen and entered the business of a well-to-do uncle in London, and since then, as the saying is, he had

30

never looked over his shoulder; fortune showered her gifts on him, and everything he touched seemed to turn to gold.

While his mother lived he had visited her regularly, but for thirty years his mother had been lying in Priorsford churchyard, and he had not cared to keep in touch with the few old friends he had. For forty-five years he had lived in London, so there was almost nothing of Priorsford left in him — nothing, indeed, except the desire to see it again before he died.

They had been forty-five quite happy years for Peter Reid. Money-making was the thing he enjoyed most in this world. It took the place to him of wife and children and friends. He did not really care much for the things money could buy; he only cared to heap up gold, to pull down barns and build greater ones. Then suddenly one day he was warned that his soul would be required of him — that soul of his for which he had cared so little. After more than sixty years of health, he found his body failing him. In great irritation, but without alarm, he went to see a specialist, one Lauder, in Wimpole Street.

He supposed he would be made to take a

holiday, and grudged the time that would be lost. He grudged also, the doctor's fee.

"Well, he said, when the examination was over, "how long are you going to keep me from my work?"

The doctor looked at him thoughtfully. He was quite a young man, tall, fair-headed, and fresh-coloured, with a look about him of vigorous health that was heartening and must have been a great asset to him in his profession.

"I am going to advise you not to go back to work at all."

"*What!*" cried Peter Reid, getting very red, for he was not accustomed to being patient when people gave him unpalatable advice. Then something that he saw — was it pity? — in the doctor's face made him white and faint.

"You — you can't mean that I'm really ill?"

"You may live for years — with care."

"I shall get another opinion," said Peter Reid.

"Certainly — here, sit down." The doctor felt very sorry for this hard, little business man whose world had fallen about his ears. Peter Reid sat down heavily on the chair the doctor gave him. "I tell you, I don't feel ill — not to speak of. And I've no time to be ill. I have a deal on just now that I stand to make thousands out of — thousands, I tell you."

"I'm sorry," James Lauder said.

"Of course, I'll see another man, though it means throwing away more money. But" — his face fell — "they told me you were the best man for the heart. . . . Leave my work! The thing's ridiculous. Patch me up and I'll go on till I drop. How long do you give me?"

"As I said, you may live for years; on the other hand, you may go very suddenly."

Peter Reid sat silent for a minute; then he broke out:

"Who am I to leave my money to? Tell me that."

He spoke as if the doctor were to blame for the sentence he had pronounced.

"Haven't you relations?"

"None."

"The hospitals are always glad of funds."

"I dare say, but they won't get them from me. I promise you that."

"Have you no great friends — no one you are interested in?"

33

"I've hundreds of acquaintances," said the rich man, "but no one has ever done anything for me for nothing — no one."

James Lauder looked at the hard-faced, little man and allowed himself to wonder how far his patient had encouraged kindness.

A pause.

"I think I'll go home," said Peter Reid.

"The servant will call you a taxi. Where do you live?"

Peter Reid looked at the doctor as if he hardly understood.

"Live?" he said. "Oh, in Prince's Gate. But that isn't home. . . . I'm going to Scotland."

"Ah," said James Lauder, "now you're talking. What part of Scotland is 'home' to you?"

"A place they call Priorsford. I was born there."

"I know it. I've fished all round there. A fine countryside."

Interest lit for a moment the dull, grey eyes of Peter Reid.

"I haven't fished," he said, "since I was a boy. Did you ever try the Caddon Burn? There are some fine pools in it. I once lost a big fellow in it and came over the hills a disappointed laddie. . . . I remember what a fine tea my mother had for me." He reached for his hat and gave a half-ashamed laugh.

"How one remembers things! Well, I'll go. What do you say the other man's name is? Yes — yes. Life's a short drag; it's hardly worth beginning. I wish, though, I'd never come near you, and I would have gone on happily till I dropped. But I won't leave my money to any charity, mind that!"

He walked towards the door and turned.

"I'll leave it to the first person who does something for me without expecting any return. . . . By the way, what do I owe you?"

And Peter Reid went away exceedingly sorrowful, for he had great possessions.

3

"It is the only set of the kind I ever met with in which you are neither led nor driven, but actually fall, and that imperceptibly, into literary topics, and I attribute it to this that in that house literature is not a treat for company upon invitation days, but it is actually the daily bread of the family."
— WRITTEN OF MARIA EDGEWORTH'S HOME

PAMELA RESTON stood in Bella Bathgate's parlour and surveyed it disconsolately.

It was papered in a trying shade of terra-cotta and the walls were embellished by enlarged photographs of the Bathgate family — decent, well-living people, but plain-headed to a degree. Linoleum covered the floor. A round table with a red-and-green cloth occupied the middle of the room, and two arm-chairs and six small chairs stood about stiffly like sentinels. Pamela had tried them all and found each one more unyielding than the next. The mantelshelf, painted to look like some

36

uncommon kind of marble, supported two tall glass jars, bright blue and adorned with white, raised flowers, which contained bunches of dried grasses ("silver shekels" Miss Bathgate called them), rather dusty and tired looking. A mahogany sideboard stood against one wall and was heavily laden with vases and photographs. Hard lace curtains tinted a deep cream shaded the bow-window.

"This is grim," said Pamela to herself. "Something must be done. First of all, I must get them to send me some rugs — they will cover this awful floor — and half a dozen cushions and some curtains and bits of embroidery and some table linen and sheets and things. Idiot that I was not to bring them with me! . . . And what could I do to the walls ? I don't know how far one may go with landladies, but I hardly think one could ask them to re-paper walls to each stray lodger's liking."

Miss Bathgate had not so far shown herself much inclined for conversation. She had met her lodger on the doorstep the night before, had uttered a few words of greeting, and had then confined herself to warning the man to watch the walls when he carried up the trunks, and to wondering aloud what anyone could want with so much luggage, and where in the world it was to find room. She had been asked to have dinner ready, and at eight o'clock Pamela had come down to the sitting-room to find a coarse cloth folded in two and spread on one-half of the round table. A knife, a fork, a spoon lay on the cloth, flanked on one side by an enormous cruet and on the other by four large spoons, laid crosswise, and a thick tumbler. An aspidistra in a pot completed the table decorations.

The dinner consisted of stewed steak, with turnip and carrots, and a large dish of potatoes, followed by a rice pudding made without eggs, and a glass dish of prunes.

Pamela was determined to be pleased.

"How *right* it all is," she told herself — "so entirely in keeping. All so clean and — and sufficient. I am sure all the things we hang on ourselves and round ourselves to please and beautify are very clogging — this is life at its simplest," and she rang for coffee, which came in a breakfast-cup and was made of Somebody's essence and boiling water.

Pamela had gone to bed very early, there being absolutely nothing to sit up for; and the bed was as hard as the nether millstone. As she put her tired head on a cast-iron pillow covered by a cotton pillow-slip, and lay crushed under three pairs of hard blankets topped by a patchwork quilt worked by Bella's mother and containing samples of the clothes of all the family — from the late Mrs. Bathgate's wedding-gown of puce-coloured cashmere to her youngest son's first pair of "breeks," the whole smelling strongly of naphtha from the *kist* where it had laid — regretful thoughts of other beds came to her. She felt she had not fully appreciated them — those warm, soft, embracing beds, with satin-smooth sheets and pillow-cases smelling of lavender and other sweet things, feather-light blankets, and rose-coloured eiderdowns.

She came downstairs in the morning to the bleak sitting-room filled with a distaste for simplicity which she felt to be unworthy. For breakfast there was a whole loaf on a platter, three breakfast rolls hot from the baker, and the family toast-rack full of tough, damp toast. A large pale-green duck's egg sat heavily in an egg-cup, capped, but not covered, by a strange, red flannel thing representing a cock's head, which Pamela learned later was called an "egg-cosy", and had come from the sale of work for Foreign Missions. A metal teapot and water-jug stood in two green worsted nests.

Pamela poured herself out some tea. "I'm almost sure I told her I wanted coffee in the morning," she murmured to herself; "but it doesn't matter." Already she was beginning to hold Bella Bathgate in awe. She took the top off the duck's egg and looked at it in an interested way. "It's a beautiful colour — orange — but" — she pushed it away — "I don't think I can eat it."

She drank some tea and ate a baker's roll, which was excellent; then she rang the bell.

When Bella appeared she at once noticed the headless but uneaten egg, and, taking it up, smelt it.

"What's wrang wi' the egg?" she demanded.

"Oh, nothing," said Pamela quickly. "It's a lovely egg really, such a beautiful colour, but" — she laughed apologetically — "you know how it is with eggs — either you can eat them or you can't. I always have to eat eggs with my head turned away, so to speak. There is something about the yolk so — so — " Her voice trailed away under Miss Bathgate's stolid, unsmiling gaze.

There was no point in going on being arch about eggs to a person who so obviously regarded one as a poor creature. But a stand must be taken.

" — Er — Miss Bathgate — " Pamela began.

There was no answer from Bella, who was putting the dishes on a tray. Had she addressed her rightly?

"You *are* Miss Bathgate, aren't you?"

"Ou ay," said Bella. "I'm no' mairret nor naething o' that kind."

"I see. Well, Miss Bathgate, I wonder if you would mind if Mawson — my maid, you know — carried away some of those ornaments and photographs to a safe place? It would be such a pity if we broke any of them, of course, you must value them greatly. These vases now, with the pretty grasses, it would be dreadful if anything happened to them, for I'm sure we could never replace them."

"Uch, ay," Bella interrupted. "I got them at the pig-cairt in exchange for some rags. He's plaenty mair o' the same kind."

"Oh, really," Pamela said, helplessly. "The fact is, a few things of my own will be arriving in a day or two — a cushion or two and that sort of thing — to make me feel at home, you know, so if you would very kindly let us make room for them, I should be so much obliged."

Bella Bathgate looked round the grim chamber that was to her as the apple of her eye, and sighed for the vagaries of "the gentry".

"Aweel," she said, "I'll pit them in a kist until ye gang awa'. I've never had lodgers afore." And as she carried out the tray there was a baleful gleam in her eye as if she were vowing to herself that she would never have them again.

Pamela gave a gasp of relief when the door closed behind the ungracious back of her landlady, and started when it opened again, but this time it was only Mawson.

She hailed her. "Mawson, we must get something done to this room. Lift all these vases and photographs carefully away. Miss Bathgate says she will put them somewhere else in the meantime. And we'll wire to Grosvenor Street for some cushions and rugs — this is too hopeless. Are you quite comfortable, Mawson?"

"Yes, Miss. I 'ave me meals in the kitchen, Miss, for Miss Bathgate don't want to keep another fire goin'. A nice cosy kitchen it is, Miss."

"Then I wish I could have my meals there, too."

"Oh, Miss!" cried Mawson in horror.

"Does Miss Bathgate talk to you, Mawson?"

"Not to say talk, Miss. She don't even listen much; says she can't understand my 'tongue'. Funny, ain't it? Seems to me it's 'er that speaks strange. But I expect we'll be friends in time, Miss. You do 'ave to give the Scotch time: bit slow they are. . . . What I wanted to h'ask, Miss, is where am I to put your things? That little wardrobe and chest of drawers 'olds next to nothing."

"Keep them in the trunks," said Pamela. "I think Miss Bathgate would like to see us departing with them today, but I won't be beat. In Priorsford we are, in Priorsford we remain. . . . I'll write out some wires and you will explore for a post office. I shall explore for an upholsterer who can supply me with an arm-chair not hewn from primeval rock."

Mawson smiled happily and departed to put on her hat, while Pamela sat down to compose telegrams.

These finished, she began, as was her almost daily custom, to scribble to her brother.

"c/o MISS B. BATHGATE,
HILLVIEW, PROIRSFORD,
SCOTLAND.

"BIDDY DEAR — The beds and chairs and cushions are all stuffed with cannon-balls, and the walls are covered with enlarged photographs of men with whiskers, and Bella Bathgate won't speak to me, partly because she evidently hates the look of me, and partly because I didn't eat the duck's egg she gave me for breakfast. But the yolk of it was orange, Biddy. How could I eat it ?

"I have sent out S.O.S. signals for necessaries in the way of rugs and cushions. Life as bald and unadorned as it presents itself to Miss Bathgate is really not quite decent. I wish she would speak to me, but I fear she considers me beneath contempt.

"What happens when you arrive in a place like Priorsford and stay in lodgings? Do you remain seated alone with your conscience, or do people call?

"Perhaps I shall only have Mawson to converse with. It might be worse. I don't think I told you about Mawson. She has been a housemaid in Grosvenor Street for some years, and she maided me once when Julie was on holiday, so when that superior damsel refused to accompany me on this trek I gladly left her behind and brought Mawson in her place.

"She is really very little use as a maid, but her conversation is pleasing and she has a most cheery grin. She reads the works of Florence Barclay, and doesn't care for music-halls — 'low I call them, Miss'. I asked her if she were fond of music, and she said 'Oh yes, Miss,' and then with a coy glance, 'I ply the mandoline.' I think she is about fifty, and not at all good-looking, so she will be a much more comfortable person in the house than Julie, who would have moped without admirers.

"Well, at present Mawson and I are rather like Robinson Crusoe and Man Friday on the island. . . ."

Pamela stopped and looked out of the window for inspiration. Miss Bathgate's parlour was not alluring, but the view from it was a continual feast — spreading fields, woods that in this yellowing time of the year were a study in old gold, the winding river, and the blue hills beyond. Pamela saw each detail with delight; then, letting her eyes come nearer home, she studied the well-kept garden belonging to her landlady. On the wall that separated it from the next garden a small boy and a dog were seated.

Pamela liked boys, so she smiled encouragingly to this one, the boy responding by solemnly raising his cap.

Pamela leaned out of the window.

"Good morning," she said. "What's your name?"

"My name's Gervase Taunton, but I'm called 'the Mhor'. This is Peter Jardine," patting the dog's nose.

"I'm very glad to know you," said Pamela. "Isn't that wall damp?"

"It is rather," said Mhor. "We came to look at you."

"Oh," said Pamela.

"I've never seen an Honourable before, neither has Peter."

"You'd better come in and see me quite close," Pamela suggested. "I've got some chocolates here."

Mhor and Peter needed no further invitation. They sprang from the wall and in a few seconds presented themselves at the door of the sitting-room.

Pamela shook hands with Mhor and patted Peter, and produced a box of chocolates.

"I hope they're the kind you like?" she said politely.

"I like any kind," said Mhor, "but specially hard ones. I don't suppose you have anything for Peter? A biscuit or a bit of cake? Peter's like me. He's always hungry for cake and *never* hungry for porridge."

Pamela, feeling extremely remiss, confessed that she had neither cake nor biscuits, and dared not ask Miss Bathgate for any.

"But you're bigger than Miss Bathgate," Mhor pointed out. "You needn't be afraid of her. I'll ask her, if you like."

Pamela heard him cross the passage and open the kitchen door and begin politely, "Good morning, Miss Bathgate."

"What are ye wantin' here wi' thae dirty boots?" Bella demanded. "Outside wi' ye!"

"I came in to see the Honourable, and she has nothing to give poor Peter to eat. Could he have a tea biscuit — not an Abernethy one, please, he doesn't like them — or a bit of cake?"

"Of a' the impidence!" ejaculated Bella. "D'ye think I keep tea biscuits and cake to feed dowgs wi'? Stan' there and dinna stir." She put a bit of carpet under the small, dirty boots, and as she grumbled she wiped her hands on a coarse towel that hung behind the door, and reached up for a tin box from the top shelf of the press beside the fire.

"Here, see, there's yin for yerself, an' the broken bits are for Peter. Here he comes snowkin'," as Peter ambled into the kitchen followed by Pamela. That lady stood in the doorway.

"Do forgive me coming, but I love a

kitchen. It is always the nicest place in the house, I think; the shining tins are so cheerful and the red fire." She smiled in an engaging way at Bella, who, after a second, and, as it were, reluctantly, smiled back.

"I see you have given the raider some biscuits," Pamela said pleasantly.

"He's an ill laddie." Bella Bathgate looked at the Mhor standing obediently on the bit of carpet, munching his biscuit, and her face softened. "He has neither father nor mother, puir lamb, but I must say Miss Jean never let him ken the want o' them."

"Miss Jean?"

"He bides at The Rigs wi' the Jardines — juist next door here. She's no bad lassie, Miss Jean, and wonderfu' sensible considerin' . . . Are ye finished, Mhor? Weel, wipe yer feet and gang ben to the room an' let me get on wi' ma work."

Pamela, feeling herself dismissed, took her guest back to the sitting-room, where Mhor at once began to examine the books piled on the table, while Peter sat himself on the rug to await developments.

"You've a lot of books," said Mhor. "I've a lot of books, too — as many as a hundred, perhaps. Jean teaches me poetry. Would you like me to say some?"

"Please," said Pamela, expecting to hear some childish rhymes. Mhor took a long breath and began:

" 'O take me to the Mountain O,
  Past the great pines and through the
    wood,
  Up where the lean hounds softly go,
  A whine for wild things' blood,
  And madly flies the dappled roe.
  O God, to shout and speed them
    there
  An arrow by my chestnut hair
  Drawn tight, and one keen glittering
    spear —
  Ah, if I could!' "

For some reason best known to himself Mhor was very sparing of breath when he repeated poetry, making one breath last so long that the end of the verse was reached in a breathless whisper — in this instance very effective.

"So that is what 'Jean' teaches you," said Pamela. "I should like to see Jean."

"Well," said Mhor, "come in with me

50

now and see her. I should be doing my lessons anyway, and you can tell her where I've been."

"Won't she think me rather pushing?" Pamela asked.

"Oh, I don't know," said Mhor carelessly. "Jean's kind to everybody — tramps and people who sing in the street and little cats with no homes. Hadn't you better put on your hat?"

So Pamela obediently put on her hat and coat and went with her new friends down the road a few steps, and up the flagged path to the front door of the funny little house that kept its back turned to its parvenu neighbours, and its eyes lifted to the hills.

In Mhor led her, Peter following hard behind, through a square, low-roofed entrance hall with a polished floor, into a long room with one end coming to a point in an odd-shaped window, rather like the bow of a ship.

A girl was sitting in the window with a large basket of darning beside her.

"Jean," cried Mhor as he burst in, "here's the Honourable. I asked her to come in and see you. She's afraid of Bella Bathgate."

51

"Oh, do come in," said Jean, standing up with the stocking she was darning over one hand. "Take this chair; it's the most comfortable. I do hope Mhor hasn't been worrying you?"

"Indeed he hasn't," said Pamela; "I was delighted to see him. But please don't let me interrupt your work."

"The boys make such big holes," said Jean, picking up a damp handkerchief that lay beside her; and then with a tremble in her voice, "I've been crying," she added.

"So I see," said Pamela. "I'm sorry. Is anything wrong?"

"Nothing in the least wrong," Jean said, swallowing hard; "only that I'm so silly." And presently she found herself pouring out her troubled thoughts about David, about the lions that she feared stood in his path at Oxford, about the hole his going made in the little household at The Rigs. It was a comfort to tell it all to this delightful-looking stranger who seemed to understand so wonderfully.

"I remember when my brother Biddy went to Oxford," Pamela told her. "I felt just as you do. Our parents were dead, and

I was five years older than my brother, and took care of him just as you do of your David. I was afraid for him, for he had too much money, and that is much worse than having too little — but he didn't get changed or spoiled, and to this day he is the same, my own, old Biddy."

Jean dried her eyes and went on with her darning, and Pamela walked about looking at the books and talking, taking in every detail of this girl and her so individual room, the golden-brown hair, thick and wavy, the golden-brown eyes, "like a trout-stream in Connemara", that sparkled and lit and saddened as she talked, the mobile, humorous mouth, the short, straight nose and pointed chin, the straight-up-and-down belted brown frock, the whole toning so perfectly with the room with its polished floor and old Persian rugs, the pale yellow walls (even on the dullest day they seemed to hold some sunshine) hung with coloured prints in old rosewood frames — "Saturday Morning", engraved (with many flourishes) to His Serene Highness the Reigning Landgrave of Hesse Darmstadt; "The Cut Finger", by David Wilkie — those and many others. The furniture was old and good, well kept and well polished, so that the shabby, friendly room had that comfortable air of well-being that only careful housekeeping can give. Books were everywhere: a few precious ones behind glass doors, hundred in low bookcases round the room.

"I needn't ask you if you are fond of reading," Pamela said.

"Much too fond," Jean confessed. "I'm a 'rake at reading'. "

"You know the people," said Pamela, "who say, 'Of course I *love* reading, but I've no time, alas!' as if everyone who loves reading doesn't make time."

As they talked, Pamela realised that this girl who lived year in and year out in a small country town was in no way provincial, for all her life she had been free of the company of the immortals. The Elizabethans she knew by heart, poetry was as daily bread. Rosalind in Arden, Viola in Illyria, were as real to her as Bella Bathgate next door. She had taken to herself as friends (being herself all the daughters of her father's house) Maggie Tulliver, Ethel Newcome, Beatrix Desmond, Clara Middleton, Elizabeth Bennet —

The sound of the gong startled Pamela to her feet.

"You don't mean to say it's luncheon-time already? I've taken up your whole morning."

"It has been perfectly delightful," Jean assured her. "Do stay a long time at Hillview and come in every day. Don't let Bella Bathgate frighten you away. She isn't used to letting her rooms, and her manners are bad, and her long upper lip very quelling; but she's really the kindest soul on earth. . . . Would you come in to tea this afternoon? Mrs. M'Cosh — that's our retainer — bakes rather good scones. I would ask you to stay to luncheon, but I'm afraid there mightn't be enough to go round."

Pamela gratefully accepted the invitation to tea, and said as to luncheon she was sure Miss Bathgate would be awaiting her with a large dish of stewed steak and carrots saved from the night before — so she departed.

Later in the day, as Miss Bathgate sat for ten minutes in Mrs. M'Cosh's shining kitchen and drank a dish of tea, she gave her opinion of the lodger.

"Awfu' English an' wi' a' the queer daft ways o' gentry. 'Oh, Miss Bathgate,' a' the time. They tell me Miss Reston's considered a beauty in London. It's no' ma idea o' beauty — a terrible lang neck an' a wee shilpit bit face, an' sic a height! I'm fair feared for ma gasaliers. An' forty if she's a day. But verra pleasant, ye ken. I aye think there maun be something wrang wi' folk that's as pleasant as a' that — ower sweet to be wholesome, like a frostit tattie! . . . The maid's ca'ed Miss Mawson. She speaks even on. The wumman's a fair clatter-vengeance, an' I dinna ken the one-hauf she says. I think the puir thing's *defeecient!*"

4

". . . Ruth, all heart and tenderness
Who wept, like Chaucer's Prioress,
When Dash was smitten:
Who blushed before the mildest men,
Yet waxed a very Corday when
You teased the kitten."
AUSTIN DOBSON

BEFORE seeking her stony couch at the end of her first day at Priorsford, Pamela finished the letter begun in the morning to her brother.

". . . . I began this letter in the morning and now it is bedtime. Robinson Crusoe is no longer solitary: the island is inhabited. My first visitors arrived about 11 a.m. — a small boy and a dog — an extremely good-looking little boy and a well-bred fox-terrier. They sat on the garden wall until I invited them in, when they ate chocolates and the boy offered to repeat poetry. I expected 'Casabianca' or the modern equivalent, but instead I got the

57

song from Hippolytus, 'O take me to the Mountain, O'. It was rather surprising, but when he invited me to go with him to his home, which is next door, it was more surprising still. Instead of finding another small villa like Hillview, with a breakneck stair and poky little rooms, I found a real old cottage. The room I was taken into was about the nicest I ever saw. I think it would have fulfilled all your conditions as to the proper furnishing of a room; indeed, now that I think of it, it was quite a man's room.

"It had a polished floor and some good rugs, and creamy yellow walls with delicious coloured prints. There were no ornaments except some fine old brass: solid chairs and a low, wide-seated sofa, and books everywhere.

"The shape of the room is delightfully unusual. It is long and rather low-ceilinged, and one end comes almost to a point like the bow of a ship. There is a window with a window-seat in the bow, and as the house stands high on a slope and faces west, you look straight across the river to the hills, and almost have the feeling that you are sailing into the sunset.

"In this room a girl sat, darning stockings and crying quietly to herself — crying because her brother David had gone to Oxford the day before, and she was afraid he would find it hard work to live on his scholarship with the small help she could give him, afraid that he might find himself shabby and feel it bitter, afraid that he might not come back to her the kind, clear-eyed boy he had gone away.

"She told me all about it as simply as a child. Didn't seem to find it in the least odd to confide in a stranger, didn't seem at all impressed by the sudden appearance of my fashionably dressed self!

"People, I am often told, find themselves rather in awe of me. I know that they would rather have me for a friend than an enemy. You see, I can think of such extraordinary nasty things to say about people I don't like. But this little girl treated me as if I had been an older sister or a kind big brother, and — well, I found it rather touching.

"Jean Jardine is her funny little name. She looks a mere child, but she tells me she is twenty-three and she has been head of the house since she was nineteen.

"It is really the strangest story. The father, one Francis Jardine, was in the Indian Civil Service — pretty good at his job, I gather — and these three children, Jean and her two brothers, David and Jock, were brought up in this cottage — The Rigs it is called — by an old aunt of the father's, Great-aunt Alison. The mother died when Jock was a baby, and after some years the father married again, suddenly and unpremeditatedly, a beautiful and almost friendless girl whom he met in London when home on leave. Jean offered no comment on the wisdom or the unwisdom of the match, but she told me the young Mrs. Jardine had sent for her (Jean was then a school-girl of fourteen) and had given her a good time in London before she sailed with her husband for India. Rather unusual when you come to think of it! It isn't every young wife who has thought on the honeymoon for school-girl step-daughters, and Jean had seen that it was kind and unselfish, and was grateful. The Jardines sailed for India, and were hardly landed when Mr. Jardine died of cholera. The young widow stayed on — I suppose she liked the life and had little to bring her back to England — and when the first year of her widowhood was over she married a young soldier, Gervase Taunton. I'm almost sure I remember meeting him about — good-looking, perfect dancer, crack polo player. They seem, in spite of lack of money, to have been supremely happy for about three years, when young Taunton was killed playing polo. The poor girl broke her heart and slipped out of life, leaving behind one little boy. She had no relations, and Captain Taunton had no one very near, and when she was dying she had left instructions. 'Send my boy to Scotland. Ask Jean to bring him up. She will understand.' I suppose she had detected even in the school-girl of fourteen Jean's most outstanding quality, steadfastness, and entrusted the child to her without even a qualm.

"So the baby of two was sent to the child of eighteen, and Jean glows with gratitude and tells you how good it was of her at-one-time stepmother to think of her! That is how she seems to take life: no suspecting of motives: looking for, therefore perhaps finding, kindness on every side. It is rather absurd in this wicked world, but I shouldn't wonder if it made for happiness.

"The Taunton child has, of course, no shadow of claim on the Jardines, but he is to them a most treasured little brother. 'The Mhor', as they call him, is their great amusement and delight. He is quite absurdly good-looking, with great, grave, green eyes and a head most wonderfully set on his shoulders. He has a small income of his own, which Jean keeps religiously apart so that he may be able to go to a good school when he is old enough.

"The great-aunt who brought up the Jardines must have been an uncommon old woman. She died (perhaps luckily) just as the young Gervase Taunton came on the scene.

"It seems she always dressed in rustling black silk, sat bolt upright on the edge of chairs for the sake of her figure, took the greatest care of her hands and complexion, and was a great age. She had, Jean said, 'come out at the Disruption'. Jean was so impressive over it that I didn't like to ask what it meant. Do you suppose she made her début then?

"Perhaps 'the Disruption' is a sort of

religious *tamasha*. Anyway, she was frightfully religious — a strict Calvinist — and taught Jean to regard everything from the point of view of her own death-bed. I mean to say, the child had to ask herself, 'How will this action look when I am on my death-bed?' Every cross word, every small disobedience, she was told, would be a 'thorn in her dying pillow'. I said, perhaps rather rudely, that Great-aunt Alison must have been a horrible old ghoul, but Jean defended her hotly. She seems to have had a great admiration for her aged relative, though she owned that her death was something of a relief. Unfortunately, most of her income died with her.

"I think perhaps it was largely this training that has given Jean her particular flavour. She is the most happy change from the ordinary, modern girl. Her manners are delightful — not noisy, but frank and gay like a nice boy's. She neither falls into the Scylla of affection nor the Charybdis of off-handness. She has been nowhere and seen very little; books are her world, and she talks of book-people as if they were everyday acquaintances. She adores Dr. Johnson and quotes him continually.

"She has no slightest trace of accent, but she has that lilt in her voice — I have noticed it once or twice before in Scots people — that makes one think of winds over heathery moorlands, and running water. In appearance she is like a wood elf, rather small and brown, very light and graceful. She is so beautifully made that there is great satisfaction in looking at her. (If she had all the virtues in the world I could never take any interest in a girl who had a large head, or short legs, or thick ankles!) She knows how to dress, too. The little brown frock was just right, and the ribbon that was tied round her hair. I'll tell you what she reminded me of a good deal — Romney's 'Parson's Daughter'.

"What a find for my first day at Priorsford!

"I went to tea with the Jardines and I never was at a nicer tea-party. We said poems to each other most of the time. Mhor's rendering of Chesterton's 'The Pleasant Town of Roundabout' was very fine, but Jock loves best 'Doon John of Austria'. You would like Jock. He has a very gruff voice and such surprised blue eyes, and is fond of weird interjections like

'Gosh, Maggie!' and 'Earl's in the streets of Cork!' He is a determined foe to sentiment. He won't read a book that contains love-making or death-beds. 'Does anybody marry?' 'Does anybody die?' are his first questions about a book, so naturally his reading is much restricted.

"The Jardines have the lovable habit of becoming suddenly overpowered with laughter, crumpled up, and helpless. You have it, too; I have it; all really nice people have it. I have been refreshing myself with *Irish Memories* since dinner. Do you remember what is said of Martin Ross? 'The large conventional jest had but small power over her; it was the trivial absurdity, the inversion of the expected, the sublimity getting a little above itself and failing to realise that it had taken that fatal step over the border — those were the things that felled her, and laid her, wherever she might be, in ruins . . .'

"Bella Bathgate, I must tell you, remains unthawed. She hinted to me tonight that she thought the Hydropathic was the place for me — surely the unkindest cut of all. People dress for dinner every night there, she tells me, and most of them are

English, and a band plays. Evidently she thinks I would be at home in such company.

"Some day I think you must visit Priorsford and get to know Miss Bathgate. — Yours,

"PAM."

"I forgot to tell you that for some dark reason the Jardines call their cat Sir J. M. Barrie.

"I asked why, but got no satisfaction.

" 'Well, you see, there's Peter,' Mhor said vaguely.

"Jock looked at the cat and observed obscurely, 'It's not a sentimental beast either' — while Jean asked if I would have preferred it called Sir Rabindranath Tagore!"

5

"O, the land is fine, fine,
I could buy it a' for mine,
For ma gowd's as the stooks
in Strathairlie."

SCOTS SONG

WHEN Peter Reid arrived at Priorsford Station from London he stood for a few minutes looking about him in a lost way, almost as if after thirty years he expected to see a "kent face" coming to meet him. He had no notion where to go; he had not written for rooms; he had simply obeyed the impulse that sent him — the impulse that sends a hurt child to its mother. It is said that an old horse near to death turns towards the the pastures where he was foaled. It is true of human beings. "Man wanders back to the fields which bred him."

After a talk with a helpful porter he found rooms in a temperance hotel in the Highgate — a comfortable quiet place.

The next day he was too tired to rise,

and spent rather a dreary day in his rooms with *The Scotsman* for sole companion.

The landlord, a cheery little man, found time once or twice to talk for a few minutes, but he had only been ten years in Priorsford and could tell his guest nothing of the people he had once known.

"Do you know a house called The Rigs?" he asked him.

The landlord knew it well — a quaint cottage with a pretty garden. Old Miss Alison Jardine was living in it when he first came to Priorsford; dead now, but the young folk were still in it.

"Young folk?" said Peter Reid.

"Yes," said the landlord, "Miss Jean Jardine and her brothers. Orphans, I'm told. Father an Anglo-Indian. Nice people? Oh, very. Quiet and inoffensive. They don't own the house, though. I hear the landlord is a very wealthy man in London. By the way, same name as yourself, sir."

"Do I look like a millionaire?" asked Peter Reid, and the landlord laughed pleasantly and non-committally.

The next day was sunny and Peter Reid went out for a walk. It was a different

Priorsford that he had come back to. A large draper's shop with plate-glass windows occupied the corner where Jenny Baxter had rolled her toffee-balls and twisted her "gundy", and where old Davy Linton had cut joints and weighed out mince-collops accompanied by wise weather-prophecies, a smart fruiterer's shop now stood furnished with a wealth of fruit and vegetables unimagined in his young days. There were many handsome shops, the streets were wider and better kept, unsightly houses had been demolished; it was a clean, prosperous-looking town, but it was different.

Peter Reid (of London) would have been the first to carp at the tumbledown irregular old houses, with their three steps up and three steps down, remaining, but Peter Reid (of Priorsford) missed them. He resented the new shops, the handsome villas, the many motors, all the evidences of prosperity.

And why had Cuddy Brig been altered?

It had been far liker the thing, he thought — the old hump-backed bridge with the grass and ferns growing in the crannies. He had waded in Cuddy when he was a boy, picking his way among the broken dishes and the tin cans, and finding wonderful adventures in the dark of the bridge; he had bathed in it as it wound, clear and shining, among the green meadows outside the town, and run "skirl-naked" to dry himself, in full sight of scandalised passengers in the Edinburgh train; he had slid on it in winter. The memory of the little stream had always lain in the back of his mind as something precious — and now to find it spanned by a staring new stone bridge. Those Town Councils with their improvements!

Even Tweed Bridge had not been left alone. It had been widened, as an inscription in the middle told the world at large. He leant on it and looked up the river. Peel Tower was the same, anyway. No one had dared to add one cubit to its grey stature. It was a satisfaction to look at something so unchanging.

The sun had still something of its summer heat, and it was pleasant to stand there and listen to the sound of the river over the pebbles and see the flaming trees reflected in the blue water all the way up Tweedside till the river took a wide curve before the green slope on which the castle stood. A wonderfully pretty place, Priorsford, he told himself: a home-like place — if one had anyone to come home to.

He turned slowly away. He would go and look at The Rigs. His mother had come to it as a bride. He had been born there. Though occupied by strangers, it was the nearest he had to a home. The house in Prince's Gate was well furnished, comfortable, smoothly run by efficient servants, but only a house when all was said. He felt he would like to creep into The Rigs, into the sitting-room where his mother had always sat (the other larger room, the "good room" as it was called, was kept for visitors and high days), and lay his tired body on the horsehair arm-chair by the fireside. He could rest there, he thought. It was impossible, of course. There would be no horsehair arm-chair, for everything had been sold — and there was no mother.

But, anyway, he would go and look at it. There used to be primroses — but this was autumn. Primroses come in the spring.

Thirty years — but The Rigs had not changed, at least not outwardly. Old Mrs. Reid had loved the garden and Great-aunt

Alison, and Jean after her had carried on her work.

The little house looked just as Peter Reid remembered it.

He would go in and ask to see it, he told himself.

He would tell these Jardines that the house was his and he meant to live in it himself. They wouldn't like it, but he couldn't help that. Perhaps he would be able to persuade them to go almost at once. He would make it worth their while.

He was just going to lift the latch of the gate when the front door opened and shut and Jean Jardine came down the flagged path. She stopped at the gate and looked at Peter Reid.

"Were you by any chance coming in?" she asked.

"Yes," said Mr. Reid; "I was going to ask if I might see over the house."

"Surely," said Jean. "But — you're not going to buy it, are you?"

The face she turned to him was pink and distressed.

"Did you think of buying it yourself?" Peter Reid asked.

"*Me?* You wouldn't ask that if you knew

how little money I have. But come in. I shall try to think of all its faults to tell you — but in my eyes it hasn't got any."

They went slowly up the flagged path and into the square, low-roofed hall. This was not as his mother had it. Then the floor had been covered with linoleum on which had stood two hard chairs and an umbrella-stand. Now there was an oak chest and a gate-table, old brass very well rubbed up, a grandfather clock with a "clear" face, and a polished floor with a Chinese rug on it.

"It is rather dark," said Jean, "but I like it dark. Coming in on a hot summer day it is almost like a pool; it is so cool and dark and polished."

Mr. Reid said nothing, and Jean was torn between a desire to have her home appreciated and a desire to have this stranger take an instant dislike to it, and to leave it speedily and for ever.

"You see," she pointed out, "the little staircase is rather steep and widing, but it is short; and the bedrooms are charming — not very big, but so prettily shaped and with lovely views." Then she remembered that she should miscall rather than praise, and added, "Of course, they have all got queer ceilings; you couldn't expect anything else in a cottage. Will you go upstairs?"

Mr. Reid thought not, and asked if he might see the sitting-rooms. "This," said Jean, opening a door, "is the dining-room."

It was the room his mother had always sat in, where the horsehair arm-chair had had its home, but it, too, had suffered a change. Gone was the arm-chair, gone the round table with the crimson cover. This room had an austerity unknown in the room he remembered. It was small, and every inch of space was made the most of. An old Dutch dresser held china and acted as a sideboard; a bare oak table, having in its centre a large blue bowl filled with berries and red leaves, stood in the middle of the room; eight chairs completed the furniture.

"This is the least nice room in the house," Jean told him; "but we are never in it except to eat. It looks out on the road."

"Yes," said Peter Reid, remembering that that was why his mother liked it. She could sit with her knitting and watch the passers-by. She had always "infused" the tea when she heard the click of the gate as he came home from school.

"You will like to see the living-room," said Jean, shivering for the effect its charm might have on a potential purchaser. She led him in, hoping that it might be looking its worst, but, as if in sheer contrariness, the fire was burning brightly, a shaft of sunlight lay across a rug, making the colours glow like jewels, and the whole room seemed to hold out welcoming hands. It was satisfactory (though somewhat provoking) that the stranger seemed quite unimpressed.

"You have some good furniture," he said.

"Yes," Jean agreed eagerly. "It suits the room and makes it beautiful. Can you imagine it furnished with a 'suite' and ordinary pictures, and draped curtains at the windows and silver photograph frames and a grand piano? It would simply be no sort of room at all. All its individuality would be gone. But won't you sit down and rest? That hill up from the town is steep."

Peter Reid sank thankfully into a corner of the sofa, while Jean busied herself at the writing-table so that this visitor, who looked so tired, need not feel that he should offer conversation.

Presently he said, "You are very fond of The Rigs?"

Jean came and sat down beside him.

"It's the only home we have ever known," she said. "We came here from India to live with our great-aunt — first me alone, and then David and Jock. And Father and Mother were with us when Father had leave. I have hardly ever been away from The Rigs. It's such a very *affectionate* sort of house — perhaps that is rather an absurd thing to say, but you do get so fond of it. But if I take you in to see Mrs. M'Cosh in the kitchen she will tell you plenty of faults. The water doesn't heat well, for one thing, and the range simply eats up coal, and there is no proper pantry. Your wife would want to know about these things."

"Haven't got a wife," said Peter Reid, gruffly.

"No? Well, your housekeeper, then. You couldn't possibly buy a house without getting to know all about the hot water and pantries."

"There is no question of my buying it."

"Oh, isn't there?" cried Jean joyfully. "What a relief! All the time I've been showing you the house I've been picturing us removing sadly to a villa in the Langhope Road. They are quite nice villas as villas go, but they have only tiny strips of gardens and stairs that come to meet you as you go in at the front door, and anyway no house could ever be home to us after The Rigs — not though it had hot and cold water in every room and a pantry on every floor."

"Dear me," said Peter Reid.

He felt perplexed, and annoyed with himself for being perplexed. All he had to do was to tell this girl with the frank eyes that The Rigs was his, that he wanted to live in it himself, that if they would turn out at once he would make it worth their while. Quite simple — They were nice people evidently, and would make no fuss. He would say it now — but Jean was speaking.

"I think I know why you wanted to see through this house," she was saying. "I think you must have known it long ago when you were a boy. Perhaps you loved it too — and had to leave it."

"I went to London when I was eighteen to make my fortune."

"Oh," said Jean, and into that "Oh" she put all manner of things she could not say. She had been observing her visitor, and she was sure that this shabby little man (Peter Reid cared not at all for appearances and never bought a new suit of clothes unless compelled) had returned no Whittington, Lord Mayor of London. Probably he was one of the "faithful failures" of the world, one who had tried and missed, and had come back, old and tired and shabby, to see his boyhood's home. The tenderest corner of Jean's tender heart was given to shabby people, and she longed to try to comfort and console, but dared not in case of appearing impertinent. She reflected dismally that he had not even a wife to be nice to him, and he was far too old to have a mother.

"Are you staying in Priorsford?" she asked gently.

"I'm at the Temperance Hotel for a few days. I — the fact is, I haven't been well. I had to take a rest, so I came back here — after thirty years."

"Have you really been away for thirty

years? Great-aunt Alison came to The Rigs first about thirty years ago. Do you, by any chance, know our landlord in London? Mr. Peter Reid is his name."

"I know him."

"He's frightfully rich, they say. I don't suppose you know him well enough to ask him not to sell The Rigs? It can't make much difference to him though it means so much to us. Is he old, our landlord?"

"A man in his prime," said Peter Reid.

"That's pretty old, isn't it?" said Jean — "about sixty, I think. Of course," hastily, "sixty isn't really old. When I'm sixty — if I'm spared — I expect I shall feel myself good for another twenty years."

"I thought I was," said Peter Reid, "until I broke down."

"Oh, but a rest at Priorsford will put you right."

Could he afford a holiday? she wondered. Even temperance hotels were rather expensive when you hadn't much money. Would it be very rash and impulsive to ask him to stay at The Rigs?

"Are you comfortable at the Temperance?" she asked. "Because if you don't much care for hotels we would love to put you up here. Mhor is apt to be noisy, but I'm sure he would try to be quiet when he knew that you needed a rest."

"My dear young lady," gasped Peter Reid. "I'm afraid you are rash. You know nothing of me. I might be an imposter, a burglar — "

Jean threw back her head and laughed.

"Do forgive me, but the thought of you with a jemmy and a dark lantern is so funny."

"You don't even know my name."

"I don't," said Jean, "but does that matter? You will tell me when you want to."

"My name is Reid, the same as your landlord."

"Then," said Jean, "are you a relative of his?"

"A connection." It was not what he meant to say, but he said it.

"How odd!" said Jean. She was trying to remember if she had said anything unbecoming of one relative to another. "Oh, here's Jock and Mhor," as two figures ran past the window; "you must stay and have tea with us, Mr. Reid."

"But I ought to be getting back to the

hotel. I had no intention of inflicting myself on you in this way." He rose to his feet and looked about for his hat. "The fact is — I must tell you — I am — "

The door burst open and Mhor appeared. He had forgotten to remove his cap, or wipe his muddy boots, so eager was he to tell his news.

"Jean," he shouted, oblivious in his excitement of the presence of a stranger; "Jean, there are six red puddock-stools at the bottom of the garden — bright red puddock-stools." He noticed Mr. Reid and, going up to him and looking earnestly into his face, he repeated, "Six!"

"Indeed," said Peter Reid.

He had no acquaintance with boys, and felt extremely ill at ease; but Mhor, after studying him for a minute, was seized with a violent fancy for this new friend.

"You're going to stay to tea, aren't you? Would you mind coming with me just now to look at the puddock-stools? It might be too dark after tea. Here is your hat."

"But I'm not staying to tea," cried the unhappy owner of The Rigs. Why, he asked himself, had he not told them at once that he was their landlord? A connection!

Fool that he was! He would say it now —
"I only came — "

"It was very nice of you to come," said
Jean, soothingly. "But, Mhor, don't worry
Mr. Reid. Everybody hasn't your passion
for puddock-stools."

"But you would like to see them," Mhor
assured him. "I'm going to fill a bowl with
chucky-stones and moss and stick the
puddock-stools among them, and make a
fairy garden for Jean. And if I can find any
more I'll make one for the Honourable;
she is very kind about giving me chocolates."

They were out of doors by this time, and
Mhor was pointing out the glories of the
garden.

"You see, we have a burn in our garden
with a little bridge over it; almost no one
else has a burn and a bridge of their very
own. There are minnows in it and all sorts
of things — water-beetles, you know. *And
here are my puddock-stools.*"

When Mr. Reid came back from the
garden Mhor had firm hold of his hand and
was telling him a long story about a
"mavis-bird" that the cat had caught and
eaten.

"Tea's ready," he said, as they entered the room; "you can't go away now, Mr. Reid. See these cookies? I went for them myself to Davidson the baker's, and they were so hot and new-baked that the bag burst and they all fell on the road."

"*Mhor*! You horrid little boy."

"They're none the worse, Jean. I dusted them all with me useful little hanky, and the road wasn't so very dirty."

"All the same," said Jean, "I think we'll leave the cookies to you and Jock. The other things are baked at home, Mr. Reid, and are quite safe. Mhor, tell Jock tea's in, and wash your hands."

So Peter Reid found himself, like Balaam, remaining to bless. After all, why should he turn these people out of their home? A few years (with care) was all the length of days promised to him, and it mattered little where he spent them. Indeed, so little profitable did leisure seem to him that he cared little when the end came. Mhor and his delight over a burn of his own, and a garden that grew red puddock-stools, had made up his mind for him. He would never be the angel with the flaming sword who turned Mhor out of paradise.

He had not known that a boy could be such a pleasant person. He had avoided children as he had avoided women, and now he found himself seated, the centre of interest, at a family tea-table, with Jean, anxiously making tea to his liking, while Mhor (with a well-soaped, shining face, but a high-water mark of dirt where the sponge had not reached) sat close beside him, and Jock, the big schoolboy, shyly handed him scones, and Peter walked among the feet of the company, waiting for what he could get.

Peter Reid quite shone through the meal. He remembered episodes of his boyhood, forgotten for forty years, and told them to Jock and Mhor, who listened with most gratifying interest. He questioned Jock about Priorsford Grammar School and recalled stories of the masters who had taught there in his day.

Jean told him about David going to Oxford, and about Great-aunt Alison who had "come out at the Disruption" — about her father's life in India, and about her mother, and he became every minute more human and interested. He even made one or two small jokes which were received with great applause by Jock and Mhor, who were grateful to anyone who tried, however feebly, to be funny. They would have said with Touchstone, "It is meat and drink to me to see a clown."

Jean watched with delight her rather difficult guest blossom into affability. "You are looking better already," she told him. "If you stayed here for a week and rested and Mrs. M'Cosh cooked you light, nourishing food and Mhor didn't make too much noise, I'm sure you would feel quite well again. And it does seem such a pity to pay hotel bills when we want you here."

Hotel bills! Peter Reid looked sharply at her. Did she imagine, this girl, that hotel bills were of any moment to him? Then he looked down at his shabby clothes and recalled their conversation and owned that her mistake was not unjustifiable.

But how extraordinary it was! The instinct that makes people wish to stand well with the rich and powerful he could understand and commend, but the instinct that opens wide doors to the shabby and the unsuccessful was not one that he knew anything about: it was certainly not an instinct for this world as he knew it.

Just as they were finishing tea Mrs. M'Cosh ushered in Miss Pamela Reston.

"You did say I might come in when I liked," she said as she greeted Jean. "I've had tea, thank you. Mhor, you haven't been to see me today."

"I would have been," Mhor assured her, "but Jean said I'd better not. Do you invite me to come tomorrow?"

"I do."

"There, Jean," said Mhor. "You can't *un*-vite me after that."

"Indeed she can't," said Pamela. "Jock, this is the book I told you about. . . . Please, Miss Jean, don't let me disturb you."

"We've finished," said Jean. "May I introduce Mr. Reid?"

Pamela shook hands and at once proceeded to make herself so charming that Peter Reid was galvanised into a spirited conversation. Pamela had brought her embroidery frame with her, and she sat on the sofa and sorted out silks, and talked and laughed as if she had sat there off and on all her life. To Jean, looking at her, it seemed impossible that two days ago none of them had beheld her. It seemed — absurdly enough — that the room could never have looked quite right when it had not this graceful creature with her soft gowns and her pearls, her embroidery frame and heaped, bright-hued silks, sitting by the fire.

"Miss Jean, won't you sing us a song? I'm convinced that you sing Scots songs quite perfectly."

Jean laughed. "I can sing Scots songs in a way, but I have a voice about as big as a sparrow's. If it would amuse you I'll try."

So Jean sat down at the piano and sang "Proud Maisie", and "Colin's Cattle", and one or two other old songs.

"I wonder," said Peter Reid, "if you know a song my mother used to sing — 'Strathairlie'?"

"Indeed I do. It's one I like very much. I have it here in this little book." She struck a few simple chords and began to sing: it was a lilting, haunting tune, and the words were "old and plain".

*"O, the lift is high and blue
And the new mune glints through*

On the bonnie corn-fields o' Strathairlie:
　　Ma ship's in Largo Bay
　　And I ken weel the way
Up the steep, steep banks o' Strathairlie.

　　When I sailed ower the sea
　　A laddie bold and free
The corn sprang green on Strathairlie:
　　When I come back again
　　It's an auld man walks his lane
Slow and sad ower the fields o'
　　Strathairlie.

　　O, the shearers that I see
　　No' a body kens me,
Though I kent them a' in Strathairlie:
　　An' the fisher wife I pass,
　　Can she be the braw lass
I kissed at the back o' Strathairlie?

　　O, the land is fine, fine,
　　I could buy it a' for mine,
For ma gowd's as the stooks in
　　Strathairlie
　　But I fain the lad would be
　　Wha sailed ower the saut sea
When the dawn rose grey on
　　Strathairlie."

88

Jean rose from the piano. Jock had got out his books and had begun his lessons. Mhor and Peter were under the table playing at being cave-men. Pamela was stitching at her embroidery. Peter Reid sat shading his eyes from the light with his hand.

Jean knelt down on the rug and held out her hands to the blazing fire.

"It must be sad to be old and rich," she said softly, almost as if she were speaking to herself. "It is so very certain that we can carry nothing out of this world. . . . I read somewhere of a man who, on every birthday, gave away some of his possessions, so that at the end he might not be cumbered and weighted with them." She looked up and caught the gaze of Peter Reid fixed on her intently. "It's rather a nice idea, don't you think, to give away all the superfluous money and lands, pictures and jewels, everything we have, and stand stripped, as it were, ready when we get the word to come, to leap into the beyond?"

Pamela spoke first. "There speaks sweet and twenty," she said teasingly.

"Yes," said Jean. "I know it's quite easy

for me to speak in that lordly way of disposing of possessions, for I haven't got any to dispose of."

"Then," said Pamela, "we are to take it that you are ready to spring across any minute?"

"So far as goods and gear go; but I'm rich in other things. I'm pretty heavily weighted by David, and Jock, and Mhor."

Then Peter Reid spoke, still with his hands over his eyes.

"Once you begin to make money it clings. How can you get rid of it?"

"I'm saving up for a bicycle," the Mhor broke in, becoming aware that the conversation turned on money. "I've got half a crown and a thrupenny-bit and fourpence-ha'penny in pennies: and I've got a duster to clean it with when I've got it."

Jean stroked his head. "I don't think you'll ever be overburdened with riches, Mhor, old man. But it must be tremendous fun to be rich. I love books where suddenly a lawyer's letter comes saying that someone has left them a fortune."

"What would you do with a fortune if you got it?" Peter Reid asked.

"Need you ask?" laughed Pamela. "Miss

Jean would at once make it over to David and Jock and Mhor."

"Oh, well," said Jean, "of course they would come *first*, but, oh, I would do such a lot of things! I'd find out where money was most needed and drop it on the people anonymously so that they wouldn't be bothered about thanking anyone. I would creep about like a beneficent Puck and take worried frowns away, and straighten out things for tired people, and, above all, I'd make children smile. There's no fun or satisfaction got from giving big sums to hospitals and things — that's all right for when you're dead. I want to make happiness while I'm alive. I don't think a million pounds would be too much for all I want to do."

"Aw, Jean," said Mhor, "if you had a million pounds would you buy me a bicycle?"

"A bicycle," said Jean, "and a motor and an aeroplane and a Shetland pony and a Newfoundland pup. I'll make a story for you in bed tonight all about what you would have if I were rich."

"And Jock, too?"

Being assured that Jock would not be

overlooked, Mhor grabbed Peter round the neck and proceeded to babble to him about bicycles and aeroplanes, motors and Newfoundland pups.

Jean looked apologetically at her guests. "When you're poor you've got to dream," she said. "Oh, must you go, Mr. Reid? But you'll come back tomorrow, won't you? We would honestly like you to come and stay with us."

"Thank you," said Peter Reid, "but I'm going back to London in a day or two. I am obliged to you for your hospitality, especially for singing me 'Strathairlie'. I never thought to hear it again. I wonder if I might trouble you to write me out the words."

"But take the book," said Jean, running to get it and pressing it into his hands. "Perhaps you'll find other songs in it you used to know and like. Take it to keep."

Pamela dropped her embroidery frame and watched the scene.

Mhor and Peter stood looking on. Jock listed his head from his books to listen. It was not new thing for the boys to see Jean give away her most treasured possessions; she was a born "Madam Liberality".

"But," Peter Reid objected, "it is rather a rare book. You value it yourself."

"Of course I do," said Jean, "and that is why I am giving it to *you*. I know you will appreciate it."

Peter Reid took the book as if it was something fragile and very precious. Pamela was puzzled by the expression on his face. He did not seem so much touched by the gift as sardonically amused.

"Thank you," he said. And again, "Thank you!"

"Jock will go down with you to the hotel," Jean said, explaining, when the visitor demurred, that the road was steep and not very well lighted.

"I'll go too," said Mhor, "me and Peter."

"Well, come straight back. Good-bye, Mr. Reid. I'm so glad you came to see The Rigs, but I wish you could have stayed. . . ."

"Is he an old friend?" Pamela asked, when the cavalcade had departed.

"I never saw him before today. He once lived in this house and he came back to see it, and he looks ill and I think he is poor, so I asked him to come and stay with us for a week."

"My dear child, do you invite every stranger to stay with you if you think he is poor?"

"Of course not. But he looked so lonely and lost somehow, and he doesn't seem to have anyone belonging to him, and I was sorry for him."

"And so you gave him that song book you value so much?"

"Yes," said Jean, looking rather ashamed. "But," she brightened, "he seemed pleased, don't you think? It's a pretty song, 'Strathairlie', but it's not a *pukka* old one — it's early Victorian."

"Miss Jean, it's a marvel to me that you have anything left belonging to you."

"Don't call me Miss Jean!"

"Jean, then; but you must call me Pamela."

"Oh, but wouldn't that be rather familiar? You see, you are so — so — "

"Stricken in years," Pamela supplied.

"No — but — well, you are rather impressive, you know. It would be like calling Miss Bathgate 'Bella' to her face. However — Pamela — "

6

"For 'tis a chronicle of day by day."
"THE TEMPEST"

ABOUT this time Jean wrote a letter to David at Oxford. It is wonderful how much news there is when people write every other day; if they wait for a month there is nothing that seems worth telling.

Jean wrote:

". . . You have been away now for four days, and we still miss you badly. Nobody sits in your place at the table, and it gives us such a horrid bereaved feeling when we look at it. Mhor was waiting at the gate for the post yesterday and brought your letter in, in triumph. He was particularly interested in hearing about your scout, and has added his name to the list he prays for. You will be glad to hear that he has got over his prejudice against going to heaven. It seems it was because someone told him that dogs couldn't go there, and he wouldn't desert Micawber — Peter, in other words. Jock has put it right by telling him that the translators of the Bible probably made a slip, and Mhor now prays earnestly every night: 'Let everyone in The Rigs go to heaven', hoping thus to smuggle in his dear companion.

"It is an extraordinary thing, but almost the very minute you left Priorsford things began to happen.

"I told you in the note I wrote the day you left that Bella Bathgate's lodger had arrived and that I had seen her, but I didn't realise then what a difference her coming would make to us. I never knew such a friendly person; she comes in at any sort of time — after breakfast, a few minutes before luncheon, for tea, between nine and ten at night. Did I tell you her name is Pamela Reston, and her brother, who seems to be ranging about India somewhere, is Lord Bidborough ('A lord no-less,' as Mrs. M'Cosh would say). She calls him Biddy, and seems devoted to him.

"Although she is horribly rich and an 'Honourable', and all that sort of thing, she isn't in the least grand. She never impresses one with her opulence as, for instance, Mrs. Duff-Whalley does. Her clothes are beautiful, but so much a part of her personality that you never think of them. Her pearls don't hit you in the face as most other people's do. Because she is so unconscious of them, I suppose. I think she is lovely. Jock says she is like a greyhound, and I know what he means — it is the long, swift, graceful way she has of moving. She says she is forty. I always thought forty was quite old, but now it seems to me the very prettiest age. Age doesn't really matter at all to people who have got faces and figures and manners like Pamela Reston. They will always make whatever age they are seem the perfect age.

"I do wonder what brings her to Priorsford! I rather think that having been all her life so very 'twopence coloured' she wants the 'penny plain' for a change. Perhaps that is why she likes The Rigs and us. There is no mistake about our 'penny plainness' — it jumps to the eye!

"I am just afraid she won't stay very long. There are so many pretty little houses in Priorsford, and so many kind and forthcoming landladies it was bad luck that she should choose Hillview and Bella Bathgate. Bella is almost like a stage-caricature of a Scotswoman, so dour she is and uncompromising, and she positively glories in the drab ugliness of her rooms. Ugliness means to Bella respectability; any attempt at adornment is 'daft-like'.

"Pamela (she has asked me to call her that) trembles before her, and that makes Bella worse. She wants someone to stand up to her, to laugh at her grimness; she simply thinks when Pamela is charming to her that she is a poor creature.

"She is charming to everyone, this lodger of Bella's. Jock and Mhor and Mrs. M'Cosh are all at her feet. She brings us books and papers and chocolates and fruit, and makes us feel we are conferring the favour by accepting them. She is a real charmer, for when she speaks to you she makes you feel that no one matters to her but just you yourself. And she is simple (or at least appears to be); she hasn't that Now-I-am-going-to-be-charming manner that is so difficult to bear. It is such fun talking to her, for she is very — pliable I think is the word I want. Accustomed to converse with people who constantly pull one up short with an 'Ah, now I don't agree', or 'There, I think you are quite wrong', it is wonderfully soothing to discuss things with someone who has the air of being convinced by one's arguments. It is weak, I know, but I'm afraid I agree with Mrs. M'Cosh, who described a friend as 'a rale nice buddy. She clinks wi' every word ye say'.

"I am thinking to myself how Great-aunt Alison would have dreaded Pamela's influence. She would have seen in her the personification of the World, the Flesh, and the Devil — albeit she would have been much impressed by her long descent: dear Aunt Alison.

"All the same, Davie, it is odd what an effect one's early training has. D'you remember how discouraged Great-aunt Alison was about our levity — especially mine? She once said bitterly that I was like the ell-woman — hollow — because I laughed in the middle of the Bible lesson. And how antiquated and stuffy we thought her views, and took pleasure in assuring ourselves that we had got far beyond them, and you spent an evening tea-less in your room because you said you would rather be a Buddhist than a Disruption Worthy — do you remember that?

"Yes; but Great-aunt Alison had builded better than she knew. When Pamela laughs 'How Biblical' or says in her pretty, soft voice that our Great-aunt's religion must have been a hard and ugly thing, I get hot with anger and feel I must stick unswervingly to the antiquated views. Is it because poor Great-aunt isn't here to make me? I don't know.

"Mhor is really surprisingly naughty. Yesterday I heard angry shouts from the road, and then I met Mhor sauntering in, on his face the seraphic expression he wears when some nefarious scheme has prospered and in his hand the brass breakfast kettle. He had been pouring water on the passers-by from the top of the wall. 'Only,' he explained to me, 'on the men who wore hard black hats, who could swear.'

"I told him the police would probably visit us in the course of the afternoon, and pointed out to him how ungentlemen-like was his behaviour, and he said he was sorry; but I'm afraid he will soon think of some other wickedness.

"He thinks he can do anything he hasn't

been told not to do, but how could I foresee that he would want to pour water on men with hard black hats, capable of swearing?

"I had almost forgotten to tell you, an old man came yesterday and wanted to see over the house. You can imagine what a scare I got — I made sure he wanted to buy it; but it turned out that he had lived at The Rigs as a boy, and had come back for old times' sake. He looked ill and rather shabby, and I don't believe life had been very good to him. I did want to try and make up a little, but he was difficult. He was staying at the Temperance, and it seemed so forlorn that he should have no one of his own to come home to. He didn't look as if anybody had ever made a fuss of him. I asked him to stay with us for a week, but he wouldn't. I think he thought I was rather mad to ask him, and Pamela laughed at me about it. . . . She laughs at me a good deal and calls me a 'senti-mentalist'. . . .

"There is the luncheon bell.

"We are longing for your letter tomorrow to hear how you are settling down. Mrs. M'Cosh has baked some shortbread for you, which I shall post this afternoon.

"Love from each of us, and Peter —
Your

"JEAN."

7

"Is this a world to hide virtues in ?"
"TWELFTH NIGHT"

"YOU should never wear a short string of beads when you are wearing big earrings," Pamela said.

"But why?" asked Jean.

"Well, see for yourself. I am wearing big round earrings — right. I put on the beads that match — quite wrong. It's a question of line."

"I see," said Jean, thoughtfully. "But how do you learn those things?"

"You don't learn them. You either know them, or you don't. A sort of instinct for dress, I suppose."

Jean was sitting in Pamela's bedroom. Pamela's bedroom it was now, certainly not Bella Bathgate's.

The swinging looking-glass had been replaced by one which, according to Pamela, was at least truthful. "The other one," she complained, pulling a wry face, "made me look pale green and drowned."

A cloth of fine linen and lace covered the toilet-table, which was spread with brushes and boxes in tortoiseshell and gold, quaint-shaped bottles for scent, and roses in a tall glass.

A jewel-box stood open and Pamela was pulling out earrings and necklaces, rings and brooches for Jean's amusement.

"Most of my things are at the bank," Pamela was saying as she held up a pair of Spanish earrings made of rows of pearls. "They generally are there, for I don't care a bit about ordinary jewels. These are what I like — odd things, old things, things picked up in odd corners of the world, things that have a story and a meaning. Biddy got me these turquoises in Tibet; that is a devil charm: isn't that jade delicious? I think I like Chinese things best of all."

She threw a string of cloudy amber round Jean's neck and cried, "My dear how it becomes you. It brings out all the golden lights in your hair and eyes."

Jean sat forward in her chair and looked at her reflection in the glass with a pleased smile.

"I do like dressing-up," she confessed.

"Pretty things are a great temptation to me. I'm afraid if I had money I would spend a lot in adorning my vile body."

"I simply don't know," said Pamela, "how people who don't care for clothes get through their lives. Clothes are a joy to the prosperous, a solace to the unhappy, and an interest always — even to old age. I knew a dear old lady of ninety-four whose chief diversion was to buy a new bonnet. She would sit before the mirror discarding model after model because they were 'much too old' for her. One would have thought it difficult to find anything too old for ninety-four."

Jean laughed, but shook her head.

"Doesn't it seem to you rather awful to care about bonnets at ninety-four?"

"Not a bit," said Pamela. She was powdering her face as she spoke. "I like to see old people holding on, not losing interest in their appearance, making a brave show to the end. . . . Did you never see anyone use powder before, Jean? Your eyes in the glass look so surprised."

"Oh, I beg your pardon," said Jean, in great confusion, "I didn't mean to stare — " She hastily averted her eyes.

Pamela looked at her with an amused smile.

"There's nothing actively immoral about powdering one's nose, you know, Jean. Did Great-aunt Alison tell you it was wrong?"

"Great-aunt Alison never talked about such things," Jean said, flushing hotly. "I don't think it's wrong, but I don't see that it's an improvement. I couldn't take any pleasure in myself if my face were made up."

Pamela swung round on her chair and laid her hands on Jean's shoulders.

"Jean," she said, "you're within an ace of being a prig. It's only the freckles on your little unpowdered nose, and the yellow lights in your eyes, and the way your hair curls up at the ends that save you. Remember, please, that three-and-twenty with a perfect complexion has no call to reprove her elders. Just wait till you come to forty years."

"Oh," said Jean, "It's absurd of you to talk like that. As if you didn't know that you are infinitely more attractive than any younger girl. I never know why people talk so much about *youth*. What does being young matter if you're awkward and dull and shy as well. I'd far rather be middle-aged and interesting."

"That," said Pamela, as she laid her treasures back in the box, "is one of the minor tragedies of life. One begins by being bored with being young, and as we begin to realise what an asset youth is, it flies. Rejoice in your youth, little Jean-girl, for it's stuff will not endure. . . . Now we'll go downstairs. It's too bad of me keeping you up here."

"How you have changed this room," exclaimed Jean. "It smells so nice."

"It is slightly less forbidding. I am quite attached to both my rooms, though when Mawson and I are both here to-gether I sometimes feel I must poke my arms out of the window or thrust my head up the chimney like Bill the Lizard in order to get room. It is a great disadvantage to be too large for one's surroundings."

Jean was quick to notice that the parlour was as much changed as the bedroom.

The round table with the red-and-green cover that filled up the middle of the room had been banished and a small card-table stood against the wall ready to be brought out for meals. A Persian carpet covered the linoleum and two comfortable wicker chairs filled with cushions stood by the fireside. The sideboard had been converted into a stand for books and flowers. The blue vases had gone from the mantelshelf and two tall candlesticks and a strip of embroidery took their place. A writing-table stood in the window, from which the hard muslin curtains had been removed; there were flowers wherever a place could be found for them, and new books and papers lay about.

Jean sank into a chair with a book, but Pamela produced some visiting-cards and read aloud:

"MRS. DUFF-WHALLEY,
MISS. DUFF-WHALLEY,
THE TOWERS,
PRIORSFORD."

"Who are they, please? and why do they come to see me?"

Jean shut her book, but kept her finger in as if hoping to get back to it soon, and smiled broadly.

"Mrs. Duff-Whalley is a wonderful woman," she said. "She knows everything about everybody and simply scents out social opportunities. Your name would draw her like a magnet."

"Why is she called Duff-Whalley? and where does she live? I'm frightfully intrigued."

"As to the first," said Jean, "there was no thought of pleasing either you or me when she was christened — or rather when the late Mr. Duff-Whalley was christened. And I pointed out the house to you the other day. You asked what the monstrosity was, and I told you it was called The Towers."

"I remember. A staring red-and-white house with about thirty bow-windows and twenty turrets. It defiles the landscape."

"Wait," said Jean, "till you see it close at hand. It's the most naked, newest thing you ever saw. Not a creeper, not an ivy leaf is allowed to crawl on it; weather seems to have no effect on it; it never gets to look any less new. And in summer it is worst, for then round about it blaze the reddest geraniums and the yellowest calceolarias and the bluest lobelias that it's possible to imagine."

"Ghastly! What is the owner like?"

"Small, with yellowish hair turning grey. She has a sharp nose, and her eyes seem to dart out at you, take you all in, and then look away. She is rather like a ferret, and she has small, sharp teeth like a ferret. I'm never a bit sure she won't bite. She really is rather a wonderful woman. She hasn't been here very many years, but she dominates everyone. At whatever house you meet her she has the air of being hostess. She welcomes you and advises you where to sit, makes suitable conversation, and finally bids you good-bye, and you feel yourself murmuring to her the grateful 'Such a pleasant afternoon', that was due to the real hostess. She is in constant conflict with the other prominent matrons in Priorsford, but she always gets her own way. At a meeting she is quite insupportable. She just calmly tells us what we are to do. It's no good saying we are busy; it's no good saying anything. We walk away with a great district to collect and a pile of pamphlets under one arm. . . . Her nose is a little on one side, and when I sit and look at her presiding at a meeting I toy with the thought that someone goaded to madness by her calm persistence had once heaved something at her, and wish I had been there to see. Really, though, she is rather a blessing in the place; she keeps us from stagnation. I read somewhere that when they bring tanks of cod to this country from wherever cod abound, they put a cat-fish in beside them, and it chases the cod round all the time, so that they arrive in good condition. Mrs. Duff-Whalley is our cat-fish."

"I see. Has she children?"

"Three. A daughter, married in London — Mrs. Egerton-Thompson — a son at Cambridge, and a daughter, Muriel, at home. I think it must be very bad for the Duff-Whalleys living in such a vulgar, restless-looking house."

Pamela laughed. "Do you think all the little pepper-pot towers must have an effect on the soul? I doubt it, my dear."

"Still," said Jean, "I think more will be expected at the end from the people who have all their lives lived in and looked at lovely places. It always worries me, the thought of people who live in the dark places of big cities — children especially, growing up like 'plants in mines that never saw the sun'. It is so dreadful that sometimes I feel I *must* go and help."

"What could you do?"

"That's what common sense always asks. I could do nothing alone, but if all the decent people tried their hardest it would make a difference. . . . It's the thought of the cruelty in the world that makes me sick. It's the hardest thing for me to keep from being happy. Great-aunt Alison said I had a light nature. Even when I ought to be sad my heart jumps up in the most unreasonable way, and I am happy. But sometimes it feels as if we comfortable people are walking on a flowery meadow that is really a great quaking morass, and underneath there is black slime full of unimagined horrors. A paragraph in the newspaper makes a crack and you see down: women who take money for keeping little babies and allow them to die, men who torture; tales of horror and terror. The War made a tremendous crack. It seemed then as if we were all to be drawn into the slime, as if cruelty had got its fangs into the heart of the world. When you knelt to pray at nights you could only cry and cry. The courage of the men who grappled in the slime with the horrors was the one thing that kept one from despair. And the fact that they could *laugh*. You know about the dying man who told his nurse some joke and finished, 'This is *the* War for laughs'."

Pamela nodded. "It hardly bears thinking of yet — the War and the fighters. Later on it will become the greatest of all sagas. But I want to hear about Priorsford people. That's a clean, cheerful subject. Who lives in the pretty house with the long ivy-covered front?"

"The Knowe it is called. The Jowetts live there — retired Anglo-Indians. Mr. Jowett is a funny, kind little man, with a red face and rather a nautical air. He is so busy that often it is afternoon before he reads his morning's letters."

"What does he do?"

"I don't think he does anything much: taps the barometer, advises the gardener, fusses with fowls, potters in the garden, teaches the dog tricks. It makes him happy to feel himself rushed, and to go carrying unopened letters at tea-time. They have no children. Mrs. Jowett is a dear. She collects servants as other people collect prints or old china or Sheffield plate. They are her hobby, and she has the most wonderful knack of managing them. Even now, when good servants seem to have become extinct, and people who need five or six are grubbing away miserably with one and a charwoman, she has four pearls with soft voices and gentle ways, experts at their job. She thinks about them all the time, and considers their comfort, and dresses them in pale grey with the daintiest spotted muslin aprons and mob caps. It is a pleasure to go to the Jowett's for a meal, everything is so perfect. The only drawback is if anyone makes the slightest mark on the cloth one of the silver-grey maids brings a saucer of water and wipes it off, and it is apt to make one nervous. I shall never forget going there to a children's party with David and Jock. Great-aunt Alison warned us most solemnly before we left home about marking the cloth, so we went rather tremblingly. There was a splendid tea in the dining-room, with silver candlesticks and pink shades, and lovely china, and a glittering cloth, and heaps of good things to eat — grown-up things like sandwiches and rich cakes, such as we hardly ever saw. Jock was quite small and loved his food, even more than he does now, dear lamb. A maid handed round the egg-shell china — if only they had given us mugs — and as she was putting down Jock's cup he turned round suddenly and his elbow simply shot it out of her hand, and sent it flying across the table. As it went it spattered everything with weak tea and then smashed itself against one of the candlesticks.

"I wished at that moment that the world would come to an end. There seemed no other way of clearing up the mess. I was so ashamed, and so sorry for my poor Jock, I couldn't lift my eyes, but Mr. Jowett rose to the occasion and earned my affection and unending gratitude. He pretended to find it a very funny episode, and made so many jokes about it that stiffness vanished from the party, and we all became riotously happy. And Mrs. Jowett, whose heart must have been wrung to see the beautiful table ruined at the outset, so mastered her emotion as to be able to smile and say no harm had been done. . . . You must go with me and see Mrs. Jowett, only don't tell her anything in the very least sad: she weeps at the slightest provocation."

"Tell me more," said Pamela — "tell me about all the people who live in those houses on the hill. It's like reading a nice *Cranfordy* book."

"But," Jean objected, "we're not in the least like people in a book. I often wonder why Priorsford is so unlike a story-book little town. We're not nearly interested enough in each other for one thing. We don't gossip to excess. Everyone goes his or her own way. In books people do things or are suspected of doing things, and are immediately cut out by a feverishly interested neighbourhood. I can't imagine that happening in Priorsford. No one ever does anything very striking, but if they did I'm sure they wouldn't be ostracised. Nobody would care much, except perhaps Mrs. Hope, and she would only be amused."

"Mrs. Hope?"

"Have you noticed a whitewashed house standing among trees about half a mile down Tweed from the bridge? That is Hopetoun, and Mrs. Hope and her daughter live there."

"Nice?"

Jean nodded her head like a wise mandarin. "You must meet Mrs. Hope.

To describe her is far beyond my powers."

"I see. Well, go on with the houses on the hill. Who lives in the one at the corner with the well-kept garden?"

"The Prestons. Mr. Preston is a lawyer, but he isn't much like a lawyer in appearance — not yellow and parchmenty, you know. He's a good shot and an ardent fisher, what Sir Walter would have called 'a just leevin' man for a country writer'. There are several daughters, all musical, and it is a very hospitable, cheerful house. Next the Prestons live the Williamsons. Ordinary nice people. There is really nothing to say about them. . . . The house after that is Woodside, the home of the two Miss Spiers. They are not ordinary. Miss Althea is a spiritualist. She sees visions and spends much of her time with spooks. Miss Clarice is a Buddhist. Their father, when he lived, was an elder in the U.F. Church. I sometimes wonder what he would say to his daughters now. When he died they left the U.F. Church and became Episcopalians, then Miss Clarice found that she couldn't believe in vicarious sacrifice and went over to Buddhism. She took me into her bedroom once. There was a thick yellow carpet, and a bed with a tapestry cover, and almost no furniture, except — is it impious to call Buddha furniture? — a large figure of Buddha, with a lamp burning before it. It all seemed to me horribly unfresh. Both ladies provide much simple amusement to the townsfolk with their clothes and their antics."

"I know the Spiers' type," said Pamela. "Foolish virgins."

"Next to Woodside is Craigton," went on Jean, "and there live three spinsters — the very best brand of spinsters — the Duncans, Miss Mary, Miss Janet, and Miss Phemie. I don't know what Priorsford would do without these good women. Spinsters they are, but they are also real mothers in Israel. They have time to help everyone. Benign Miss Mary is the housekeeper — and such a housekeeper! Miss Janet is the public one, sits on all the Committees. Miss Phemie does the flowers and embroiders beautiful things and is like a tea-cosy, so soft and warm and comfortable. Somehow they always seem to be there when you want them. You never go to their door and get a dusty answer. There is the same welcome for everyone, gentle and simple, and always the bright fire, and the kind, smiling faces, and tea with thick cream and cake of the richest and freshest. . . . You know how some people beg you to visit them, and when you go they seem to wear a surprised look, and you feel unexpected and awkward? The Duncans make you feel so pleased with yourself. They are so unselfishly interested in other people's concerns; and they are grand laughers. Even the dullest warm to something approaching wit when surrounded by that appreciative audience of three. They don't talk much themselves, but they have made of listening a fine art."

"Jean," said Pamela, "do you actually mean to tell me that everybody in Priorsford is nice? Or are you merely being charitable? I don't know anything duller than your charitable person who always says the kind thing."

Jean laughed. "I'm sorry, but I'm afraid the Priorsford people are all more or less nice. At least, they seem so to me, but perhaps I'm not very discriminating. You will tell me what you think of them when you meet them. All these people I've been telling you about are rich people, 'in a large way', as Priorsford calls it. They have all large motor-cars and hot-houses and rich things like that. Mrs. M'Cosh says Priorsford is a 'real tone-y wee place', and we do fancy ourselves a good deal. It's a community largely made up of women and middle-aged retired men. You see, there is nothing for the young men to do; we haven't even mills like so many of the Tweedside towns."

"Will people call on me?" Pamela asked. "Is Priorsford sociable?"

Jean pursed up her mouth in an effort to look worldly wise. "I think *you* will find it sociable, but if you had come here obscure and unknown, your existence would never have been heard of, even if you had taken a house and settled down. Priorsford hardly looks over its shoulder at a newcomer. Some of the 'little' people might call and ask you to tea — the kind 'little' people — but — "

"Who do you call the 'little' people?"

"All the people who aren't 'in a large way', all the dwellers in the snug little villas — most of Priorsford, in fact," Jean got up to go. "Dear me, look at the time! The boys will be home from school. May

I have the book you spoke of? Priorsford would be enraged if it heard me calmly discussing its faults and foibles." She laughed softly. "Lewis Elliot says Priorsford is made up of three classes — the dull, the daft, and the devout."

Pamela, looking for the book she wanted to lend to Jean, stopped and stood still as if arrested by the name.

"Lewis Elliot!"

"Yes, of Laverlaw. D'you know him, by any chance?"

"I used to know a Lewis Elliot who had some connection with Priorsford, but I thought he had left it years ago."

"Our Lewis Elliot inherited Laverlaw rather unexpectedly some years ago. Before that he was quite poor. Perhaps that is what makes him so understanding. He is a sort of distant cousin of ours. Great-aunt Alison was his aunt too — at least, he called her aunt. It will be fun if he turns out to be the man you used to know."

"Yes," said Pamela. "Here is the book, Jean. It's been so nice having you this afternoon. No, dear, I won't go back with you to tea. I'm going to write letters. Good-bye. My love to the boys."

But Pamela wrote no letters that evening. She sat with a book on her knee and looked into the fire: sometimes she sighed.

8

"I have, as you know, a general prejudice against all persons who do not succeed in the world."

JOWETT OF BALLIOL

MRS. DUFF-WHALLEY was giving a dinner-party. This was no uncommon occurrence, for she loved to entertain. It was her real pleasure to provide a good meal and to see her guests enjoy it. "Besides," as she often said, "what's the use of having everything solid for the table, and a fine house and a cook at sixty pounds a year, if nobody's any the wiser?"

It will be seen from this remark that Mrs. Duff-Whalley had not always been in a position to give dinner-parties; indeed, Mrs. Hope, that terror to the newly risen, who traced everyone back to their first rude beginnings (generally "a wee shop"), had it that the late Mr. Duff-Whalley had begun life as a "Johnnie-a'-things" in Leith, and that his wife had been his landlady's daughter.

But the "wee shop" was in the dim past, if, indeed, it had ever existed except in Mrs. Hope's wicked, wise old head, and for many years Mrs. Duff-Whalley had ruffled it in a world that asked no questions about the origin of money so obviously there.

Most people are weak when they come in contact with a really strong-willed woman. No one liked Mrs. Duff-Whalley, but few, if any, withstood her advances. It was easier to give in and be on calling and dining terms than to repulse a woman who never noticed a snub, and who would never admit the possibility that she might not be wanted. So Mrs. Duff-Whalley could boast with some degree of truth that she knew "everybody", and entertained at The Towers "very nearly the highest in the land".

The dinner-party I write of was not one of her more ambitious efforts. It was a small and (with the exception of one guest) what she called "a purely local affair". That is to say, the people who were to grace the feast were culled from the big villas on the Hill, and were not "county".

Mrs. Duff-Whalley was an excellent

manager, and left nothing to chance. She saw to all the details herself. Dressed and ready quite half an hour before the time fixed for dinner, she had cast her eagle glance over the dinner-table, and now sailed into the drawing-room to see that the fire was at its best, the chairs comfortably disposed, and everything as it should be. Certainly no one could have found fault with the comfort of the room this evening. A huge fire blazed in the most approved style of grate, the electric light (in the latest fittings) also blazed, lighting up the handsome oil-paintings that adorned the walls, the many photographs, the china in the cabinets, the tables with their silver treasures. Everywhere stood vases of heavy-scented hot-house flowers. Mrs. Duff-Whalley approved of hot-house flowers; she said they gave a tone to a room.

The whole room glittered, and its mistress glittered with it as she moved about in a dress largely composed of sequins, a diamond necklace, and a startling ornament in her hair.

She turned as the door opened and her daughter came into the room, and looked her carefully up and down. She was a pretty girl dressed in the extreme of fashion, and under each arm she carried a tiny barking-dog.

Muriel was a good daughter to her mother, and an exemplary character in every way, but the odd thing was that few people liked her. This was the more tragic as it was the desire of her heart to be popular. Her appearance was attractive, and strangers usually began acquaintance with enthusiasm, but the attraction rarely survived the first hour's talk. She was like a very well-coloured and delightful-looking apple that is without flavour. She was never natural — always aping some-one. Her enthusiasms did not ring true, her interest was obviously feigned, and she had that most destroying of social faults — she could not listen with patience, but let her attention wander to the conver-sation of her neighbours. It seemed as if she could never talk at peace with anyone for fear of missing something more inter-esting in another quarter.

"You look very nice, Muriel! I'm glad I told you to put on that dress, and that new way of doing your hair is very be-coming." One lovable thing about Mrs.

Duff-Whalley was the way she sincerely and openly admired everything that was hers. "Now, see and do your best to make the evening go. Mr. Elliot takes a lot of amusing, and the Jowett's aren't very lively either."

"Is that all that's coming?" Muriel asked.

"I asked the new Episcopalian parson — what's his name? — yes — Jackson — to fill up."

"You don't often descend to the clergy, mother."

"No; but Episcopalians are slightly better fitted for society than Presbyterians, and this young man seems quite a gentleman — such a blessing, too, when they haven't got wives. Dear, dear, I told Dickie not to send in any more of that plant — what d'you call it?" (It was a peculiarity of Mrs. Duff-Whalley that she never could remember the names of any but the simplest flowers.) "I don't like its perfume. What was I saying? Of course, I only got up this dinner on the spur of the moment, so to speak, when I met Mr. Elliot in the Highgate. He comes and goes so much, you never know when he's at Laverlaw; if you write or telephone he's always got another engagement. But when I met him face to face I just said, 'Now, when will you dine with us, Mr. Elliot?' and he hummed and hawed a bit and then fixed tonight."

"Perhaps he didn't want to come," Muriel suggested, as she snuggled one of the small dogs against her face. "And did it love its own mummy, then, darling snub-nose pet?"

Her mother scouted the idea.

"Why should he not want to come? Do put down those dogs, Muriel. I never get used to see you kissing them. A good dinner and everything comfortable, and you to play the piano to him taught by the best masters — he's ill to please. And he's not very well off, though he does own Laverlaw. It's the time the family has been there that gives him the standing. I must say, he isn't in the least genial, but he gets that from his mother. A starchier old woman I never met. I remember your father and I were staying at the Hydro when old Elliot died, and his son was killed before that, shooting lions or something in Africa, so this Lewis Elliot, who was a nephew, inherited. We thought we would go and ask if by any chance they wanted to sell the place, so we called in a friendly way, though we didn't know them, of course. It was old Mrs. Elliot we saw, and my word, she was cold. As polite as you like, but as icy as the North Pole. Your father had some vulgar sayings I couldn't break him of, and he said as we drove out of the lodge gates, 'Well, that old wife gave us our head in our laps and our lugs to play wi'.' "

"Why, mother!" Muriel cried, astonished. Her mother was never heard to use a Scots expression and thought even a Scots song slightly vulgar.

"I know — I know," said Mrs. Duff-Whalley, hastily. "It just came over me for a minute how your father said it. He was a very amusing man, your father, very bright to live with, though he was too fond of low Scots expressions for my taste; and he *would* eat cheese to his tea. It kept us down, you know. I've risen a lot in the world since your father left us, though I miss him, of course. He used to laugh at Minnie's ideas. It was Minnie got us to send Gordon to an English school and then to Cambridge, and take the hyphen. Your father had many a laugh at the hyphen, and before the servants too! You see, Minnie went to a high-class school and made friends with the right people, and learned how things should be done. She had always assurance, had Minnie. The way she could order the waiters about in those grand London hotels! And then she married Egerton-Thomson. But you're better looking, Muriel."

Muriel brushed aside the subject of her looks.

"What made you settle in Priorsford?" she asked.

"Well, we came out first to stay at the Hydro — you were away at school then — and your father took a great fancy to the place. He was making money fast, and we always had a thought of buying a place. But there was nothing that just suited us. We thought it would be too dull to be right out in the country at the end of a long drive — exclusive, you know, but terribly dreary, and then your father said, 'Build a house to suit ourselves in Priorsford, and we'll have shops and a station and everything quite near.' His idea was to have a house as like a hydropathic as possible, and to call it The Towers. 'A fine big, red house,

Aggie,' he often said to me, 'with plenty of bow-windows and turrets and a hot-house off the drawing-room and a sweep of gravel in front and a lot of geraniums and those yellow flowers — what do'you call 'em? — good lawns, and a flower garden and a kitchen garden and a garage, and what more d'you want?' Well, well, he got them all, but he didn't live long to enjoy them. I think myself that having nothing to do but take his meals killed him. I hear wheels! That'll be the Jowetts. They're always so punctual. Am I all right?"

Muriel assured her that nothing was wrong or lacking, and they waited for their guests.

The door opened and the servant announced, "Mr. and Mrs. Jowett."

Mrs. Jowett walked very slowly and delicately, and her husband pranced behind her. It might have been expected that in their long walk together through life Mr. Jowett would have got accustomed to his wife's deliberate entrances, but no — it always seemed as if he were just on the point of giving her an impatient push from behind.

She was a gentle-looking woman with

soft, white hair and a pink-and-white complexion — the sort of woman one always associates with old lace. In her youth it was said that she had played the harp, and one felt that the "grave, sweet melody" would have well become her. She was dressed in pale shades of mauve, and had a finely finished look. The Indian climate and curries had affected Mr. Jowett's liver, and made his temper fiery, but his heart remained the sound, childlike thing it had always been. He quarrelled with everybody (though never for long), but people in trouble gravitated to him naturally, and no one had ever asked him anything in reason and been refused; children loved him.

Mr. Jackson, the Episcopalian clergyman, followed hard behind the Jowetts, and was immediately engaged in an argument with Mr. Jowett as to whether or not choral communion, which had recently been started and which Mr. Jowett resented, as he resented all new things, should be continued.

"Ridiculous!" he shouted — "utterly ridiculous! You will drive the people from the church, sir."

Then Mr. Elliot arrived. Mrs. Duff-Whalley greeted him impressively, and dinner was announced.

Lewis Elliot was a man of forty-five, tall and thin and inclined to stoop. He had short-sighted blue eyes and a shy, kind smile. He was not a sociable man, and resented being dragged from his books to attend a dinner-party. Like most people he was quite incapable of saying No to Mrs. Duff-Whalley when that lady desired an affirmative answer, but he had condemned himself roundly to himself as a fool as he drive down the glen from Laverlaw.

Mrs. Duff-Whalley always gave a long and pretentious meal, and expected everyone to pay for their invitation by being excessively bright and chatty. It was not in the power of the present guests to be either the one thing or the other. Mrs. Jowett was pensive and sweet, and inclined to be silent; her husband gave loud barks of disagreement at intervals; Mr. Jackson enjoyed his dinner and answered when spoken to, while Lewis Elliot was rendered almost speechless by the flood of talk his hostess poured over him.

"I'm very sorry, Mr. Elliot," she remarked in a pause, "that the people I wanted to meet you couldn't come. I asked Sir John and Lady Tweedie, but they were engaged — so unfortunate, for they are such an acquisition. Then I asked the Olivers, and they couldn't come. You would really wonder where the engagements come from in this quiet neighbourhood." She gave a little, unbelieving laugh. "I had evidently chosen an unfortunate evening for the County."

It was trying for everyone: for Mr. Elliot, who was left with the impression that people were apt to be engaged when asked to meet him; for the Jowetts, who now knew that they had received a "fiddler's bidding", and for Mr. Jackson, who felt that he was only there because nobody else could be got.

There was a blank silence, which Lewis Elliot broke by laughing, cheerfully. "That absurd rhyme came into my head," he explained. "You know:

" 'Miss Smarty gave a party,
    No one came.
    Her brother gave another,
    Just the same.' "

134

Then, feeling suddenly that he had not improved matters, he fell silent.

"Oh," said Mrs. Duff-Whalley, rearing her head like an affronted hen, "the difficulty, I assure you, is not to find guests but to decide which to select."

"Quite so, quite so, naturally," murmured Mr. Jackson, soothingly; he had laughed at the rhyme and felt apologetic. Then, losing his head completely under the cold glance his hostess turned on him, he added, "Go ye into the highways and hedges and compel them to come in."

Mrs. Jowett took a bit of toast and broke it nervously. She was never quite at ease in Mrs. Duff-Whalley's company. Incapable of an unkind thought or a bitter word, so refined as to be almost inaudible, she felt jarred and bumped in her mind after a talk with that lady, even as her body would have felt after bathing in a rough sea among rocks. Realising that the conversation had taken an unfortunate turn, she tried to divert it into more pleasing channels.

Turning to Mr. Jackson, she said: "Such a sad thing happened today. Our dear old dog, Rover, had to be put away.

He was sixteen, very deaf and rather cross, and the Vet. said it wasn't *kind* to keep him; and of course after that we felt there was nothing to be said. The Vet. said he would come this morning at ten o'clock, and it quite spoiled my breakfast, for dear Rover sat beside me and begged, and I felt like an executioner; and then he went out for a walk by himself — a thing he hadn't done since he had become frail — and when the Vet. came there was no Rover."

"Dear, dear!" said Mr. Jackson, helping himself to an entrée.

"The really dreadful thing about it," continued Mrs. Jowett, refusing the entrée, "was that Johnston — the gardener, you know — had dug the grave where I had chosen he should lie, dear Rover, and — you have heard the expression, Mr. Jackson — a yawning grave? Well, the grave *yawned*. It was too heart-rending. I simply went to my room and cried, and Tim went in one direction and Johnston in another, and the maids looked too, and they found the dear doggie, and the Vet. — a most obliging man called Davidson — came back . . . and dear Rover is *at rest*."

Mrs. Jowett looked sadly round and

found that the whole table had been listening to the recital.

Few people have not loved a dog and known the small tragedy of parting with it when its all too short day was over, and even the "lamentable comedy" of Mrs. Jowett's telling of the tale drew no smile.

Muriel leant forward, genuinely distressed. "I'm so frightfully sorry, Mrs. Jowett, you'll miss dear old Rover dreadfully."

"It's a beastly business putting away a dog," said Lewis Elliot. "I always wish they had the same lease of life as we have. Three score years and ten. And it's none too long for such faithful friends."

"You must get another, Mrs. Jowett," her hostess told her, bracingly. "Get a dear little toy Pekingese or one of those Japanese what-do-you-call 'ems? that you carry in your arms. So smart."

"If you do, Janetta," her husband warned her, "you must choose between the brute and me. I refuse to live in the same house with one of those pampered, trifling little beasts. If we decide to fill old Rover's place, I suggest that we get a rough-haired

Irish terrier." He rolled the "r's" round his tongue. "Something robust that can bark and chase cats, and not lie all day on a cushion, like one of those dashed Chinese . . ." His voice died away in muttered thunder.

Again Mrs. Duff-Whalley reared her head, but Muriel interposed, laughing. "You mustn't really be so severe, Mr. Jowett. I happen to possess two of the 'trifling beasts', and you must come and apologise to them after dinner. You can't imagine more perfect darlings, and *of course* they are called Bing and Toutou. You won't be able to resist their little sweet faces — too utterly darling!"

"Shan't I?" said Mr. Jowett, doubtfully. "Well, I apologise. Nobody likes to hear their dog miscalled. . . . By the way, Jackson, that's an abominable brute of yours. Bit three milk girls and devastated the Scott's hen-house last week, I hear."

"Yes," said Mr. Jackson. "Four murdered fowls they brought to me, and I had to pay for them; and they didn't give me the corpses, which I felt was too bad."

"What?" said Mrs. Duff-Whalley, deeply interested. "Did you actually pay for the damage done and let them keep the fowls?"

"I did," Mr. Jackson owned gloomily, and the topic lasted until the fruit was handed round.

"I wonder," said Mrs. Jowett to her hostess, as she peeled a pear, "if you have met a newcomer in Priorsford — Miss Reston? She has taken Miss Bathgate's rooms."

"You mean the Honourable Pamela Reston? She is a daughter of the late Lord Bidborough of Bidborough Manor, Surrey, and Mintern Abbas, Oxfordshire, and sister of the present peer: I looked her up in Debrett. I called on her, feeling it my duty to be civil to a stranger, but it seems to me a very odd thing that's a peer's daughter would care to live in such a humble way. Mark my words, there's something shady about it. Perhaps she's an absconding lady's maid. She was out when I called anyway, so I didn't see her."

"Oh, indeed," said Mrs. Jowett, blushing pink, "Miss Reston is no imposter. When you have seen her you will realise that. I met her yesterday at the Jardines'. She is the most delightful creature, *so*

charming to look at, so wonderfully graceful — "

"I think," said Lewis Elliot, "that that
must be the Pamela Reston I used to know.
Did you say she was living in Priorsford?"

"Yes; in a cottage called Hillview, next
to The Rigs, you know," Mrs. Jowett
explained. "Mhor made friends with her
whenever she arrived, and took her in to
see Jean. You can imagine how attractive
she found the whole household."

"The Jardines are very unconventional,"
said Mrs. Duff-Whalley, "if you call that
attractive. Jean doesn't know how to keep
her place with people at all. I saw her walking beside a tinker woman the other day,
helping her with her bundle; and I'm sure,
I've simply had to give up calling at The
Rigs, for you never knew who you would
have to shake hands with. I'm sorry for
Jean, poor little soul. It seems a pity that
there is no one to dress her and give her a
chance. She's a plain little thing at best,
but clothes might transform her."

"There I totally disagree," shouted Mr.
Jowett. "Jean, to my mind, is the best-
looking girl in Priorsford. She walks so well
and has such an honest jolly look. She's the

kind of a girl a man would like to have for a daughter."

"But what," asked Mrs. Duff-Whalley, "can Miss Reston have in common with people like the Jardines? I don't believe they have more than £300 a year, and such a plain little house, and one queer old servant. Miss Reston must be accustomed to things so very different. We must ask her here to meet some of the County."

"The County?" growled Mr. Jowett. "Except for Elliot here, and the Hopes and the Tweedies and the Olivers, there are practically none of the old families left. I tell you what it is — "

But Mrs. Duff-Whalley had had enough for the moment of Mr. Jowett's conversation, so she nodded to Mrs. Jowett, and with an arch admonition to the men not to stay too long, she swept the ladies before her to the drawing-room.

9

"I will the country see
Where old simplicity,
Though hid in grey
Doth look more gay
than foppery in plush and scarlet clad."*
THOMAS RANDOLPH, 1605–35

A LETTER from Pamela Reston to her brother:

" . . . It was a tremendous treat to get your budget this morning after three mails of silence. I got your cable saying you were back before I knew you comtemplated going, so I never had to worry. I think the War has shaken my nerves in a way I hadn't realised. I never used to worry about you very much, knowing your faculty of falling on your feet, but now I tremble.

"Sikkim must be marvellous, and to try an utterly untried route was thrilling, but what uncomfortable times men do give themselves! To lie in a tiny tent in the soaking rain with your bedding crawling with leeches, 'great cold, well-nourished fellows'. Ugh! And yet, I suppose you counted the discomforts as nothing when you gazed at Everest while yet the dawn 'walked tiptoe on the mountains' and even more wonderful, as you describe it, must have been the vision from below the Aluk-thang glacier, when the mists slowly un-veiled the face of Pandim to the moon. . . .

"And I shall soon hear of it all by word of mouth. It is the best of news that you are coming home. I don't think you must go away again without me. I have missed you dreadfully these last six months.

"Besides, you ought to settle at home for a bit now, don't you think? First, your long exploring expedition and then the War: haven't you been across the world away long enough to make you want to stay at home? You are one of the very worst specimens of an absentee landlord. . . . After profound calculations I have come to the conclusion that you will get two letters from me from Priorsford before you leave India. I am sending this to Port Said to make sure of not missing you. You will have lots of time to read it on board ship if it is rather long.

"Shall I meet you in London? Send me a wire when you get this. What I should like to do would be to conduct you personally to Priorsford. I think you would like it. The countryside is lovely, and after a week or two we could go somewhere for Christmas. The Champertouns have asked me to go to them, and of course their invitation would include you. They are second or third cousins, and we've never seen them, but they are our mother's people, and I have always wanted to see where she was brought up. However, we can settle all that later on. . . .

"I feel myself quite an old resident in Priorsford now, and have become acquainted with some of the people — well-to-do, hospitable, not at all interesting (with a few exceptions), but kind.

"The Jardines remain my great interest. What a blessing it is when people improve by knowing — so few do. I see the Jardines once everyday, sometimes oftener, and I like them more every time I see them.

"I've been thinking, Biddy, you and I haven't had a vast number of people, to be fond of. There was Aunt Eleanor, but I defy anyone to be fond of her. Respect her one might, fear her we did, but love her — it would have been as discouraging as petting a steam road-roller. We hadn't even a motherly old nurse, for Aunt Eleanor liked machine-made people like herself to serve her. I don't think it did you much harm, you were such a sunny-tempered, affectionate little boy, but it made me rather inhuman.

"As we grew up we acquired crowds of friends and acquaintances, but they were never like real home-people to whom you show both your best and your worst side, and who love you simply because you are you. The Jardines give me that homey feeling.

"The funny thing is I thought I was going to broaden Jean, to show her what a narrow, little Puritan she is, bound in the Old Testament thrall of her Great-aunt Alison — but not a bit of it. She is very receptive, delighted to be told about people and clothes, cities, theatres, pictures, but on what she calls 'serious things' she is an absolute rock. It is like finding a Round-head delighting in Royalist sports and plays, or a Royalist chanting Roundhead Psalms — if you can imagine an evangelical

145

Royalist. Anyway, it is rather a fine combination.

"I only wish I could help to make things easier for Jean. I have far more money than I want; she has so little. I'm afraid she has to plan and worry a good deal how to clothe and feed and educate those boys. I know that she is very anxious that David should not be too scrimped for money at Oxford, and consequently spends almost nothing on herself. A warm coat for Jock; no evening gown for Jean. David finds he must buy certain books and writes home in distress. 'That can easily be managed,' says Jean, and goes without a new winter hat. She and Mrs. M'Cosh are wonders of economy in housekeeping, and there is always abundance of plain, well-cooked food.

"I told you about Mrs. M'Cosh? She is the Jardines' one servant — an elderly woman, a widow from Glasgow. I like her way of showing in visitors. She was a pew-opener in a church at one time, which may account for it. When you ask if Jean is in, she puts her head on one side in a consider-ing way and says, 'I'm no' juist sure,' and ambles away, leaving the visitor quite undecided whether she is intended to re-main on the doorstep or follow her in. I know now that she means you to remain meekly on the doorstep, for she lately recounted to me with glee of another caller, 'I'd went awa' up the stair to see if Miss Jean wis in, whit d'ye think? When I lukit roond the wumman wis at ma heels.' The other day workmen were in the house doing something, and when Mrs. M'Cosh opened the door to me she said, 'Ye see the mess we're in. D'ye think ye should come in?' leaving it to my better nature to decide whether to bide or come another day.

"She is always serene, always smiling. The great love of her life is Peter, the fox-terrier, one of the wickedest and nicest of dogs. He is always in trouble, and she is sorely put to it sometimes to find excuses for him. 'He's a great wee case, is Peter,' she generally finishes up. 'He means no ill' (this, after it had been proved that he has chased sheep, killed hens, and bitten message-boys); 'he's juist a wee thing playful.'

"Peter attends every function in Priors-ford — funerals, marriages, circuses. He meets all the trains and escorts strangers to the objects of interest in the neighbourhood. He sees people off, and wags his tail in farewell as the train moves out of the station.

"He and Mhor are fast friends, and it is an inspiring sight to see them of a morning, standing together in the middle of the road with the whole wide world before them, wondering which would be the best way to take for adventures. Mhor has had much liberty lately as he has been infectious after whooping-cough, but now he has gone back to the little school he attends with some twenty other children. I'm afraid he is a very unwilling scholar.

"You will be glad to hear that Bella Bathgate (I'm taking a liberty with her name I don't dare take in speaking to her) is thawing me slightly. It seems that part of the reason for her distaste to me was that she thought I would probably demand a savoury for dinner! If I did ask for such a thing — which Heaven forbid! — she would probably send me in a huge pudding dish of macaroni and cheese. Her cooking is not the best of Bella.

"She and Mawson have become fast

friends. Mawson has asked Bella to call her Winifred, and she calls Miss Bathgate 'Beller'.

"Miss Bathgate spends any leisure moments she has in doing long strips of crochet, which eventually become a bedspread, and considers it a waste of time to read anything but the Bible, *The Scotsman*, and *The Missionary Magazine* (she is very keen on Foreign Missions), but she doesn't object to listening to Mawson's garbled accounts of the books she reads. I sometimes overhear their conversations as they sit together by the kitchen fire in the long evenings.

" 'And,' says Mawson, describing some particularly lurid work of fiction, 'Evangeline was left shut up in the picture-gallery of the 'ouse.'

" 'D'ye mean to tell me hooses hev picture-galleries?' says Bella.

" 'Course they 'ave — all big 'ouses.'

" 'Juist like the Campbell Institution — sic a bother it must be to dust!'

" 'Well,' Mawson goes on; 'Evangeline finds 'er h'eyes attracted — '

"Again Bella interrupts. 'Wha was Evangeline? I forget aboot her.'

" 'Oh, don't you remember? The golden-'aired 'eroine with vilet eyes.'

" 'I mind her noo. The yin wi' the black hair was the bad yin.'

" 'Yes, she was called 'Ermione. Well, Evangeline finds 'er h'eyes attracted to the picture of a man dressed like a cavalier.'

" 'What's that?'

" 'I don't rightly know,' Mawson confesses. 'Kind of a fancy dress, I believe, but anyway, 'er h'eyes were attracted to the picture, and as she fixed 'er h'eyes on it the *h'eyes in the picture moved.*'

" 'Oh, murder!' says Bella, much thrilled.

" 'You may say it. Murder it was, h'attempted murder, I should say, for of course it would never do to murder the vilet-h'eyed 'eroine. As it 'appened . . .' and so on. . . .

"One of the three months gone! Perhaps at the beginning of the year I shall have had more than enough of it, and go gladly back to the fleshpots of Egypt and the Politician.

"It is a dear thing a little town, 'a lovesome thing, God wot', and Priorsford is the pick of all little towns. I love the shops and the kind, interested way the shopkeepers serve one. I have shopped in most European cities, but I never realised the full delight of shopping till I came to Priorsford. You can't think what fun it is to order in all your own meals, to decide whether you will have a 'finnan-haddie' or a 'kipper' for breakfast — much more exciting than ordering a ball gown.

"I love the river, and the wide bridge, and the old castle keeping watch and ward, and the *pends* through which you catch sudden glimpses of the solemn round-backed hills. And most of all I love the lights that twinkle out in the early darkness, every light meaning a little home, and a warm fireside and kindly people round it.

"To live, as you and I have done all our lives, in houses where all the difficulties of life are kept in oblivion, and existence runs on well-oiled wheels is very pleasant, doubtless, but one misses a lot. I love the *nearness* of Hillview, to hear Mawson and B.B. converse in the kitchen, to smell (this is the most comfortable and homely smell) the ironing of clean clothes, and to know (also by the sense of smell) what I am going to have for dinner hours before it comes.

"Of course you will say, and probably with truth, that what I enjoy is the *newness* of it, that if I knew that my life would be spent in such surroundings I would be profoundly dissatisfied.

"I daresay. But in the meantime I am happy — happy in a contented, quiet way that I never knew before.

"It is strange that our old friend Lewis Elliot is living near Priorsford, a place called Laverlaw, about five miles up Tweed from here. Do you remember what good times we used to have with him when he came to stay with the Greys? That must be more than twenty years ago — you were a little boy and I was a wild colt of a girl. I don't think you have ever seen much of him since, but I saw a lot of him in London when I first came out. Then he vanished. Some years ago his uncle died and he inherited Laverlaw. He came to see me the other day, not a bit changed, the same dreamy, unambitious creature — rather an angel. I sometimes wonder if little Jean will one day go to Laverlaw. It would be very nice and fairy-tale-ish!"

10

"You that are old," Falstaff reminds the
Chief Justice,
*"consider not the capacities of us that are
young."*
"KING HENRY THE FOURTH PART 2"

ONE afternoon Jean called for Pamela to take her to see Mrs. Hope.

It was a clear, blue-and-white day, with clouds scudding across the sky, and a cold, whistling wind that blew the fallen leaves along the dry roads — a day that made people walk smartly, and gave the children apple-red cheeks and tangled curls.

Mhor and Peter were seated on The Rigs garden wall as Pamela and Jean came out of Hillview gate. Peter wagged his tail in recognition, but Mhor made no sign of having seen his sister and her friend.

"Aren't you cold up there?" Pamela asked him.

"Very cold," said Mhor, "but we can't come down. We're on sentry duty on the city wall till sundown," and he shaded his eyes with his hand and pretended to peer into space for lurking foes.

Peter looked wistfully up at him and hunched himself against the scratched bare knees now blue with cold.

"When the sun touches the top of West Law," said Jean, pointing to a distant blue peak, "it has set. See — there. . . . Now run in, sonny, and tell Mrs. M'Cosh to let you have some currant-loaf for tea. Pamela and I are going to tea at Hopetoun."

"Aw," said Mhor, "I hate when you go out to tea. So does Jock. So does Peter. Look out! I'm going to jump."

He jumped and fell prostrate, barking his chin, but no howl came from him, and he picked himself up with dignity, merely asking for the loan of a handkerchief, his own "useful little hanky" as he explained, having been used to mop up a spilt inkbottle.

Fortunately Jean had a spare handkerchief, and Pamela promised that on her return he should have a reel of stickingplaster for his own use, so, battered but content, he returned to the house, Peter remaining behind to investigate a mole-heap.

"What a cheery day for November," Pamela remarked as they took the road by Tweedside. "Look at that beech tree against the blue sky, every black twig silhouetted. Trees are wonderful in winter."

"Trees are wonderful always," said Jean. " 'Solomon spake of trees' — I do wonder what he said. I suppose it would be the cedars of Lebanon he 'spake' of, and the hyssop that grows in the walls, and sycamores, but he would have been worth hearing on a rowan tree flaming red against a blue September sky. Look at that newly ploughed field so softly brown, and the faded gold of the beech hedge. November *is* a cheery time. The only depressing time of the year to me is when the swallows go away. I can't bear to see them wheeling round and preparing to depart. I want so badly to go with them. It always brings back to me the feeling I had as a child when people read Hans Andersen to me — the storks in *The Marsh King's Daughter*, talking about the mud in Egypt. Imagine Priorsford swallows in Egypt! . . . As the song says:

> *'It's dowie at the hint o' hair'st*
> *At the way-gaun o' the swallow.' "*

"What a lovely sound Lowland Scots has," said Pamela. "I like to hear you speak it. Tell me about Mrs. Hope, Jean. I do hope we shall see her alone. I don't like Priorsford tea-parties: they are rather like a foretaste of eternal punishment. With no choice you are dumped down beside the most irrelevant sort of person, and there you remain. I went to return Mrs. Duff-Whalley's call the other day, and fell into one. Before I could retreat I was wedged into a chair beside a woman whom I hope I shall never see again. She was one of those bleak people who make the thought of getting up in the morning and dressing quite insupportable. I don't think there was a detail in her domestic life that she didn't touch on. She told me all her husband could eat and couldn't eat; she called her children 'little tots', and said she couldn't get so much as a 'serviette' washed in the house. I thought nobody talked of serviettes outside Wells and Arnold Bennett. Mrs. Duff-Whalley rescued me in the nick of time before I could do anything desperate, and then *she* cross-examined me as to my reasons for coming to Priorsford."

Jean laughed. "What a cheery afternoon! But it will be all right today. Mrs. Hope never sees more than one or two people at a time. She is pretty old, you see, and frail, though she has such an extraordinary gift of being young. I do hope you will like each other. She has an edge to her tongue, but she is an incomparable friend. The poor people go to her in flocks, and she scolds them roundly, but always knows how to help them in the only wise way. Her people have been in Priorsford for ages; she knows every soul in the place, and is vastly amused at all the little snobberies that abound in a small town. But she laughs kindlily. Pretentious people are afraid of her; simple people love her."

"Am I simple, Jean?"

Jean laughed and refused to give an opinion on the subject beyond quoting the words of Autolycus — "How blessed are we that are not simple men".

There were in the Hopetoun Woods now, and at the end of the avenue could see the house standing on a knoll by the river, whitewashed, dignified, homelike.

"Talk to Mrs. Hope about the view," Jean advised. "She is as proud of the Hopetoun Woods as if she had made them. Isn't it a nice place ? Old and proud and honourable — like Mrs. Hope herself."

"Are there sons to inherit ?"

Jean shook her head. "There were three sons. Mrs. Hope hardly ever talks about them, but I've seen their photographs, and of course I have often been told about them — by Great-aunt Alison, and others — and heard how they died. They were very clever and good-looking and well liked — the kind of sons mothers are very proud of, and they all died imperially, if that is an expression to use. Two died in India, one — a soldier — in one of the Frontier skirmishes; the other — an I.C.S. man — for overworking in a famine-stricken district. The youngest fell in the Boer War . . . so you see Mrs. Hope has the right to be proud. Aunt Alison used to tell me that she made no moan over her wonderful sons. She shut herself up for a short time, and then faced the world again, her kindly, sharp-tongued self. She is one of those splendid people who take the stings and arrows thrown at them by outrageous fortune and bury them deep in their hearts and go on, still able to laugh, still able to take an interest. Only you mustn't speak to her of what she has lost. That would be too much."

"Yes," said Pamela. "I can understand that."

She stopped for a minute and stood looking at the river full of "wan water from the Border hills", at the stretches of lawn ornamented here and there by stone figures, at the trees *thrawn* with winter and rough weather, and she thought of the three boys who had played here, who had lived in the white-washed house (she could see the barred nursery windows), bathed and fished in the Tweed, thrown stones at the grey stone figures on the lawn, climbed the trees in the Hopetoun Woods, and who had gone out with their happy young lives to lay them down in a far country.

Mrs. Hope was sitting by the fire in the drawing-room, a room full of flowers and books, and lit by four long windows. Two of the windows looked on to the lawns, and the stone figures chipped by generations of catapult-owning boys; the other two looked across the river into the

Hopetoun Woods. The curtains were not drawn though the lamps were lit, for Mrs. Hope liked to keep the river and the woods with her as long as light lasted, so the warm, bright room looked warmer and brighter in contrast with the cold, ruffled water and the wind-shaken trees outside.

Mrs. Hope has been a beautiful woman in her day, and was still an attractive figure, her white hair dressed high and crowned with a square of lace tied in quaint fashion under her chin. Her black dress was soft and becoming to her spare figure. There was nothing unsightly about her years; she made age seem a lovely, desirable thing. Not that her years were so very many, but she had lived every minute of them; also she had given lavishly and un-sparingly of her store of sympathy and energy to others: and she had suffered grievously.

She kissed Jean affectionately, upbraiding her for being long in coming, and turned eagerly to Pamela. New people still interested her vividly. Here was a newcomer who promised well.

"Ah, my dear," she said in greeting, "I have wanted to know you. I'm told you are the most interesting person who ever came to this little town."

Pamela laughed. "There I am sure you have been misled. Priorsford is full of exciting people. I expected to be dull, and I have rarely been so well amused."

Mrs. Hope studied the charming face bent to her own. Her blue eyes were shrewd, and though she stood so near the end of the way she had lost none of her interest in the comings and goings of Vanity Fair.

"Is Priorsford amusing?" she asked. "Well," (complacently), "we have our points. As Jane Austen wrote of the Misses Bingley, 'Our powers of conversation are considerable — we can describe an entertainment with accuracy, relate an anecdote with humour, and laugh at our acquaintances with spirit.' "

"Laugh!" Jean groaned. "Pamela, I must warn you that Mrs. Hope's laughter scares Priorsford to death. We speak her fair in order that she won't give us away to our neighbours, but we have no real hope that she doesn't see through us. Have we, Miss Augusta?" addressing the daughter of the house, who had just come into the room.

"Ah," said Mrs. Hope, "if everyone was as transparent as you, Jean."

"Ah, don't," Jean pleaded. "You remind me that I am quite uninteresting when I am trying to make believe that I am subtle, or 'subtile', as the Psalmist says of the fowler's snare."

"Absurd child! Augusta, my dear, this is Miss Reston."

Miss Hope shook hands in her gentle, shy way, and busied herself putting small tables beside her mother and the two guests as the servant brought in tea. Her life was spent in doing small services.

Once, when Augusta was a child, someone asked her what she would like to be, and she had replied, "A lady like mamma." She had never lost the ambition, though very soon she had known that it could not be realised. It was difficult to believe that she was Mrs. Hope's daughter, for she had no trace of the beauty and sparkle with which her mother had been endowed. Augusta had a long, kind, patient face — a drab coloured face — but her voice was beautiful. She had never been young; she was born an anxious pilgrim, and now, at fifty, she seemed infinitely older than her ageless mother,

Pamela, watching her as she made the tea, saw all Augusta's heart in her eyes as she looked at her mother, and saw, too, the dread that lay in them — the dread of the days that she must live after the light had gone out for her.

During the tea Mrs. Hope had many questions to ask about David's time at Oxford, and Jean was only too delighted to recount every single detail.

"And how is my dear Jock? He is my favourite."

"Not the Mhor?" asked Pamela.

"No. Mhor is 'a'body's body'. He will never lack for admirers. But Jock is my own boy. We've been friends since he came home from India, a white-headed baby with the same surprised blue eyes that he has now. He was never out of scrapes at home, but he was always good with me. I suppose I was flattered by that."

"Jock," said Jean, "is very nearly the nicest thing in the world, and the funniest. This morning Mrs. M'Cosh caught a mouse alive in a trap, and Jock, while dressing, heard her say she would drown it. Down he went, like an avalanche, in pyjamas, drove Mrs. M'Cosh into the scullery, and let the mouse away in the garden. He would fight any number of boys of any size for an ill-treated animal. In fact, all his tenderness is given to dumb animals. He has no real liking for mortals. They affront him with their love-making and their marriages. He has to leave the room when anything bordering on sentiment is read aloud. 'Tripe,' he calls it in his low way. *Do* you remember his scorn of knight-errants who rescued distressed damsels? They seemed to him so little worth rescuing."

"I never cared much for sentiment myself," said Mrs. Hope. "I wouldn't give a good adventure yarn for all the love-stories ever written."

"Mother remains very boyish," said Augusta. "She likes something vivid in the way of crime."

"And now," said her mother, "you are laughing at an old done woman, which is very unseemly. Come and sit beside me, Miss Reston, and tell me what you think of Priorsford."

"Oh," said Pamela, drawing a low chair to the side of her hostess; "it's not for me to talk about Priorsford. They tell me you know more about it than anyone."

"Do I? Well, perhaps; anyway, I love it more than most. I've lived here practically all my life, and my forebears have been in the countryside for generations, and that all counts. Priorsford . . . I sometimes stand on the bridge and look and look, and tell myself that I feel like a mother to it."

"I know," said Pamela. "There is something very appealing about a little town: I never lived in one before."

"But," said Mrs. Hope, jealous as a mother for her own, "I think there is something very special about Priorsford. There are few towns as beautiful. The way the hills cradle it, and Peel Tower stands guard over it, and the links of Tweed water it, and even the streets aren't ordinary — they have such lovely glimpses. From the East Gate you look up to the East Law, pine trees, grey walls, green terraces; in the Highgate you don't go many yards without coming to a *pend*, with a view of blue distances that takes your breath, just as in Edinburgh when you look down an alley and see ships tacking for the Baltic. . . . But I wish I had known Priorsford as it was in my mother's young days, when the French prisoners were here. The genteel supper-parties and assemblies must have been vastly entertaining. It has changed, even in my day. I don't want to repeat the old folks' litany, 'No times like the old times', but it does seem to me — or is it only distance lending enchantment? — that the people I used to know were more human, more interesting; there was less worship of money, less running after the great ones of the earth, certainly less vulgarity. We were content with less, and happier."

"But Mrs. Hope," said Pamela, laying down her cup, "this is most depressing hearing. I came here to find simplicity."

"You needn't expect to find it in Priorsford. We aren't so provincial as all that. I just wish Mrs. Duff-Whalley could hear you. Simplicity indeed! I'm not able to go out much now, but I sit here and watch people, and I am astonished at the number of restless eyes. So many people spend their lives striving to keep in the swim. They are miserable in case anyone gets before them, in case a neighbour's car is a

better make, in case a neighbour's entertainments are more elaborate. . . . Two
girls came to see me this morning — nice
girls, pretty girls — but even my old eyes
could see the powder on their faces and
their touched-up eyes. And their whole
talk was of daft-like dances, and bridge,
and absurdities. If they had been my
daughters I would have whipped them for
their affected manners. And when I think
of their grandmother! A decent woman
was Mirren Somerville. She lived with her
father in that ivy-covered cottage at our
gates, and she did sewing for me before
she married Banks. She wasn't young when
she married. I remember she came to ask
my advice. "D'you care for him, Mirren?'
I asked. 'Well, mem, it's no' as if I were a
young lassie. I'm forty, and near by caring.
But he's a dacent man, and it's lonely now
ma faither's awa, an' I'm a guid cook, an'
he would aye come in to a clean fireside.'
So she married him and made a good wife
to him, and they had one son. And Mirren's
son is now Sir John Banks, a baronet and
an M.P. Tuts, the thing's ridiculous. . . .
Not that there's anything wrong with the
man. He's a soft-tongued, stuffed-looking,

butler-like creature with a lot of that low cunning that is known as business instinct, but he was good to his mother. He didn't marry till she died, and she kept house for him in his grand new house — the dear soul with her caps and her broad south-country accent. She managed wonderfully, for she had great natural dignity, and aped nothing. It was the butler killed her. She could cope with the women servants but when Sir John felt that his dignity required a butler she gave it up. I dare say she was glad enough to go. . . . 'Eh, mem, I am effrontit,' she used to say to me if I went in and found her spotless kitchen disarranged, and I thought of her today when I saw those silly little painted faces, and was glad she had been spared the sight of her descendants. . . . But what am I raging about? What does it matter to me when all's said? Let the lassies dress up as long as they have the heart; they'll have long years to learn sense if they're spared. . . . Miss Reston, did you ever see anything bonnier than Tweed and Hopetoun Woods? Jean, my dear, Lewis Elliot brought me a book last night which really delighted me. Poems by Violet Jacob. If anyone could do for Tweeddale what she has done for Angus I would be glad. . . .

"You must care for poetry, Miss Reston ? In Priorsford it's considered rather a slur on your character to care for poetry. Novels we may discuss, sensible people read novels, even now and again essays or biography, but poetry — there we have to dissemble. We pretend, don't we, Jean ? — that poetry is nothing to us. Never a quotation or an allusion escapes us. We listen to tales of servants' misdeeds, we talk of clothes and the ongoings of our neighbours, and we never let on that we would rather talk of poetry. No; No. A daft-like thing for either an old woman or a young one to speak of. Only when we are alone — Jean and Augusta and Lewis Elliot and I — we 'tire the sun with talking and send it down the sky'. . . . Miss Reston, Lewis Elliot tells me he knew you very well at one time."

"Yes; away at the beginning of things. I adored him when I was fifteen and he was twenty. He was wonderfully good to me and Biddy — my brother. It is delightful to find an old friend in a new place."

"I'm very fond of Lewis," said Mrs.

Hope, "but I wish to goodness he had never inherited Laverlaw. He might have done a lot in the world with his brain and his heart and his courage, but there he is contentedly settled in that green glen of his, and greatly absorbed in sheep. Sheep! The country is run by the Sir John Bankses, and the Lewis Elliots think about sheep. It's all wrong. It's all wrong. The War wakened him up, and he was in the thick of it both in the East and in France, but never in the limelight, you understand, just doggedly doing his best in the background. If he would marry a sensible wife with some ambition, but he's about as much sentiment in him as Jock. It would take an earthquake to shake him into matrimony."

"Perhaps," said Pamela, "he is like your friend Mirren — 'bye caring'."

"Nonsense," said Mrs. Hope briskly. "He's 'bye' the fervent stage, if he ever was a prisoner in that cage of rushes, which I doubt, but there are long years before him, I hope, and if there isn't a fire of affection on the hearth, and someone always about to listen and understand, it's a dowie business when the days draw in and the nights get longer and colder, and the light departs."

"But if it's dreary for a man," Pamela argued, "what about us? What of the 'left ladies', as I once heard a child describe spinsters?"

Mrs. Hope's blue eyes callously calm, surveyed the three spinsters before her.

"You will get no pity from me," she said. "It's practically always the woman's own fault if she remains unmarried. Besides, a woman can do fine without a man. A woman has so much within herself, she is a constant entertainment to herself. But men are helpless souls. Some of them are born bachelors and they do very well, but the majority are lost without a woman. And angry they would be to hear me say it! . . . Are you going, Jean?"

"Mhor's lessons," said Jean. "I'm frightfully sorry to take Pamela away."

"May I come again?" Pamela asked.

"Surely. Augusta and I will look forward to your next visit. Don't tire of Priorsford yet awhile. Stay amongst us and learn to love the place." Mrs. Hope smiled very kindly at her guest and Pamela, stooping down, kissed the hand that held her own.

11

Lord Clincham waved a careless hand. A small portion of blood royal flows in my veins, he said, but it does not worry me at all, and after all, he added piously, at the Day of Judgement what will be the odds?
Mr. Salteena heaved a sigh. I was thinking of this world, he said.

"THE YOUNG VISITERS"

"I WOULD like," said Pamela, "to get to know my neighbours. There are six little houses, each exactly like Hill-view, and I would like to be able to nod to the owners as I pass. It would be more friendly."

Pamela and Jean, with Mhor and Peter, were walking along the road that contained Hillview and The Rigs.

"Every house in this road is a twin," said Mhor, "except The Rigs. It's different from every other house."

They were coming home from a long walk, laden with spoils from the woods: moss for the bowls of bulbs, beautiful bare branches such as Jean loved to stand in blue jars against the creamy walls. Mhor and Peter had been coursing about like two puppies, covering at least four times the ground their elders covered, and were now lagging, weary-footed, much desiring their midday meal.

"I don't know," said Jean, pondering on the subject of neighbours, "how you could manage to be friends with them. You see, they are busy people and — it sounds very rude — they haven't time to be bothered with you. Just smile tentatively when you see them and pass the time of day casual-like; you would soon get friendly. There is one house, the one called 'Balmoral', with the very much decorated windows and the basket of ferns hanging in the front door, where the people are at leisure, and I know would deeply value a little friendliness. Two sisters live in it — Watson is the name most kindly and hospitable creatures with enough to live on comfortable and keep a small servant, and ample leisure after they have, what Mrs. M'Cosh calls, 'dockit up the hoose', to entertain and be entertained. They are West country — Glasgow, I think, or Greenock — and they find Priorsford just a little stiff. They've been here about three years, and I'm afraid are rather disappointed that they haven't made more progress socially. I love them personally. They are so genteel, as a rule, but every little while the raciness natural to the West country breaks out."

"You are nice to them, Jean, I'm sure."

"Oh, yes, but the penalty of being more or less nice to everyone is that nobody values your niceness: they take it for granted. Whereas the haughty and exclusive if they do condescend to stoop are hailed as gods among mortals."

"Poor Jean!" laughed Pamela. "That is rather hard. It's a poor thing human nature."

"It is," Jean agreed. "I went to the dancing class the other day to see a most unwilling Mhor trip fantastically, and I saw a tiny girl take the hand of an older girl and look admiringly up at her. The older child, with the awful heartlessness of childhood, wriggled her hand away and turned her back on her small admirer. The poor mite stood trying not to cry, and presently a still tinier mite came snuggling up to her and took her hand. 'Now', I thought, 'having learned how cruel a thing a snub is, will she be kind?' Not a bit of it. With the selfsame gesture the older girl had used she wriggled away her hand and turned her back."

"Cruel little wretches," said Pamela, "but it's the same with us older children. Apart from sin altogether, it must be hard for God to pardon our childishness. . . . But about the Miss Watsons — d'you think I might call on them?"

"Well, they wouldn't call on you, I'm sure of that. Suppose I ask them to meet you, and then you could fix a day for them to have tea with you? It would be a tremendous treat for them, and pleasant for you too — they are very entertaining."

So it was arranged. The Miss Watsons were asked to The Rigs, and to their unbounded satisfaction spent a most genial hour in the company of Miss Reston, whose comings and goings they had watched with breathless interest from behind the elegant sash curtain of Balmoral. On their way home they borrowed a copy of Debrett and studied it all evening.

It was very confusing at first, but at last they ran their quarry to earth. "Here she is. . . . She's the daughter (dau. must mean daughter) of Quintin John, 10th Baron Bidborough. And this'll be her brother, Quintin Reginald Feurbras — what names! *Teenie*, her mother was an earl's daughter!"

"Oh, mercy!" wailed Miss Teenie, quite overcome.

"Yes, see here. Sixth Earl of Champertoun — a Scotch earl too! Lady Ann was her name. Fancy that now!"

"And her so pleasant!" said Miss Teenie.

"It just lets you see," said Miss Watson, "the higher up you get in the social scale, the pleasanter and freer people are. You see, they've been there so long they're accustomed to it; their position never gives them a thought: it's the people who have climbed up who keep on wondering if you're noticing how grand they are."

"Well, Agnes," said Miss Teenie, "it's a great rise in the world for you and me to be asked to tea with an earl's granddaughter. There's no getting over that. I'm thinking we'll need to polish up our manners. I've an awful habit of drinking my tea with my mouth full. It seems more natural somehow to give it a *synd* down than to wait to drink till your mouth's empty."

"Of course it's more natural," said her sister, "but what's natural's never refined. That's a queer thing when you think of it."

The Miss Watsons called on all their friends in the next few days, and did not fail to mention in each house, accidentally, as it were, that on Wednesday they expected to take tea with Miss Reston, and led on from the fact to glowing details of Miss Reston's ancestry.

The height of their satisfaction was reached when they happened to meet Mrs. Duff-Whalley, who, remembering yeoman service rendered by the sisters at a recent bazaar, stopped them, and, greatly condescending, said, "Ah, er — Miss Watson — I'm asking a few local ladies to The Towers on Wednesday afternoon to discuss the subject of a sale of work for the G.F.S. A cup of tea, you understand, and a friendly chat in my own drawing-room. You will both join us, I hope?" Her tone held no doubt of their delighted acceptance, but Miss Watson, who had suffered much from Mrs. Duff-Whalley, who had been made use of and then passed unnoticed, taken up when needed and dropped, replied with great deliberation, "Oh, thank you, but we are going to tea with Miss Reston that afternoon. I dare say we shall hear from someone what has been decided about the sale of work."

The epoch-making Wednesday dawned at last.

Great consultations had gone on between The Rigs and Hillview how best to make it an enjoyable occasion. Pamela wanted Jean to be present, but Jean thought it better not to be. "It would take away from the glory of the occasion. I'm only a *chota Miss*, and they are too accustomed to me. Ask Mrs. Jowett. She wouldn't call on the Watsons — the line must be drawn somewhere even by the gentle Mrs. Jowett — but she will be very sweet and nice to them. And Miss Mary Dawson. She is such a kind, comfortable presence in a room — I think that would be a nice little party."

Pamela obediently promised to do as Jean suggested.

"I've sent to Fullers' for some cakes, though I don't myself consider them a patch on the Priorsford cakes, but they will be a change and make it more of an occasion. Mawson can make delicious sandwiches, and Bella Bathgate has actually offered to bake some scones. I'll make the room look as smart as possible with flowers."

"You've no photographs of relations? They would like photographs better than anything."

"People they never heard of before," cried Pamela. "What an odd taste! However, I'll do what I can."

By 11 a.m. the ladies in Balmoral had laid out all they meant to wear — skirts spread neatly on beds, jackets over chair-backs, even to the very best handkerchiefs on the dressing-table waiting for a sprinkle of scent.

At two o'clock they began to dress.

Miss Teenie protested against this disturbance of their afternoon rest, but her sister was firm.

"It'll take me every minute of the time, Teenie, for I've all my underclothing to change."

"But, mercy me, Miss Reston'll not see your underclothes!"

"I know that, but when you've on your very best things underneath you feel a sort of respect for yourself, and you're better able to hold your own in whatever company you're in. I don't know what you mean to do, but I'm going to change *to the skin*."

Miss Teenie nearly always followed the lead of her elder sister, so she meekly went off to look out and air her most self-respecting under-garments, though she protested, "Not half aired they'll be, and as likely as not I'll catch my death," and added bitterly, "It's not all pleasure knowing the aristocracy."

They were ready to the last glove-button half an hour before the time appointed, and sat stiffly on two high chairs in their little dining-room. "I think," said Miss Watson, "we'd be as well to think on something that'll interest Miss Reston. I wish I knew more about the Upper Ten."

"I'd better not speak at all," said Miss Teenie, who by this time was in a very bad temper. "I never could mind the names of the Royal family, let alone the aristocracy. I always thought there was a weakness about the people who liked to read in the papers and talk about those kind of folk. I'm sure when I do read about them they're always doing something kind of indecent, like getting divorced. It seems to me they never even make an attempt to be respectable."

She looked round the cosy room and thought how pleasant it would have been if she and her sister had been sitting down to tea as usual, with no need to think of topics. It had been all very well to tell their obviously surprised friends where they were going for tea, but when it came to the point she would infinitely have preferred to stay at home.

"She'll not likely have any notion of a proper tea," Miss Watson said. "Scraps of thin bread and butter, mebbe, and a cake, so don't you look disappointed, Teenie, though I know you like your tea. Just toy with it, you know."

"No, I don't know," said Miss Teenie, crossly. "I never 'toyed' with my tea yet, and I'm not going to begin. It'll likely be China tea anyway, and I'd as soon drink dish-water."

Miss Watson looked bitterly at her sister.

"You'll never rise in the world, Teenie, if you can't give up a little comfort for the sake of refinement. Fancy making a fuss about China tea when it's handed to you by an earl's grand-daughter."

Miss Teenie made no reply to this except to burst — as was a habit of hers — into a series of violent sneezes, at which her sister's wrath broke out.

"That's the most uncivilised sneeze I ever heard. If you do that before Miss Reston, Teenie, I'll be tempted to do you an injury."

Miss Teenie blew her nose pensively. "I doubt I've got a chill changing my underclothes in the middle of the day, but 'a little pride and a little pain', as my mother used to say when she screwed my hair with curl-papers. . . . I suppose it'll do if we stay an hour?"

Things are rarely as bad as we anticipate, and, as it turned out, not only Miss Watson, but the rebellious Miss Teenie, looked back on that tea-party as one of the pleasantest they had ever taken part in, and only Heaven knows how many tea-parties the good ladies had attended in their day.

They were judges of china and fine linen, and they looked appreciatively at the table. There were the neatest of tea-knives, the daintiest of spoons, jam glowed crimson through crystal, butter was there in a lordly dish, cakes from London, delicate sandwiches, Miss Bathgate's best and lightest in the way of scones, shortbread crisp from the oven of Mrs. M'Cosh.

And here was Miss Reston looking lovely and exotic in a wonderful tea-frock, a class of garment hitherto unknown to the Miss Watsons, who thrilled at the sight. Her welcome was so warm that it seemed to the guests, accustomed to the thus-far-and-no-further manner of the Priorsford great ladies, almost exuberant. She led Miss Teenie to the most comfortable chair, she gave Miss Watson a footstool and put a cushion at her back, and talked so simply, and laughed so naturally, that the Miss Watsons forgot entirely to choose their topics and began on what was uppermost in their minds, the fact that Robina (the little maid) had actually managed that morning to break the gazogene.

Pamela, who had not a notion what a gazogene was, gasped the required surprise and horror and said "But how did she do it?" which was the safest remark she could think of.

"Banged it in the sink," said Miss Watson, with a dramatic gesture, "and the bottom came out. I never thought it was possible to break a gazogene with all that wire-netting about it."

"Robina," said Miss Teenie gloomily, "could break a steam-roller let alone a gazogene."

"It'll be an awful miss," said her sister. "We've had it so long, and it always stood on the sideboard, with a bottle of lemon syrup beside it."

Pamela was puzzling to think what this could be that stood on a sideboard companioned by lemon syrup and compassed with wire-netting when Mawson showed in Mrs. Jowett, and with her Miss Mary Dawson, and the party was complete.

The Miss Watsons greeted the newcomers brightly, having met them on bazaar committees and at Red Cross work parties, and having always been treated courteously by both ladies. They were quite willing to sink at once into a lower place now that two denizens of the Hill had come, but Pamela would have none of it.

They were the reason of the party; she made that evident at once.

Miss Teenie did not attempt the impossible and "toy" with her tea. There was no need to. The tea was delicious, and she drank three cups. She tried everything on the table and pronounced everything excellent. Never had she felt herself so entertaining, such a capital talker as now, with Pamela smiling and applauding every effort. Mrs. Jowett too, gentle lady, listened with most gratifying interest, and Miss Mary Dawson threw in kind, sensible remarks at intervals. There was no arguing, no disagreeing, everybody "clinked" with everybody else — a most pleasant party.

"And isn't it awful," said Miss Watson in a pause, "about our minister marrying?"

Pamela waited for further information before she spoke, while Mrs. Jowett said, "Don't you consider it a suitable match?"

"Oh, well," said Miss Watson, "I just meant that it was awful unexpected. He's been a bachelor so long, and then to marry a girl twenty years younger than himself and a 'Piscipalian into the bargain."

"But how sporting of him," Pamela said.

"Sporting?" said Miss Watson doubtfully, vague thoughts of guns and rabbits floating through her mind. "Of course you're a 'Piscipalian too, Miss Reston, so is Mrs. Jowett: I shouldn't have mentioned it."

"I'm afraid I'm not much of anything," Pamela confessed, "but Jean Jardine has great hopes of making me a Presbyterian. I have been going with her to hear her own most delightful parson — Mr. Macdonald."

"A dear old man," said Mrs. Jowett; "he does preach so beautifully."

"Mr. Macdonald's church is the old Free Kirk, now U.F., you know," said Miss Watson in an instructive tone. "The Jardines are great Free Kirk people, like the Hopes of Hopetoun — but the Parish is far more class, you know what I mean? You've more society there."

"What a delightful reason for worshipping in a church!" Pamela said. "But please tell me more about your minister's bride — does she belong to Priorsford?"

"English," said Miss Teenie, "and smokes, and plays golf, and wears skirts near to her knees. What in the world she'll look like at the missionary work party or attending the prayer meeting — I cannot think. Poor Mr. Morrison must be demented, and he is such a good preacher."

"She will settle down," said Miss Dawson in her slow, sensible way. "She's really a very likeable girl; and if she puts all the energy she uses to play games into church-work she will be a great success. And it will mean an interest having a young wife at the manse."

"I don't know," said Miss Watson, doubtfully. "I always think a minister's wife should have a little money and a strong constitution and be able to play the harmonium."

Miss Watson had not intended to be funny, and was rather surprised at the laughter of her hostess.

"It seems to me," she said, "that the poor woman *would* need a strong constitution."

"Well, anyway," said Miss Teenie, "she would need the money; ministers have so many claims on them. And they've a position to keep up. Here, of course, they have manses, but in Glasgow they sometimes live in flats. I don't think that's right. . . . A minister should always live in a villa, or at least in a 'front door'."

"Is your minister's bride pretty?" Pamela asked.

Miss Watson got in her word first. "Pretty," she said; "but not in a ministerial way, if you know what I mean. I wouldn't call her ladylike."

"What would you call 'ladylike'?" Pamela asked.

"Well, a good height, you know, and a nice figure and a pleasant face and tidy hair. The sort of person that looks well in a grey coat and skirt and a feather boa."

"I know exactly. What a splendid description!"

"Now," continued Miss Watson, much elated by the praise, "Mrs. Morrison is very conspicuous looking. She's got yellow hair and a bright colour, and a kind of bold way of looking."

"She's a complex character," sighed Mrs. Jowett: "she wears snakeskin shoes. But you must be kind to her, Miss Watson. I think she would appreciate kindness."

"Oh, so we are kind to her. The congregation subscribed and gave a grand piano for a wedding-present. Wasn't that good? She is very musical, you know, and plays the violin beautifully. That'll be very useful at church meetings."

"I can't imagine," said Miss Dawson, "why we should consider a minister's wife and her talents as the property of the congregation. A doctor's wife isn't at the beck and call of her husband's patients, a lawyer's wife isn't briefed along with her husband. It doesn't seem to me fair."

"How odd," said Pamela; "only yesterday I was talking to Mrs. Macdonald — Jean's minister's wife — and I said just what you say, that it seems hard that the time of a minister's wife should be at the mercy of everyone, and she said, 'My dear, it's our privilege, and if I had my life to live again I would ask nothing better than to be a hard-working minister's hardworking wife.' I stand hat in hand before that couple. When you think what they have given all these years to this little town — what qualities of heart and head. The tact of an ambassador (Mrs. Macdonald has that), the eloquence of a Wesley, a largesse of sympathy and help and encouragement, not to speak of more material things to everyone in need, all at the rate of £250 per annum. Prodigious!"

"Yes," said Miss Dawson, "they have been a blessing to Priorsford for more than forty years. Mr. Macdonald is a saint, but a saint is a great deal the better of a practical wife. Mrs. Macdonald is an example of what can be accomplished by a woman both in a church and at home. I sit rebuked before her."

"Oh, my dear," said Mrs. Jowett, "no one could possibly be more helpful than you and your sisters. It's I who am the drone. . . . Now I must go."

The Miss Watsons outstayed the other guests, and Pamela, remembering Jean's advice, produced a few stray photographs of relations which were regarded with much interest and some awe. The photograph of her brother, Lord Bidborough, they could hardly lay down. Finally, Pamela presented them with flowers and a basket of apples newly arrived from Bidborough Manor, and they returned to Balmoral walking on air.

"Such *pleasant* company and *such* a tea," said Miss Watson. "She had out all her best things."

"And Mrs. Jowett and Miss Dawson were asked to meet *us*," exulted Miss Teenie.

"And very affable they were," added her sister.

But when the sisters had removed their best clothes and were seated in the dining-room with the cloth laid for supper, Miss Teenie said, "All the same, it's fine to be back in our own house and not to have to heed about manners." She pulled a low chair close to the fire as she spoke, and spread her skirt back over her knee and, thoroughly comfortable and at peace with the world, beamed on her sister, who replied:

"What do you say to having some toasted cheese to our supper?"

12

"I hear the whaups on windy days
Cry up among the peat
Whaun, on that road that spiels and braes,
I've heard ma ain sheep's feet.
An' the bonnie lambs wi' their canny ways
And the silly yowes that bleat."
"SONGS OF ANGUS"

MHOR, having but lately acquired the art of writing, was fond of exercising his still very shaky pen where and when he could.

One morning, by reason of neglecting his teeth, and a few other toilet details, he was able to be downstairs ten minutes before breakfast, and spent the time in the kitchen, plaguing Mrs. M'Cosh to let him write an inscription in her Bible.

"What wud ye write?" she asked, suspiciously.

"I would write," said Mhor — "I would write 'From Gervase Taunton to Mrs. M'Cosh,'"

"That wud be a lee," said Mrs. M'Cosh, "for I got it frae ma sister Annie, her that's in Australia. Here see, there's a post-caird for ye. It's a rale nice yin — Sauchiehall Street, Glasgow. There's Annackers' shop, as plain's plain."

Mhor looked discontentedly at the offering.

"I wish," he said slowly — "I wish I had a postcard of a hippopotamus being sick."

"Ugh, you want unnaitural post-cairds. Think on something wise-like, like a guid laddie."

Mhor considered. "If you give me a sheet of paper and an envelope I might write to the Lion at the Zoo."

For the sake of peace, Mrs. M'Cosh produced the materials, and Mhor sat down at the table, his elbows spread out, his tongue protruding. He had only managed "Dear Lion", when Jean called him to go upstairs and wash his teeth and get a clean handkerchief.

The sun was shining into the dining-room, lighting up the blue china on the dresser, and catching the yellow lights in Jean's hair.

"What a silly morning for November," growled Jock. "What's the sun going on shining like that for? You'd think it thought it was summer."

"In winter," said Mhor, "the sky should always be grey. It's more suitable."

"What a couple of ungrateful creatures you are," Jean said; "I'm ashamed of you. And as it happens, you are going to have a great treat because of the good day. I didn't tell you because I thought it would very likely pour. Cousin Lewis said if it was a good day he would send the car to take us to Laverlaw to luncheon. It's really because of Pamela; she has never been there. So you must ask to get away at twelve, Jock, and I'll go up with Pamela and collect Mhor."

Mhor at once left the table and, without making any remark, stood on his head on the hearthrug. Thus did his joy find vent. Jock, on the other hand, seemed more solemnised than gleeful.

"That's the first time I've ever had a prayer answered," he announced. "I couldn't do my Greek last night, and I prayed that I wouldn't be at the class — and I won't be. Gosh, Maggie!"

"Oh, Jock," his sister protested, "that's not what prayers are for."

"Mebbe not, but I've managed it this time," and, unrepentant, Jock started on another slice of bread and butter.

Jean told Pamela of Jock's prayers as they went together to fetch Mhor from school.

"But Mhor is a much greater responsibility than Jock. You know where you are with Jock; underneath is a bedrock of pure goodness. You see, we start with the enormous advantage of having had forebears of the very decentest — not great, not noble, but men who feared God and honoured the King — men who lived justly and loved mercy. It would be most uncalled-for of us to start out on bypaths with such a straight record behind us. But Mhor, bless him, is different. I haven't a notion what went to the making of him. I seem to see behind him a long line of men and women who danced and laughed and gambled and feasted, light-hearted, charming people. I sometimes think I hear them laugh as I teach Mhor, *What is the chief end of man?* . . . I couldn't love Mhor more if he really were my little brother, but I know that my hold over him is of the frailest. It's only now that I have him. I must make the most of the present — the little boy days — before life takes him away from me."

"You will have his heart always," Pamela comforted her. "He won't forget. He has been rooted and grounded in love."

Jean winked away the tears that had forced their way into her eyes, and laughed.

"I'm bringing him up a Presbyterian. I did try him with the Creed. He listened politely, and said carelessly, 'It all seems rather sad — Pilate is a nice name, but not Pontius.' Then Jock laughed at him learning, 'What is your name, A or B?' and Mhor himself preferred to go to the root of the matter with our Shorter Catechism, and answer nobly if obscurely — *Man's chief end is to glorify God and to enjoy Him for ever*. Indeed, he might be Scots in his passion for theology. The other night he went to bed very displeased with me, and said, 'You needn't read me any more of that narsty Bible,' but when I went up to say good-night he greeted me with, '*How* can I keep the commandments when I can't even remember what they are?' . . .

This is Mhor's school, or rather Miss Main's school."

They went up the steps of a pretty, creeper-covered house.

"It once belonged to an artist," Jean explained. "There is a great, big, light studio at the back which makes an ideal schoolroom. It's an ideal school altogether. Miss Main and her young step-sister are born teachers, full of humour and understanding, as well as being brilliantly clever — far too clever really for this job; but if they don't mind we needn't complain. They get the children on most surprisingly, and teach them all sorts of things outside their lessons. Mhor is always astonishing me with his information about things going on in the world. . . . Yes, do come in. They won't mind. You would like to see the children."

"I would indeed. But won't Miss Main object to us interrupting — "

Miss Main at once reassured her on that point, and said that both she and the scholars loved visitors. She took them into the large schoolroom where twenty small people of various sizes sat with their books, very cheerfully imbibing knowledge.

Mhor and another small boy occupied one desk.

Jean greeted the small boy as "Sandy", and asked him what he was studying at that moment.

"I don't know," said Sandy.

"Sandy," said Miss Main, "don't disgrace your teachers. You know you are learning the multiplication table. What are three times three?"

Sandy merely looked coy.

"Mhor?"

"Six," said Mhor, after some thought.

"Hopeless," said Miss Main. "Come and speak to my sister Elspeth, Miss Reston."

"My sister Elspeth" was a tall, fair girl, with merry blue eyes.

"Do you teach the Mhor?" Pamela asked her.

"I have that honour," said Miss Elspeth, and began to laugh. "He always arrives full of ideas. This morning he had thought out a plan to stop the rain. The sky, he said, must be gone over with glue, but he gave it up when he remembered how sticky it would be for the angels. . . . He has the most wonderful feeling for words of any child I ever taught. He can't, for instance, bear to hear a Bible story told in everyday language. The other children like it broken down to them, but Mhor pleads for 'the real words'. He likes the swing and majesty of them. . . . I was reading them Kipling's story, *Servants of the Queen*, the other day. You know where it makes the oxen speak of the walls of the city falling, 'and the dust went up as though many cattle were coming home'. I happened to look up, and there was Mhor with lamps lit in those wonderful green eyes of his, gazing at me. He said, 'I like that bit. It's a nice bit. I think it should be at the end of a sad story.' And he uses words well himself, have you noticed? The other day he came and thrust a dead field-mouse into my hand. I squealed and dropped it, and he said, 'Afraid? And of such a calm little gentleman?' "

Pamela asked if Mhor's behaviour was good.

"Only fair," said pretty Miss Elspeth. "He always means to be good, but he is inhabited by an imp of mischief that prompts him to do the most improbable things. He certainly doesn't make for peace in the school, but he keeps 'a body frae languor'. I like a naughty boy myself much better than a good one. He's the 'more natural beast of the twain'."

Outside, with the freed Mhor capering before them, Pamela was enthusiastic over the little school and its mistresses.

"Miss Main looks like an old miniature, with her white hair and her delicate colouring, and is wise and kind and sensible as well; and as for that daffodil girl, Elspeth, she is a sheer delight."

"Yes," Jean agreed. "Hasn't she charming manners? It is so good for the children to be with her. She is so polite to them that they can't be anything but gentle and considerate in return. Heaps of girls would think school-marming very dull, but Elspeth makes it into a sort of daily entertainment. They manage, she and her sister, to make the dullest child see some glimmer of reason in learning lessons. I do wish I had had a teacher like that. I had a governess who taught me like a parrot. She had no notion how to make the dry bones live. I thought I scored by learning as little as I possibly could. The consequence is I'm almost entirely illiterate. . . . There's the car waiting, and Jock prancing impatiently. Run in for your thick coat, Mhor. No, you can't take Peter. He chased sheep last time and fought the other dogs and made himself a nuisance."

Mhor was now pleading that he might sit in the front beside the chauffeur and cry "Honk, honk," as they went round corners.

"Well," said Jean, "choose whether it will be going or coming back. Jock must sit there one time."

Mhor, as he always did, grasped the pleasure of the moment, and clambered into the seat beside the chauffeur, an old and valued friend, whom he greeted familiarly as "Tam".

The road to Laverlaw ran through the woods behind Peel, dipped into the Manor Valley and, emerging, made straight for the hills, which closed down round it as though jealous of the secrets they guarded. It seemed to a stranger as if the road led nowhere, for nothing was to be seen for miles except bare hillsides and a brawling burn. Suddenly the road took a turn, a white bridge spanned the noisy Laverlaw Water, and there at the opening of a wide, green glen stood the house.

Lewis Elliot was waiting at the doorstep to greet them. He had been out all morning, and with him were his two dogs, Rab and Wattie. Jock and Mhor threw themselves on them with many endearing names, before they even looked at their host.

"Is luncheon ready?" was Mhor's greeting.

"Why? Are you hungry?"

"Oh, yes, but it's not that. I wondered if there would be time to go to the stables. Tam says there are some new puppies."

"I'd keep the puppies for later, if I were you," Lewis Ellist advised. "You'd better have luncheon while your hands are fairly clean. Jean will be sure to make you wash them if you go mucking about in the stables."

Mhor nodded. He was no Jew, and took small pleasure in the outward cleansing of the cup and platter. Soap and water seemed to him almost quite unnecessary, and he had greatly admired and envied the Laplanders since Jock had told him that that hardy race rarely, if ever, washed.

"I hope you weren't cold in that open car," Lewis Elliot said as he helped Pamela and Jean to remove their wraps. "D'you mind coming into my den? It's warm, if untidy. The drawing-room is so little used that it's about as cheerful as a tomb."

He led them through the panelled hall, down a long passage hung with sporting prints, into what was evidently a much-liked and much-used room.

Books were everywhere, lining the walls, lying in heaps on tables, some even piled on the floor, but a determined effort had evidently been made to tidy things a little, for papers had been collected into bundles, pipes had been thrust into corners, and bowls of chrysanthemums stood about to sweeten the tobacco-laden atmosphere.

A large fire burned on the hearth, and Lewis pulled up some masculine-looking arm-chairs and asked the ladies to sit in them, but Jean along with Jock and Mhor were already engrossed in books, and their neglected host looked at them with disgust.

"Such are the primitive manners of the Jardine family," he said to Pamela. "If you want a word out of them you must lock up all printed matter before they approach. Thank goodness, that's the gong! They can't read while they're feeding."

"Honourable," said Mhor, as they ate

their excellent luncheon. "Isn't Laverlaw a lovely place?"

Pamela agreed. "I never saw anything so indescribably green. It wears the fairly livery. I can easily picture True Thomas walking by that stream."

"Long ago," said Jock in his gruff voice, "there was a keep at Laverlaw instead of a house, and Cousin Lewis' ancestors stole cattle from England, and there were some fine fights in this glen. Laverlaw Water would run red with blood."

"Jock," Jean protested, "you needn't say it with such relish."

Pamela turned to her host.

"Priorsford seems to think you find yourself almost too contented at Laverlaw. Mrs. Hope says you are absorbed in sheep."

Lewis Elliot looked amused. "I can imagine the scorn Mrs. Hope put into her voice as she said 'sheep'. But one must be absorbed in something — why not sheep?"

"I like a sheep," said Jock, and he quoted:

" 'Its conversation is not deep
But then, observe its face.'"

"You may be surprised to hear," said Lewis, "that sheep are almost like fine ladies in their ways: they have megrims, it appears. I found one the other day lying on the hill more or less dead to the world, and I went a mile or two out of my way to tell the shepherd. All he said was, 'I ken that yowe. She aye comes ower dwamy in an east wind'. . . . But tell me, Jean, how is Miss Reston conducting herself in Priorsford?"

"With the greatest propriety, I assure you," Pamela replied for herself. "Aren't I, Jean? I have dined with Mrs. Duff-Whalley and been introduced to 'the County'. You were regrettably absent from that august gathering, I seem to remember. I have lunched with the Jowetts, and left the table without a stain either on the cloth or my character, but it was a great nervous strain. I thought of you, Jock, old man, and deeply sympathised with your experience. I have been to quite a lot of tea-parties, and I have given one or two. Indeed, I am becoming as absorbed in Priorsford as you are in sheep."

"You have been to Hopetoun, I know."

"Yes; but don't mix that up with

ordinary tea-parties. That is an experience to keep apart. She holds the imagination, that old woman, with her sharp tongue, and her haggard, beautiful eyes, and her dead sons. To know Mrs. Hope and her daughter is something to be thankful for."

"I quite agree. The Hopes do much to leaven the lump. But I expect you find it rather a lump."

"Honestly, I don't. I'm not being superior, please don't think so, or charitable, or pretending to find good in everything, but I do like the Priorsford people. Some of them are interesting, and nearly all of them are dears."

"Even Mrs. Duff-Whalley?"

"Well, she is rather a caricature, but there are oddly nice bits about her, if only she weren't so overpoweringly opulent. The ospreys in her hat seem to shriek money, and her furs smother one, and that house of hers remains so starkly new. If only creepers would climb up and hide its staring red-and-white face, and ivy efface some of the decorations, but no — I expect she likes it as it is. But there is something honest about her very vulgarity. She knows what she wants and goes straight for it; and she isn't a fool. The daughter is. She was intended by nature to be a dull young woman with a pretty face, but not content with that she puts on an absurdly skittish manner — oh, so ruthlessly bright — talks what she thinks is smart slang, poses continually, and wears clothes that would not be out of place at Ascot, but are a positive offence to the little grey town. I hadn't realised how gruesome provincial smartness could be until I met Muriel Duff-Whalley."

"Oh, poor Muriel!" Jean protested. "You've done for her, anyway. But you're wrong in thinking her stupid. She only comes to The Rigs when she isn't occupied with smart friends, and is rather dull — I don't see her in her more exalted moments; but I assure you, after she has done talking about 'the County', and after the full blast of 'dear Lady Tweedie' is over, she is a very pleasant companion, and has nice delicate sorts of thoughts. She's really far too clever to be as silly as she sometimes is — I can't quite understand her. Perhaps she does it to please her mother."

"Jean's disgustingly fond of finding out the best in people," Pamela objected.

"Priorsford is a most charming town," said Mr. Elliot; "but I never find its inhabitants interesting."

"No," Jean said, "but you don't try, do you? You stay here in your 'wild glen sae green', and only have your own friends to visit you — "

"Are you," Pamela asked Lewis, "like a woman I know who boasts that she knows no one in her country place, but gets her friends and her fish from London?"

"No; I'm not in the least exclusive, only rather *blate*, and, I suppose, uninterested. Do you know I was rather glad to hear you begin to slang the unfortunate Miss Duff-Whalley. It was more like the Pamela Reston I used to know. I didn't recognise her in the tolerant, all-loving lady."

"Oh," said Pamela, "you are cruel to the girl I once was. The years mellow. Surely you welcome improvement, even while you remind me of my sins and faults of youth."

"I don't think," Lewis Elliot said slowly, "that I ever allowed myself to think that the Pamela Reston I knew needed improvement. That would have savoured of sacrilege. . . . Are we finished? We might have coffee in the other room."

Pamela looked at her host as she rose from the table, and said, "Years have brought clearer eyes for faults."

"I wonder," said Lewis Elliot, as he put a large chocolate into Mhor's ever-ready mouth.

Before going home they went for a walk up the glen. Jean and the boys, very much at home, were in front, while Lewis named the surrounding hills and explained the lie of the land to Pamela. They fell into talk of younger days, and laughed over episodes they had not thought of for twenty years.

"And, do you know, Biddy's coming home?" Pamela said. "I keep remembering that with a most delightful surprise. I haven't seen him for more than a year — my beloved Biddy!"

"He was a most charming boy," Lewis said. "I suppose he would be about fifteen when last I saw him. How old is he now?"

"Thirty-five. But such a young thirty-five. He has always been doing the most youth-preserving things, chasing over the world after adventures, like a boy after butterflies, seeing new peoples, walking in untrodden ways. If he had lived in more spacious days he would have sailed with Francis Drake and helped to singe the King of Spain's beard. Oh, I do think you will still like Biddy. The charm he had at fifteen he hasn't lost one little bit. He has still the same rather shy manner and slow way of speaking and sudden, affection-winning smile. The War has changed him, of course, emptied and saddened his life, and he isn't the light-foot lad he was six years ago. When it was all over he went off for one more year's roving. He has a great project which I don't suppose will ever be accomplished — to climb Everest! He and three great friends had arranged it all before the War, but everything of course was stopped, and whatever happens he will never climb it with those three friends. They had to scale greater heights than Everest. It is a sober and responsible Biddy who is coming back, to settle down and look after his places, and go into politics, perhaps — ”

They walked together in comfortable silence.

Jean, in front, turned round and waved to them.

"I'm glad," said Lewis, "that you and Jean have made friends. Jean — " He stopped.

Pamela stood very still for a second, and then said encouragingly, "Yes?"

"Jean and her brothers are sort of cousins of mine. I've always been fond of them, and my mother and I used to try to give them a good time when we could, for Great-aunt Alison's was rather an iron rule. But a man alone is such a helpless object, as Mrs. Hope often reminds me. It isn't fair that Jean shouldn't have her chance. She never gets away, and her youth is being spoiled by care. She is such a quaint little person with her child-like face and motherly ways! I do wish something could be done."

"Jean must certainly have her chance," said Pamela. She took a long breath, as if she had been under water and had come to the surface. "I've said nothing about it to anyone, but I am greatly hoping that some arrangement can be made about sending the boys away to school and letting me carry off Jean. I want her to forget that she ever had to think about money worries. I want her to play with other boys and girls. I want her to marry."

"Yes; that would be a jolly good scheme." Lewis Elliot's voice was hearty in its agreement. "It really is exceedingly kind of you. You've lifted a weight from my mind — though what business I have to push my weights on to you. . . . Yes, Jean, perhaps we ought to be turning back. The car is ordered for four o'clock. I wish you would stay to tea, but I expect you are dying to get back to Priorsford. That little town has you in its thrall."

"I wish," said Jock, "that The Rigs could be lifted up by some magician and plumped down in Laverlaw Glen."

"Oh, Jock, wouldn't that be fine?" sighed the Mhor. "Plumped right down at the side of the burn, and then we could fish out of the windows."

The sun had left the glen, the Laverlaw Water ran wan; it seemed suddenly to have become a wild and very lonely place.

"Now I can believe about the raiders coming over the hills in an autumn twilight," said Pamela. "There is something haunted about this place. In Priorsford we are all close together and cosy; that's what I love about it."

"You've grown quite suburban," Lewis taunted her. "Jean, I was told a story about two Priorsford ladies the other day. They were in London and went to see Pavlova dance at the Palace, for the first time. It was her last appearance that season, and the curtain went down on Pavlova embedded in bouquets, bowing her thanks to an enraptured audience, the house rocking with enthusiasm. The one Priorsford lady turned to the other Priorsford lady and said, 'Awfully like Mrs. Wishart!'"

As the car moved off, Jock's voice could be heard asking, "And who *was* Mrs. Wishart?"

13

"Hast any philosophy in thee?"
"AS YOU LIKE IT"

MISS BELLA BATHGATE was a staunch supporter of the Parish Kirk. She had no use for any other denomination, and no sympathy with any but the Presbyterian form of worship. Episcopalians she regarded as beneath contempt, and classed them in her own mind with "Papists" — people who were more mischievous and almost as ignorant as "the heathen", for whom she collected small sums quarterly, and for whom the minister prayed as "sitting in darkness". Miss Bathgate had developed a real, if somewhat contemptuous, affection for Mawson, her lodger's maid, but she never ceased to pour scorn on her "English ways" and her English worship. If Mawson had not been one of the gentlest of creatures she would not have tolerated it for a day.

One wet and windy evening Bella sat

waiting for Mawson to come in to supper. She had gone to a week-night service at the church, greatly excited because the Bishop was to be present. The supper was ready and keeping hot in the oven, the fire sparkled in the bright range, and Bella sat crotcheting and singing to herself, "From Greenland's icy mountains". For Bella was passionately interested in missions. The needs of the heathen lay on her heart. Every penny she could scrape together went into "the box". The War had reduced her small income, and she could no longer live without letting her rooms; but whatever she had to do without, her contributions to missions never faltered; indeed, they had increased. Missions were the romance of her life. They put a scarlet thread into the grey. The one woman she had ever envied was Mary Slessor of Calabar, and she had read all that had been written about her intrepid countrywoman.

Mawson came in much out of breath, having run up the hill to get out of the darkness.

"Weel, and hoo's the Bishop?" Bella said in jocular tones.

"Ow, 'e was lovely. 'E said the Judgement was 'anging over all of us."

"Oh, wumman," said Bella as she dumped a loaf viciously on the platter, "d'ye need a Bishop to tell ye that? I'm sure I've kent it a' ma days."

"It gives me the creeps to think of it. Imagine standin' h'up before h'all the earth and 'aving all your little bits o' sins fetched out against you! But" — hopefully — "I don't see myself 'ow there'll be time."

"Ay, there'll be time! There'll be a' Eternity afore us, and as far as I can see there'll be naething else to do."

"Ow," Mawson wailed. "You do make it sound so 'orrid, Bella. The Bishop was much more comfortable, and 'e 'as such a nice rosy face you can't picture anything very bad 'appening to 'im. But I suppose Bishops'll be judged like everyone else."

"They will that." Bella's tone was emphatic, almost tinged with vindictiveness.

"Oh, well," said Mawson, who looked consistently on the bright sides, "I dare say they won't pay much h'attention to the likes of us when they've Kings and Bishops and M.P.'s and London ladies to judge.

Their sins will be a bit more interestin' than my little lot. . . . Well, I'll be glad of a cup of tea, for it's thirsty work listening to sermons. I'll just lay me 'at and coat down 'ere, if you don't mind, Beller. Now, this is cosy. I was thinkin' of this as I came paddin' over the bridge, listening to the sound of the wind and the water. A river's a frightenin' sort of thing at night and after 'earin' about the Judgement too."

Miss Bathgate took a savoury-smelling dish from the oven and put it, along with two hot plates, before Mawson, then put the teapot before herself and they began.

"Whaur's Miss Reston the nicht?" Bella asked, as she helped herself to hot buttered toast.

"Dinin' with Sir John and Lady Tweedie. She's wearin' a lovely new gown, sort of yellow. It suited her a treat. I must say she did look noble. She is 'andsome, don't you think?"

"Terrible lang and lean," said Miss Bathgate. "But I'm no denyin' that there's a kind o' look aboot her that's no common. She would mak' a guid queen if we had ony need o' anither."

"She makes a good mistress, anyway," said loyal Mawson.

"Oh, she's no bad," Bella admitted. "An' I must say she disna gie much trouble — but it's an idle life for ony wumman. I canna see why Miss Reston, wi' a' her faculties aboot her, needs you hingin' round her. Mercy me, what's to hinder her pu'in ribbons through her ain underclothes, if ribbons are necessary, which they're not. There's Mrs. Muir next door, wi' six bairns, an' a' the wark o' the hoose to dae an' washin's forbye, an' here's Miss Reston never liftin' finger except to pu' silk threads through a bit stuff. That's what makes folk Socialists."

Mawson, who belonged to that fast disappearing body, the real servant class, and who, without a thought of envy, delighted in the possession of her mistress, looked sadly puzzled.

"But, Beller, don't you think things work out more h'even than they seem? Mrs. Muir next door works very 'ard. I've seen her put out a washin' by seven o'clock in the morning, but then she 'as a good 'usband and an 'ealthy family and much pleasure in 'er work. Miss Reston lies soft and drinks her mornin' tea in comfort, but she never knows the satisfied feelin' that Mrs. Muir 'as when she takes in 'er clean clothes."

"Weel, mebbe you're right. I'm nae Socialist masel'. There maun aye be rich and poor, Dives in the big hoose an Lazarus at the gate. But so long as we're sure that Dives'll catch it in the end, and Lazarus lie soft in Abraham's bosom, we can pit up wi' the unfairness here. An' speaking aboot Miss Reston, I dinna mind her no' working. Ye can see by the look of her that she never was meant to work, but just to get everything done for her. Can ye picture her peelin' tatties? The verra thocht's rideeclus. She's juist for lookin' at, like the floors and a' the bonnie things. . . . But it's thae new folk that pit up ma birse. That Mrs. Duff-Whalley, crouse cat! Rollin' aboot wrap up in furs in a great caur, patronisin' everybody that's daft enough to let theirselves be patronised by her. Onybody could see she's no used to it. She's so ta'en up wi' hersel'. It's kinda play-actin' for her. . . . An' there's naebody gives less to charitable objects. I suppose when ye've paid and fed sae mony servants, and dressed yersel' in silks and satins, and bocht every denty ye can think of, and kept up a great big hoose an' a great muckle caur, there's no' that much left for the kirk-plate, or the heathen, or the hospitals. . . . Oh, it's peetifu'!"

Mawson nodded wisely. "There's plenty Mrs. Duff-Whalleys about; you be thankful you've only one in the place. Priorsford is a very charitable place, *I* think. The poor people here don't know they're born after London, and the clergy seem very active, too."

"Oh, they are that. I daur say they're as guid as is gaun. Mr. Morrison is a fine man if marriage disna ruin him."

"Oh, surely not!"

"There's no sayin'," said Bella gloomily. "She's young and flighty, but there's wan thing she has no money. I ken a minister — he was a kinda cousin o' ma father's — an' he mairret a heiress and they had late denner. I tell ye that late denner was the ruin o' that man. It fair got between him an' his jidgment. He couldna veesit his folk at a wise-like hour in the evening because he was gaun to hev his denner, and he couldna get oot late because his leddy-wife wanted him to be at hame efter denner. There's mony a thing to cause a minister to stumble, for they're juist human beings after a', but his rich marriage was John Allison's undoing."

"Marriage," sighed Mawson, "is a great risk. It's often as well to be single, but I sometimes think Providence must ha' meant me to 'ave an 'usband — I'm such a clingin' creature."

Such sentiments were most distasteful to Miss Bathgate, that self-reliant spinster, and she said bitterly:

"Ma wumman, ye're ill off for something to cling to! I never saw the man yet that I wud be pitten up wi'."

"Ho! I shouldn't say that, but I must say I couldn't ever bring myself to fancy a h'undertaker. Just imagine 'im 'andlin' the dead and then 'andlin' me!"

"Eh, ye nesty cratur," said Bella much disgusted. "But I suppose ye're meaning *English* undertakers — men that does naething but work wi' funerals — a fearsome ill job. Here it's the jiner that does a'thing, so it's faur mair homely."

"Speakin' about marriages," said Mawson, who preferred cheerful subjects; "I do enjoy a nice weddin'. The motors and the bridesmaids and the flowers. Is there no chance of a weddin' 'ere?"

Miss Bathgate shook her head.

"Why not Miss Jean?" Mawson suggested.

Again Miss Bathgate shook her head.

"Nae siller," she said briefly.

"What! No money, you mean? But h'every gentleman ain't after money." Mawson's expression grew softly sentimental as she added, "Many a one marries for love, like the king and the beggar-maid."

"Mebbe," said Bella; "but the auld rhyme's oftener true:

" 'Be a lassie ne'er sae black
　　Gie her but the name o' siller,
Set her up on Tintock tap
　　An' the wind'll blaw a man till her.

Be a lassie ne'er sae fair,
　　Gin she hinna penny-siller,
A flea may fell her in the air
　　Ere a man be eavened till her.' "

"I would like fine to see Miss Jean get a guid man, for she's no' a bad lassie, but I doot she'll never manage't."

"Oh, Beller, you do take an 'opeless view of things. I think it's because you wear black so much. Now I must say I like a bit o' bright colour. I think it gives one bright thoughts."

"I aye wear black," said Bella firmly, as she carried the supper dishes to the scullery, "and then, as the auld wifie said, 'Come daith, come sacrament, I'm ready!' "

14

*"Pray you sir, how much carnation ribbon
may a man buy for a remuneration ?"*
"COMEDY OF ERRORS"

THE living-room at The Rigs was the
stage of many plays. Its uses ranged
from the tent of a menagerie or the
wigwam of an Indian brave to the Forest of
Arden.

This December night it was a "wood
near Athens", and to Mhor, if to no one
else, it faithfully represented the original.
That true Elizabethan needed no aids to
his imagination. "This is a wood," said
Mhor, and a wood it was. "Is all our company here ?" and to him the wood was
peopled by Quince and Smug, by Bottom
the weaver, by Puck and Oberon. Titania
and her court he reluctantly admitted were
necessary to the play, but he did not try to
visualise them, regarding them privately as
blots. The love-scenes between Hermia and
Lysander, Helena and Demetrius, were

omitted, because Jock said they were
"*awful* silly".

It was Friday evening, so Jock had put
off learning his lessons till the next day,
and, as Bully Bottom, was calling over the
names of his caste.

"Are we all met?"

"Pat, pat," said Mhor, who combined in
his versatile person all the other parts; "and
here's a marvellous convenient place for our
rehearsal. This green plot shall be our
stage, this hawthorn brake our tiring-
house; and we will do it in action as we
will do it before the duke."

Pamela Reston, in her usual place, the
corner of the sofa beside the fire, threaded
her needle with a bright silk thread, and
watched the players amsuedly.

"Did you ever think," she asked Jean,
who sat on a footstool beside her — a glowing figure in a Chinese coat given her by
Pamela, engaged rather incongruously in
darning one of Jock's stockings — "did you
ever think what it must have been like to
see a Shakespeare play for the first time?
Was the Globe filled, I wonder, with a
quite unexpected first night audience?
And did they realise that the words they

heard were deathless words? Imagine hearing for the first time:

" '*When daisies pied and violets blue*
And lady-smocks all silver white. . . .'"

and then — 'The words of Mercury are harsh after the songs of Apollo'. Did you ever try to write, Jean?"

"Pamela," said Jean, "if you drop from Shakespeare to me in that sudden way, you'll be dizzy. I have thought of writing and trying to give a truthful picture of Scottish life — a cross between *Drumtochty* and *The House with the Green Shutters* — but I'm sure I shall never do it. And if by any chance I did accomplish it, it would probably be reviewed as a 'feebly written story of life in a Scots provincial town', and then I would beat my pen into a hatpin and retire from the literary arena. I wonder how critics can bear to do it. I couldn't sleep at nights for thinking of my victims — "

"You sentimental little absurdity! It wouldn't be honest to praise poor work."

Jean shook her head. "They could always be a little kind. . . . Pamela, I love

226

myself in this coat. You can't think what a delight colours are to me." She stopped, and then said shyly, "You have brought colour into all our lives. I can see now how drab they were before you came."

"Oh, dear, no, Jean, your life was never drab. It could never be drab whatever your circumstances, you have so much happiness within yourself. I don't think anything in life could ever quite down you, and even death — what of death, Jean?"

Jean looked up from her stocking. "As Boswell said to Dr. Johnson. 'What of death, Sir?' and the great man was so angry that the little twittering genius should ask lightly of such a terrifying thing that he barked at him and frightened him out of the room! I suppose the ordinary thing is never to think about death at all, to keep the thought pushed away. But that makes people so *afraid* of it. It's such a bogey to them. The Puritans went to the other extreme and dressed themselves in their grave-clothes every day. Wasn't it Samuel Rutherford who advised people to 'forefancy their latter end'? I think that's where Great-aunt Alison got the idea; she certainly made us 'forefancy' ours! But apart from what death may mean to each of us — life itself gets all its meaning from death. If we didn't know that we had all to die we could hardly go on living, could we?"

"Well," said Pamela, "it would certainly be difficult to bear with people if their presence and our own were not utterly uncertain. And if we knew with surety when we rose in the morning that for another forty years we would go on getting up, and having a bath and dressing, we would be apt to expire with ennui. We rise with alacrity because we don't know if we shall ever put our clothes on again."

Jean gave a little jump of expectation. "It's frightfully interesting. You never do know when you get up in the morning what will happen before night."

"Most people find that a little wearing. It isn't always nice things that happen, Jean."

"Not always, of course, but far more nice things happen than nasty ones."

"Jean, I'm afraid you're a chirping optimist. You'll reduce me to the depths of depression if you insist on being so bright. Rather help me to rail against fate, and so cheer me."

"Do you realise that Davie will be home next week?" said Jean, as if that were reason enough for any amount of optimism. "I think on the whole, he has enjoyed his first term, but he was pretty homesick at first. He never actually said so, but he told us in one letter that he smelt the tea when he made it, for it was the one thing that reminded him of home. And another time he spoke with passionate dislike of the pollarded trees, because such things are unknown on Tweedside. I'm so glad he has made quite a lot of friends. I was afraid he might be so shy and unforthcoming that he would put people off, but he writes enthusiastically about the men he is with. It is good for him to be made to leave his work, and play games; he is keen about his footer and they think he will row well! The man who has rooms on the same staircase seems a very good sort. I forget who he is — it's quite a well-known family — but he has been uncommonly kind to Davie. He wants him to go home with him next week, but of course Davie is keen to get back to Priorsford. Besides, you can't visit the stately homes of England on thirty shillings, and that's about Davie's limit, dear lamb! Jock and Mhor are looking forward with joy to hear him speak. They expect his accent to have suffered an Oxford change, and Jock doesn't think he will be able to remain in the room with him and not laugh."

"I expect Jock will be 'affronted'," said Pamela. "But you aren't the only one who is expecting a brother, Jean girl. Any moment I may hear that Biddy is in London. He wired from Port Said that he would come straight to Priorsford. I wonder whether I should take rooms for him in the Hydro, or in one of these nice old hotels in the Nethergate? I wish I could crush him into Hillview, but there isn't any room, alas!"

"I wish," said Jean, and stopped. She had wanted, in her hospitable way, to say that Pamela's brother must come to The Rigs, but she checked the impulse with a fear that it was an absurd proposal. She was immensely interested in this brother of Pamela's. All she had heard of him appealed to her imagination, for Jean, cumbered as she was with domestic cares, had an adventurous spirit, and thrilled to hear of the perils of the mountains, the treks behind the ranges for something hidden, all the daring escapades of an adventure-loving young man with time and money at his disposal. She had made a hero of Pamela's "Biddy", but now that she was to see him she shrank from the meeting. Suppose he were a supercilious sort of person who would be bored with the little town and the people in it. And the fact that he had a title complicated matters, Jean thought. She could not imagine herself talking naturally to Lord Bidborough. Besides, she thought, she didn't know in the least how to talk to men; she so seldom met any.

"I expect," she broke out after a silence, "your brother will take you away?"

"For Christmas, I think," said Pamela; "but I shall come back again, never fear. Do you realise that I've been here two months, Jean?"

"Does it seem so short to you?"

"In a way it does; the days have passed so pleasantly. And yet I seem to have been here all my life; I feel so much a part of Priorsford, so akin to the people in it. It must be the Border blood in my veins. My mother loved her own country dearly. I have heard my aunt say that she never felt at home at Bidborough or Mintern

Abbas. I am sure she would have wanted us to know her Scots home, so Biddy and I are going to Champertoun for Christmas. My mother never had any brothers, and everything went to a distant cousin. He and his wife seem friendly people and they urge us to visit them.''

"That will mean a lovely Christmas for you,'' Jean said, genuine warmth in her voice.

Here Mhor stopped being an Athenian reveller to ask that the sofa might be pushed back. The larger stage now became the palace of Theseus, and Mhor, as the Prologue, was addressing an imaginary audience with — "Gentles, perchance you wonder at this show''.

Pamela and Jane removed themselves to the window-seat and listened while Jock, covered with an old skin rug gave a realistic presentment of the lion, that very gentle beast, and of a good conscience.

The "tedious brief'' scene was drawing to an end, when the door opened and a fluttering Mrs. M'Cosh, with a scared look in her eyes and an excited squeak in her voice, announced, "Lord Bidborough.''

A slim, dark young man stood in the

doorway, regarding the dishevelled room. Jock and Mhor were still writhing on the floor, the chairs were pushed in all directions, Pamela's embroidery frame had alighted on the bureau, and the rugs were pulled here and there.

Pamela gave a cry and rushed at her brother, forgetting everything in the joy of seeing him. Then, remembering her hostess, she turned to Jean, who still sat on the window-seat, her face flushed and her eyes dark with excitement, the blood-red mandarin's coat with its embroidery of blue and mauve and gold vivid against the dark curtains, and said, "Jean, this is Biddy!"

Jean stood up and held out a shy hand.

"And this is Jock — and Mhor!"

"Having a great game, aren't you?" said the newcomer, smiling broadly.

"Not a game," Mhor corrected him, "a play, *Midsummer Night's Dream*."

"No; are you? I once played in it at the O.U.D.S. I wanted to be Bully Bottom, but I wasn't much good, so they made me Snug the joiner. I shall always remember the man who played Puck — he was a wonder, about as light on his feet and as swift as the real Puck. A jolly play."

"Biddy," said his sister, "why didn't you wire to me? I have taken no rooms."

"Oh, that's all right — a porter at the station, a most awfully nice chap, put me into a sort of fly and sent me to one of the hotels — a jolly good little inn it is — and they can put me up. Then I asked for Hillview, mentioning the witching name of Miss Bella Bathgate, and they sent a boy with me to find the place. Miss Bathgate sent me on here. Beautifully managed, you see."

He smiled lazily at his sister, who cried:

"The same casual old Biddy! What about dinner?"

"Mayn't I feed with you? I think Miss Bathgate would like me to. And I'm devoted to stewed beef and carrots. After cold storage food, it will be a most welcome change. But," turning to Jean, "please forgive me arriving on you like this, and discussing board and lodgings. It's the most frightful cheek on my part, but, you see, Pam's letters have made me so well acquainted with The Rigs and everyone in it that I'm afraid I don't feel the least need of ceremony".

"We shouldn't know what to do with

ceremony here," said Jean. "But I do wish the room had been tidier. You will get a bad impression of our habits — and we are really quite neat as a rule. Jock, take that rug back to Mrs. M'Cosh and put the sofa right. And Mhor, do wash your face; you've got it all smeared with black."

As Jean spoke she moved about putting things to rights, lifting cushions, brightening the fire, brushing away fallen cinders.

"That's better. Now don't stand about so uncomfortably. Pamela, sit in your corner; and this is a really comfortable chair, Lord Bidborough."

"I want to look at the books, if I may," said Lord Bidborough. "It's always the first thing I do in a room. You have a fine collection here."

"They are nearly all my father's books," Jean explained. "We don't add to them, except of course on birthdays and at Christmas, and never valuable books."

"You have some very rare books — this, for instance."

"Yes. Father treasured that — and have you seen this?"

They browsed among the books for a little, and Jean, turning to Pamela, said,

"I remember the first time you came to see us; you did this, too, walked about and looked at the books."

"I remember," said Pamela; "history repeats itself."

Lord Bidborough stopped before a shelf. "This is a catholic selection."

"Those are my favourite books," said Jean — "modern books, I mean."

"I see." He went along the shelf, naming each book as he came to it. "*The Long Roll* and *Cease Firing*. Two great books. I should like to read them again now."

"Now one could read them," said Jean. "Through the War I tried to, but I had to stop. The writing was too good — too graphic, somehow. . . ."

"Yes; it would be too poignant. . . . *John Splendid*. I read that one autumn in Argyle — slowly — about two chapters a day, making it last as long as I could."

"Isn't it fine?" said Jean. "John Splendid, who never spoke the truth except to an enemy! Do you remember the scene with the blind widow of Glencoe? And John Splendid was so gallant and tactful: 'dim in the sight', he called her, for he wouldn't say 'blind'; and then was terrified when he heard that plague had been in the house, and would have left without touching the outstretched hand, and Gordon, the harsh-mannered minister, took it and kissed it; and the blind woman cried, 'O Clan Campbell, I'll never call ye down — ye may have the guile they claim for ye, but ye have the way with a women's heart,' and poor John Splendid went out covered with shame."

Jean's eyes were shining, and she had forgotten to be awkward and tongue-tied.

"I remember," said Lord Bidborough. "And the wonderful descriptions — 'I know corries in Argyle that whisper silken' . . . do you remember that ? And the last scene of all when John Splendid rides away ?"

"Do you cry over books, Jean ?" Pamela asked. She was sitting on the end of the sofa, her embroidery frame in her hand and her cloak on, ready to go when her brother had finished looking at Jean's treasures.

Jean shook her head. "Not often. Great-aunt Alison said it was the sign of a feeble mind to waste tears over fiction, but I have cried. Do you remember the end of *The Mill on the Floss*? Tom and Maggie have been estranged, and the flood comes, and Tom goes to save Maggie. He is rowing when he sees the great mill machinery sweeping down on them, and he takes Maggie's hand, and calls her the name he had used when they were happy children together — '*Magsie*!' "

Pamela nodded. "Nothing appeals to you so much as family affection, Jean, girl. What have you got now, Biddy? *Nelly's Teachers*?"

"Oh, that," said Jean, getting pink — "that's a book I had when I was a child, and I still like it so much that I read it through every year."

"Oh, Jean, you babe!" Pamela cried. "Can you actually still read goody-goody girls' stories?"

"Yes," said Jean defiantly, "and enjoy them too."

"And why not?" asked Lord Bidborough. "I enjoy *Huckleberry Finn* as much now as I did when I was twelve; and I often yearn after the books I had as a boy and never see now. I used to lie on my face poring over them. *The Clipper of the Clouds*, and *Sir Ludar*, and a fairy story called *Rigmarole in Search of a Soul*, which, I remember, was quite beautiful, but can't lay hands on anywhere."

Jean looked at him gratefully, and thought to herself that he wasn't going to be a terrifying person after all. For his age — Jean knew that he was thirty-five, and had expected something much more mature — he seemed oddly boyish. He had an expectant young look in his eyes, as if he were always waiting for some chance of adventure to turn up, and there were humorous lines about his mouth which seemed to say that he found the world a very funny place, and was exceedingly well amused.

He certainly seemed very much at home at The Rigs, fondling the rare old books with the hands of a book-lover, inspecting the coloured prints, chaffing Jock and Mhor, who fawned round him like two puppy dogs. Peter had at once made friends with him, and Mrs. M'Cosh, coming into the room on some errand, edged her way out backwards, her eyes fixed on the newcomer with an approving stare. As she told Jean later: "For a' Andra pit me against lords, I canna see muckle wrang wi' this yin. A rale pleasant fellow I tak' him to be, lord or no lord. If they were a' like him, we wudna need to be Socialists. It's queer I've aye hed a hankerin' after thae high-born kinna folk. It's that interestin' to watch them. Ye niver ken whit they'll dae next, or whit they'll say — they're that audacious. We wud mak' an awfu' dull warld o' it if we pit them a' awa to Ameriky or somewhere. I often tell't Andra that, but he said it wud be a guid riddance . . . I'm wonderin' what Bella Bathgate thinks o' him. It'll be great to hear her breath on't. She's quite comin' roond to Miss Reston. She was tellin' me she disna think there's onything veecious about her, and she's gettin' quite used to her manners."

When Pamela departed with her brother to partake of a dinner cooked by Miss Bathgate (a somewhat doubtful pleasure), Mhor went off to bed, and Jock curled himself up on the sofa with Peter, for his Friday night's extra hour with a story-book, while Jean resumed her darning of stockings.

Her thoughts were full of the sister and brother who had just left. "Queer they are!" she thought to herself. "If Davie came back to me after a year in India, I wouldn't have liked to meet him in somebody else's house. But they seemed quite happy to look at books, and talk about just anything, and play with Jock and Mhor and tease Peter. Now I expect they'll be talking about their own affairs, but I would have rushed at the pleasure of hearing all about everything — I couldn't have waited. Pamela has such a leisured air about everything she does. It's nice and sort of aloof and quiet — but I could never attain to it. I'm little and bustling and rather Martha-like."

Here Jean sighed, and put her fingers through a large hole in the toe of a stocking.

"I'm only fit to keep house and darn and worry the boys about washing their ears. . . . Anyway, I'm glad I had on my Chinese coat."

15

"Her gown should be of goodliness
Well ribboned with renown,
Purfilled with pleasures in ilk place
Furred with fine fashion.

Her hat should be of fair having,
And her tippit of truth,
Her patclet of good pansing
Her neck ribbon of ruth.

Her sleeves should be of esperance
To keep her from despair:
Her gloves of the good governance
To guide her fingers fair.

Her shoes should be of sickerness
In syne she should not slide:
Her hose of honesty, I guess
I should for her provide.
"THE GARMENT OF GOOD LADIES, 1568"

JOCK and Mhor looked back on the time
Lord Bidborough spent in Priorsford as
one long, rosy dream.

It is true they had to go to school as
usual, and learn their home-lessons, but

their lack of attention in school hours must have sorely tried their teachers, and their home-lessons were crushed into the smallest space of time so as not to interfere with the crowded hours of glorious living that Lord Bidborough managed to make for them.

That nobleman turned out to be the most gifted player that Jock and Mhor had ever met. There seemed no end to the games he could invent, and he played with a zest that carried everyone along with him.

Mhor's great passion was for trains. He was no budding engineering genius; he cared nothing about knowing what made the wheels go round; it was the trains themselves, the glorious, puffing, snorting engines, the comfortable guards' vans, and the signal-boxes that enchanted him. He thought a signalman's life was one of delirious happiness; he thrilled at the sight of a porter's uniform, and hoped that one day he too might walk abroad dressed like that, wheel people's luggage on a trolley, and touch his hat when given tips. It was his great treat to stand on the iron railway-bridge and watch the trains snorting deliriously underneath; but the difficulty was that he might not go alone, and as everyone in the house fervently disliked the task of accompanying him, it was a treat that came all too seldom for the Mhor.

It turned out that Lord Bidborough also delighted in trains, and he not only stood patiently on the bridge watching goods-trains shunting up and down, but he made friends with the porters, and took Mhor into prohibited areas such as signal-boxes and goods sheds, and showed him how signals were worked, and ran him up and down on trolley's.

One never-to-be-forgotten day a sympathetic engine-driver lifted Mhor into the engine and, holding him high above the furnace, told him to pull a chain, where-upon the engine gave an anguished hoot. Mhor had no words to express his unbounded pleasure, but in an ecstasy of gratitude he had spontaneously seized the engine-driver's grimy hand and kissed it, leaving that honest workman, who was not accustomed to such displays of affection, considerably confused.

Jock did not share Mhor's interest in "base mechanic happenings"; his passion was for the world at large; his motto, "For to admire and for to see". He had long made up his mind that he must follow some profession that would take him to far places. Mrs. Hope suggested the Indian Army, while Mr. Jowett loyally recommended the Indian Civil Service, though he felt bound in duty to warn Jock that it wasn't what it was in his young days, and was indeed hardly fit now for a white man.

Jock felt that Mrs. Hope and Mr. Jowett were wise and experienced, but they were old. In Lord Bidborough he found one who had come hot-foot from the ends of the earth. He had seen with his own eyes, and he could tell Jock such fascinating tales that made the coveted far lands come to life before him; and Jock fell down and worshipped.

Through the day, while the two boys were interned in school, Pamela took her brother the long walks over the hills that had delighted her days in Priorsford. Jean sometimes went with them, but more often she stayed at home. It was her mission in life, she said, to stay at home and have meals ready for people when they returned, and it was much better that the brother and sister should have their walks alone, she told herself. Excessive self-confidence was not one of Jean's faults. She was much afraid of boring people by her presence, and shrank from being the third that constitutes "a crowd".

One afternoon Lewis Elliot called at The Rigs.

"Sitting alone, Jean? Well, it's nice to find you in. I thought you would be out with your new friends."

"Lord Bidborough has motored Pamela down Tweed to see some people," Jean explained. "They asked me to go with them, but I thought I might perhaps be in the way. Lord Bidborough is frightfully pleased to be able to hire a motor to drive. On Saturday he has promised to take the boys to Dryburgh and to the Eildon Hills. Mhor is very keen to see for himself where King Arthur is buried, and make a search for the horn!"

"I see. It's a pity it isn't a better time of year. December days are short for excursions. . . . Isn't Biddy a delightful fellow?"

"Yes. Jock and Mhor worship him. One word from him is more to them than all the wisdom I'm capable of. It isn't quite fair. After all, I've had them so long, and they've only known him for a day or two. No, I don't think I'm jealous. I'm — I'm hurt!" and to Lewis Elliot's great discomfort Jean took out her handkerchief and openly wiped her eyes, and then, putting her head on the table, cried.

He sat in much embarrassment, making what he meant to be comforting ejaculations, until Jean stopped crying and laughed through her tears.

"It's wretched of me to make you so uncomfortable. I don't know what's happened to me. I've suddenly got so silly. And I don't think I like charming people. Charm is a merciless sort of gift . . . and I know he will take Pamela away, and she made things so interesting. Every day since he came I seem to have got lonelier and lonelier, and the sight of your familiar face and the sound of your kind voice finished me. . . . I'm quite sensible now, so don't go away. Tea will be in, in a minute, and the boys. Isn't it fine Davie will be home tomorrow? D'you think he'll be changed?"

Lewis Elliot stayed to tea, and Jock and

Mhor fell on him with acclamation, and told him wonderful tales of their new friend, and never noticed the marks of tears on Jean's face.

"Jean, can you tell me? What is Lord Bidborough's Christian name?" Jock asked.

"Oh, I don't know. Richard Plantagenet, I should think."

"Really, Jean?"

"Why not? But you'd better ask him. Are you going, Cousin Lewis? When will you come and see Davie?"

"Let me see. I'm lunching at Hillview on Friday. May I come in after luncheon? Thanks. You must all come up to Laverlaw one day next week. The puppies are growing up, Mhor, and you're missing all their puppyhood; that's a pity."

Later in the evening, just before Mhor's bedtime, Lord Bidborough came to The Rigs. Pamela was resting, he explained, or writing letters, or doing something else, and he had come in to pass the time of day with them.

"The time of night, you mean," said Mhor, ruefully. "In ten minutes I'll have to go to bed."

"Had you a nice time this afternoon?" Jean asked.

"Oh, ripping! Coming up by Tweed in the darkening was heavenly. I wish you had been with us, Miss Jean. Why wouldn't you come?"

"I had things to do," said Jean, primly.

"Couldn't the things have waited? Good days in December are precious, Miss Jean — and Pam and I are going away next week. Promise you will go with us next time — on Saturday, to the Eildon Hills."

"What's your Christian name, please?" Jock broke in suddenly, remembering the discussion. "Jean says it's Richard Plantagenet — *is* it?"

Jean flushed an angry pink, and said sharply:

"Don't be silly, Jock. I was only talking nonsense."

"Well, what is it?" Jock persisted.

"It's not quite Richard Plantagenet, but it's pretty bad. My name given me by my godmother and godfathers is — Quintin Reginald Fuerbras."

"Gosh Maggie!" ejaculated Jock, mouth agape. "Earls in the streets of Cork!"

"I knew," said Jean, "that it would be something very twopence-coloured."

"It's not, I grant, such a jolly name as yours," said Lord Bidborough — "Jean Jardine."

"Oh, mine is Penny-plain," said Jean hurriedly.

"Must we always call you Lord?" Mhor asked.

"Of course you must," Jean said. "Really, Mhor, you and Jock are sometimes very stupid."

"Indeed you must not," said Lord Bidborough. "Forgive me, Miss Jean, if I am undermining your authority, but, really, one must have some say in what one is to be called. Why not call me Biddy?"

"That might be too familiar," said Jock. "I think I would rather call you Richard Plantagenet."

"Because it isn't my name?"

"It sort of suits you," Jock said.

"I like long names," said Mhor.

"Will you call me Richard Plantagenet, Miss Jean?"

The yellow lights in Jean's eyes sparkled. "If you'll call me Penny-plain," she said.

"Then that's a bargain, though I don't

think either of us is well suited. However —
now that we are really friends, what did you
do this afternoon that was so very important ?"

"Talked to Lewis Elliot for one thing;
he came to tea."

"I see. An excellent fellow, Lewis. He's
a relation of yours, isn't he ?"

"A very distant one, but we have so few
relations; we are only too glad to claim
him. He has been a very good friend to us
always. . . . Mhor, you really must go to
bed now."

"Oh, all right, but I don't think it's very
polite to go to bed when a visitor's in. It
might make him think he ought to go
away."

Lord Bidborough laughed, and assured
Mhor that he appreciated his delicacy of
feeling.

"There's a thing I want to ask you,
anyway," said Mhor. — "Yes, I'm going
to bed, Jean. Whether do you think
Quentin Durward or Charlie Chaplin
would be the better man in a fight ?"

Lord Bidborough gave the matter some
earnest thought, and decided on Quentin
Durward.

"I told you that," said Jock to Mhor. "Now, perhaps, you'll believe me."

"I don't know," said Mhor, still doubtful. "Of course Quentin Durward had his sword — but you know that way Charlie has with a stick?"

"Well, anyway, go to bed," said Jean, "and stop talking about that horrible little man. He oughtn't to be mentioned in the same breath as Quentin Durward."

Mhor went out of the room still arguing.

The next day David came home.

The whole family including Peter were waiting on the platform to welcome him, but Mhor was too interested in the engine and Jock too afraid of showing sentiment to pay much attention to him, and it was left to Jean and Peter to express joy at the traveller's return.

At first it seemed to Jean that it was a different David who had come back. There was an indefinable change, even in his appearance. True, he wore the same Priorsford clothes that he had gone away in, but he carried himself better, with more assurance. His round, boyish face had taken on a slightly graver and more responsible look, and his accent certainly had an Oxford touch. Enough, anyhow, to send Jock and Mhor out of the room to giggle convulsively in the lobby. To Jean's relief David noticed nothing; he was too busy telling Jean his news to trouble about the eccentric behaviour of the two boys.

David would hardly have been human if he had not boasted a little that first night. He had often pictured it to himself just how it would be. Jean would sit by the fire and listen, and he would sit on the old comfortable sofa and recount all the doings of his first term, tell of his friends, his tutors, his rooms, the games, the fun — all the details of the wonderful new life. And it had happened just as he had pictured it — lucky David! The room had looked as he had known it would look, with a fire that sparkled as only Jean's fires ever sparkled and Jean's eyes — Jean's "doggy" eyes, as Mhor called them — were lit with interest; and Jock and Mhor and Peter crept in after a little and lay on the rug and gazed up at him, a quiet and most satisfactory audience.

Jean felt a little in awe of this younger brother of hers, who had suddenly grown a man and spoke with an air of authority.

She had an ache at her heart for the Davie who had been a little boy and content to lean; she seemed hardly to know this new David. But it was only for a little. When Jock and Mhor had gone to bed, the brother and sister sat over the fire talking, and David forgot all his new importance and ceased to "buck", and told Jean all his little devices to save money, and how he had managed just to scrape along fairly well.

"If only everyone else were poor as well," said Jean, "then it wouldn't matter."

"That's just it; but it's so difficult doing things with men who have loads of money. It never seems to occur to them that other people haven't got it. Of course, I just say I can't afford to do things, but that's awkward too, for they look so surprised and sort of ashamed, and it makes me feel a prig and a fool. I think having a lot of money takes away people's imagination."

"Oh, it does," Jean agreed.

"Anyway," David went on, "it's up to me to make some money. I hate sponging on you, old Jean, and I'm not going to do it. I've been trying my hand at writing lately and — I've had two things accepted."

Jean all but fell into the fire in her surprise and delight.

"Write! You! Oh, Davie, how utterly splendid!"

A torrent of questions followed, which David answered as well as he could.

"Yes; they are printed, and paid for, and what's more I've spent the money." He brought out from his pocket a small leather case which he handed to his sister.

"For me? Oh, David!" Her hands shook as she opened the box and disclosed a small brooch, obviously inexpensive but delicately designed.

"It's nothing," said David, walking away from the emotion in his sister's face. "With the rest of the money I got presents for the boys and Mrs. M'Cosh and Peter, but they'd better be kept out of sight till Christmas Day."

Truth to tell, he had meant to keep the brooch also out of sight till Christmas, but the temptation to see Jean's pleasure had been to strong. This Jean divined and, with happy tears in her eyes, handed it back to him to keep till the proper giving-day arrived.

The next day David was introduced to

Pamela and her brother, and was pleased to pronounce well of them. He had been inclined to be distrustful about the entrance of such exotic creatures as they sounded into the quiet of Priorsford, but having seen and talked to them he assured his sister they were quite all right.

Why, Lord Bidborough had been at David's own college — that alone was recommendation enough. His feats, too, were still remembered, not feats of scholarship — oh no, but of mountaineering on the college roofs. He had not realised when Jean mentioned Lord Bidborough in her letters that it was the same man who was still spoken of by undergraduates with bated breath.

Of Pamela, David attempted no criticism. How could he? He was at her feet, and hardly dared lift his eyes to her face. A smile or two, a few of Pamela's softly spoken sentences, and David had succumbed. Not that he allowed her — or anyone else — to know what was in his heart. He kept at a respectable distance, and worshipped in silence.

One evening while Pamela sat stitching at her embroidery in the little parlour at

Hillview her brother laid down the book he was reading, lit a cigarette, and said suddenly, "What of the Politician, Pam?"

Pamela drew the thread in and out several times before she answered.

"The Politician is safe so far as I'm concerned. Only last week I wrote and explained matters to him. He wrote a very nice letter in reply. I think, on the whole, he is much relieved, though he expressed polite regret. It must be rather a bore at sixty to become possessed of a wife, even though she might be able to entertain well and manage people . . . It was a ridiculous idea always; I see that now."

Lord Bidborough regarded his sister with an amused smile. "I always did regard the Politician as a fabulous monster. But tell me, Pam, how long is this to continue? Are you so enamoured of the simple life that you can go on indefinitely living in Miss Bathgate's parlour and eating stewed steak and duck's eggs?"

Pamela dropped her embroidery frame, looked at her brother with a puzzled frown, and gave a long sigh.

"Oh, I don't know," she said — "I don't know. Of course it can't go on indefinitely, but I do hate the thought of going away and leaving it all. I love the place. It had given me a new feeling about life; it has taught me contentment; I have found peace here. If I go back to the old restless, hectic life I shall be, I'm afraid, just as restless and feverishly anxious to be happy as I used to be. And yet, I suppose, I must go back. I've almost had the three months I promised myself. But I'm going to try and take Jean with me. Lewis Elliot and I mean to arrange things so that Jean can have her chance."

"Why should Lewis Elliot have anything to do with it?"

Her brother's tone brought a surprised look into Pamela's eyes.

"Lewis is a relation as well as a very old friend. Naturally he is interested. I should think it could easily be managed. The boys will go to school, Mrs. M'Cosh will stay on at The Rigs, Jean will see something of the world. Imagine the joy of taking Jean about! She will make everything worth while. I don't in the least expect her to be what is known as a 'success'. I can picture her at a ball thinking of her latter end! Up-to-date revues she will hate, and I can't see her indulging in whatever is the latest artistic craze of the moment. She is a very *select* little person, Jean. But she will love the plays and pictures, and shops and sights. And she has never been abroad — picture that! There are worlds of things to show her. I find that her great desire — a very modest one — is to go some April to the Shakespeare Festival at Stratford-on-Avon. She worships Shakespeare hardly on this side of idolatry."

"Won't she be disappointed? There is nothing very romantic about Stratford of today."

"Ah, but I think I can stage-manage so that it will come up to her expectations. A great many things in this world need a little stage-management. Oh, I hope my plans will work out. I *do* want Jean."

"But, Pamela — I want Jean too."

Lord Bidborough had risen from his chair, and now stood before the fire, his hands in his pockets, his head thrown back, his eyes no longer lazy and amused, but keen and alert. This was the man of action who attempted impossible things — and did them.

It is never an easy moment for a sister

when she realises that an adored brother no longer belongs to her.

Pamela, after one startled look at her brother, dropped her eyes and tried to go on with her embroidery, but her hand trembled, and she made stitches at random.

"Pam, dear, you don't mind? You don't think it an unfriendly act? You will always be Pam, my only sister; someone quite apart. The new love won't lessen the old."

"Ah, my dear" — Pamela held out her hands to her brother — "you mustn't mind if at first . . . You see, it's a great while ago since the world began, and we've been wonderful friends all the time, haven't we, Biddy?" They sat together silent for a minute, and then Pamela said, "And I'm actually crying, when the thing I most wanted has come to pass: what an idiot! Whenever I saw Jean I wanted her for you. But I didn't try to work it at all. It all just happened right, somehow. Jean's beauty isn't for the multitude, nor her charm, and I wondered if she would appeal to you. You have seen so many pretty girls, and have been almost surfeited with charm, and remained so calm that I wondered if you ever would fall in love. The 'manoeuvring mamaws', as Bella Bathgate calls the ladies with daughters to marry, quite lost hope where you were concerned; you never seemed to see their manoeuvres, poor dears. . . . And I was so thankful, for I didn't want you to marry the modern type of girl . . . But I hardly dared to hope you would come to Priorsford and love Jean at sight. It's all as simple as a fairy-tale."

"Oh, *is* it ? I very much doubt if Jean will look at me. I sometimes think she rather avoids me. She keeps out of my way, and hardly ever addresses a remark to me."

"She has never mentioned you to me," said Pamela, "and that's a good sign. I don't say you won't have to wait. I'm pretty certain she won't accept you when you ask her. Even if she cares — and I don't think she realises yet that she does — her sense of duty to the boys, and other things, will hold her back, and your title and possessions will tell against you. Jean is the least mercenary of creatures. Ask her before you leave, and if she refuses you appear to accept her refusal. Don't say you will try again and that sort of thing : it gives a girl a caged feeling. Go away for a while and make no sign. I know what I'm talking about, Biddy . . . and she is worth waiting for."

"I would serve for her as Jacob served for Rachel, and not grudge one minute of the time, but the nuisance is I'm twelve years older than she is. I can't afford to wait. I'm afraid she will think me too old."

"Nonsense, a boy would never do for Jean. Although she looks such a child, she is a woman, and a woman with a brain. Otherwise she would never do for you. You would tire of a doll in a week, no matter how curly the hair or flawless the complexion. . . . You realise, of course, that Jean is an uncompromising little Puritan ? Mercy is as plain as bread and honour is as hard as stone to Jean — but she has a wide tolerance for sinners. I can imagine it won't always be easy to be Jean's husband. She is so full of compassion that she will want to help every unfortunate, and fill the house with the broken and the unsuccessful. But she won't be a wearisome wife. She won't pall. She will always be full of surprises, and an infinite variety, and find such numbers of things to laugh about . . . You know how she mothers those boys —

can't you see Jean with babies of her own? . . . To me she is like a well of spring-water, a continual refreshment for weary souls."

Pamela stopped. "Am I making too much of an ordinary little country girl, Biddy?"

Her brother smiled and shook his head, and after a minute he said:

"A garden enclosed is my love."

16

"What's to be said to him, lady?
He is fortified against any denial."
"TWELFTH NIGHT"

THE day before Pamela and her
brother left Priorsford .for their
visit to Champertoun was a typical
December day, short and dark and dirty.

There was a party at Hopetoun in honour
of David's home-coming, and Pamela and
her brother were invited, along with the
entire family from The Rigs.

They all set off together in the early
darkening, and presently Pamela and the
three boys got ahead, and Jean found
herself alone with Lord Bidborough.

Weather had little or no effect on Jean's
spirits, and today, happy in having David
at home, she cared nothing for the depressing mist that shrouded the hills, or the
dank drip from the trees on the carpet of
sodden leaves, or the sullen swirl of Tweed
coming down big with spate, foaming
against the supports of the bridge.

"As dull as a great thaw," she quoted to her companion cheerfully. "It does seem a pity the snow should have gone away before Christmas. Do you know, all the years of my life I've never seen snow on Christmas. I do wish Mhor wouldn't go on praying for it. It's so stumbling for him when Christmas comes mild and muggy. If we could only have it once as you see it in pictures and read about it in books — "

She broke off to bow to Miss Watson and her sister, Miss Teenie, who passed Jean and her companion with skirts held well out of the mud and eyes, after the briefest glance, demurely cast down.

"They are going out to tea," Jean explained to Lord Bidborough. "Don't they look nice and tea-partyish? Fur capes over their best dresses and snow boots over their slippers. Those little black satin bags hold their work, and I expect they have each a handkerchief edged with Honiton lace and scented with White Rose. Probably they are going to Mrs. Henderson's. She gives wonderful teas, and they will be taken to a bedroom to take off their outer coverings, and they'll probably stay till about eight o'clock and then go home to supper."

Lord Bidborough laughed. "I begin to see what Pam means when she talked of the lovableness of a little town. It is cosy, as she says, to see people go out to tea and know exactly where they are going, and what they'll do when they get there."

"I should think," said Jean, "that it would rather appeal to you. Your doings have always been on such a big scale — climbing the highest mountains in the world, going to the very farthest places — that the tiny and the trivial ought to be rather fascinating by contrast."

Lord Bidborough admitted that it was so, and silence fell between them.

"I wonder," said Jean politely, having cast round in her mind for a topic that might interest — "I wonder what you will attempt next? Jock says you want to climb Everest. He is frightfully excited about it, and wishes you would wait a few years till he is grown up and ready."

"Jock is a jewel, and he will certainly go with me when I attempt Everest, if that time ever comes."

They had reached the entrance to Hopetoun: the avenue to the house was short. "Would you mind," said Lord Bidborough, "walking on with me for a little bit ? . . ."

"But why?" asked Jean, looking along the dark, uninviting road. "They'll wonder what's become of us, and tea will be ready, and Mrs. Hope doesn't like to be kept waiting."

"Never mind," said Lord Bidborough, his tone somewhat desperate. "I've got something I want to say to you, and this may be my only chance. Jean, could you ever — I mean, d'you think it possible — oh, Jean, will you marry me?"

Jean backed away from him, her mouth open, her eyes round with astonishment. She was too much surprised to be anything but utterly natural.

"Are you asking me to marry you? But how *ludicrous*!"

The answer restored them both to their senses.

Lord Bidborough laughed ruefully and said, "Well, that's not a pretty way to take a proposal," while Jean, flushed with shame at her own rudeness, and finding herself suddenly rather breathless, gasped out, "but you shouldn't give people such frights. How could I know you were going to say anything so silly? And it's my first proposal, and I've *got on goloshes*!"

"Oh, Jean! What a blundering idiot I am! I might have known it was a wrong moment, but I'm hopelessly inexperienced, and, besides, I couldn't risk waiting; I so seldom see you alone. Didn't you see, little blind Jean, that I was head over ears in love with you? The first night I came to The Rigs and you spoke to me in your singing voice I knew you were the one woman in the world for me."

"No," said Jean. "No."

"Ah, don't say that. You're not going to send me away, Penny-plain?"

"Don't you see," said Jean, "I mustn't *let* myself care for you, for it's quite impossible that I could ever marry you. It's no good even speaking about such a thing. We belong to different worlds."

"If you mean my stupid title, don't let that worry you. A second and the Socialists alter that! A title means nothing in these days."

"It isn't only your title: it's everything — oh, can't you *see*?"

"Jean, dear, let's talk it over quietly. I

confess I can't see any difficulty at all — if you care for me a little. That's the one thing that matters."

"My feelings," said Jean, "don't matter at all. Even if there was nothing else in the way, what about Davie and Jock and the dear Mhor? I must always stick to them — at least until they don't need me any longer."

"But, Jean, beloved, you don't suppose I want to take you away from them? there's room for them all . . . I can see you at Mintern Abbas, Jean, and there's a river there, and the hills aren't far distant — you won't find it unhomelike — the only thing that is lacking is a railway for the Mhor."

"Please don't," said Jean. "You hurt me when you speak like that. Do you think I would let you burden yourself with all my family? I would never be anything but a drag on you. You must go away, Richard Plantagenet, and take your proper place in the world, and forget all about Priorsford and Penny-plain, and marry someone who will help you with your career and be a fit mistress for your great houses, and I'll just stay here. The Rigs is my proper setting."

"Jean," said Lord Bidborough, "will you tell me — is there any other man?"

"No. How could there be? There aren't any men in Priorsford to speak of."

"There's Lewis Elliot."

Jean stared. "You don't suppose *Lewis* wants to marry me, do you? Men are the *stupidest* things! Don't you know that Lewis..."

"What?"

"Nothing. Only you needn't think he ever looks the road I'm on. What a horrid conversation this is! It's a great mistake ever to mention love and marriage. It makes the nicest people silly. I simply daren't think what Jock would say if he heard us. He would be what Bella Bathgate calls 'black affrontit'."

"Jean, will it always matter to you more than anything in the world what David and Jock and Mhor think? Will you never care for anyone as you care for them?"

"But they are my charge," Jean explained. "They were left to me. Mother said, before she went away that last time, 'I trust you, Jean, to look after the boys,' and when father didn't come back, and Great-aunt Alison died, they had only me."

"Can't you adopt me as well? Do you know, Penny-plain, I believe it is all the fault of your Great-aunt Alison. You are thinking that on your death-bed you will like to feel that you sacrificed yourself to others — "

"Oh," cried Jean, "did Pamela actually tell you about Great-aunt Alison? That wasn't quite fair."

"She wasn't laughing. She only told me because she knew I was interested in every detail of your life, and Great-aunt Alison explains a lot of things about her grand-niece."

Jean pondered on this for a little and then said:

"Pam once said I was on the verge of being a prig, and I'm not sure that she wasn't right, and it's a hateful thing to be. D'you think I'm priggish, Richard Plantagenet? Oh no, don't kiss me. I hate it . . . Why do you want to behave like that? It isn't nice."

"I'm sorry, Jean."

"And now your voice sounds as if you did think me a prig . . . Here we are at last, and I simply don't know what to say kept us."

"Don't say anything: leave it to me. I'll be sure to think of some lie. Do you realise that we are only ten minutes behind the others?"

"Is that all?" cried Jean, amazed. "It seems like *hours*."

Lord Bidborough began to laugh, helplessly.

"I wonder if any man ever had such a difficult lady," he said, "or one so uncompromisingly truthful?"

He rang the bell, and as they stood on the doorstep waiting, the light from the hall-door fell on his face, and Jean, looking at him, suddenly felt very low. He was going away, and she might never see him again. The fortnight he had been in Priorsford had given her an entirely new idea of what life might mean. She had not been happy all the time; she had been afflicted with vague discontents and jealousies such as she had not known before, but at the back of them all she was conscious of a shining happiness, something that illuminated and gave a new value to all the commonplace daily doings. Now, as in a flash, while they waited for the door to open, Jean knew what had caused the happiness, and realised that with her own hand she was shutting the door on the light, shutting herself out to a perpetual twilight.

"If only you hadn't been a man," she said miserably, "we might have been such friends."

A servant opened the door and they went in together.

17

"When icicles hang by the wall
And Dick the shepherd blows his nail
And Tom bears logs into the hall
And milk comes frozen home in pail.
When blood is nipp'd and ways be foul,
Then nightly sings the staring owl,
Tu whit tu whu, a merry note
While greasy Joan doth keel the pot."
"LOVE'S LABOUR'S LOST"

MHOR began to look forward to Christmas whenever the days began to shorten and the delights of summer to fade; and the moment the Hallowe'en "dooking" for apples was over he and Jock were deep in preparations.

As is the way with most things, the looking forward and preparing were the best of it. It meant weeks of present-making, weeks of wrestling with delicious things like paints and pasteboard and glue. Then came a week or two of walking on tiptoe into the little spare room where the presents were stored, just to peep, and make sure that they really were there and had not been spirited away, for at Christmas-time you never knew what knavish sprites were wandering about. The spare room became the most interesting place in the house. It was all so thrilling: the pulling out of the drawer, the breathless moment until you made sure that the presents were safe, the smell that came out of the drawer to meet you, an indescribable smell of lavender and well-washed linen, of furniture polish and cedarwood. The dressing-table had a row of three little drawers on either side, and in these Jean kept the small eatables that were to go into the stockings — things made of chocolate, packets of almonds and raisins, big sugar "bools". To Mhor a great mystery hung over the dressing-table. No mortal hand had placed those things there; they were fairy things, and might vanish any moment. On Christmas morning he ate his chocolate frog with a sort of reverence, and sucked the sugar "bools" with awe.

A caller at The Rigs had once exclaimed in astonishment that an intelligent child like Mhor still believed in Santa Claus, and Jean had replied with sudden and startling ferocity, "If he didn't believe I would beat him till he did." Happily there was no need for such extreme measures: Mhor believed implicity.

Jock had now grown beyond such beliefs, but he did nothing to undermine Mhor's trust. He knew that the longer you can believe in such things the nicer the world is.

The Jardines always felt about Christmas Day that the best of it was over in the morning — the stockings and the presents and the postman, leaving long, over-eaten, irritable hours to be got through before bedtime and oblivion.

This year Jock had drawn out a timetable to insure that the day held no longueurs.

7.30	*Stockings.*
8.30	*Breakfast.*
9	*Postman.*
10–12	*Deliver small presents to various friends.*
1	*Luncheon at the Jowetts'.*
4	*Tea at home at present-giving.*
5–9	*Devoted to supper and variety entertainment.*

This programme was strictly adhered to, except by the Mhor in the matter of his stocking, which was grabbed from the bedpost and cuddled into bed beside him at least two hours before the scheduled time; and by the postman, who did not make his appearance till midday, thereby greatly disarranging things.

The day passed very pleasantly: the luncheon at the Jowett's was everything a Christmas meal should be, Mrs. M'Cosh surpassed herself with bakemeats for the tea, the presents gave lively satisfaction, but *the* feature of the day was the box that arrived from Pamela and her brother. It was waiting when the family came back from the Jowett's, standing in the middle of the little hall with a hammer and a screwdriver laid on the top by thoughtful Mrs. M'Cosh — a large white wooden box which thrilled one with its air of containing treasures. Mhor sank down beside it, hardly able to wait until David had taken off his coat and was ready to tackle it. Off came the lid, and out came the packing paper on the top, and in Jock and Mhor dived.

It was really a wonderful box. In it

there was something for everybody, including Mrs. M'Cosh and Peter, but Mhor's was the most striking present. No wonder the box was large. It contained a whole railway — a train, lines, signal-boxes, a station, even a tunnel.

Mhor was rendered speechless with delight. Jean wished Pamela had been there to see the lamps lit in his green eyes. Mrs. M'Cosh's beautiful tea was lost on him: he ate and drank without being aware of it, his eyes feasting all the time on this great new treasure.

"I wish," he said at last, "that I could do something for the Honourable and Richard Plantagenet. I only sent her a wee poetry-book. It cost a shilling. It was Jean's shilling, really, for I hadn't anything left, and I wrote in it, 'Wishing you a pretty New Year.' I forgot about 'happy' being the word; d'you think she'll mind awfully?"

"I think Pamela will prefer it called 'pretty'," Jean said. "You are lucky, aren't you?—and so is Jock with that gorgeous knife."

"It's an explorer's knife," said Jock. "You see, you can do almost everything with it. If I was wrecked on a desert island I could pretty nearly build a house with it. Feel the blades — "

"Oh, do be careful. I would put away the presents in the meantime and get everything ready for the charade. Are you quite sure you know what you're going to do? You mustn't just stand and giggle."

Jean had asked three guests to come to supper — three lonely women who otherwise would have spent a solitary evening — and Mrs. M'Cosh had asked Bella Bathgate to sup with her and afterwards to witness what she dubbed "a chiraide".

The living-room had been made ready for the entertainment, all the chairs placed in rows, the deep window-seat doing duty for a stage; but Jean was very doubtful about the powers of the actors, and hoped that the audience would be both easily amused and long-suffering.

Jock and Mhor protested that they had chosen a word for the charade, and knew exactly what they meant to say; but they would divulge no details, advising Jean to wait patiently, for something very good was coming.

The little house looked very festive, for

the boys had decorated earnestly, the square hall was a bower of greenery, and a gaily coloured Chinese lantern hanging in the middle added a touch of gaiety to the scene. The supper was the best that Jean and Mrs. M'Cosh could devise, the linen and the glass and silver shone, the flowers were charmingly arranged, Jean wore her gay mandarin's coat, and the guests — when they arrived — found themselves in such a warm and welcoming atmosphere that they at once threw off all stiffness and prepared to enjoy the evening.

The entertainment was to begin at eight, and Mrs. M'Cosh and Miss Bathgate took their seats "on the chap", as the latter put it. The two Miss Watsons, surprisingly enough, were also present. They had come along after supper with a small present for Jean, had asked to see her, and stood lingering on the doorstep refusing to come farther, but obviously reluctant to depart.

"Just a little bag, you know, Miss Jean, for you to put your work in if you're going out to tea, you know. No; it's not at all kind. You've been so nice to us. No, no, we won't come in; we don't want to disturb you — just ran along — you've friends, anyway. Oh, well, if you put it that way . . . we might just sit down for five minutes — if you're sure we're not in the way . . ." And still making a duet of protest they sank into seats.

A passage had been arranged with screens, between the door and the window-seat, and much traffic went along that way; the screens bumped and bulged and seemed on the point of collapsing, while smothered giggles were frequent.

At last the curtains were jerked apart, and revealed what seemed to be a funeral pyre. Branches were piled on the window-seat, and on the top, wrapped in an eider-down quilt, with a laurel wreath bound round his head, lay David. Jock, with bare legs and black boots, draped in an old-fashioned circular waterproof belonging to Mrs. M'Cosh, stood with arms folded looking at him; while Mhor, almost de-nuded of clothing, and supported by Peter (who sat with his back to the audience to show his thorough disapproval of the pro-ceedings), stood at one side.

When the murmured comments of the spectators had ceased, Mhor, looking extra-ordinarily Roman, held up his hand as if appealing to a raging mob, and said, "Peace, ho! Let us hear him," whereupon Jock, breathing heavily in his brother's face, proceeded to give Antony's oration over Caesar. He did it very well, and the Mhor as the Mob supplied appropriate growls at intervals; indeed, so much did Antony's eloquence inspire Mhor that, when Jock shouted, "Light the pyre!" (a sentence introduced to bring in the charade word), instead of merely pretending with an un-lighted taper, Mhor dashed to the fire, lit the taper, and before anyone could stop him thrust it among the dry twigs, which at once began to light and crackle. Im-mediately all was confusion. "Mhor!" shouted Jean, as she sprang towards the stage. "Gosh Maggie!" Jock yelled, as he grabbed the burning twigs, but it was "Imperial Caesar, dead and turned to clay", who really put out the fire by rolling on it wrapped in an eiderdown quilt.

"Eh, ye ill callant," said Bella Bathgate.

"Ye wee deevil," said Mrs. M'Cosh, "ye micht hev had us a' burned where we sat, and it Christmas, too!"

"What made you do it, sonny?" Jean asked.

"It made it so real," Mhor explained, "and I knew we could always throw them out of the window if they really blazed. What's the use of having a funeral pyre if you don't light it ?"

The actors departed to prepare for the next performance, Jock coming back to put his head in at the door to ask if they had guessed the first part of the word.

Jean said she thought it must be incenddiarism.

"Funeral," said Miss Watson, brightly.

"Huch," said Jock; "it's a word of one syllable."

"I think," Jean said as the door shut on Jock — "I think I know what the word is — pyre."

"Oh, really," said Miss Watson, "I'm all shaking yet with the fright I got. He's an awful bad wee boy that — sort of regardless. He needs a man to look after him."

"I'll never forget," said Miss Teenie, "once I was staying with a friend of ours, a doctor; his mother and our mother were cousins, you know, and when I looked — I was doing me hair at the time — I found that the curtain had blown across the gas and was blazing. If I had been in our own house I would just have rushed out screaming, but when you're away from home you've more feeling of responsibility, and I just stood on a chair and pulled at the curtain till I brought it down and stamped on it. My hands were all scorched and of course the curtain was beyond hope, but when the doctor saw it, he said, 'Teenie,' he said — his mother and ours were cousins, you know — 'you're just a wee marvel.' That was what he said — 'a wee marvel.' "

Jean said, "You *were* brave," and one of the guests said that presence of mind was a wonderful thing, and then the next act was ready.

The word had evidently something to do with eating, for the three actors sat at a Barmecide feast and quaffed wine from empty goblets, and carved imaginary haunches of venison. So far as could be judged from the conversation, which was much obscured by the smothered laughter of the actors, they seemed to belong to Robin Hood's merry men.

The third act took place on board ship — a ship flying the Jolly Roger — and it was obvious to the meanest intelligence that the word was pirate.

"Very good," said Miss Teenie, clapping her hands; "but," addressing the Mhor, "don't you go lighting any more funeral pyres. Boys who do that have to go to jail."

Mhor looked coldly at her, and half-opened his mouth to reply, only to be restrained by a single quelling glance from Jean who said hastily:

"You must show everyone your wonderful present, Mhor. I think the hall would be the best place to put it up in."

The second part of the programme was of a varied character. Jean led off with the old carol:

"*There comes a ship far sailing then,*
St. Michael was the steersman,"

and Mhor followed with a poem, "In Time of Pestilence", which had captivated this strange small boy's soul, and which he had learned for the occasion. Everyone felt it to be singularly inappropriate, and Miss Watson said it gave her quite a turn to hear the relish with which he knolled out:

> *"Wit with his wantonness*
>   *Tasteth death's bitterness:*
>   *Hell's executioner*
>   *Hath no ears for to hear*
>   *What vain art can reply!*
>   *I am sick, I must die —*
>   *God have mercy on us."*

From the safe haven of her spinsterdom she regarded him with disapproving eyes as a thoroughly uncomfortable and revolutionary character.

One of the guests sang a drawing-room ballad in which the words "dear heart" and the fervent clasping of the hands to the bosom seemed to occur with astonishing frequency. Then the entertainment took a distinctly lower turn.

David and Jock sang a song composed by themselves and set to a hymn tune, a somewhat ribald production. Mhor then volunteered the information that Mrs. M'Cosh could sing a song. Mrs. M'Cosh said, "Awa wi' ye, laddie", and "Sic havers", but after much urging owned that she knew a song which had been a favourite with her Andra. It was sung to the tune of "When the kye come hame", and was obviously a parody on that lyric, beginning:

> "Come a' ye Hieland pollismen
> That whustle through the street,
> An' A'll tell ye a' aboot a man
> That's got triple expansion feet.
>
> He's got braw, braw tartan whuskers
> That defy the shears and kaim;
> There's an awfu' row in Brigton
> When M'Kay comes hame."

Despite some youthful laughter Mrs. M'Cosh went on to tell how:

> "John M'Kay works down in Singers's,
> He's a ceevil engineer,
> But his wife's no verra ceevil
> When she's had some ginger-beer.
> When he missed the last Kilbowie train
> And had to walk hame lame.
> There wis Home Rule wi' the poker
> When M'Kay cam hame."

Mrs. M'Cosh sang four verses and stopped, in spite of the rapturous applause of a section of the audience.

"There's aboot nineteen mair verses," she explained, "an' they get kinna worse as they gang on, so I'd better stop," which she did, to Jean's relief, for she saw that her guests showed signs of restlessness, feeling perhaps that this was not an entertainment such as the Best People indulged in.

"And now Miss Bathgate will sing," said Mhor.

"I will not sing," said Miss Bathgate. "I've mair pride than make a fool o' mysel' to please folk."

"Oh, come on," Jock begged. "Look at Mrs. M'Cosh!"

Miss Bathgate snorted.

"Ay," said Mrs. M'Cosh, with imperturbable good-humour, "she seen me, and she thinks yin auld fool is enough at a time. Never heed, Bella, juist gie us a verse."

Miss Bathgate protested that she knew no songs, and had no voice, but under persuasion she broke into a ditty, a sort of recitative:

"*Gang further up the toon,*
Geordie Broon, Geordie Broon,
Gang further up the toon, Geordie Broon:
Gang further up the toon

Til, ye's spent yer hale hauf-croon,
And then come singin' doon,
Geordie Broon, Geordie Broon."

"I remember that when I was a child," Jean said. "We used to be put to sleep with it; it is very soothing. Thank you so much, Miss Bathgate. . . . Now I think we should have a game."

"Forfeits," Miss Teenie suggested.

"That's a silly game," said Mhor; "there's kissing in it."

"Perhaps we might have a quiet game," Jean said. "What was that one we played with Pamela, you remember, Jock? We took a subject, and tried who could say the most obvious thing about it."

"Oh, nothing clever, for goodness' sake," pleaded Miss Watson. "I've no head for anything but fancy-work."

" 'Up Jenkins' would be best," Jock decreed; so a table was got in, and "up Jenkins" was played with much laughter until the clock struck ten, and the guests all rose in a body to go.

"Well," said Miss Watson, "it's been a very pleasant evening, though I wouldn't wonder if I had a nightmare about that funeral pyre. . . . I always think, don't you, that there's something awful pathetic about Christmas? You never know where you may be before another."

One of the guests, a little music teacher, said:

"The worst of Christmas is that it brings back to one's mind all the other Christmasses and the people who were with us then. . . ."

Bella Bathgate's voice was heard talking to Mrs. M'Cosh at the door: "I dinna believe in keeping Christmas; it's a popish festival. New Year's the time. Ye can eat yer currant-bun wi' a relish then. Guidnicht, then, and see ye lick that ill laddie for near settin' the hoose on fire. It's no' safe, I tell ye, to live anywhere near him noo that he's begun thae tricks. Baith Peter an' him are fair Bolsheviks. . . . Did I tell ye that Miss Reston sent me a grand feather-boa — grey, in a present? I've aye had a notion o' a feather-boa, but I dinna ken how she kent that. And this is no' yin o' the skimpy kind; it's fine and fussy and soft. . . . Here, did the Lord send Miss Jean a present? . . . I doot he's aff for guid. Weel, weel, guid-nicht."

With a heightened colour Jean said good-night to her guests, separated Mhor from his train, and sent him with Jock to bed.

As she went upstairs, Bella Bathgate's words rang in her ears dismally: "I doot he's aff for guid."

It was what she wanted, of course; she had told him so. But she had half hoped that he might send her a letter or a little remembrance on Christmas Day.

Better not, perhaps, but it would have been something to keep. She sometimes wondered if she had not dreamt the scene in the Hopetoun Woods, and only imagined the words that were constantly in her ears. It was such a very improbable thing to happen to such a commonplace person.

Her room was very restful-looking that night to Jean, tired after a long day's junketing. It was a plain little upper chamber, with white walls and Indian rugs on the floor. A high south wind was blowing (it had been another of poor Mhor's snowless Christmasses!), making the curtains billow out into the room, and she could hear through the open window the sound of Tweed rushing between its banks. On the dressing-table a new novel with a vivid paper cover. Jean gave it a little disgusted push. Someone had lent it to her, and she had been reading it between Christmas preparations, reading it with deep distaste. It was about a duel for a man between a woman of forty-five and a girl of eighteen. The girl was called Noel, and was "pale, languid, passionate". The older woman gave up before the end, and said Time had "done her in". There were pages describing how she looked in the mirror "studying with a fearful interest the little hard lines and markings there beneath their light coating of powder, fingered and smoothed the slight looseness and fullness of the skin below her chin", and how she saw herself going down the years, "powdering a little more, painting a little more, touching up her hair till it was all artifice, holding on by every little device. . . ."

A man had written that. What a trade for a man to practise, Jean thought.

She was glad she lived among people who had the decency to go on caring for each other in spite of lines and wrinkles — comfortable couples whose affection for each other was a shelter in the time of storm, a shelter built of common joys, of "fireside talks and counsels in the dawn", cemented by tears shed over common sorrows.

She smiled to herself as she remembered a little woman who had told her with a great pride that, to celebrate their silver wedding, her husband was giving her a complete set of artificial teeth. "And," she had finished impressively, "you know what teeth cost now."

And why not? It was as much a token of love as a pearl necklace, and, looked at in the right way, quite as romantic.

"I'd better see how it finishes," Jean said to herself, opening the book a few pages from the end.

Oh, yes, there they were at it. Noel, "pale, languid, passionate", and the man "moved beyond control". "He drew her so close that he could feel the throbbing of her heart. . . ." And the other poor woman with the hard lines and marking beneath the light coating of powder, where had she gone?

Jean pushed the book away, and stood leaning on the dressing-table studying her face in the glass. This was no heroine, "pale, languid, passionate". She saw a fresh-coloured face with a pointed chin, wide-apart eyes as frank and sunny as a moorland burn, an innocent mouth. It seemed to Jean a very uninteresting face. she was young, certainly, but that was all — not beautiful, or brilliant and witty. Lord Bidborough must see scores of lovely girls. Jean seemed to see them walking past her in a procession — girls who had maids to do their hair in the most approved fashion, constantly renewed girls whose clothes were a dream of daintiness, all charming, all witty, all fitted to be wife to a man like Lord Bidborough. What was he doing now, Jean wondered. Perhaps dancing, or sitting out with someone. Jean could see him so clearly, listening, smiling, with lazy, amused eyes. By now he must be thankful that the penny-plain girl at Priorsford had not snatched at the offer he had made her, but had had the sense to send him away. It must have been a sudden madness on his part. He had never said a word of love to her — then suddenly in the rain and mud, when she was looking her very plainest, muffled up in a thick coat, clogged by goloshes, to ask her to marry him!

Jean nodded at the girl in the glass.

"What you've got to do is to put him out of your head, and be thankful that you have lots to do, and a house to keep, and boys to make happy, and aren't a heroine writhing about in a novel."

But she sighed as she turned away. Doing one's duty is a dreary business for three-and-twenty. It goes on for such a long time.

18

"It was told me I should be rich by the fairies."
"A WINTER'S TALE"

JANUARY is always a long flat month: the Christmas festivities are over, the bills are waiting to be paid, the weather is very often of the dreariest, spring is yet far distant. With February, hope and the snowdrops begin to spring, but January is a month to be *warstled* through as best we can.

This January of which I write Jean felt to be a peculiarly long, dull month. She could not understand why, for David was at home, and she had always thought that to have the three boys with her made up the sum of her happiness. She told herself that it was Pamela she missed. It made such a difference knowing that the door would not open to admit that tall figure; the want of the embroidery frame seemed to take a brightness from the room, and the lack of that little gay laugh of Pamela's left a dullness that the loudest voices did nothing to dispel.

Pamela wrote that the vist to Champertoun had been a signal success. The hitherto unknown cousins were delightful people, and she and her brother were prolonging their stay till the middle of January. Then, she said, she hoped to come back to Priorsford for a little, while Biddy went on to London.

How easy it all sounded, Jean thought. Historic houses full of all things lovely, leisured, delightful people, the money and the freedom to go where one listed: no pinching, no striving, no sordid cares.

David's vacation was slipping past; and Jean was deep in preparations for his departure. She longed vehemently for some money to spend. There were so many things that David really needed and was doing without, so many of the things he had were so woefully shabby. Jean understood better now what a young man wanted; she had studied Lord Bidborough's clothes. Not that the young man was anything of a dandy, but he had always looked right for every occasion. And Jean thought that probably all the young men at Oxford looked like that — poor David! David himself never grumbled. He meant to make money by his pen in spare moments, and his mind was too full of plans to worry much about his shabby clothes. He sometimes worried about his sister, and thought it hard that she should have the cares of a household on her shoulders at an age when other girls were having the times of their lives; but he solaced himself with the thought that some day he would make it up to Jean, that some day she should have everything that now she was missing, full measure pressed down and running over. It never occurred to the boy that Jean's youth would pass, and whatever he might be able to give her later, he could never give her that back.

Pamela returned to Hillview in the middle of the month, just before David left.

Bella Bathgate owned that she was glad to have her back. That indomitable spinster had actually missed her lodger. She was surprised at her own pleasure in seeing the boxes carried upstairs again, in hearing the soft voice talking to Mawson, in sniffing the faint sweet scent that seemed to hang about the house when Miss Reston was in it, conquering the grimmer odour of naphtha and boiled cabbage which generally held sway.

Bella had missed Mawson, too. It was fine to have her back again in her cosy kitchen, enjoying her supper and full of tales of the glories of Champertoun. Bella's face grew even longer than it was naturally as she heard of the magnificence of that ancient house, of the chapel, of the ball-room, of the number of bedrooms, of the man-servants and maid-servants, of the motors and horses.

"Forty bedrooms!" she said, in scandalised tones. "The thing's rideeclous. Mair like an institution than a private hoose."

"Oh, it's a *gentleman's* 'ouse," said Mawson proudly — "the sort of thing Miss Reston's accustomed to. At Bidborough, I'm told, there's bedrooms to 'old a regiment, and the same at Mintern Abbas, but I've never been there yet. It was all the talk in the servants' 'all at Champertoun 'oo would be Lady Bidborough. There were several likely young ladies there, but 'e didn't seem partial to any of them."

"Whaur's he awa to the noo?"

"Back to London for a bit, I 'eard, and later on we're joining 'im at Bidborough. Beller, I was thinking to myself when they were h'all talking, what if Lady B. should be a Priorsford lady? His lordship did seem h'attentive in at The Rigs. Wouldn't it be a fine thing for Miss Jean?"

Miss Bathgate suddenly had a recollection of Jean as she had seen her pass that morning — a wistful face under a shabby hat.

"Hut," she said, tossing her head and lying glibly. "It's ma opeenion that the Lord askit Miss Jean when he was in Priorsford, and she simply sent him to the right about."

She took a drink of tea, with a defiant twirl of her little finger, and pretended not to see the shocked expression on Mawson's face. To Mawson it sounded like sacrilege for anyone to refuse anything to his lordship.

"Oh, Beller! Mis Jean would 'ave jumped at 'im!"

"Naething o' the kind," said Miss Bathgate fiercely, forgetting all about her former pessimism as to Jean's chance of getting a man, and desiring greatly to champion her cause. "D'ye think Miss Jean's sittin' here waitin' to jump at a man like a cock at a grossit? Na! He'll be a lucky man that gets her, and weel his lordship kens it. She's no pented up to the een-holes like thae London Jezebels. Her looks'll stand wind and water. She's a kind wise lassie, and if she condescends to the Lord, I'm sure I hope he'll be guid to her. For ma ain pairt I wud faur rather see her marry a dacent, ordinary man like a minister or a doctor — but we've nane o' thae kind needin' wives in Priorsford the noo, so Miss Jean'll mebbe hev to fa' back on a lord. . . ."

On the afternoon of the day this conversation took place in Hillview kitchen, Jean sat in the living-room of The Rigs, a very depressed little figure. It was one of those days in which things seem to take a positive pleasure in going wrong. To start with, the kitchen range could not go on, as something had happened to the boiler, and that had shattered Mrs. M'Cosh's placid temper. Also the bill for mending it would be large, and probably the landlord would make a fuss about paying it. Then Mhor had put a newly-soled boot right on the hot bar of the fire and burned it across, and

Jock had thrown a ball and broken a precious Spode dish that had been their mother's. But the worst thing of all was that Peter was lost, had been lost for three days, and now they felt they must give up hope. Jock and Mhor were in despair (which may have accounted for their abandoned conduct in burning boots and breaking old china), and in their hearts felt miserably guilty. Peter had wanted to go with them that morning three days ago; he had stood patiently waiting before the front door, and they had sneaked quietly out at the back without him. It was really for his own good, Jock had told Mhor; it was because the gamekeeper had said if he got Peter in the Peel woods again he would shoot him, and they had been going to the Peel woods that morning — but nothing brought any comfort either to Jock or Mhor. For two nights Mhor had sobbed himself to sleep openly, and Jock had lain awake and cried when everyone else was sleeping.

They scoured the country in the day-time, helped by David and Mr. Jowett and other interested friends, but all to no purpose.

"If I knew God had him I wouldn't mind," said Mhor, "but I keep seeing him in a trap watching for us to come and let him out. Oh, Peter, *Peter*. . . ."

So Jean felt completely demoralised this January afternoon and sat in her most unbecoming dress, with the fire drearily, if economically banked up with dross, hoping that no one would come near her. And Mrs. Duff-Whalley and her daughter arrived to call.

It was at once evident that Mrs. Duff-Whalley was on a very high horse indeed. Her accent was at its most superior — not at all the accent she used on ordinary occasions — and her manner was an excellent imitation of that of a lady she had met at one of the neighbouring houses and greatly admired. Her sharp eyes were all over the place, taking in Jean's poor little home-made frock, the shabby slippers, the dull fire, the depressed droop of her hostess's shoulders.

Jean was sincerely sorry to see her visitors. To cope with Mrs. Duff-Whalley and her daughter one had to be in a state of robust health and high spirits.

"We ran in, Jean — positively one has

time for nothing these days — just to wish you a Happy New Year, though a fortnight of it has gone. And how are you? I do hope you had a very gay Christmas, and loads of presents. Muriel quite passed all limits. I told her I was quite ashamed of the shoals of presents, but of course the child has so many friends. The Towers was full for Christmas. Dear Gordon brought several Cambridge friends, and they were so useful at all the festivities. Lady Tweedie said to me, 'Mrs. Duff-Whalley, you really are a godsend with all these young men in this unmanned neighbourhood.' Always so witty, isn't she? dear woman. By the way, Jean, I didn't see you at the Tweedies' dance, or the Olivers' theatricals."

"No. I wasn't there. I hadn't a dress that was good enough, and I didn't want to be at the expense of hiring a carriage."

"Oh, really! We had a small dance at The Towers on Christmas night — just a tiny affair, you know, really just our own house-party and such old friends as the Tweedies and the Olivers. We would have liked to ask you and your brother — I hear he's home from Oxford — but you know what it is to live in a place like Priorsford:

if you ask one you have to ask everybody — and we decided to keep it entirely County — you know what I mean?"

"Oh, quite," said Jean; "I'm sure you were wise."

"We were so sorry," went on Mrs. Duff-Whalley, "that dear Lord Bidborough and his charming sister couldn't come. We have got so fond of both of them. Muriel and Lord Bidborough have so much in common — music, you know, and other things. I simply couldn't tear them away from the piano at The Towers. Isn't it wonderful how simple and pleasant they are considering their lineage? Actually living in that little dog-hole of a Hillview. I always think Miss Bathgate's such an insolent woman; no notion of her proper place. She looks at me as if she actually thought she was my equal, and wasn't she positively rude to you, Muriel, when you called with some message?"

"Oh, frightful woman!" said Muriel, airily. "She was most awfully rude to me. You would have thought that I wanted to burgle something." She gave an affected laugh. "I simply stared through her. I find that irritates that class of person frightfully. . . . How do you like my sables, Jean? Yes — a present."

"They are beautiful," said Jean, serenely; but to kerself she muttered bitterly, "Opulent *lumps*!"

"David goes back to Oxford next week," she said aloud, the thought of money recalling David's lack of it.

'Oh, really! How exciting for him," Mrs. Duff-Whalley said. "I suppose you won't have heard from Miss Reston since she went away!"

"I had a letter from her a few days ago."

Mrs. Duff-Whalley waited expectantly for a moment, but as Jean said nothing more she continued:

"Did she talk of future plans? We simply must fix them both up for a week at The Towers. Lord Bidborough told us he had quite fallen in love with Priorsford and would be sure to come back. I thought it was so sweet of him. Priorsford is such a dull little place."

"Yes," said Jean; "it was very condescending of him."

Then she remembered Richard Plantagenet, her friend, his appreciation of everything, his love for the Tweed, his passion for the hills, his kindness to herself and the boys — and her conscience pricked her. "But I think he meant it," she added.

"Well," Muriel said, "I fail to see what he could find to admire in Priorsford. Of all the provincial little holes! I'm constantly upbraiding Mother for letting my father build a house here. If they had gone two or three miles out; but to plant themselves in a little dull town, always knocking up against the dull little inhabitants! Positively it gets on my nerves. One can't go out without having to talk to Mrs. Jowett, or a Dawson, or some of the villa dwellers. As I said to Lady Tweedie yesterday when I met her in the Eastgate, 'Positively,' I said, 'I shall *scream* if I have to say to any-one else, "Yes, isn't it a nice quiet day for the time of the year?'" I'm just going to pretend I don't see people now."

"Muriel, darling, you mustn't make yourself unpopular. It's not like London, you know, where you can pick and choose. I quite agree that the Priorsford people need to be kept in their places, but one needn't be rude. And some of the people, the aborigines, as dear Gordon calls them, are really quite nice. There are about half a dozen men one can ask to dinner, and that new doctor — I forget his name — is really quite a gentleman. Plays bridge."

Jean laughed, suddenly, and Mrs. Duff-Whalley looked inquiringly at her.

"Oh," she said, blushing, "I remembered the definition of a gentleman in the Irish R.M. — 'a man who has late dinner and takes in the London *Times*'. . . . Won't you stay to tea?"

"Oh, no, thank you, the car is at the gate. We are going on to tea with Lady Tweedie. 'You simply must spare me an afternoon, Mrs. Duff-Whalley,' she said to me the other day, and I rang her up and said we would come today. Life is really such a rush. And we are going abroad in February and March. We must have some sunshine. Not that we need it for our health, for we're both as strong as ponies. I haven't been a day in bed for years, and Muriel the same, I'm thankful to say. We've never had to waste money on doctors. And the War kept us so cooped up, it's really pleasant to feel we can get about again. I thought on our way south we would make a tour of the battle-fields. I think one owes it to the men who fought for us to go and visit their graves — poor fellows! I saw Mrs. Macdonald — you go to their church, don't you? — at a meeting yesterday, and I said if she would give me particulars I'd try and see her boy's grave. They won't be able to go themselves, poor souls, and I thought it would be a certain consolation to them to know that a friend had gone. I must say, I think she might have shown more gratitude. She was really quite offhand. I think ministers' wives have often bad manners; they deal so much with the working classes. . . ."

Jean thought of a saying she had read of Dr. Johnson's: "He talked to me at the Club one day concerning Catiline's conspiracy — so I withdrew my attention and thought about Tom Thumb." When she came back to Mrs. Duff-Whalley that lady was saying:

"Did you say that Miss Reston is coming back to Priorsford soon?"

"Yes, any day."

"Fancy! And her brother, too?"

Jean said she thought not: Lord Bidborough was going to London.

"Ah! then we shall see him there. I don't know when I met anyone with whom I felt so instantly at home. He has such easy manners. It really is a pleasure to meet a gentleman. I do wish my boy Gordon had seen more of him. I'm sure they would have been friends. So good for a boy, you know, to have a man of the world to go about with. Well, good-bye, Jean. You really look very washed out. What you really need is a thorough holiday and change of scene. Why, you haven't been away for years. Two months in London would do wonders for you — "

The handle of the door turned and a voice said, "May I come in?" and without waiting for permission Pamela Reston walked in, bare-headed, wrapped in a cloak, and with her embroidery frame under her arm, as she had come many times to The Rigs during her stay at Hillview.

When Jean heard the voice it seemed to her as if everything was transformed. Mrs. Duff-Whalley and Muriel, their sables and their Rolls-Royce, ceased to be great weights crushing life and light out of her, and became small, ordinary, rather vulgar figures; she forgot her own home-made frock and shabby slippers; and even the fire seemed to feel that things were brightening, for a flame struggled through the backing and gave promise of future cheerfulness.

"Oh, Pamela!" cried Jean. There was more of relief and appeal in her voice than she knew, and Pamela, seeing the visitors, prepared to do battle.

"I thought I should surprise you, Jean girl. I came by the two train, for I was determined to be here in time for tea." She slipped off her coat and took Jean in her arms. "It is good to be back. . . . Ah, Mrs. Duff-Whalley, how are you? Have you kept Priorsford lively through the Christmas-time, you and your daughter?"

"Well, I was just telling Jean we've done our best. My son, Gordon, and his Cambridge friends, delightful young fellows, you know, *perfect* gentlemen. But we did miss you and your brother. Is dear Lord Bidborough not with you?"

"My brother has gone to London."

"Naturally," said Mrs. Duff-Whalley, nodding her head, knowingly. "All young men like London, so gay, you know, restaurants and theatres and nightclubs — "

"Oh, I hope not," laughed Pamela. "My brother's rather extraordinary; he cares very little for London pleasures. The open road is all he asks — a born gipsy."

"Fancy! Well, it's a nice taste, too. But I would rather ride in my car than tramp the roads. I like my comforts. Muriel and I are going to London shortly, on our way to the Continent. Will you be there?"

"Probably, and if I am, Jean will be with me. Do you hear that, Jean?" and paying no attention to the dubious shake of Jean's head she went on: "We must give Jean a very good time and have lots of parties. Perhaps, Mrs. Duff-Whalley, you will bring your daughter to one of Jean's parties when you are in London? You have been so very kind to us that we should greatly like to have an opportunity of showing you some hospitality. Do let us know your whereabouts. It would be fun— wouldn't it, Jean? — to entertain Priorsford friends in London?"

For a moment Mrs. Duff-Whalley looked very like a ferret that wanted to bite; then she smiled and said:

"Well, really, it's most kind of you. I'm sure Jean should be very grateful to you. You're a kind of fairy godmother to this little Cinderella. Only Jean must remember that it isn't very nice to come back to drudgery after an hour or two at the ball," and she gave an unpleasant laugh.

"Ah, but you forget your fairy tale," said Pamela. "Cinderella had a happy ending. She wasn't left to the drudgery, but reigned with the prince in the palace."

"It's hardly polite, surely," Muriel put in, "to liken poor little Jean to a cinder-witch."

Jean laughed and held out a foot in a shabby slipper. "I've felt like one all day. It's been such a grubby day, no kitchen range on, no hot water, and Mrs. M'Cosh actually out of temper. Now you've come, Pamela, it will be all right — but it has been wretched. I hadn't the spirit to change my frock or put on decent slippers, that's why I've reminded you all of Cinderella. . . . Are you going, Mrs. Duff-Whalley. Good-bye."

Mrs. Duff-Whalley had, with an effort, regained her temper, and was now all smiles.

"We must see you often at The Towers while you are in Priorsford, dear Miss Reston. Muriel and I are on our way to tea with Lady Tweedie. She will be so excited to hear you are back. You have made quite a *place* for yourself in our little circle. Good-bye, Jean, we shall be seeing you some time. Come, Muriel. Well — t'ta."

When the visitors had rolled away in their car Jean told Pamela about Peter.

"I couldn't tell you before those opulent, well-pleased people. It's absolutely breaking our hearts. Mrs. M'Cosh looks ten years older, and Jock and Mhor go about quite silent thinking out wicked things to do to relieve their feelings. David has gone over all the hills looking for him, but he may be lying trapped in some wood. Come and speak to Mrs. M'Cosh for a minute. Between Peter and the boiler she is in despair."

They found Mrs. M'Cosh baking with the gas oven.

"It's a scone for the tea. When I seen Miss Reston it kinna cheered me up. Hae ye tell't her aboot Peter?"

"He will turn up yet, Mrs. M'Cosh," Pamela assured her. "He's such a clever dog. Even if he is trapped I believe he will manage to get out."

314

"It's to be hoped so, for the want o' him is something awful."

A knock came to the back door and a boy's voice said, "Is Peter in?" It was a message boy who knew all Peter's tricks — knew that however friendly Peter was with a message boy on the road, he felt constrained to jump out at him when he appeared at the back door with a basket. The innocent question was too much for Mrs. M'Cosh.

"Na," she said bitterly. "Peter's no' in, so ye needna hold on to the door. Peter's lost. Deid, as likely as not." She turned away in bitterness of heart, leaving Jean to take the parcels from the boy.

The boys came in quietly after another fruitless search. They did not ask hopefully as they had done at first if Peter had come home, and Jean did not ask how they had fared.

The sight of Pamela cheered them a good deal.

"Does she know?" Jock asked, and Jean nodded.

Pamela kept the talk going through tea, and told them so many funny stories that they had to laugh.

"If only," said Mhor, "Peter was here now the Honourable's back we would be happy."

"There's a big box of hard chocolates behind that cushion," Pamela said, pointing to the sofa.

It was at that moment that the door opened, and Mrs. M'Cosh put her head in. Her face wore a broad smile.

"The wanderer hes returned," she said.

At that moment Jean thought the Glasgow accent the most delightful thing on earth, and the smile on Mrs. M'Cosh's face the most beautiful. With a shout they all made for the kitchen.

There was Peter, thin and dirty, but in excellent spirits, wagging his tail so violently that his whole body wagged.

"See," said Mrs. M'Cosh, "he's been in a trap, but he's gotten out. Peter's a cliver lad."

Jock and Mhor had no words. They lay on the linoleum-covered floor, while Mrs. M'Cosh fetched hot milk, and crushed their faces against the little black-and-white body they had thought they might never see again, while Peter licked his own torn paw and their faces in turn.

It was wonderfully comfortable to see Pamela settle down in the corner of the sofa with her embroidery, and ask news of all her friends. Jean had been a little shy of meeting Pamela, wondering if Lord Bidborough had told her anything, wondering if she were angry that Jean should have had such an offer, or resentful that she had refused it. But Pamela talked quite naturally about her brother, and gave no hint that she knew of any reason why Jean should blush when his name was mentioned.

"And how are all the people — the Jowetts and the Watsons and the Dawsons? And the dear Macdonalds? I picked up a book in Edinburgh that I think Mr. Macdonald will like. And Lewis Elliot — have you seen him lately, Jean?"

"He's away. Didn't you know? He went just after you did. He was in London at Christmas — at least, that was the postmark on the parcels, but he has never written a word. He was always a bad correspondent, but he'll turn up one of these days."

Mrs. M'Cosh came in with the letters from the evening post.

"Actually a letter for me," said Jean,

"from London. I expect it's from that landlord of ours. Surely he won't be giving us notice to leave. Pamela, I'm afraid to open it. It looks like a lawyer's letter."

"Open it then."

Jean opened it slowly and read the enclosure with a puzzled frown; then she dropped it with a cry.

Pamela looked up from her work to see Jean with tears running down her face. Jock and Mhor stopped what they were doing and came to look at her. Peter rubbed himself against her legs by way of comfort.

"My dear," said Pamela, "is there anything wrong?"

"Oh, do you remember the little, old man who came one day to look at the house and stayed to tea and I sang 'Strathairlie' to him? He's dead." Jean's tears flowed afresh as she said the words.

"How I wish I had been kinder to him. I somehow felt he was ill."

"And why have they written to tell you?" Pamela asked.

Jean stooped and picked up the letter which had fallen on the floor.

"It's from his lawyer, and he says he has

left me money. . . . Read it, Pamela. I don't seem able to see the words."

So Pamela read aloud the letter that converted poverty-stricken Jean into a very wealthy woman.

Jean's face was dead white, and she lay back as if stunned, while Jock gave solemn utterance "Goodness-gracious-mercy-Moses!"

Mhor said nothing, but stared with grave, green eyes at the stricken figure of the heiress.

"It's awful," Jean moaned.

"But, my dear," said Pamela, "I thought you wanted to be rich."

"Oh — rich in a gentle way, a few hundred a year — but this — "

"Poor Jean, buried under bullion."

"You're all looking at me differently already," cried poor Jean. "Mhor, it's just the same me. Money can't make any real difference. Don't stare at me like that."

"Will Peter have a diamond collar now?" Mhor asked.

"Awful effect of sudden riches," said Pamela. "Bear up, Jean — I've no doubt you'll be able to get rid of your money. Just think of all the people you will be able to help. You needn't spend it on yourself, you know."

"No, but suppose it's the ruin of the boys! I've often heard of sudden fortunes making people go all wrong."

"Now, Jean, does Jock look as if anything so small as a fortune could put him wrong? And David — by the way, where is David?"

"Out," said Jock, "getting something at the stationer's. Let me tell him when he comes in."

"Then I'll tell Mrs. M'Cosh," cried Mhor and, followed by Peter, rushed from the room.

The colour was beginning to come back to Jean's face, and the stunned look to go out of her eyes.

"Why in the world has he left it to me?" she asked Pamela.

"You see, the lawyer suggests coming to see you. He will explain it all. It's a wonderful stroke of luck, Jean. No wonder you can't take it in."

"I feel like the little old woman in the nursery-rhyme who said, 'This is none of I.' I'm bound to wake up and find I've dreamt it. . . . Oh, Mrs. M'Cosh!"

"It's the wee laddie Scott to say his mother canna come and wash the morn's mornin'; she's no' weel. It's juist as well, seein' the biler's gone wrang. I suppose I'd better gie the laddie a piece?"

"Yes, and a penny." Then Jean remembered her new possessions. "No, give him this, please, Mrs. M'Cosh."

Mrs. M'Cosh took the coin and gasped. "Hauf a croon!" she said.

"Silver," said Pamela, "is to be more accounted of than it was in the days of Solomon!"

"D'ye ken whit ye'll dae?" said Mrs. M'Cosh. "Ye'll get the laddie taen up by the pollis. Gie him thruppence — it's mair wise like."

"Oh, very well," said Jean, thwarted at the very beginning of her efforts in philanthropy. "I'll go and see his mother tomorrow and find out what she needs. Have you heard the news, Mrs. M'Cosh?"

Mrs. M'Cosh came farther into the room, prepared to gossip.

"Weel, Mhor came in and tell't me some kinna story aboot a lot o' money, but I thocht he was juist bletherin'. Is't a fac'?"

"It would seem to be. The lawyer in

London writes that Mr. Peter Reid — d'you perhaps remember an old man who came here to tea one day in October? — he came from London and lived at the Temperance — has left me all his fortune, which is a large one. I can't think why. . . . And I thought he was so poor, I wanted to have him here to stay, to save him paying hotel bills. Poor man, he must have been very friendless when he left his money to a stranger."

"It's a queer turn up onyway. I juist hope it's a' richt. But I would see it afore ye spend it. I wis readin' a bit in the papers the ither day about a wumman who got word o' a fortune sent her, and went and got a' sorts o' braw claes and things ower the heid o't, and here it wis a' begunk. And a freend o' mine had a husband oot aboot Canada somewhere, and she got word o' his death, and she claimed the insurance, and got verra braw blacks, and here wha should turn up but his lordship, as leevin' as you or me! Eh, puir thing, she wis awfu' annoyed. . . . You be carefu', Miss Jean, and see the colour o' yer money afore ye begin gien' awa' hauf-croons instead o' pennies."

19

*"O, I wad like to ken — to the beggar-wife
    says I —
Why chops are guid to brander and nane sae
    guid to fry.
An' siller, that's sae braw to get, is brawer
    still to gie.*
'It's gey an' easy spierin'.' *says the beggar-
    wife to me."*

ROBERT LOUIS STEVENSON

IT is always easier for poor human
nature to weep with those who weep
than to rejoice with those who rejoice.
Into our congratulations to our more
fortunate neighbour we often manage to
squeeze something of the "hateful rind of
resentment", forgetting that the cup of
life is none too sweet for any of us, and
needs nothing of our bitterness added.

Jean had not an enemy in the world,
almost everyone wished her well, but in
very few cases was there any marked
enthusiasm about her inheritance. "Ridiculous" was the most frequent comment: or

"Fancy that little thing!" It seemed altogether too absurd that such an unimportant person should have had such a large thing happen to her.

Pamela was frankly disgusted with the turn things had taken. She had intended giving Jean such a good time; she had meant to dress her and amuse her and settle her in life. Peter Reid had destroyed all her plans, and Jean would never now be dependent on her for the pleasures of life.

She wrote to her brother:

"Jean seems to be one of the people that all sorts of odd things happen to, and now fortune has played one of her most impish tricks and Jean has become a very considerable heiress. And I was actually there, oddly enough, when the god in the car alighted, so to speak at The Rigs.

"One afternoon, just after I came to Priorsford, I went in after tea and found the Jardines entertaining a shabby-looking elderly man. They were all so very nice to him that I thought he must be some old family friend, but it turned out that none of them had seen him before that afternoon. He had asked to look over the house, and told Jean that he had lived in it as a boy, and Jean, remarking his rather shabby clothes and frail appearance, jumped to the conclusion that he had failed in life and — you know Jean — was at once full of tenderness and compassion. At his request she sang to him a song he had heard his mother sing, and finished by presenting him with the song-book containing it — a somewhat rare collection which she valued.

"This shabby old man, it seems, was one Peter Reid, a wealthy London business man, and owner of The Rigs, born and bred in Priorsford, who had just heard from his doctor that he had not long to live, and had come back to his childhood's home meaning to die there. He had no relations and few friends, and had made up his mind to leave his money to the first person who did anything for him without thought of payment. (He seems to have been a hard, suspicious type of man who had not attracted kindness.) So Fate guided his steps to Jean, and this is the result. Yes, rather far-fetched, I agree, but Fate is often like a novelette.

"Mr. Peter Reid had meant to ask the Jardines to leave The Rigs and let him settle there, but — there must have been a soft part somewhere in the hard little man — he hadn't the heart to do it when he found how attached they were to the place.

"I was at The Rigs when the lawyer's letter came. Jean as an heiress is very funny and, at the same time, horribly touching. At first she could think of nothing but that the lonely old man she had tried to be kind to was dead, and wept bitterly. Then as she began to realise the fact of the money she was aghast, suffocated with the thought of her own wealth. She told us piteously that it wouldn't change her at all. I think the poor child already felt the golden barrier that wealth builds round its owners. I don't think Mr. Peter Reid was kind, though, perhaps he meant to be. Jean is such a conscientious, anxious pilgrim at any time, and I'm afraid the wealth will hang round her neck like the Ancient Mariner's albatross.

". . . I have been wondering, Biddy, how this will affect your chances. I know you felt as I did how nice it would be to give Jean all the things that she has never had and which money can buy. I admit I am horribly disappointed about it, but I'm not at all sure that this odd trick of fortunes won't help you. Her attitude was that marriage with you was unthinkable; you had so much and she had so little. Well, this evens things up. *Don't come. Don't write.* Leave her alone to try her wings. She will want to try all sorts of schemes for helping people, and I'm afraid the poor child will get many bad falls. So long as she remains in Priorsford with people like Mrs. Hope and the Macdonalds to watch over her, she can't come to any harm. Don't be anxious. Honestly, Biddy, I think she cares for you. I'm glad you asked her when she was poor."

When the news of Jean's fortune broke over Priorsford, tea-parties had no lack of material for conversation.

Miss Watson and Miss Teenie, much more excited than Jean herself, ranged gaily round the circle of their acquaintances, drank innumerable cups of tea, and discussed the matter in all its bearings.

"Isn't it strange to think of Miss Jean as an heiress ? Such a plain little thing — in her clothes, I mean, for she has a bit sweet, wee face. I don't know how she'll ever do in a great big house with butlers and things. I expect she'll leave The Rigs now. It's no place for an heiress. Perhaps she'll build a house like The Towers. No; you're right. She'll look for an old house; she always had such queer ideas about liking old things and plain things. . . . Well, when she had a wee house it had a wide door. I hope when she gets a big house it won't have a narrow door. Money sometimes changes people's very natures. . . . It's funny business; you never really know what'll happen to you in this world. Anyway I don't grudge it to Miss Jean, though; mind you, I don't think myself that she'll carry off money well. She hasn't presence enough, if you know what I mean. She'll never look the thing in a big motor, and you can't imagine her being haughty to people poorer than herself. She has such a wonderful way of putting herself beside folk — even a tinker-body on the road!"

Miss Bathgate heard the news with sardonic laughter.

"So that's the latest! Miss Jean's gaun to be upsides wi' the best o' them! Puir lamb, puir lamb! I hope the siller'll bring her happiness, but I doot it. . . . I yince kent some folk that got a fortune left them. He was a beadle in the K.F. Kirk at

Kirkcaple, a dacent man wi' a wife and dochter, an' by some queer chance they came into a heap o' siller, an' a hoose — a mansion hoose, ye ken. They never di mair guid, puir bodies. The hoose was that big that the only kinda cosy place they could see to sit in was the butler's pantry, an' they took to drink, fair for want o' anything else to dae. I've heard tell that they took whisky to their porridges; but that's, mebbe, a lee. Onyway, the faither and mither sune died off, and the dochter went to board wi' the minister an' his wife, to see if they could dae onything wi' her. I mind seein' her yince. She sittin' horn-idle, an' I said to her, 'D'ye niver tak' up a stockin'?' and she says, 'I dinna *need* to dae naething.' 'But,' I says, 'a stockin' keeps your hands busy, an' keeps ye frae wearyin',' but she juist said, 'I tell ye I dinna need to dae naething. I whiles taks a ride in a carriage.' . . . It was a sorry sicht, I can tell ye, to see a dacent lass ruined wi' siller. . . . Weel, Miss Jean'll get a man noo. Nae fear o' that," and Miss Bathgate repeated her cynical lines about the lass "on Tintock tap".

Mrs. Hope was much excited when she

heard of Jean's good fortune, more especially when she found out who her benefactor was.

"Reids who lived in The Rigs thirty years ago? But I knew them. I know all about them. It was I who suggested to Alison Jardine that the cottage would suit her. She had lost a lot of money and wanted a small place. . . . Why, bless me, Augusta, Mrs. Reid, this man's mother, came from Corlaw; her people were tenants of my father's. What was the name? I used to be taken to their house by my nurse and get an oatcake with sugar sprinkled on it — a great luxury, I thought. Yes, of course, Laidlaw. She was Jeannie Laidlaw. When I married and came to Hopetoun I often went to see Mrs. Reid. She reminded me of Corlaw, and could talk of my father, and I liked that. . . . Her husband was James Reid. He must have had some money, and I think he was retired. He had a beard and came from Fife. I remember the east-country tone in his voice. They went to the Free Kirk, and I overheard, one day a man say to him as we came out of church (where a retiring collection for the next Sunday had been announced), 'There's an awfu' heap o' collections in oor kirk,' and James Reid replied, 'Ou ay, but ma way is to pay no attention.' When I told your father he was delighted and said that he must take that for his motto through life — 'Ma way is to pay no attention'."

Mrs. Hope took off her glasses and smiled to herself over her recollections. . . . "Mrs. Reid was a nice creature, 'fair bigoted', as they say here, on her son Peter. He was her chief topic of conversation. Peter's cleverness, Peter's kindness to his mother, Peter's good looks, Peter's fine voice: when I saw him — well, I thought we should all thank God for our mothers, for no one else will ever see us with such kind eyes. . . . And it's this Peter Reid — Jeannie Laidlaw's son — who has enriched Jean. Well, Augusta, I must say I consider it rather a liberty."

Augusta looked at her mother with an amused and understanding smile.

"Yes, Augusta, it was a pushing, interfering sort of thing to do. What is the child to do with a great fortune? I'm not afraid of her being spoiled. Money won't vulgarise Jean as it does so many people, but it may turn her into a very burdened, anxious pilgrim. She is happier poor. The pinch of too little money is a small thing compared to the burden of too much. The doing without is good for both body and soul, but the great possessions are apt to harden our hearts and make our souls small and meagre. Who would have thought that little Jean would have had the hard hap to become heir to them? But she has a high heart. She may make a success of being a rich woman! She has certainly made a success of being a poor one."

"I think," said Augusta, in her gentle voice, "that Peter Reid was a wise man to leave his money to Jean. Only the people who have been poor know how to give, and Jean has imagination and an understanding heart. Haven't you noticed what a wonderful way she has with the poor people? She is always welcome in the cottages. . . . And think what a delight she will have in spending money on the boys! But I hope Pamela Reston will do as she had planned and carry Jean off for a real holiday. I should like to see her for a little while spend money like water, buy all manner of useless, lovely things, and dine and dance and go to plays."

Mrs. Hope put up her glasses to regard her daughter with open disapproval.

"Dear me, Augusta, am I hearing right? Who is more severe than you on the mad women who dance, and sup, and frivol their money away? But there's something in what you say. The bairn needs a play-time. . . . To think that Jeannie Laidlaw's son should change the whole of Jean's life. Preposterous!"

Mrs. Duff-Whalley was having tea with Mrs. Jowett when the news was broken to her. It was a party, but only, as Mrs. Duff-Whalley herself would have put it, "a purely local affair", meaning some people on the hill.

Mrs. Jowett sat in her soft-toned room, pouring out tea into fragile cups with hands that seemed to demand lace ruffles, so white were they and transparent. The room was like herself, exquisitely fresh and dainty; white walls hung with pale water-colours in gilt frames, Indian rugs of soft pinks and blues and greys, plump cushions in worked muslin covers that looked as if they were put on fresh every morning. Photographs stood about of women looking

333

sweetly into vacancy over the heads of pretty children, and books of verses, bound daintily in white and gold, lay on carved tables.

Mrs. Duff-Whalley did not care for Mrs. Jowett's tea-parties, and she always felt irritated by her drawing-room. The gentle voice of her hostess made her want to speak louder than usual, and she thought the conversation insipid to a degree. How could it be anything but insipid with Mrs. Jowett saying only "How nice", or "What a pity" at intervals? She did not even seem to care to hear Mrs. Duff-Whalley's news of "the County", and "dear Lady Tweedie", merely murmuring, "Oh, really," when told the most interesting and even startling facts.

"Uninterested idiot," thought Mrs. Duff-Whalley to herself as she turned from her hostess to Miss Mary Duncan, who at least had some sense, though both she and her sisters had a lamentable lack of style.

Miss Duncan's kind face beamed pleasantly. She was quite willing to listen to Mrs. Duff-Whalley as long as that lady pleased. She thought she needed soothing, so she agreed with everything she said, and made sensible little remarks at intervals. Mrs. Jowett was pouring out a second cup of tea for Mrs. Duff-Whalley when she said, "And have you heard the latest about our dear little Jean Jardine?"

"Has anything happened to her? I saw her the other day and she was all right."

"She's quite well, but haven't you heard? She has inherited a large fortune."

Mrs. Duff-Whalley said nothing for a minute. She could not trust herself to speak. Despised Jean, whom she had not troubled to ask to her parties, whom she had always felt she could treat anyhow, so poor was she and of no account. It had been bad enough to know that she was on terms of intimacy with Pamela Reston and her brother: to hear Miss Reston say that she meant to take her to London and entertain for her, and to hear her suggest that Muriel might go to Jean's parties had been galling; but she had thrust the recollection from her, reflecting that fine ladies said much that they did not mean, and that probably the promised visit to London would never materialise. And now to be told this! A fortune: Jean — it was too absurd!

When she spoke, her voice was shrill with anger in spite of her efforts to control it.

"It can't be true. The Jardines have no relations that could leave them money."

"This isn't a relation," Mrs. Jowett explained. "It's someone Jean was kind to quite by chance. I think it is *so* sweet. It quite makes one want to cry, *Dear* Jean!"

Mrs. Duff-Whalley looked at the sentimental woman before her with bitter scorn.

"It would take more than that to make me cry," she snorted. "I wonder what fool wanted to leave Jean money. Such an unpractical creature! She'll simply make ducks and drakes of it, give it away to all and sundry. Pauperise and unsettle the whole neighbourhood, I shouldn't wonder."

"Oh, I don't think so," Miss Duncan broke in. "She has had a hard training, poor child. Such a pathetic mite she was when her great-aunt died and left her with David and Jock and the little Gervase Taunton! No one thought she could manage, but she did, and she has been so plucky; she deserves all the good fortune that life can bring her. I'm longing to hear what Jock says about this. I do like that boy."

"They are, all three, dear boys," said Mrs. Jowett. "Tim and I quite feel as if they were our own. Tim, dear," to that gentleman, who had bounced suddenly and violently into the room, "we are talking about the great news — Jean's fortune — "

"Ah, yes, yes," said Mr. Jowett, distributing brusque nods to the women present. "What I want is a bit of thick string." (His wife's delicate drawing-room hardly seemed the place to look for such a thing.) "No, no tea, my dear. I told you I wanted a bit of *thick string*. . . . Yes, let's hope it won't spoil Jean, but I think it's almost sure to. Fortune-hunters, too. Bad thing for a girl to have money. . . . Yes, yes, I asked the servants, and Chart brought me the string basket, but it was all thin stuff. I'll lose the post, but it's always the way. Every day more rushed than another. Remind me, Janetta, to get some thick string tomorrow. I've no time to go down to the town today. Why, bless me, my morning letters are hardly looked at yet," and he fussed himself out of the room.

Mrs. Duff-Whalley rose to go.

"Then, Mrs. Jowett, I can depend on you to look after that collecting? And please be firm. I find that collectors are apt to be very lazy and unconscientious. Indeed, one told me frankly that in her district she only went to the people she knew. That isn't the way to collect. The only way is to get into each house — to stand on the doorstep is no use, they can so easily send a maid to refuse — and sit there till they give a subscription. Every year since I took it on, there has been an increase, and I'll be frightfully disappointed if you let it go back."

Mrs. Jowett looked depressed. She knew herself to be one of the worst collectors on record. She was guiltily aware that she often advised people not to give; that is, if she thought their circumstances straitened!

"I don't know," she began; "I'm afraid I could never sit in a stranger's house and insist on being given money. It's so — so high-handed, like a highwayman or something."

"Think of the cause," said Mrs. Duff-Whalley, "not of your own feelings."

"Yes, of course, but . . . well, if there is a deficit, I can always raise my own subscription to cover it." She smiled happily at this solution of the problem.

Mrs. Duff-Whalley sniffed.

" 'The cronies are a feeble folk,' " she quoted, rudely. "Well, good-bye. I shall send over all the papers and collecting books tomorrow. Muriel and I go off to London on Friday *en route* for the south. It will be pleasant to have a change and meet some interesting people. Muriel was just saying it's a cabbage's life we live in Priorsford. I often wonder we stay here. . . ."

Mrs. Duff-Whalley went home a very angry woman. After dinner, sitting with Muriel before the fire in the glittering drawing-room, she discussed the matter.

"I know what'll be the end of it," she said. "You saw what a fuss Miss Reston made of Jean the other day when we called? Depend upon it, she knew the money was coming. I dare say she and her brother are as poor as church mice — those aristocrats usually are — and Jean's money will come in useful. Oh, we'll see her Lady Bidborough yet. . . . I tell you what it is, Muriel, the way this world's managed is past speaking about."

Mrs. Duff-Whalley was knitting a stocking for her son, Gordon (her hands were seldom idle), and she waved it in her exasperation as she talked.

"Here are you, meant, as anyone can see, for the highest position, and instead that absurd little Jean is to be cocked up — a girl with no more dignity than a sparrow, who couldn't keep her place with a washerwoman. I've heard her talking to these cottage women as if they were her sisters."

Muriel leant back in her chair and seemed absorbed in balancing her slipper on her toe.

"My dear mother," she said, "why excite yourself? It isn't clever of you to be so openly annoyed. People will laugh. I don't say I like it any better than you do, but I hope I have the sense to purr congratulations. We can't help it, anyway. You and I aren't attracted to Jean; but there's no use denying, most people are. And what's more, they keep on liking her. She isn't a person people get easily tired of.

I wish I knew her secret. I suppose it is charm — a thing that can't be acquired."

"What nonsense you do talk, Muriel! I wonder to hear you. I'd like to know who has charm if you haven't. It is a ridiculous word, anyway."

Muriel shook her head. "It's no good posing when we are by ourselves. As a family we totally lack charm. Minnie tries to make up for it by a great deal of manner and a loud voice. Gordon — well, it doesn't matter so much for a man, but you can see his friends don't really care about him much. They take his hospitality and say he isn't a bad sort. They know he is a snob, and when he tries to be funny, he is often offensive, poor Gordon! I've got a pretty face, and I play games well, so I am tolerated, but I have hardly one real friend. The worst of it is I know all the time where I am falling short, and I can't help it. I feel myself jar on people. I once heard old Mrs. Hope say very wisely that it doesn't matter how vulgar we are, so long as we know we are being vulgar. But that isn't true. It's not much fun to know you are being vulgar and not be able to help it."

Mrs. Duff-Whalley gave a convulsed

ejaculation, but her daughter went on.

"Sometimes I've gone in of an afternoon to see Jean, and found her darning stockings in her shabby frock, with a look on her face as if she knew some happy secret: a sort of contented, brooding look — and I've envied her. And so I talked of all the gaieties I was going to, of the new clothes I was getting, of the smart people we know, and all the time I was despising myself for a fool, for what did Jean care! She sat there with her mind full of books and poetry and those boys she is so absurdly devoted to; it was nothing to her how much I bucked; and this fortune won't change her. Money is nothing — "

Mrs. Duff-Whalley gasped despairingly to hear her cherished daughter talking, as she thought, rank treason.

"Oh, Muriel, how you can! And your poor father working so hard to make a pile so that we could all be nice and comfortable. And you were his favourite, and I've often thought how proud he would have been to see his little girl so smart and pretty and able to hold her own with the best of them. And I've worked, too. Goodness knows, I've worked hard. It isn't as easy as it looks to keep your end up in Priorsford and keep the villa-people in their places, and force the County to notice you. If I had been like Mrs. Jowett you would just have had to be content with the people on the Hill. Do you suppose I haven't known they didn't want to come here and visit us? Oh, I knew, but I *made* them. And it was all for you. What did I care for them and their daft-like ways and their uninteresting talk about dogs and books and things! It would have been far nicer for me to have made friends with the people in the little villas. My! I've often thought how I would relish a tea-party at the Watsons'! Your father used to have a saying about it being better to be at the head of the commonalty than at the tail of the gentry, and I know it's true. Mrs. Duff-Whalley, of The Towers, would be a big body at the Miss Watsons' tea-parties, and I know fine I'm only tolerated at the Tweedies' and the Olivers' and all the others."

"Poor Mother! You've been splendid!"

"If you aren't happy, what does anything matter? I'm fair disheartened, I tell you. I believe you're right. Money isn't much of a blessing. I've never said it to you because you seemed so much a part of all the new life, with your accent and your manners and your little dogs; but over and over when people snubbed me, and I had to talk loud and brazen because I felt so ill at ease, I've thought of the old days when I helped your father in the shop. Those were my happiest days — before the money came. I had a girl to look after the house and you children, and I went between the house and the shop, and I never had a dull minute. Then we came into some money, and that helped your father to extend and extend. First, we had a house in Murrayfield — and, my word, we thought we were fine. But I aimed at Drumsheugh Gardens, and we got there. Your father always gave in to me. Eh, he was a hearty man, your father. If it's true what you say that none of you have charm, though I'm sure I don't know what you mean by it, it's my blame, for your father was popular with everyone. He used to laugh at me and my ambition, for, mind you, I was always ambitious; but his was kindly laughter. Often and often when I've been sitting all dressed up at some dinner-party, like to yawn my head off with the dull talk, I've thought of the happy days when I helped in the shop and did my own washing — eh, I little thought I would ever live in a house where we never even know when it's washing day — and went to bed tired and happy, and fell asleep behind your father's broad back. . . ."

"Oh, Mother, don't cry. It's beastly of me to discourage you when you've been the best of mothers to me. I wish I had known my father better, and I do wish I could remember when we were all happy in the little house. You've never been so very happy in The Towers, have you, Mother?"

"No; but I wouldn't leave it for the world. Your father was so proud of it. 'It's as like a hydro as a private house can be,' he often said, in such a contented voice. He just liked to walk round and look at all the contrivances he had planned, all the hot-rails and things in the bath-rooms and cloak-rooms, and radiators in every room, and the wonderful pantries — 'tippy' he called them. He couldn't understand people making a fuss about old houses, and old furniture, grey walls half tumbling down and mouldly rooms. He liked the new look of The Towers, and he said to me, 'Mind, Aggie, I'm not going to let you grow any nonsense like or ivy creepers up this fine new house. They're all very well for holding together tumbledown old places, but The Towers doesn't need them.' And I'm sure he would be pleased today if he saw it. The times people have advised me to grow ivy — even Lady Tweedie, the last time she came to tea — but I never would. It's as new looking as the day he left it. . . . You don't ever want to leave The Towers do you Muriel?"

"No — o, but — don't you think, Mother, we needn't work quite so hard for our social existence? I mean, let's be more friendly with the people round us, and not strive so hard to keep in with the County set. If Miss Reston can do it, surely we can."

"But don't you see," her mother said, "Miss Reston can do it just because she is Miss Reston. If you're a Lord's daughter you can be as eccentric as you like, and make friends with anyone you choose. If we did it, they would just say, 'Oh, so they've come off their perch!' and once we let ourselves down we would never raise ourselves again. I couldn't do it, Muriel. Don't ask me."

"No. But we've go to be happier somehow. Climbing is exhausting work." She stooped and picked up the two small dogs that lay on a cushion beside her. "Isn't it, Bing? Isn't it, Toutou? You're happy, aren't you? A warm fire and a cushion and some mutton-chop bones are good enough for you. Well, we've got all these and we want more. . . . Mother, perhaps Jean would tell us the secret of happiness."

"As if I'd ask her," said Mrs. Duff-Whalley.

20

*"Marvell, who had both pleasure and success,
who must have enjoyed life if ever man did, . . .
found his happiness in the garden where he was*
From "THE TIMES LITERARY SUPPLEMENT"

MRS. M'COSH remained extremely sceptical about the reality of the fortune until the lawyer came from London, "yin's errand to see Miss Jean," as she explained importantly to Miss Bathgate, and he was such an eminently solid, safe-looking man that her doubts vanished.

"I wud say he wis an elder in the kirk, if they've onything as respectable as an elder in England," was her summing up of the lawyer.

Mr. Dickson (of Dickson, Staines, & Dickson), though a lawyer and used to such missions, was also a human being, and was able to meet Jean with sympathy and understanding when she tried to explain to him her wishes.

First of all, she was very anxious to know

if Mr. Dickson thought it quite fair that she should have the money. Was he *quite* sure that there were no relations, no one who had a real claim ?

Mr. Dickson explained to her what a singularly lonely, self-sufficing man Peter Reid had been, a man without friends, almost without interests — except the piling up of money.

"I don't say he was unhappy; I believe he was very content, absolutely absorbed in his game of money-making. But when he couldn't ignore any longer the fact that there was something wrong with his health, and went to the specialist and was told to give up work at once, he was completely bowled over. Life held nothing more for him. I was very sorry for the poor man . . . he had only one thought — to go back to Priorsford, his boyhood home."

"And I didn't know," said Jean, "or we would all have turned out there and then and sat on our boxes in the middle of the road, or roosted in the trees like crows, rather than keep him for an hour out of his own house. He came and asked to see The Rigs and I was afraid he meant to buy it: it was always our nightmare that the landlord in London would turn us out. . . . He looked frail and shabby, and I jumped to the conclusion that he was poor. Oh, I do wish I had known . . ."

"He told me," Mr. Dickson went on, "when he came to see me on his return, that he had come with the intention of asking the tenants to leave The Rigs, but that he hadn't the heart to do it when he saw how attached you were to the place. He added that you had been kind to him. He was rather gruff and ashamed about his weakness, but I could see that he had been touched to receive kindness from utter strangers. He was amused in a sardonic way that you had thought him a poor man and had yet been kind to him; he had an unhappy notion that in this world kindness is always bought . . . He had no heir, and I think I explained to you in my letter that he had made up his mind to leave his whole fortune to the first person who did anything for him without expecting payment. You turned out to be that person, and I congratulate you, Miss Jardine, most heartily. I would like to tell you that Mr. Reid planned everything so that it would be as easy as possible for you, and asked me to come and see you and explain in person. He seemed very satisfied when all was in order. I saw him a few days before he died and I thought he looked better, and told him so. But he only said, 'It's a great load off my mind to get everything settled, and it's a blessing not to have an heir to step into my shoes, and grudging me a few years longer on the earth.' Two days later he passed away in his sleep. He was a curious, hard man whom few cared about, but at the end there was something simple and rather pathetic about him. I think he died content."

"Thank you for telling me about him," Jean said, and there was silence for a minute.

"And now may I hear your wishes?" said Mr. Dickson.

"Can I do just as I like with the money? Well, will you please divide it into four parts? That will be a quarter for each of us — David, Jock, Mhor, me."

Jean spoke as if the fortune was a lump of dough and Mr. Dickson the baker, but the lawyer did not smile.

"I understood you had only two brothers?"

351

"Yes; David and Jock, but Mhor is an adopted brother. His name's Gervase Taunton."

"But — has he any claim on you?"

Jean's face got pink. "I should think he has. He's *exactly* like our own brother."

"Then you want him to have a full share?"

"Of course. It's odd how people will assume one is a cad! When Mhor's mother died (his father had died before) he came to us — his mother *trusted him* to us — and people kept saying. 'Why should you take him? He has no claim on you.' As if Mhor wasn't the best gift we ever got . . . And when you have divided it, I wonder if you would take a tenth off each share? We were brought up to give a tenth of any money we had to God. I'm almost sure the boys would give it themselves. I *think* they would, but perhaps it would be safer to take it off first and put it aside."

Jean looked very straight at the lawyer. "I wouldn't like any of us to be unjust stewards," she said.

"No," said the lawyer; "no."

"And perhaps," Jean went on, "the boys had better not get their shares until they are twenty-five. David could have it now, so far as sense goes, but it's the responsibility I'm thinking about."

"I would certainly let them wait until they are twenty-five. Their shares will accumulate, of course, and be very much larger when they get them."

"But I don't want that," said Jean. "I want the interest on the money to be added to the tenths that are laid away. It's better to give more than the strict tenth. It's so horrid to be shabby about giving."

"And what are the 'tenths' to be used for?"

"I'll tell you about that later, if I may. I'm not quite sure myself. I shall have to ask Mr. MacDonald, our minister. He'll know. I'm never quite certain whether the Bible means the tenth to be given in charity, or kept entirely for churches and missions . . . And I want to buy some annuities, if you will tell me how to do it. Mrs. M'Cosh, our servant — perhaps you noticed her when you came in? I want to make her absolutely secure and comfortable in her old age. I hope she will stay with us for a long time yet, but it will be nice for her to feel that she can have a home of her own whenever she likes. And there are others . . . but I won't worry you with them just now. It was most awfully kind of you to come all this way from London to explain things to me, when you must be very busy."

"Coming to see you is part of my business," Mr. Dickson explained, "but it has been a great pleasure, too . . . By the way, will you use the house in Prince's Gate or shall we let it?"

"Oh, do anything you like with it. I shouldn't think we would ever want to live in London, it's such a noisy, overcrowded place, and there are always hotels . . . I'm quite content with The Rigs. It's such a comfort to feel it is our own."

"It's a charming cottage," Mr. Dickson said; "but won't you want something roomier? Something more imposing for an heiress?"

"I hate imposing things," Jean said, very earnestly. "I want to go on just as we were doing, only with no scrimping, and more treats for the boys. We've only got £350 a year now, and the thought of all this money dazes me. It doesn't really mean anything to me yet."

"It will soon. I hope your fortune is going to bring you much happiness, though I doubt if you will keep much of it to yourself."

"Oh, yes," Jean assured him. "I'm going to buy myself a musquash coat with a skunk collar. I've always wanted one frightfully. You'll stay and have luncheon with us, won't you?"

Mr. Dickson stayed to luncheon, and was treated with great respect by Jock and Mhor. The latter had a notion that somewhere the lawyer had a cave in which he kept Jean's fortune, great casks of gold pieces and trunks of precious stones, and that any lack of manners on his part might lose Jean her inheritance. He was disappointed to find him dressed like an ordinary man. He had had a dim hope that he would look like Ali Baba and wear a turban.

After Mr. Dickson had finished saying all he had come to say, and had gone to catch his train, Jean started out to call on her minister. Pamela met her at the gate.

"Well, Jean, and whither away? You look very grave. Are you going to tell the King the sky's falling?"

"Something of that kind. I'm going to

see Mr. Macdonald. I've got something I want to ask him."

"I suppose you don't want me to go with you? I love an excuse to go and see the Macdonalds. Oh, but I have one. Just wait a moment, Jean, while I run back and fetch something."

She joined Jean after a short delay, and they walked on together. Jean explained that she was going to ask Mr. Macdonald's advice how best to use her money.

"Has the lawyer been?" Pamela asked. "Do you understand about things?"

Jean told of Mr. Dickson's visit.

"It's a fearful lot of money, Pamela. But when it's divided into four, that's four people to share the responsibility."

"And what are you going to do with your share?"

"I'll tell you what I'm not going to do. I'm not going to take a house and fill it with guests who will be consistently unpleasant, as the Benefactress did. And I'm not going to build a sort of fairy palace and commit suicide from the roof like the millionaire in that book *Midas*, something or other. And I *hope* I'm not going to lose my imagination and forget what it feels like to be poor, and send a girl with a small dress allowance half a dozen muslin handkerchiefs at Christmas."

"I suppose you know, Jean — I don't want to be discouraging — that you will get very little gratitude, that the people you try to help will smarm to your face and blackguard you behind your back? You will be hurt and disappointed times without number. . . . You see, my dear, I've had money for quite a lot of years, and I know."

Jean nodded.

They were crossing the wide bridge over Tweed, and she stopped and, leaning her arms on the parapet, gazed up at Peel Tower.

"Let's look at Peel for a little," she said. "It's been there such a long time and must have seen so many people trying to do their best and only succeeding in making mischief. It seems to say, 'Nothing really matters: you'll all be in the toad's hole in less than a hundred years. I remain, and the river and the hills.' "

"Yes," said Pamela, "they are a great comfort, the unchanging things — these placid round-backed hills, and the river and the grey town — to us restless mortals

. . . Look, Jean, I want you to tell me if you think this miniature is at all like Duncan Macdonald. You remember I asked you to let me have that snapshot of him that you said was so characteristic, and I sent it to London to a woman I know who does miniatures well. I thought his mother would like to have it. But you must tell me if you think it good enough."

Jean took the miniature and looked at the pictured face, a laughing boy's face, fresh-coloured, frank, with flaxen hair falling over a broad brow.

When, after a minute, she handed it back she assured Pamela that the likeness was wonderful.

"She has caught it exactly, that look in his eyes as if he were telling you it was 'fair time of day' with him. Oh, dear Duncan! It's fair time of day with him now, I am sure, wherever he is . . . He was twenty-two when he fell three years ago . . . You've often heard Mrs. Macdonald speak of her sons. Duncan was the youngest by a lot of years — the baby. The others are frightfully clever, but Duncan was a lamb. They all adored him, but he wasn't spoiled . . . Life was such a joke to Duncan. I can't

358

even now think of him as dead. He was so full of abounding life one can't imagine him lying still — quenched. You know that odd little poem:

> "*And Mary's the one that never liked angel stories,*
> *And Mary's the one that's dead. . . .*"

Death and Duncan seem such a long way apart. Many people are so dull and apathetic that they never seem more than half alive, so they don't leave much of a gap when they go. But Duncan — The Macdonalds are brave, but I think living to them is just a matter of getting through now. The end of the day will mean Duncan. I am glad you thought about getting the miniature done. You do have such nice thoughts, Pamela."

The Macdonalds' manse stood on the banks of Tweed, a hundred yards or so below Peel Tower, a square house of grey stone in a charming garden.

Mr. Macdonald loved his garden and worked in it diligently. It was his doctor, he said. When his mind got stale and sermon-writing difficult, when his head ached and people became a burden, he put on an old coat and went out to dig, or plant or mow the grass. He grew wonderful flowers, and in July when his lupins were at their best he took a particular pleasure in enticing people out to see the effect of their royal blue against the silver of Tweed.

He had been a minister in Priorsford for close on forty years and had never had more than £250 of a salary, and on this he and his wife had brought up four sons who looked, as an old woman in the church said, "as if they'd aye got their meat". There had always been a spare place at every meal for any casual guest, and a spare bedroom looking over Tweed that was seldom empty. And there had been no lowering of the dignity of a manse. A fresh, wise-like, middle-aged woman opened the door to visitors, and if you had asked her, she would have told you she had been in service with the Macdonalds since she was fifteen, and Mrs. Macdonald would have added that she never could have managed without Agnes.

The sons had worked their way with bursaries and scholarships through school and college, and now three of them were in positions of trust in the government of their country. One was in London, two

India — and Duncan lay in France, that Holy Land of our people.

It was a nice question his wife used to say before the War (when hearts were lighter and laughter easier) whether Mr. Macdonald was prouder of his sons or his flowers, and when, as sometimes happened, he had them all with him in the garden, his cup of content had been full.

And now it seemed to him that when he was in the garden Duncan was nearer him. He could see the little figure in a blue jersey marching along the paths with a wheelbarrow, very important because he was helping his father. He had called the big clump of azaleas "the burning bush". . . . He had always been a funny little chap.

And it was in the garden that he had said good-bye to him that last time. He had been twice wounded, and it was hard to go back again. There was no novelty about it now, no eagerness or burning zeal, nothing but a dogged determination to see the thing through. They had stood together looking over Tweed to the blue ridge of Cademuir, and Duncan had broken the silence with a question:

"What's the psalm, Father, about the

man 'who going forth doth mourn'?"

And with his eyes fixed on the hills the old minister had repeated:

> " *'That man who bearing precious seed*
> *In going forth doth mourn,*
> *He, doubtless, bringing back the sheaves*
> *Rejoicing will return.'* "

And Duncan had nodded his head and said, "That's it. 'Rejoicing will return.' " And he had taken another long look at Cademuir.

Many wondered what had kept such a man as John Macdonald all his life in a small town like Priorsford. He did more good, he said, in a little place; he would be of no use in a city. But the real reason was he knew his health would not stand the strain. For many years he had been a martyr to a particularly painful kind of rheumatism. He never spoke of it if he could help it, and tried never to let it interfere with his work, but his eyes had the patient look that suffering brings, and his face often wore a twisted, humorous smile, as if he were laughing at his own pain. He was now sixty-four. His sons, so far as they were allowed, had smoothed the way for their parents, but they could not induce their father to retire from the ministry. "I'll give up when I begin to feel myself a nuisance," he would say. "I can still preach and visit my people, and perhaps God will let me die in harness, with the sound of Tweed in my ears."

Mrs. Macdonald was, in Bible words, a "succourer of many". She was a little stout woman with the merry heart that goes all the way, combined with heavy-lidded, sad eyes, and a habit of sighing deeply. She affected to take a sad view of everything, breaking into irrepressible laughter in the middle of the most pessimistic utterances, for she was able to see the humorous side of her own gloom. Mrs. Macdonald was a born giver; everything she possessed she had to share. She was miserable if she had nothing to bestow on a parting guest, small gifts like a few new-laid eggs or a pot of home-made jam.

"You know yourself," she would say, "what a satisfied feeling it gives you to come away from a place with even the tiniest gift."

Her popularity was immense. Sad

people came to her because she sighed with them and never tried to cheer them: dull people came to her because she was never in offensive high spirits or in a boastful mood — not even when her sons had done something particularly striking — and happy people came in to her, for, though she sighed and warned them that nothing lasted in this world, her eyes shone with pleasure, and her interest was so keen that every detail could be told and discussed and gloated over with the comfortable knowledge that Mrs. Macdonald would not say to her next visitor that she had been simple *deaved* with talk about So-and-so's engagement.

Mrs. Macdonald believed in speaking her mind — if she had anything pleasant to say, and she was sometimes rather startling in her frankness to strangers. "My dear, how pretty you are," she would say to a girl visitor, or, "Forgive me, but I must tell you I don't think I ever saw a nicer hat."

The women in the congregation had no comfort in their new clothes until Mrs. Macdonald had pronounced on them. A word was enough. Perhaps at the church door some congregational matter would be discussed; then, at parting, a quick touch on the arm and — "Most successful bonnet I ever saw you get," or, "The coat's worth all the money." or, "Everything new, and you look as young as your daughter."

Pamela and Jean found the minister and his wife in the garden. Mr. Macdonald was pacing up and down the path overlooking the river with his next Sunday's sermon in his hand; while Mrs. Macdonald raked the gravel before the front door (she liked the place kept so tidy that her sons had been wont to say bitterly, as they spent an hour of their precious Saturdays helping, that she dusted the branches and wiped the faces of the flowers with a handkerchief) and carried on a conversation with her husband which was of little profit, as the rake on the stones dimmed the sense of her words.

"Wasn't that right, John?" she was saying as her husband came near her.

"Dear me, woman, how can I tell? I haven't heard a word you've been saying. Here are callers. I'll get away to my visiting. Why! It's Jean and Miss Reston — this is very pleasant."

Mrs. Macdonald waved her hand to her visitors as she hurried away to put the rake in the shed, reappearing in a moment like a stout little whirlwind.

"Come away my dears. Up to the study, Jean; that's where the fire is today. I'm delighted to see you both. What a blessing Agnes is baking pancakes. It seemed almost a waste, for neither John nor I eat them; but, you see, they had just been meant for you . . . I wouldn't go just now, John. We'll have an early tea and that will give you a long evening."

Jean explained that she specially wanted to see Mr. Macdonald.

"And would you like me to go away?" Mrs. Macdonald asked. "Miss Reston and I can go to the dining-room."

"But I want you as much as Mr. Macdonald," said Jean. "It's your advice I want — about the money, you know."

Mrs. Macdonald gave a deep sigh. "Ah, money," she said — "the root of all evil."

"Not at all, my dear," her husband corrected. "The love of money is the root of all evil — a very different thing. Money can be a very fine thing."

"Oh," said Jean, "that's what I want you to tell me. How can I make this money a blessing?"

Mr. Macdonald gave his twisted smile.

"And am I to answer you in one word, Jean? I fear it's a word too wide for a mouth of this age's size. You will have to make mistakes and learn by them and gradually feel your way."

"The most depressing thing about money," put in his wife, "is that the Bible should say so definitely that a rich man can hardly get into heaven. Oh, I know all about a needle's eye being a gate, but I've always a picture in my own mind of a camel and an ordinary darning-needle, and anything more hopeless could hardly be imagined."

Mrs. Macdonald had taken up a half-finished sock, and, as she disposed of the chances of all the unfortunate owners of wealth, she briskly turned the heel.

Jean knew her hostess too well to be depressed by her, so she smiled at her minister, who said, "Heaven's gate is too narrow for a man and his money; that goes without saying, Jean."

Jean leant forward and said eagerly,

"What I really want to know is about the tenth we are to put away as not being our own. Does it count if it is given in charity, or ought it to be given to Church things and missions?"

"Whatever is given to God will 'count', as you put it — lighting, where you can, candles of kindness to cheer and warm and lighten."

"I see," said Jean. "Of course, there are heaps of things one could slump money away on, hospitals and institutions and missions, but these are all so impersonal. I wonder, would it be pushing and *furritsome*, do you think, if I tried to help ministers a little? — ministers, I mean, with wives and families and small incomes shut away in country places and in the poor parts of big towns? It would be such pleasant helping to me."

"Now," said Mrs. Macdonald, "that's a really sensible idea, Jean. There's no manner of doubt that the small salaries of the clergy are a crying scandal. I don't like ministers to wail in the papers about it, but the laymen should wail until things are changed. Ministers don't enter the Church for the loaves and fishes, but the labourer is worthy of his hire, and they must have enough to live on decently. Living has doubled. I couldn't manage as things are now, and I'm a good manager, though I says it as shouldn't . . . The fight I've had all my life nobody will ever know. Now that we have plenty, I can talk about it. I never hinted it to anybody when we were struggling through; indeed, we washed our faces and anointed our heads and appeared not unto men to fast! The clothes and the boots and the butcher's bills! It's pleasant to think of now, just as it's pleasant to look from the hilltop at the steep road you've come. The boys sometimes tell me that they are glad we were too poor to have a nurse, for it meant that they were brought up with their father and me. We had our meals together, and their father helped them with their lessons. Indeed, it's only now I realise how happy I was to have them all under one roof."

She stopped and sighed, and went on again with a laugh. "I remember one time a week before the Sustentation Fund was due, I was down to one sixpence. And of course a collector arrived! D'you remember that, John? . . . And the boys worked so hard to educate themselves. All except Duncan. Oh, but I am glad with all my heart that my little laddie had an easy time — when it was to be such a short one."

"He always wanted to be a soldier," Mr. Macdonald said. "You remember, Anne, when you tried to get him to say he would be a minister? He was about six then, I think. He said, 'No, it's not a white man's job,' and then looked at me apologetically, afraid that he had hurt my feelings. When the War came he went 'most jocund, apt, and willingly', but without any ill-will in his heart to the Germans.

" *'He left no will but good will*
And that to all mankind. . . .'"

Mrs. Macdonald stared into the fire with tear-blurred eyes and said: "I sometimes wonder if they died in vain. If this is the new world it's a far worse one than the old. Class hatred, discontent, wild extravagance in some places, children starving in others, women mad for pleasure, and the dead forgotten already except by the mothers — the mothers who never to their dying day will see a fresh-faced boy without a sword piercing their hearts and a cry rising to their lips, 'My son! My son!' "

"It's all true, Anne," said her husband, "but the sacrifice of love and innocence can never be in vain. Nothing can ever dim that sacrifice. The country's dead will save the country as they saved it before. Those young lives have gone in front to light the way for us."

Mrs. Macdonald took up her sock again, with a long sigh.

"I wish I could comfort myself with thoughts as you can, John, but I never had any mind. No, Jean, you needn't protest so politely. I'm a good housewife, and I admit my shortbread is 'extra', as Duncan used to say. Duncan was very sorry as a small boy that he had left heaven and come to stay with us. He used to say with a sigh, 'You see, heaven's extra.' I don't know where he picked up the expression. But what I was going to say is that people are so wretchedly provoking. This morning I was really badly provoked. For one thing, I was very busy doing the accounts of the Girls' Club (you know I have no head for figures), and Mrs. Morton strolled in to see me, to cheer me up, she said. Cheer me up!

She maddened me. I haven't been forty years a minister's wife without learning patience, but it would have done me all the good in the world to take that woman by her expensive fur coat and walk her rapidly out of the room. She sat there breathing opulence, and told me how hard it was for her to live — she, a lone woman with six servants to wait on her, and a car and a chauffeur! 'I am not going to give to this War memorial,' she said. 'At this time it seems rather a wasteful proceeding, and it won't do the men who have fallen any good.' . . . I could have told her that surely it wasn't *waste* the men were thinking about when they poured out their youth like wine that she and her like might live and hug their bank books."

Mr. Macdonald had moved from his chair in the window, and now stood with one hand on the mantelshelf, looking into the fire. "Do you remember," he said, "that evening in Bethany when Mary took a box of spikenard, very costly, and anointed the feet of Jesus, so that the odour of the ointment filled the house? Judas — that same Judas who carried the bag and was a robber — was much concerned about the waste. He said that the box might have been sold for three hundred pence and given to the poor. And Jesus, rebuking him, said, 'The poor always ye have with you, but Me ye have not always.' "

He stopped abruptly and went over to his writing-table and made as though he were arranging papers. Presently he said, "Anne, you've been here." His tone was accusing.

"Only writing a post card," said his wife quickly. "I can't have made much of a mess." She turned to her visitors and explained: "John is a regular old maid about his writing-table; everything must be so tidy and unspotted."

"Well, I can't understand," said her husband, "why anyone so neat handed as you are should be such a filthy creature with ink. You seem positively to sling it about."

"Well," said Mrs. Macdonald, changing the subject, "I like your idea of helping ministers, Jean. I've often thought if I had the means I would know how to help. A cheque to a minister in a city-charge for a holiday; a cheque to pay a doctor's bill and ease a little for a worn-out wife. You've a great chance, Jean."

"I know," said Jean, "if you will only tell me how to begin."

"I'll soon do that," said practical Mrs. Macdonald. "I've got several in my mind this moment that I just ache to give a hand to. But only the very rich can help. You can't in decency take from people who have only enough to go on with . . . Now, if you'll excuse me, I'll see if Agnes is getting the tea. I want you to taste my rowan and crab-apple jelly, Miss Reston, and, if you like it, you will take some home with you."

As they left the manse an hour later, laden with gifts, Pamela said to Jean, "I would rather be Mrs. Macdonald than anyone else I know. She is a practising Christian. If I had done a day's work such as she has done, I think I would go out of the world pretty well pleased with myself."

"Yes," Jean agreed. "If life is merely a chance of gaining love she will come out with high marks. Did you give her the miniature?"

"Yes, just as we left, when you had walked on to the gate with Mr. Macdonald. She was so absurdly grateful she made me cry. You would have thought no one had ever given her a gift before."

"The world," said Jean, "is divided into two classes, the givers and the takers. Nothing so touches and pleases and surprises a 'giver' as to receive a gift. The 'takers' are too busy standing on their hind legs (like Peter at tea-time) looking wistfully for the next bit of cake to be very appreciative of the biscuit of the moment."

"Bless me!" said Pamela, "Jean among the cynics!"

21

*"The soul's dark cottage, batter'd and
decay'd,
Lets in the light through chinks that time
has made:
Stronger by weakness wiser men become
As they draw nearer to their eternal home:
Leaving the old, both worlds at once they view
That stand upon the threshold of the new."*

EDMUND WALLER

ONE day Pamela walked down to Hopetoun to lunch with Mrs. Hope. Augusta had gone away on a short visit and Pamela had promised to spend as much time as possible with her mother.

"You won't be here much longer," Mrs. Hope had said, "so spend as much time with me as you can spare, and we'll talk books and quote poetry and," she had finished defiantly, "I'll miscall my neighbours if I feel inclined."

It was February now, and there was a hint of spring in the air. The sun was shining as if trying to make up for the days

376

it had missed, the green shoots were pushing daringly forth, and a mavis in a holly-bush was chirping loudly and cheerfully. Tomorrow they might be plunged back into winter, the green things nipped and discouraged, the birds silent — but today it was spring.

Pamela lingered by Tweedside listening to the mavis, looking back at the bridge spanning the river, the church steeple high against the pale blue sky, the little town pouring its houses down to the water's edge. Hopetoun woods were still bare and brown, but soon the larches would get their pencils, the beeches would unfurl tiny leaves of living green, and the celandines begin to poke their yellow heads through the carpet of last year's leaves.

Mrs. Hope was sitting close to the window that looked out on the Hopetoun Woods. The spring sunshine and the notes of the mavis had brought to her a rush of memories.

> *"For what can spring renew*
> *More fiercely for us than the need of you."*

Her knitting lay on her lap, a pile of new books stood on the table beside her, but her hands were idly folded, and she did not look at the books, did not even notice the sunshine; her eyes were with her heart, and that was far away across the black dividing sea in the last resting-places of her sons. Wild laddies they had been, never at rest, never out of mischief, and now — "a' quaitit noo in the grave".

She turned to greet her visitor with her usual whimsical smile. She had grown very fond of Pamela; they were absolutely at ease with each other, and could enjoy talking, or sitting together in silence.

Today the conversation was brisk between the two at luncheon. Pamela had been with Jean to Edinburgh and Glasgow on shopping expeditions, and Mrs. Hope was keen to hear all about them.

"I could hardly persuade her to go," Pamela said. "Her argument was, 'Why get clothes from Paris if you can get them in Priorsford?' She only gave in to please me, but she enjoyed herself mightily. We went first to Edinburgh — my first visit except just waiting a train."

"And weren't you charmed? Edinburgh is our own town, and we are inordinately proud of it. It's full of steep streets and east winds and high houses, and you can't move a step without treading on a W.S., but it's a fine place for all that."

"It's a fairy-tale place to see," Pamela said. "The castle at sunset, the sudden glimpses of the Forth, Holyrood dreaming in the mist — these are pictures that will remain with one always. But Glasgow — "

"I know almost nothing of Glasgow," said Mrs. Hope, "but I like the people that come from it. They are not so devoured by gentility as our Edinburgh friends; they are more living, more human . . ."

"Are Edinburgh people very refined ?"

"Oh, some of them can hardly see out of their eyes for gentility. I delight in it myself, though I've never attained to it. I'm told you see it in its finest flower in the suburbs. A friend of mine was going out by train to Colinton, and she overheard two girls talking. One said, 'I was at a dence lest night.' The other, rather condescendingly, replied, 'Oh, really! And who do you dence with out at Colinton ?' 'It depends,' said the first girl. 'Lest night, for instance, I was up to my neck in advocates.' . . . Priorsford's pretty genteel, too. You know the really genteel by the way they say

'Good-bai.' The rest of us who pride ourselves on not being provincial say — you may have noticed — 'Good-ba — a.' "

Pamela laughed, and said she had noticed the superior accent of Priorsford.

"Jean and I were much interested in the difference between Edinburgh and Glasgow shops. Not in the things they sell — the shops in both places are most excellent — but in the manner of selling. The girls in the Edinburgh shops are nice and obliging — the war-time manner doesn't seem to have reached shop-assistants in Scotland, luckily — but quite Londonish with their manners and their 'Moddom'. In Glasgow, they give one such a feeling of personal interest. You would really think it mattered to them what you chose. They delighted Jean by remarking as she tried on a hat, 'My, you look a treat in that!' We bought a great deal more than we needed, for we hadn't the heart to refuse what was brought with such enthusiasm. 'I don't know what it is about that hat, but it's awful nice somehow. Distinctive, if you know what I mean. I think when you get it home you'll like it awful well — ". Who would refuse a hat after such a recommendation ?"

"Who, indeed! Oh, they're a hearty people. Has Jean got the fur coat she coveted?"

"She hasn't. It was a great disappointment, poor child. She was so excited when she saw them being brought in rich profusion, but when she tried them on all desire to possess one left her: they became her so ill. They buried her, somehow. She said herself she looked like 'a mouse under a divot', whatever that may be, and they really did make her look like five out of any six women one meets in the street. Fur coats are very levelling things. Later on, when I get her to London we'll see what can be done. Jean needs careful dressing to bring out that very real but elusive beauty of hers. I persuaded her in the meantime to get a soft cloth coat made with a skunk collars and cuffs . . . She was so funny about under-things. I wanted her to get some sets of *crêpe-de-Chine* things, but she was adamant. She didn't at all approve of them, and said she liked under-things that would *boil*. She has always had very dainty things made by herself; Great-aunt Alison taught her to do beautiful, fine sewing . . . Jean is a delightful person to do things with; she brings such a freshness to everything, is never bored, never blasé. I was glad to see her so deeply interested in new clothes. I confess to having a deep distrust of a woman who is above trying to make herself attractive. She is an insufferable thing."

"I quite agree, my dear. A woman deliberately careless of her appearance is an offence. But, on the other hand, the opposite can be carried too far. Look at Mrs. Jowett!"

"Oh, dear Mrs. Jowett, with her lace and her delicate, faded tints; and her tears of sentiment and her marvellous maids!"

"A good woman," said Mrs. Hope, "but silly. She fears a draught more than she does the devil. I'm always reminded of her when I read *Weir of Hermiston*. She has many points in common with Mrs. Weir — 'a dwaibly body'. Of the two, I really prefer Mrs. Duff-Whalley. *Her* great misfortune was being born a woman. With all that energy and perfect health, that keen brain and the indomitable strain that never knows when it is beaten, she might have done almost anything. She might have been a Lipton or a Coats, or even gone out and discovered the South Pole, or contested Lloyd George's Welsh seat in the Conservative interest. As a woman she is cribbed and cabined. What she has set herself to do is to force what she calls 'The County' to recognise her, and marry off her girl as well as possible. She has accomplished the first part through sheer perseverance, and I've no doubt she will accomplish the second; the girl is pretty and well dowered. I have a liking for the woman, especially if I haven't seen her for a little. There is some bite in her conversation. Mrs. Jowett is a sweet woman; but to me she is like a vacuum cleaner. When I've talked to her for ten minutes my head feels like a cushion that has been cleaned — a sort of empty, yet swollen feeling. I never can understand how Mr. Jowett has gone through life with her and kept his reason. But there's no doubt men like sweet, sentimental women, and I suppose they are restful in a house. . . . Shall we have coffee in the drawing-room? It's cosier."

In the drawing-room they settled down before the fire very contentedly silent. Pamela idly reached out for a book and read a little here and there as she sipped her coffee, while her hostess looked into the fire. The room seemed to dream in the spring sunshine. Generations of Hopes had lived in it, and each mistress had set her mark on the room. Beautiful old cabinets stood against the white walls, while beaded ottomans worked in the early days of Victoria jostled slender Chippendale chairs and tables. A large comfortable Chesterfield and down-cushioned armchairs gave the comfort moderns ask for. Nothing looked out of place, for the room with its gracious proportions took all the incongruities — the family Raeburns, the Queen Anne cabinets, the miniatures, the Victorian atrocities, the weak water-coloured sketches, the framed photographs of whiskered gentlemen and ladies with bustles, and made them into one pleasing whole. There is no charm in a room furnished from showrooms, though it be correct in every detail of the period chosen. Much more human is the room that is full of things, ugly, perhaps, in themselves but which link one generation to another. The ottoman worked so laboriously by a ringletted great-aunt stood with its ugly mahogany legs beside a Queen Anne chair, over whose faded wool-work seat a far-off beauty had pricked her dainty fingers — and both of the workers were Hopes; while by Pamela's side stood a fire-screen stitched by Augusta, the last of the Hopes.

"I wonder," said Mrs. Hope, breaking the silence, "what has become of Lewis Elliot? I haven't heard from him since he went away. Do you know where he is just now."

Pamela shook her head.

"Why don't you marry him, Pamela?"

"For a very good reason — he hasn't asked me."

"Hoots!" said Mrs. Hope, "as if that mattered!"

Mamela lifted her eyebrows. "It is generally considered rather necessary, isn't it?" she asked mildly.

"You know quite well that he would ask you tomorrow if you gave him the slightest encouragement. The man's afraid of you, that's what's wrong."

Pamela nodded.

"Is that why you have remained Pamela Reston? My dear, men are fools, and blind. And Lewis is modest as well. But . . . forgive me blundering. I've a long tongue, but you would think at my age I might keep it still."

"No, I don't mind your knowing. I don't think anyone else had a suspicion of it. And I thought myself I had long since got over it. Indeed, when I came here I was contemplating marrying someone else."

"Tell me, did you know Lewis was here when you came to Priorsford?"

"No — I'd completely lost trace of him. I was too proud ever to inquire after him, when he suddenly gave up coming near us. Priorsford suggested itself to me as a place to come for a rest, chiefly, I suppose, because I had heard of it from Lewis, but I had no thought of seeing him. Indeed, I had no notion that he had still a connection with the place. And then Jean suddenly said his name. I knew then I hadn't forgotten; my heart leapt up in the old unreasonable way. I met him — and thought he cared for Jean."

"Yes. I used sometimes to wonder why Lewis didn't fall in love with Jean. Of course he was too old for her, but it would have been quite a feasible match. Now I know that he cared for you all the time. No, I'm not surprised that he looked at no

one else. But that you should have waited
. . . There must have been so many
suitors. . . ."

"A few. But some people are born faithful. Anyway, I'm so glad that when I thought he cared for Jean it made no difference in my feelings for her. I should have felt so humiliated if I had been petty enough to hate her for what she couldn't help. My brother Biddy wants to marry Jean, and I've great hopes that it may work out all right."

Mrs. Hope sat forward in her chair.

"I had my suspicions. Jean has changed lately; nothing to take hold of, but I have felt a difference. It wasn't the money — that's an external thing — the change was in Jean herself, a certain reticence where there had been utter frankness; a laugh more frequent, but not quite so gay and light-hearted. Has he spoken to her?"

"Yes, but Jean wouldn't hear of it."

"Dear me! I could have sworn she cared."

"I think she does, but Jean is proud. What a silly thing pride is! However, Biddy is very tenacious, and he isn't at all down-hearted about his rebuff. He's quite sure that Jean and he were meant for each other, and he has great hopes of convincing Jean. I've never mentioned the subject to her, she is so tremendously reticent and shy about such things. I talk about Biddy in a casual way, but if I hadn't known from Biddy, I would have learned from Jean's averted eyes that something had happened. The child gives herself away every time."

"This, I suppose, happened before the fortune came. What effect will the money I wonder?"

"I wonder too," said Pamela. "Now that Jean feels she has something to give it may make a difference. I wish she would speak to me about it, but I can't force her confidence."

"No," said Mrs. Hope. "You can't do that. As you say, Jean is very reticent. I think I'm rather hurt that she hasn't confided in me. She is almost like my own. . . . She was a little child when the news came that Sandy my youngest boy, was gone. . . . I'm reticent too, and I couldn't mention his name, or speak about my sorrow, and Jean seemed to understand. She used to garden beside me, and chatter about her baby affairs, and ask me questions, and I sometimes thought she saved my reason. . . ."

Pamela sat silent. It was well known that no one dared mention her sons' names to Mrs. Hope. Figuratively she removed her shoes from off her feet, for she felt that it was holy ground.

Mrs. Hope went on. "I dare say you have heard about — my boys. They all died within three years, and Augusta and I were left alone. Generally I get along, but today — perhaps because it is the first spring day, and they were so young and full of promise — it seems as if I must speak about them. Do you mind ?"

Pamela took the hand that lay on the black silk lap and kissed it. "Ah, my dear," she said.

"Archie was my eldest son. His father and I dreamed dreams about him. They came true, though not in the way we would have chosen. He went into the Indian Civil Service — the Hopes were always a far-wandering race — and he gave his life fighting famine in his district. . . . And Jock would be nothing but a soldier — *my* Jock with his warm heart and his sudden rages and his passion for animals! (Jock Jardine reminds me of him just a little.) There never was anyone more lovable, and he was killed in a Frontier raid — two in a year. Their father was gone, and for that I was thankful; one can bear sorrow oneself, but it is terrible to see others suffer. Augusta was a rock in a weary land to me; nobody knows what Augusta is but her mother. We had Sandy, our baby left, and we managed to go on. But Sandy was a soldier too, and when the Boer War broke out, of course he had to go. I knew when I said good-bye to him that whoever came back it wouldn't be my laddie. He was too shining-eyed, too much all that was young and innocent and brave to win through. . . . Archie and Jock were men, capable, well equipped to fight the world, but Sandy was our baby — he was only twenty. . . . Of all the things the dead possessed it is the thought of their gentleness that breaks the heart. You can think of their qualities of brain and heart and be proud, but when you think of their gentleness and their youth you can only weep and weep. I think our hearts broke — Augusta's and mine — when Sandy went. . . . He had been, they told us later, the life of his company. His spirits never went down. It was early morning, and he was singing 'Annie Laurie' when the bullet killed him — like a lark shot down in the sun-rising. . . . His great friend came to see us when everything was over. He was a very honest fellow, and couldn't have made up things to tell us if he had tried. He sat and racked his brains for details, for he saw that we hungered and thirsted for anything. At last he said, 'Sandy was a funny fellow. If you left a cake near him he ate all the currants out of it.' . . . My little boy, my little, *little* boy! I don't know why I should cry. We had him for twenty years. Stir the fire, will you, Pamela, and put on a log — I don't like it when it gets dull. Old people need a blaze even when the sun is outside."

"You mustn't say you are old," Pamela said, as she threw on a log and swept the hearth, shading her eyes, smarting with tears, from the blaze. "You must stay with Augusta for a long time. Think how everyone would miss you. Priorsford wouldn't be Priorsford without you."

"Priorsford would never look over its shoulder. Augusta would miss me, yes, and some of the poor folk, but I've too illscrapit a tongue to be much liked. Sorrow ought to make people more tender, but it made my tongue bitter. To an unregenerate person with an aching heart like myself it is a relief to slash out at the people who annoy one by being too correct, or too consciously virtuous. I admit it's wrong, but there it is. I've prayed for charity and discretion, but my tongue always runs away with me. And I really can't be bothered with those people who never say an ill word of anyone. It makes conversation as savourless as porridge without salt. One needn't talk scandal. I hate scandal — but there is no harm in remarking on the queer ways of your neighbours: anyone who likes can remark on mine. Even when you are old and done and waiting for the summons it isn't wrong surely to get amusement out of the other pilgrims — if you can. Do you know your *Pilgrim's Progress*, Pamela? Do you remember where Christiana and the others reach the Land of Beulah? It is the end of the journey, and they have nothing to do but wait, while the children go into the King's gardens and gather there sweet flowers. . . . It is all true. I know, for I have reached the land of Beulah. 'How welcome is death,' says Bunyan, 'to them that have nothing to do but die'. For the last twenty-five years the way has been pretty hard. I've stumbled along very lamely, followed my Lord on crutches like Mr. Fearing, but now the end is in sight and I can be at ease. All these years I have never been able to read the letters and diaries of my boys — they tore my very heart — but now I can read them without tears, and rejoice in having had such sons to give. I used to be tortured by dreams of them, when I thought I held them and spoke to them, and woke to weep in agony, but now when they come to me I can wake and smile, satisfied that very soon they will be mine again. Sorrow is a wonderful thing. It shatters this old earth, but it makes a new heaven. I can thank God now for taking my boys. Augusta is a saint and acquiesced from the first, but I was rebellious. I see that Heaven and myself had part in my boys; now Heaven has all, and all the better it is for the boys. I hope God will forgive my bitterness, and all the grief I have given with words. 'No suffering is for the present joyous . . . nevertheless after-wards . . .' When the Great War broke out and the terrible casualty lists became longer and longer, and 'with rue our hearts were laden', I found some of the 'peaceable fruits' we are promised. I found I could go without impertinence into the house of mourning even when I hardly knew the people, and ask them to let me share their grief, and I think sometimes I was able to help just a little."

"I know how you helped," said Pamela; "the Macdonalds told me. Do you know, I think I envy you. You have suffered much but you have loved much. Your life has meant something. Looking back I've nothing to think on but social successes that now seem very small and foolish, and years of dressing and talking and dancing and laughing. My life seems like a brightly coloured bubble — as light and as useless."

"Not useless. We need the flowers and the butterflies and the things that adorn. . . . I wish Jean would give herself over to pleasure for a little. Her poor little head is full of schemes — quite practical schemes they are too, she has a shrewd head — about helping others. I tell her she will do it all in good time but I want her to forget the woes of the world for a little and rejoice in her youth."

"I know," said Pamela. "I was astonished to find how responsible she felt for the misery in the world. She is determined to build a heaven in hell's despair! It reminds one of Saint Theresa setting out holding her little brother's hand to convert the Moors! . . . Now I've stayed too long and tired you, and Augusta will have me assassinated. Thank you, my very dear lady, for letting me come to see you, and for — telling me about your sons. Bless you . . ."

22

"For never anything can be amiss
When simpleness and duty tender it."
"AS YOU LIKE IT"

THE lot of the conscientious philanthropist is not an easy one. The kind but unthinking rich can strew their benefits about, careless of their effect on the recipients, but the path of the earnest lover of his fellows is thorny and difficult, and dark with disappointment.

To Jean in her innocence it had seemed that money was the one thing necessary to make bright the lives of her poorer neighbours. She pictured herself as a sort of fairy godmother going from house to house carrying sunshine and leaving smiles and happiness in her wake. She soon found that her dreams had been rosy delusions. Far otherwise was the result of her efforts.

"It's like something in a fairy-tale," she complained to Pamela. "You are given a fairy palace, but when you try to go to it mountains of glass are set before you and you can't reach it. You can't think how different the people are to me now. The very poor whom I thought I could help don't treat me any longer like a friend to whom they can tell their troubles in a friendly way. The poor-spirited ones whine, with an eye on my pocket, and where I used to get welcoming smiles I now only get expectant grins. And the high-spirited ones are so afraid that I'll offer them help that their time is spent in snubbing me and keeping me in my place."

"It's no use getting down about it," Pamela told her. "You are only finding what thousands have found before you, that it's the most difficult thing in the world to be wisely charitable. You will never remove mountains. If you can smooth a step here and there for people, and make your small corner of the world as pleasant as possible, you do very well."

Jean agreed with a sigh. "If I don't finish by doing harm. I have awful thoughts sometimes about the dire effects money may have on the boys — on Mhor especially. In any case it will change their lives entirely. It's a solemnising thought," and she laughed, ruefully.

Jean plodded on her well-doing way, and knocked her head against many posts, and blundered into pitfalls, and perhaps did more good and earned more real gratitude than she had any idea of.

"It doesn't matter if I'm cheated ninety-nine times if I'm some real help the hundredth time," she told herself. "Puir thing," said the recipients of her bounty, in kindly tolerance, "she means weel, and it's a kindness to help her awa' wi' some of her siller. A' she gies us is juist like tippence frae you or me."

One woman, at any rate, blessed Jean in her heart, though her stiff, ungracious lips could not utter a word of thanks. Mary Abbot lived in a neat cottage surrounded by a neat garden. She was a dressmaker in a small way, and had supported her mother till her death. She had been very happy with her work and her bright, tidy house and her garden and her friends, but for more than a year a black fear had brooded over her. Her sight, which was her living, was going. She saw nothing before her but the workhouse. Death she would have welcomed, but this was shame. For months she had fought it out, as her eyes grew dimmer, letting no one know of the anxiety that gnawed at her heart. No one suspected anything wrong. She was always neatly dressed at church, she always had her small contribution ready for collectors, her house shone with rubbing, and as she did not seem to want to take in sewing now, people thought that she must have made a competency and did not need to work so hard.

Jean knew Miss Abbot well by sight. She had sat behind her in church all the Sundays of her life, and had often admired the tidy appearance of the dressmaker, and thought that she was an excellent advertisement of her own wares. Lately she had noticed her thin and ill-coloured and Mrs. Macdonald had said one day, "I wonder if Miss Abbot is all right. She used to be such a help at the sewing meeting, and now she doesn't come at all, and her excuses are lame. When I go to see her she always says she is perfectly well, but I am not at ease about her. She's the sort of woman who would drop before she made a word of complaint. . . ."

One morning when passing the door Jean saw Miss Abbot polishing her brass knocker. She stopped to say good-morning.

"Are you keeping well, Miss Abbot? There is so much illness about."

"I'm in my usual, thank you," said Miss Abbot, stiffly.

"I always admire the flowers in your window," said Jean. "How do you manage to keep them so fresh looking? Ours get so mangy. May I come in for a second and look at them?"

Miss Abbot stood aside and said coldly that Jean might come in if she liked, but her flowers were nothing extra.

It was the tidiest of kitchens she entered. Everything shone that could be made to shine. A hearth-rug made by Miss Abbot's mother lay before the fireplace, in which a mere handful of fire was burning. An armchair with cheerful red cushions stood beside the fire. It was quite comfortable, but Jean felt a bareness. There were no pots on the fire — nothing seemed to be cooking for dinner.

She admired the flowers and got instructions from their owner when to water and when to refrain from watering, and then, seating herself in a chair, she proceeded to try to make Miss Abbot talk. That lady stood bolt upright waiting for her visitor to go, but Jean, having got a footing, was determined to remain.

"Are you very busy just now?" she asked. "I was wondering if you could do some sewing for me? I don't know whether you ever go out by the day?"

"No," said Miss Abbot.

"We could bring it you here if you would do it at your leisure."

"I can't take in any more work just now. I'm sorry."

"Oh, well, it doesn't matter. Perhaps later on. . . . I'm keeping you. It's Saturday morning and you'll want to get on with your work."

"Yes."

There was a silence, and Jean reluctantly rose to go. Miss Abbot had turned her back and was looking into the fire.

"Good-morning, Miss Abbot. Thank you so much for letting me know about the flowers." Then she saw that Miss Abbot was crying — crying in a hopeless, helpless way that made Jean's heart ache. She went to her and put her hand on her arm. "Won't you tell me what's wrong? Do sit down here in the arm-chair. I'm sure you're not well."

Miss Abbot allowed herself to be led to the arm-chair. Having once given way she was finding it no easy matter to regain control of herself.

"Is it that you aren't well?" Jean asked. "I know it's a wretched business trying to go on working when one is seedy."

Miss Abbot shook her head. "It's far worse than that. I have to refuse work for I can't see to do it. I'm losing my sight and . . . and there is nothing before me but the workhouse."

Over and over again in the silence of the night she had said those words to herself; she had seen them written in letters of fire on the walls of her little room; they had seemed seared into her brain, but she had never meant to tell a soul, not even the minister, and here she was telling this strip of a girl.

Jean gave a cry and caught her hands. "Oh no, no! Never that!"

"I've no relations," said Miss Abbot. She was quiet now and calm, and hopeless. "And if I had, I couldn't be a burden on them. Nobody wants a penniless, half-blind woman. I've had to use up all my savings this winter . . . it will just have to be the workhouse."

"But it shan't be," said Jean. "What's the use of me if I'm not to help? No. Don't stiffen and look at me like that. I'm not offering you charity. Perhaps you may have heard that I've been left a lot of money — in trust. It's your money as much as mine; if it's anybody's it's God's money. I felt I just couldn't pass your door this morning, and I spoke to you, though I was frightfully scared — you looked so stand-offish. . . . Now listen. All I've got to do is to send your name to my lawyer — he's in London, and he knows nothing about anybody in Priorsford, so you needn't worry about him — and he will arrange that you get a sufficient income all your life. No, it isn't charity. You fought hard all your life for others, and it's high time you got a rest. Everyone should get a rest and a competency when they are sixty. (Not that you are nearly that, of course.) Some day that happy state of affairs will be. Now the kettle's almost boiling, and I'm going to make you a cup of tea. Where's the caddy?"

There was a spoonful of tea in the caddy, but in the cupboard there was only the heel of a loaf — no butter, no cheese, no jam.

"I'm at the end of my tether," Miss Abbot admitted. "And unless I touch the money laid away for my rent, I haven't a penny in the house."

"Then," said Jean, "it was high time I turned up." She heated the teapot and poked the bit of coal into a blaze. "Now here's your tea" — she reached for her bag that lay in the table — "and here's some money to go on with. Oh, please don't let's go over it all again. Do, my dear, be reasonable."

"I doubt it's charity," said poor Miss Abbot, "but I cannot refuse. Indeed, I don't seem to take it in. . . . I've whiles dreamed something like this, and cried when I wakened. This last year has been something awful — trying to hide my failing sight, and pretending I didn't need sewing when I was near starving and always seeing the workhouse before me. When I got up this morning there seemed to be a high wall in front of me, and I knew I had come to the end. I thought God had forgotten me."

"Not a bit of it," said Jean. "Put away that money like a sensible body, and I'll write to my lawyer today. And the next thing to do is to go with me to an oculist, for your eyes may not be as bad as you think. You know, Miss Abbot, you haven't treated your friends well, keeping them all at arm's length because you were in trouble. Friends do like to be given the chance of being useful. . . . Now I'll tell you what to do. This is a nice fresh day. You go and do some shopping, and be sure and get something nice for your supper, and fresh butter and marmalade and things, and then go for a walk along Tweedside and let the wind blow on you, and then drop in and have a cup of tea and a gossip with one of the friends you've been neglecting lately, and you see if you don't feel heaps better. . . . Remember nobody knows anything about this but you and me. I shan't even tell Mr. Macdonald. . . . You will get papers and things to sign, I expect, from the lawyer, and if you want anything explained you will come to The Rigs, won't you? Perhaps you would rather I didn't come here much. Good-morning, Miss Abbot," and Jean went away. "For all the world," as Miss Abbot said to herself, "as if lifting folk from the miry clay and setting them on a rock was all in the day's work."

The days slipped away and March came and David was home again; such a smart David in new clothes and (like Shakespeare's Town Clerk) "everything handsome about him."

He immediately began to entice Jean into spending money. It was absurd, he said, to have no one but Mrs. M'Cosh: a smart housemaid must be got.

"She would only worry Mrs. M'Cosh," Jean protested, "and there isn't room for another maid, and I hate smart maids anyway. I like to help in the house myself."

"But that's so absurd," said David, "with all your money. You should enjoy life now."

"Yes," said Jean meekly, "but smart maids wouldn't help me to — quite the opposite. . . . And don't you get ideas into your head about smartness, Davie. The Rigs could never be smart: you must go to The Towers for that. So long as we live at The Rigs we must be small, plain people. And I hope I shall live here all my life — and so that's that!"

David, greatly exasperated, bounded from his chair the better to harangue his sister.

"Jean, anybody would think you were a hundred to hear you talk! You'll get nothing out of life except perhaps a text on your tombstone, 'She hath done what she could', and that's a dull prospect. . . . Why aren't you more like other girls? Why don't you do your hair the new way, all sort of — oh I don't know, and wear earrings . . . you know you don't dress smartly."

"No," said Jean.

"And you haven't any tricks. I mean you don't try and attract attention to yourself."

"No," said Jean.

"You don't talk like other girls, and you're not keen on the new dances. I think you like being old-fashioned."

"I'm afraid I'm a failure as a girl," Jean confessed, "but perhaps I'll get more charming as I get older. Look at Pamela!"

"Oh, *Miss Reston*," said David, in the tone that he might have said "Helen of Troy". . . . "But seriously, Jean, I think you are using your money in a very dull way. You see, you're so dashed *helpful*. What makes you want to think all the time about slum children? . . . I think you'd better present your money all in a lump to the Government as a drop in the ocean of the National Debt."

"I'll not give it to the Government," said Jean, "but we may count ourselves lucky if they don't thieve it from us. I'm at one with Bella Bathgate when she says, 'I'm no verra sure aboot thae politicans, Liberal *or* Tory.' I think she fears that any day they may grab Hillview from her."

"Anyway," David persisted, "we might have a car, I learned to drive at Oxford. It would be frightfully useful you know, a little car."

"Useful!" laughed Jean. "Have you written any more, Davie?"

David explained that the term had been a very busy one, and that his time had been too much occupied for any outside work, and Jean understood that the stimulus of poverty having been removed David had fallen into easier ways. And why not — at nineteen?

"We must think about a car. Do you

know all about the different makes? We mustn't be rash."

David assured her that he would make all inquiries, and went out of the room whistling blithely.

Jean, left alone, sat thinking. Was the money to be a treasure to her or the reverse? It was fine to give David what he wanted, to know that Jock and Mhor could have the best of everything, but their wants would grow and grow; simple tastes and habits were easily shed, and luxurious ways easily learned. Would the possession of money spoil the boys? She sighed, and then smiled rather ruefully as she thought of David and his smart maids and motors. It was very natural and very boyish of him. "He'll have the face ett off me," said Jean, quoting the Irish R.M. . . . Richard Plantagenet hadn't minded her being old-fashioned.

It was odd how empty her life felt when it ought to feel so rich. She had the three boys beside her. Pamela was next door; she had all manner of schemes in hand to keep her thoughts occupied — but there was a great want somewhere. Jean owned to herself that the blank had been there ever since Lord Bidborough went away. It was frightfully silly, but there it was; and probably by this time he had quite forgotten her. It had amused him to imagine himself in love, something to pass the time in a dull little town. She knew from books that men had a roving fancy — but even as she said it to herself, her heart rebuked for her disloyalty. Richard Plantagenet's eyes, laughing, full of kindness and honest — oh, honest, she was sure! — looked into hers. She thrilled again as she seemed to feel the touch of his hand and heard his voice saying, "Oh, Penny-plain, are you going to send me away?" Why hadn't he written to congratulate her on the fortune? He might have done that surely . . . And Pamela hardly spoke of him. Didn't seem to think Jean would be interested — Jean, whose heart leapt into her throat at the mere casual mention of his name.

Jean looked up quickly, hearing a step on the gravel. It was Pamela sauntering in, smiling over her shoulder at Mhor, who was swinging on the gate, with Peter by his side.

"Oh, Pamela, I am glad to see you.

David says I am using the money in such a stuffy way. Do you think I am?"

"What does David want you to do?" Pamela asked, as she threw off her coat and knelt before the fire to warm her hands.

" *To eat your supper in a room*
Blazing with lights, four Titians on the wall
And twenty naked girls to change your plate' ?"

Jean laughed. "Something like that, I suppose. Anyway he wants a smart parlour-maid at once, and a motor car. Also he wants me to wear earrings, and talk slang, and wear the newest sort of clothes."

"Poor Penny-plain, are you going to be forced into being twopence coloured? But I think you should get another maid; you have too much to do. And a car would be a great interest to you. Jock and Mhor would love it, too; you could go touring all round in it. You must begin to see the world now. I think, perhaps, David is right. It is rather stuffy to stick in the same place (even if that place is Priorsford) when the whole wide world is waiting to be looked at . . . I remember a dear old curé in Switzerland who, when he retired from his living at the age of eighty, set off to see the world. He told me he did it because he was quite sure when he entered heaven's gate the first question God would put to him would be, 'And what did you think of My world?' and he wanted to be in a position to answer intelligently . . . He was an old dear. When you come to think of it, it is a little ungrateful of you, Jean, not to want to taste all the pleasures provided for the inhabitants of this earth. There is no sense in useless extravagance, but there is a certain fitness in things. A cottage is a delicious thing, but it is meant for the lucky people with small means; the big houses have their uses, too. That's why so many rich people have discontented faces. It's because to them £200 a year and a cottage is 'paradise enow', and they are doomed to the many mansions and the many servants."

Jean nodded. "Mrs. M'Cosh often says, 'There's many a lang gant in a cairriage,' and I dare say it's true. I don't want to be ungrateful, Pamela. I think it's about the worst sin one can commit — ingratitude.

And I don't want to be stuffy, either, but I think I was meant for small ways."

"Poor Penny-plain! Never mind. I'm not going to preach any more. You shall do just as you please with your life. I was remembering, Jean, your desire to go to the Shakespeare Festival at Stratford in April. Why not motor there? It is a lovely run. I meant to take you myself, but I expect you would enjoy it much better if you went with the boys. It would be great fun for you all, and take you away from your philanthropic efforts and let you see round everything clearly."

Jean's eyes lit with interest, and Pamela, seeing the light in them, went on:

"Everybody should make a pilgrimage in spring: it's the correct thing to do. Imagine starting on an April morning, through new roads, among singing birds and cowslips and green new leaves, and stopping at little inns for the night — lovely, Jean."

Jean gave a great sigh.

"Lovely," she echoed. Lovely, indeed, to be away from house-keeping and poor people and known paths for a little, and into leafy Warwick lanes and the rich English country which she had never seen.

"And then," Pamela went on, "you would come back appreciating Priorsford more than you have ever done. You would come back to Tweed and Peel Tower and the Hopetoun Woods with a new understanding. There's nothing so makes you appreciate your home as leaving it . . . Bother! That's the bell. Visitors!"

It was only one visitor — Lewis Elliot.

"Cousin Lewis!" cried Jean. "Where in the world have you been? Three whole months since you went away and never a word from you. You didn't even write to Mrs. Hope."

"No," said Lewis: "I was rather busy." He greeted Pamela and sat down.

"Were you so very busy that you couldn't write as much as a post card? And I don't believe you know that I'm an heiress?"

"Yes: I heard that, but only the other day. It was a most unexpected windfall. I was delighted to hear about it." Jean looked at him and wondered if he were well. His long holiday did not seem to have improved his spirits; he was more absent-minded than usual and disappointingly uninterested.

"I didn't know you were back in Priorsford," he said, addressing Pamela, "till I met your brother in London. I called on you just now, and Miss Bathgate sent me over here."

"Is Biddy amusing himself well?" Pamela asked.

"I should think excellently well. I dined with him one night and he seemed in great spirits. He seemed to be very much in request. He wanted to take me about a bit, but I've got out of London ways. I don't seem to know what to talk about to this new generation, and I yawn. I'm better at home at Laverlaw among the sheep."

Mrs. M'Cosh came in to lay the tea, and Jean said: "You'll have tea here, Cousin Lewis, though this isn't my visit, and then you can go over to Hillview with Pamela and pay your visit to her. You mustn't miss the opportunity of killing two birds with one stone. Besides, Pamela's time in Priorsford is so short now; you mayn't have another chance of paying a visit of ceremony."

"Well, if I may — "

"Yes; do come. I expect Jean has had enough of me for one day. I've been lecturing her . . . By the way, where are the boys today? Mhor was swinging on the gate as I came in. He told me he was going somewhere, but his speech was obstructed by a large piece of toffee, and I couldn't make out what he said."

"He was waiting for Jock," said Jean. "Did you notice that he was very clean, and that his hair was sleeked down with brilliantine? They are invited to bring Peter to tea at the Miss Watsons', and are in great spirits about it. They generally hate going out to tea, but Jock discovered recently that the Watsons had a father who was a sea captain. That fact has thrown such a halo round the two ladies that he can't keep away from them. They have allowed him to go to the attic and rummage in the big sea-chests which, he says, are chockful of treasures like ostrich eggs and lumps of coral and Chinese idols. It seems the Miss Watsons won't have these treasures downstairs as they don't look genteel among the 'new art' ornaments admired in Balmoral. All the treasures are to be on view today (Jock has great hopes of persuading the dear ladies to give him one to bring home, what he calls a 'Chinese scratcher' — it certainly sounds far from genteel) and a gorgeous spread as well — Jock confided to me that he thought there might even be sandwiches; and Peter being invited has filled Mhor's cup of happiness to the brim. So few people welcome that marauder."

"I wish I could be there to hear the conversation," said Pamela. "Jock with his company manners is a joy."

An hour later Lewis Elliot accompanied Pamela back to Hillview.

"It's rather absurd," he protested. "I'm afraid I'm inflicting myself on you, but if you will give me half an hour of your time I shall be grateful."

"You must tell me about Biddy," Pamela said, as she sat down in her favourite chair. "Draw up that basket chair, won't you? and be comfortable. You look as if you were just going to dart away again. Did Biddy say anything in particular?"

"He told me to come and see you . . . I won't take a chair, thanks. I would rather stand . . . Pamela, I know it's the most frightful cheek, but I've cared for you exactly twenty-five years. You never had a notion of it, I know, and of course I never said anything, for to think of your marrying a penniless, dreamy sort of idiot was absurd — you who might have married anybody! I couldn't stay near you, loving you as I did, so I went right out of your life. I don't suppose you ever noticed I had gone; you had always so many round you waiting for a smile . . . I used to read the lists of engagements in *The Times*, dreading to see your name. No; that's not the right word, because I loved you well enough to wish happiness for you, whoever brought it. I sometimes heard of you from one and another, and I never forgot — never for a day. Then my uncle died and my cousin was killed, and I came back to Priorsford and settled down at Laverlaw, and was content and quite fairly happy. The war came, and of course I offered my services. I wasn't much use but, thank goodness, I got out to France and got some fighting — a second lieutenant at forty! It was the first time I had ever felt myself of some real use . . . Then that finished and I was back at Laverlaw among my sheep — and you came to

Priorsford. The moment I saw you, I knew that my love for you was as strong and young as it was twenty years ago . . ."

Pamela sat fingering a fan she had taken up to protect her face from the blaze and looking into the fire.

"Pamela. Have you nothing to say to me?"

"Twenty-five years is a long time," Pamela said, slowly. "I was fifteen then and you were twenty. Twenty years ago I was twenty and you were twenty-five — why didn't you speak then, Lewis? You went away and I thought you didn't care. Does a man never think how awful it is for a woman who has to wait without speaking? You thought you were noble to go away . . . I suppose it must have been for some wise reason that the good God made men blind, but it's hard on the women. You might at least have given me the chance to say No."

"I was a coward. But it was unbelievable that you could care. You never showed me by word or look."

"Was it likely? I was proud and you were blind, so we missed the best. We lost our youth — and I very nearly lost my soul. After you left, nothing seemed to matter but enjoying myself as best I could. I hated the thought of growing old, and I looked at the painted restless faces round me and wondered if they were afraid, too. Then I thought I would marry and have more of a reason for living. A man offered himself — a man with a great position — and I accepted him and it was worse than ever, so I fled from it all — to Priorsford. I loved it from the first, the little town and the river and the hills, and Bella Bathgate's grim honesty and poor cookery! And you came into my life again and I found I couldn't marry the other man and his position . . ."

"Pamela, can you really marry a fool like me? . . . It's my fault that we've missed so much, but thank God we haven't missed everything. I think I could make you happy. I wouldn't ask you to stay at Laverlaw for more than a month or two at a time. We would live in London if you wanted to. I could even stick London if I had you."

Pamela looked at him, with laughter in her eyes.

"And you couldn't say fairer than that, my dear. No, no, Lewis. If I marry you, we'll live at Laverlaw. I love your green glen already; it's a place after my own heart. We won't trouble London much, but spend our declining years among the sheep — unless you become suddenly ambitious for public honours and, as Mrs. Hope desires, enter Parliament."

"There's no saying what I may do now. Already I feel twice the man I was."

They talked in the firelight and Pamela said: "I'm not sure that our happiness won't be the greater because it has come twenty years late. Twenty years ago we would have taken it pretty much as a matter of course. We would have rushed at our happiness and swallowed it whole, so to speak. Now, with twenty lonely, restless years behind us, we shall go slowly, and taste every moment and be grateful. Years bring their compensation . . . It's a funny world. It's a *nice*, funny world."

"I think," said Lewis, "I know something of what Jacob must have felt after he had served all the years, and at last took Rachel by the hand — "

" 'Served' is good," said Pamela in mocking tones. But her eyes were tender.

23

*"It was high spring, and, all the way
Primrosed and hung with shade. . . ."*
HENRY VAUGHAN

*"There is no private house in which people
can enjoy themselves so well as at a capital
tavern . . . No, Sir, there is nothing which
has yet been contrived by man by which so
much happiness is produced as by a good
tavern."*

DR. JOHNSON

PAMELA and David between them
carried the day, and a motor car was
bought. It was not the small useful
car talked about at first, but one which had
greatly taken the fancy of the Jardine
family in the showroom — a large landau-
lette of a well-known make, upholstered
in palest fawn, fitted with every newest
device, very sumptuous and very shiny.

They described it minutely to Pamela
before she went with them to see and fix
definitely.

"It runs beautifully," said David.

"It's about fifty horse-power," said Jock.

"And, Honourable," said Mhor, "it's got electric light inside, just like a little house, and all sorts of lovely things — a clock and — "

"And, I suppose, hot and cold water laid on," said Pamela.

"The worst thing about it," Jean said, "is that it looks *horribly* rich — big and fat and purring — just as if it were saying, 'Out of the way, groundlings.' You know what an insolent look big cars have."

"Your small, deprecating face inside will take away from the effect," Pamela assured her; "and you need a comfortable car to tour about in. When do you go exactly ?"

"On the twentieth," Jean told her. "We take David first to Oxford, or rather he takes us, for he understands maps and can find the road; then we go on to Stratford. I wrote for rooms as you told me, and for seats for the plays, and I have heard from the people that we can have both. I do wish you were coming, Pamela — won't you think better of it ?"

"My dear, I would love it — but it can't be done. I must go to London this week. If we are to be married on first June there are simply multitudes of things to arrange. But I'll tell you what, Jean. I shall come to Stratford for a day or two, when you are there. I shouldn't be a bit surprised if Biddy were there, too. If he happened to be in England in April he always made a pilgrimage to the Shakespeare Festival. Mintern Abbas isn't very far from Stratford, and Mintern Abbas in spring is heavenly. *That's* what we must arrange — a party at Mintern Abbas. You would like that, wouldn't you, Jock?"

"Would Richard Plantagenet be there? I would like awfully to see him again. It's been so dull without him."

Mhor asked if there were any railways near Mintern Abbas, and was rather cast down when told that the nearest railway station was seven miles distant. It amazed him that anyone should, of choice, live away from railways. The skirl of an engine was sweeter to his ears than horns of elfland faintly blowing, and the dream of his life was to be allowed to live in a small whitewashed shanty which he knew of, on the railway-side, where he could spend ecstatic days watching every "passenger" and every "goods" that rushed shrieking, or dawdled shunting, along the permanent way. To him each different train had its own features. "I think," he told Jean, "that the nine train is the most good-natured of the trains; he doesn't care how many carriages and horse-boxes they stick on to him. The twelve train has always a cross, snorty look, but the five train" — his voice took the fondling note that it held for Peter and Barrie, the cat — "that little five train goes much the fastest; he's the hero of the day!"

Pamela's engagement to Lewis Elliot had made, what Mrs. M'Cosh called, "a great speak" in Priorsford. On the whole, it was felt that she had done well for herself. The Elliots were an old and honoured family, and the present laird, though shy and retiring, was much liked by his tenants, and respected by everyone. Pamela had made herself very popular in Priorsford, and people were pleased that she should remain as lady of Laverlaw.

"Ay," said Mrs. M'Cosh, "he's waited lang, but he's waled weel in the end. He's gotten a braw leddy, and she'll no be as flighty as a young yin, for Mr. Elliot likes quiet ways. An' then she has plenty siller, an' that's a help. A rale sensible marriage!"

Bella Bathgate agreed. "It'll mak' a big differ at Laverlaw," she said, "for she's the kind o' body that makes hersel' felt in a hoose. I didna want her at Hillview wi' a' her trunks and her maid and her fal-lals an' her fykey ways, but, d'ye ken, I'll miss her something horrid. She was an awfu' miss in the hoose when she was awa' at Christmas-time; I was fair kinna lost wi'out her. It'll be rale nice for Maister Elliot havin' her aye there. It's mebbe a wakeness on ma pairt, but I whiles mak' messages into the room juist to see her sittin' pittin' stitches into that embroidery, as they ca' it, an' hear her gie that little lauch o' hers! She has me fair bewitched. There's a kinna *glawmour* aboot her. An' I tell ye I culdna stand her by onything at the first . . . I even think her bonnie noo — an' she's no' that auld. I saw a pictur in a paper the ither day of a new-mairit couple, an' *baith o' them had the auld-age pension.*"

Jean looked on rather wistfully at her

friend's happiness. She was most sincerely glad that the wooing — so long delayed — should end like an old play and Jack have his Jill, but it seemed to add to the empty feeling in her own heart. Pamela's casual remark about her brother, perhaps, being at Stratford had filled her for the moment with wild joy; but hearts after leaps ache, and she had quickly reminded herself that Richard Plantagenet had most evidently accepted the refusal as final and would never be anything more to her than Pamela's brother. It was quite as it should be, but life in spite of April and a motor car was, what Mhor called a minister's life, "a dullsome job".

That year's spring came, not reluctantly, as it often does in the uplands, but generously, lavishly, scattering buds and leaves and flowers and lambs, and putting a spirit of youth into everything. The days were as warm as June, and fresh as only April days can be. The Jardines anxiously watched the sun-filled days pass, wishing they had arranged to go earlier, fearful lest they should miss all the good weather. It seemed impossible that it could go on being so wonderful, but day followed day in golden succession and there was no sign of a break.

David spent most of his days at the Depot that held the car, there being no garage at The Rigs, and Jock and Mhor worshipped with him. A chauffeur had been engaged, one Stark, a Priorsford youth, a steady young man and an excellent driver. He had never been farther than Edinburgh.

The 20th came at last. Jock and Mhor were up at an unearthly hour, parading the house, banging at Mrs. M'Cosh's door, and imploring her to rise in case breakfast was late, and thumping the barometer to see if it showed any inclination to fall. The car was ordered for nine o'clock, but they were down the road looking for it at least half an hour before it was due, feverishly anxious in case something had happened either to it or to Stark.

The road before The Rigs was quite crowded that April morning. Mrs. M'Cosh stood at the gate beside the dancing daffodils and the tulips and the opening wallflowers in the border, her hands folded on her spotless white apron, her face beaming with its accustomed kind smile, and watched her family depart.

"Keep a haud o' Peter, Mhor," she cautioned. "Ye needa come back here if ye lose him." The safety of the rest of the party did not seem to concern her.

Mr. and Mrs. Jowett were there, having breakfasted an hour earlier than usual, thus risking the wrath of their cherished domestics. Mrs. Jowett was carrying a large box of chocolates as a parting gift to the boys, while Mr. Jowett had a bottle of lavender water for Jean.

Augusta Hope had walked up from Hopetoun with her mother's love to the travellers, a basket of fruit for the boys, and a book for Jean.

The little Miss Watsons hopped forth from their dwelling with an offering of a home-baked cake, "just in case you get hungry on the road, you know."

Bella Bathgate was there, looking very saturnine, and counselling Mhor as to his behaviour. "Dinna lean oot o' the caur. Mony a body has lost their heid stickin' it oot of a caur. Here's some tea-biscuits for Peter. You'll be ower prood for onything but curranty-cake, I suppose."

Mhor assured her he was not, and gratefully accepted the biscuits. "Isn't it fun

Peter's going? I couldn't have gone either if he hadn't been allowed, but I expect I'll have to hold him in my arms a lot. He'll want to jump out at dogs."

And Mr. and Mrs. Macdonald were there — Mrs. Macdonald absolutely weighed down with gifts. "It's just a trifle for each of you," she explained. "No, no, don't thank me; it's nothing."

"I've brought you nothing but my blessing, Jean," the minister said. "You'll never be better than I wish you."

"Don't talk as if I were going away for good," said Jean, with a lump in her throat. "It's only a little holiday."

"Who can tell?" sighed Mrs. Macdonald. "It's an uncertain world. But we'll hope that you'll come back to us, Jean. Are you sure you are warmly clad? Remember it's only April, and the evenings are cold."

David packed Jean, Jock, and Mhor into the car. Peter was poised on one of the seats that let down, a cushion under him to protect the pale, fawn cloth from his paws. All the presents found places; the luggage was put on the top; Stark took his seat; David, his coat pocket bulging with maps, got in beside him; and amid a chorus of good-byes they were off.

Jean, looking back rather wistfully at The Rigs, got a last sight of Mrs. M'Cosh shaking her head dubiously at the departing car.

One of the best things in life is to start on a spring morning for a holiday. To Jock and Mhor at least life seemed a very perfect thing as the car slid down the hill, over Tweed Bridge, over Cuddy Bridge, and turned sharp to the left up the Old Town. Soon they were out of the little grey town that looked so clean and fresh with its shining morning face, and running through the deep woods above Peel Tower. Small children creeping unwillingly to school stopped to watch them, and Mhor looked at them pityingly. School seemed a thing so far removed from his present happy state as not to be worth remembering. Somewhere, doubtless, unhappy little people were learning the multiplication table, and struggling with the spelling of uncouth words, but Mhor, sitting in state in "Wilfred the Gazelle" (for so David had christened the new car), could only spare them a passing thought.

He looked at Peter sitting self-consciously virtuous on the seat opposite, he leaned across Jean to send a glance of profound satisfaction to Jock, then he raked from his pocket a cake of butter-scotch and sank back in his seat to crunch in comfort.

They followed Tweed as it ran by wood and field and hamlet, and as they reached the moorlands of the upper reaches Jean began to notice that Wilfred the Gazelle was not running as smoothly as usual. Perhaps it was imagination, Jean thought, or perhaps it was the effect of having luggage on the top; but in her inmost heart she knew it was more than that, and she was not surprised.

Jean was filled with a deep-seated distrust of motors. She felt that every motor was just waiting its chance to do its owner harm. She had started with no real hope of reaching any destination, and expected nothing less than to spend the night camping inside the car in some lonely spot. She had all provisions made for such an occurrence.

Jock said suddenly, "We're not going more than ten miles an hour," and then the car stopped altogether and David and Stark got down. Jean leaned out and asked what was wrong, and David said shortly that there was nothing wrong.

Presently he and Stark got back into their places and the car was started again. But it went slowly, haltingly, like a bird with a broken wing. They made up on a man driving a brown horse in a wagonette — a man with a brown beard and a cheerful eye — and passed him.

The car stopped again.

Again David and Stark got out and stared and poked and consulted together. Again Jean's head went out, and again she received the same short and unsatisfactory answer.

The brown bearded man and his wagonette made up on them, looked at the car in an interested way, and passed on.

Again the car started, passed the wagonette, and went on for about a mile and stopped.

Again Jean's head went out.

"David," she said, "what *is* the matter?" and it goes far to show how harassed that polished Oxonian was when he replied, "If you don't take your face out of that I'll slap it."

Jean withdrew at once, feeling that she

had been tactless and David had been unnecessarily rude — David who had never been rude to her since they were children, and had told each other home-truths without heat and without ill-feeling on either side. If this was to be the effect of owning a car —

"Wilfred the Gazelle's dead," said Mhor, and got out, followed by Jock, and in a minute or two by Jean.

They all sat down in the heather by the roadside.

Dead car notwithstanding, it was delicious sitting there in the spring sunshine. Tweed was nearing its source and was now only a trickling burn. A lark was singing high up in the blue. The air was like new wine. The lambs were very young, for spring comes slowly up that way, and one tottering little fellow was found by Mhor, and carried rapturously to Jean.

"Take it; it's just born," he said. "Jock, hold Peter tight in case he bites them."

"Did you ever see anything quite so new?" Jean said as she stroked the little head, "and yet so independent? Sheep are far before mortals. Its eyes looked so perplexed, Mhor. It's quite strange to the world and doesn't know what to make of it. That's it's mother over there. Take it to her; she's crying for it."

David came up and stood looking gloomily at the lamb. Perhaps he envied it being so young and careless and motor-less.

"Stark's busy with the car," he announced, rather needlessly, as the fact was apparent to all. "I'm dashed if I know what's the matter with the old 'bus . . . Here's that man again . . ."

Jean burst into helpless laughter as the wagonette again overtook them. The driver flourished his whip and the horse broke into a canter — it looked like derision.

There was a long silence — then Jean said:

"If it won't go, it's too big to move. We shall have to train ivy on it and make it a feature of the landscape."

"Or else," said David, savagely and irreverently — "or else hew it in pieces before the Lord."

Stark got up and straightened himself, wiped his hands and his forehead, and came, to David.

"I've found out what's wrong," he said.

"She'll manage to Moffat, but we'll have to get her put right there. It's . . ." He went into technical details incomprehensible to Jean.

They got back into the car and it sprang away as if suddenly endowed with new life. In a trice they had passed the wagonette, leaving it in a whirl of scornful dust. They ate the miles as a giant devours sheep. They passed the Devil's Beef Tub — Jock would have liked to tarry there and investigate, but Jean dared not ask Stark to stop in case they could not start again — and soon went sliding down the hill to Moffat. Hot puffs of scented air rose from the valley, they had left the moorlands and the winds, and the town was holding out arms to welcome them. They drove along the sunny, sleepy, midday High Street and stopped at an hotel.

Except David, no member of the Jardine family had ever been inside an hotel, and it was quite an adventure for them to go up the steps from the street, enter the swinging doors, and ask a polite woman, with elaborately done hair, if they might have luncheon. Yes, they might, and Peter, at present held tightly in Mhor's arms, could be fed in the kitchen if that would suit.

Stark had meantime taken the car to a motor-repairing establishment.

It was half-past three before the car came swooping up to the hotel doors. Jean gazed at it, with a sort of fearful pride. It looked very well if only it didn't play them false. Stark too, looked well — a fine impassive figure.

"Will it be all right, Stark?" she ventured to inquire, but Stark, who rarely committed himself, merely said, "Mebbe."

Stark had no manners, Jean reflected, but he had a nice face and was a teetotaller, and one can't have everything.

To Mhor's joy the road now ran for a bit by the side of the railway line, where thundered great express trains such as there never were in Priorsford. They were spinning along the fine level road, making up for lost time, when a sharp report startled them and made Mhor, who was watching a train, lose his balance and fall forward on to Peter, who was taking a sleep on the rug at their feet.

It was a tyre gone, and there was not time to mend it if they were to be at

Carlisle in time for tea. Stark put on the spare wheel and they started again.

Fortune seemed to have got tired of persecuting them, and there were no further mishaps. They ran without a pause through village after village, snatching glimpses of lovely places where they would fain have lingered, forgetting them as each place offered new beauties.

The great excitement to Jock and Mhor was the crossing of the border.

"I did it once," said Mhor, "when I came from India, but I didn't notice it."

"Rather not," said Jock; "you were only two. I was four, wasn't I, Jean? when I came from India, and I didn't notice it."

"Is there a line across the road?" Mhor asked. "And do the people speak Scots on one side and English on the other? I suppose we'll go over with a bump."

"There's nothing to show," Jock told him, "but there's a difference in the air. It's warmer in England."

"It's very uninterested of Peter to go on sleeping," Mhor said in a disgusted tone. "You would think he would feel there was something happening. And he's a Scot's dog, too."

The Border was safely crossed, and Jock professed to notice at once a striking difference in air and landscape.

"There's an English feel about things now," he insisted, sniffing and looking all round him; "and I hear the English voices . . . Mhor, this is how the Scots came over to fight the English, only at night and on horseback — into Carlisle Castle."

"And I was English," said Mhor, dreamily; "and I had a big black horse and I pranced on the Castle wall and killed everyone that came."

"You needn't boast about being English," Jock said, looking at Mhor, coldly. "I don't blame you, for you can't help it, but it's a pity."

Mhor's face got very pink and there was a tremble in his voice, though he said in a bragging tone, "I'm glad I'm English. The English are as brave as — as — "

"Of course they are," said Jean, holding Mhor's hand tight under the rug. She knew how it hurt him to be, even for a moment, at variance with Jock, his idol. "Mhor has every right to be proud of being English, Jock. His father was a soldier and he has ancestors who were great fighting men.

And you know very well that it doesn't matter what side you belong to, so long as you are loyal to that side. You two would have had some great fights if you had lived a few hundred years ago."

"Yes," said Mhor. "I'd have killed a great many Scots — but not Jock."

"Ho," said Jock, "a great many Scots would have killed you first."

"Well, it's all past," said Jean; "and England and Scotland are one, and fight together now. This is Carlisle. Not much romance about it now, is there? We're going to the Station Hotel for tea, so you will see the train, Mhor, old man."

"Mhor," said Jock, "there's one thing you would have missed if you'd lived long ago — trains."

The car had to have a tyre repaired and that took some time, so after tea the Jardines stood in the station and watched trains for what was, to Mhor at least, a blissful hour. It was thrilling to stand in the half-light of the big station and see great trains come in, and the passengers jump out and tramp about the platform and buy books and papers from the bookstall, or fruit, or chocolate, or tea and buns from the boys in uniform, who went about crying their wares. And then the wild scurrying of the passengers — like hens before a motor, Jock said — when the flag was waved and the train about to start. Mhor hoped fervently, and a little unkindly that at least one might be left behind; but they all got in, though with some it was the last second of the eleventh hour. There seemed to be hundreds of porters wheeling luggage on trolleys, guards walked about looking splendid fellows, and Mhor's eyes as he beheld them were the eyes of a lover on his mistress. He could hardly be torn away when David came to say that Stark was waiting with the car and that they could not hope to get farther than Penrith that night.

The dusk was falling and the vesper-bell ringing as they drove into the town and stopped before a very comfortable-looking inn.

It was past Mhor's bedtime, and it seemed to that youth a fit ending for the most exciting day of his whole seven years of life, to sit up and partake of mutton-chops and apple-tart at an hour when he should have been sound asleep.

He saw Peter safely away in charge of a sympathetic "boots" before he and Jock ascended to a bedroom, with three small windows in the most unexpected places; a bright, cheery paper; and two small white beds.

Next morning the sun peeped in at all the odd-shaped windows on the two boys sprawled over their beds, in the attitudes in which they said they best enjoyed slumber.

It was another crystal-clear morning, with mist in the hollows and the hill-tops sharp against the sky. When Stark, taciturn as ever, came to the door at nine o'clock, he found his party impatiently awaiting him on the doorstep, eager for another day of new roads and fresh scenes.

Jean asked him, laughingly, if Wilfred the Gazelle would live up to his name this run, but Stark received the pleasantry coldly, having no use for archness in any form.

It was wonderful to rush through the morning air, still sharp from a touch of frost in the night, ascending higher and higher into the hills. Mhor sang to himself in sheer joy of heart, and though no one knew what were the words he sang, and

Jock thought poorly of the tune, Peter snuggled up to him and seemed to understand and like it.

The day grew hot and dusty as they ran down from the Lake district, and they were glad to have their lunch beside a noisy, little burn in a green meadow, from the well-stocked luncheon-basket provided by the Penrith inn. Then they dipped into the black country, where tall chimneys belched out smoke, and car-lines ran along the streets, and pale-faced, hurrying people looked enviously at the big car with its load of youth and good looks. Everything was grim and dirty and spoiled. Mhor looked at the grimy place and said solemnly:

"It reminds me of hell."

"Haw, haw!" laughed Jock. "When did you see hell last?"

"In the *Pilgrim's Progress*," said Mhor.

One of the black towns provided tea in a café which purported to be Japanese, but the only things about it that recalled that sunny island overseas were the paper napkins, the china, and two fans nailed on the wall; the linoleum-covered floor, the hard wooden chairs, the fly-blown buns being peculiarly and bleakly British.

Before evening the grim country was left behind.

In the soft April twilight they crossed wide moorlands (which Jock was inclined to resent as being "too Scots to be English") until, as it was beginning to get dark, they slid softly into Shrewsbury.

The next day was as fine as ever. "Really," said Jean, as they strolled before breakfast, watching the shops being opened and studying the old timbered houses, "it's getting almost absurd: like Father's story of the soldier who greeted his master every morning in India with 'Another hot day, sirr'. We thought if we got one good day out of the three we were to be on the road we wouldn't grumble, and here it goes on and on . . . We must come back to Shrewsbury, Davie. It deserves more than just to be slept in . . ."

"Aren't English breakfasts the best you ever tasted?" David asked as they sat down to rashers of home-cured ham, corpulent brown sausages, and eggs poached to a nicety.

So far David had made an excellent guide. They had never once diverged from the road they meant to take, but this third

444

day of the run turned out to be somewhat confused. They started off almost at once on the wrong road and found themselves riding up a deep, green lane into a farmyard. Out again on the highway David found the number of crossroads terribly perplexing. Once he urged Stark to ask directions from a cottage. Stark did so and leapt back into his seat.

"Which road do we take?" David asked, as five offered themselves.

"Didna catch what they said," Stark remarked as he chose a road at random.

"Didna catch it," was Stark's favourite response to everything. Later on they came to the top of a steep hill ornamented by an enormous warning-post with this alarming notice — "Cyclists dismount. Many accidents. Some fatal." Stark went on unconcernedly, and Jean shouted at him, holding desperately to the side of the car, as if her feeble strength would help the brakes. "Stark! Stark! Didn't you see that placard?"

"Didna catch it," said Stark, as he swung lightheartedly down an almost perpendicular hill into the valley of the Severn.

"I do think Stark's a fool," said Jean,

bitterly, wrathful in the reaction from her fright. "He does no damage on the road, and of course I'm glad of that. I've seen him stop dead for a hen, and the wayfaring man, though a fool, is safe from him, but he cares nothing for what happens to the poor wretched people *inside* the car. As nearly as possible he had us over the parapet of that bridge."

And later, when they found from the bill at lunch-time that Stark's luncheon had consisted of "one mineral", she thought that the way he had risked all their lives must have taken away his appetite.

The car ran splendidly that day — David said it was getting into its stride — and they got to Oxford for tea and had time to go and see David's rooms before they left for Stratford. But David would let them see nothing else. "No," he said; "it would be a shame to hurry over your first sight. You must come here after Stratford. I'll take rooms for you at the Mitre. I want to show you Oxford on a May morning."

It was quite dark when they reached Stratford. To Jean it seemed strange and delicious thus to enter Shakespeare's own town, the Avon a-glimmer in the meadows.

The lights of the Shakespeare Hotel shone cheerily as they came forward. A "boots" with a wrinkled, whimsical face came out to help them in. Shaded lights and fires (for the evenings were chilly) made a bright welcome, and they were led across the stone-paved hall with its oaken rafters, gate-legged tables, and bowls of spring flowers, up a steep little staircase hung with old prints of the plays, down winding passages to the rooms allotted to them. Jean looked eagerly at the name on her door.

"Hurrah! I've got 'Rosalind'. I wanted her most of all."

Jock and Mhor had a room with two beds, rather incongruously called "Anthony and Cleopatra". Jock was inclined to be affronted, and said it was a silly-looking thing to put him in a room called after such an amorous couple. If it had been Touchstone, or Mercutio, or even Shylock, he would not have minded, but the pilgrims of love got scant sympathy from that sturdy misogynist.

24

"It was a lover and his lass,
With a hey and a ho, and a hey nonnio,
That o'er the green corn-fields did pass
In the spring-time, the only pretty
ring-time. . . . "
"AS YOU LIKE IT"

NEXT morning Jean's eyes wandered round the dining-room as if looking for someone, but there was no one she had ever seen before among the breakfasters at the little round tables in the pretty room, with its low ceiling and black oak beams. To Jean, unused to hotel life and greatly interested in her kind, it was like a peep into some thrilling book. She could hardly eat her breakfast for studying the faces of her neighbours and trying to place them at their various social levels.

Were they all ardent lovers of Shakespeare ? she wondered earnestly.

The people at the next table certainly looked as if they might be: a high-browed, thin-faced clergyman, with a sister who was clever (from her eyeglasses and the way her hair was done, Jean decided she must be very clever), and a friend with them who looked literary — at least he had a large pile of letters and a clean-shaven face; and they seemed, all three, like Lord Lilac, to be "remembering him like anything".

There were several clergymen in the room; one rather fat, with a smug look and a smartly dressed wife, Jean decided must have married an heiress; another, with very prominent teeth and kind eyes, was accompanied by an extremely aged mother and two lean sisters.

One family partly attracted Jean very much: a young-looking father and mother, with two girls, very pretty and newly grown up, and a boy like Davie. They were making plans for the day, deciding what to see and what to leave unseen, laughing a great deal, and chaffing each other, parents and children together. They looked so jolly and happy as if they had always found the world a comfortable and amusing place. They seemed rather amused to find themselves at Stratford among the worshippers. Jean concluded that they were of those "not bad of heart", who "remembered Shakespeare with a start".

Jock and Mhor were in the highest spirits. It seemed to them enormous fun to be staying in an hotel, and not an ordinary square, up-and-down hotel, but a rambling place with little stairs in unexpected places, and old parts and new parts, and bedrooms owning names, and a long, low-roofed drawing-room with a window at the far end that opened right out to the stable-yard through which pleasantries could be exchanged with grooms and chauffeurs. There was a parlour, too, off the hall — the cosiest of parlours with cream walls and black oak beams and supports, two fire-places round which were grouped inviting arm-chairs, tables with books and papers, many bowls of daffodils. And all over the house hung old prints of scenes in the plays; glorious pictures, some of them — ghosts and murders over which Mhor gloated.

They went before luncheon to the river and sailed up and down in a small steam-launch named *The Swan of Avon*. Jean thought privately that the presence of such things as steam-launches were a blot on Shakespeare's river, but the boys were delighted with them, and at once began to plan how one might be got to adorn Tweed.

In the afternoon they walked over the fields to Shottery to see Anne Hathaway's cottage.

Jean walked in a dream. On just such an April day, when shepherds pipe on oaten straws, Shakespeare himself must have walked here. It would be different, of course; there would be no streets of little, mean houses, only a few thatched cottages. But the larks would be singing as they were today, and the hawthorn coming out, and the spring flowers abloom in Anne Hathaway's garden.

She caught her breath as they went out of the sunshine into the dim interior of the cottage.

This ingle-nook . . . Shakespeare must have sat here on winter evenings and talked. Did he tell Anne Hathaway wonderful tales? Perhaps, when he was not writing and weaving for himself a garment of immortality, he was just an everyday man, genial with his neighbours, interested in all the small events of his own town, just Master Shakespeare whom the children looked up from their play to smile at as he passed.

"Oh, Jock," Jean said, clutching her brother's sleeve. "Can you really believe that *he* sat here? — actually in this little room? Looked out of the window — isn't it *wonderful*, Jock?"

Jock, like Mr. Fearing, ever wakeful on the enchanted ground, rolled his head uncomfortably, sniffed, and said, "It smells musty!" Both he and Mhor were frankly much more interested in the fact that confectionery, ginger-beer and biscuits were to be had in the cottage next door.

They mooned about all afternoon vastly content, and had tea in the garden of a sort of enchanted cottage (with a card in the window which bore the legend, *"We sell home-made lemonade, lavender, and pot-pourri"*), among apple trees and spring flowers and singing birds, and ate home-made bread and honey, and cakes with orange icing on them. A girl in a blue gown, who might have been Sweet Anne Page, waited on them, and Jean was so distressed at the amount they had eaten and at the smallness of the bill presented that she slipped an extra large tip under a plate, and fled before it could be discovered. It was a red-letter day for all three, for they were going to the theatre that night for the first time. Jean had once been at a play with her father, but it was so long ago as to be the dimmest memory, and she was as excited as the boys. Their first play was to be *As You Like It*. Oh, lucky young people to see, for the first time on an April evening, in Shakespeare's own town, the youngest, gayest play that ever was written!

They ran up to their rooms to dress, talking and laughing. They could not be silent, their hearts were so light. Jean sang softly to herself as she laid out what she meant to wear that evening. Pamela had made her promise to wear a white frock, the merest wisp of a frock made of lace and georgette, with a touch of vivid green, and a wreath of green leaves for the golden-brown head. Jean had protested. She was afraid she would look overdressed: a black frock would be more suitable; but Pamela had insisted and Jean had promised.

As she looked in the glass she smiled at the picture she made. It was a pity Pamela couldn't see how successful the frock was, for she had designed it . . . Lord Bidborough had never seen her prettily dressed. Why did Pamela never mention him? Jean realised the truth of the old saying, "Speak weel o' ma love, speak ill o' ma love, but aye speak o' him."

She looked into the boys' room when she was ready and found them only half dressed and engaged in a game of cockfighting. Having admonished them she went down alone. She went very slowly down the last flight of stairs (she was shy of going into the dining-room) — a slip of a girl crowned with green leaves. Suddenly she stopped. There, in the hall watching her, alone but for the "boots" with the wrinkled, humorous face and eyes of amused tolerance, was Richard Plantagenet.

Behind her where she stood hung a print of *Lear* — the hovel on the heath, the storm-bent trees, the figure of the old man, the shivering Fool with his "Poor Tom's a'cold". Beside her, fastened to the wall, was a letter-box, with a glass front full of letters and picture-cards waiting to be taken to the evening post. Tragedy and the commonplace things of life — but Jean, for the moment, was lifted far from either. She was seeing a new heaven and a new earth. Words were not needed. She looked into Richard Plantagenet's eyes and knew that he wanted her, and she put her hands out to him like a trusting child.

When Jock and Mhor reached the dining-room and found Richard Plantagenet seated beside Jean they were rapturous in their greetings, pouring questions on him, demanding to know how long he meant to stay.

"As long as you stay," he told them.

"Oh, good," Jock said greatly pleased. "Are you *fearfully* keen on Shakespeare? Jean's something awful. It gives me a sort of hate at him to hear it."

"Oh, Jock," Jean protested, "surely not. I'm not nearly as bad as some of the people here. I don't haver quite so much . . . I was in the drawing-room this morning and heard two women talking, an English woman and an American. The English woman remarked casually that Shakespeare wasn't a Christian, and the American protested, 'Oh, don't say. He had a great White Soul.'"

"Gosh, Maggie!" said Jock. "What a beastly thing to say about anybody! If Shakespeare could see Stratford now I expect he'd laugh — all the shops full of little heads, and pictures of his house, and models of his birthplace . . . it's enough to put anybody off being a genius."

"I was dreadfully snubbed in a shop today," said Jean, smiling at her lover. "It was a very nice mixed-up shop with cakes and crucifixes and little stucco figures, presided over by a dignified lady with black lace on her head. I remembered Mrs. Jowett's passion for stucco saints in her bedroom, and picked one up, remarking that it would be a nice remembrance of Stratford. 'Oh, surely not, madam,' said the shocked voice of the shoplady, 'surely a nobler memory' — and I found *it was a figure of Christ*."

"Jean simply rushed out of the shop," said Jock, "and she hadn't paid, and I had to go in again with the money."

"See what I've got," Mhor said, producing a parcel from his pocket. He unwrapped it, revealing a small cream-coloured bust of Shakespeare.

"It's a wee Shakespeare to send to Mrs.

M'Cosh — and I've got a card for Bella Bathgate — a funny one, a pig. Read it."

He handed the card to Lord Bidborough, who read aloud the words issuing from the mouth of the pig:

"You may push me
You may shove,
But I never will be druv
From Stratford on Avon."

"Excellent sentiment, Mhor — Miss Bathgate will be pleased."

"Yes," said Mhor complacently. "I thought she'd like a pig better than a Shakespeare one. She said she wondered Jean would go and make a fuss about the place a play-actor was born in. She says she wouldn't read a word he wrote, and she didn't seem to like the bits I said to her . . . This isn't the first time, Richard Plantagenet, I've sat up for dinner."

"Isn't it?"

"No. I did it at Penrith and Shrewsbury and last night here."

"By Jove, you're a man of the world now, Mhor."

"It mustn't go on," said Jean, "but once in a while . . ."

"And d'you know where I'm going to-night?" Mhor went on. "To a theatre to see a play. Yes. And I shan't be in bed till at least eleven o'clock. It's the first time in my life I've ever been outside after ten o'clock, and I've always wanted to see what it was like so late at night."

"No different from any other time," Jock told him. But Mhor shook his head. He knew better. After-Ten-O'clock Land *must* be different . . .

"This a great night for us all," Jean said. "Our first play. You have seen it often, I expect. Are you going?"

"Of course I'm going. I wouldn't miss Jock's face at a play for anything . . . Or yours," he added, leaning towards her. "No Mhor. There's no hurry. It doesn't begin for another half-hour . . . we'll have coffee in the other room."

Mhor was in a fever of impatience, and quite ten minutes before the hour they were in their seats in the front row of the balcony. Oddly enough, Lord Bidborough's seat happened to be adjoining the seats taken by the Jardines, and Jean and he sat together.

It was a crowded house, for the play was being played by a new company for the first time that night. Jean sat silent, much too content to talk, watching the people round her, and listening idly to snatches of conversation. Two women, evidently inhabitants of the town, were talking behind her.

"Yes," one woman was saying; "I said to my sister only today, 'What would we do if there was a sudden alarm in the night?' If we needed a doctor or a policeman? You know, my dear, the servants are as old as we are. I don't really believe there is anyone in our road that can run."

The other laughed comfortably and agreed, but Jean felt chilled a little, as if a cloud had obscured for a second the sun of her happiness. In this gloriously young world of unfolding leaves and budding hawthorns and lambs and singing birds and lovers, there were people old and done who could only walk slowly in the sunshine, in whom the spring could no longer put a spirit of youth, who could not run without being weary. How ugly age was? Grim, menacing: Age, I do abhor thee ...

The curtain went up.

The youngest son of Sir Rowland de

Boys, the young Orlando, "a youth un-schooled and yet learned, full of noble device, of all sorts enchantingly beloved," talked to old Adam, and then to his own most unnatural brother. The scene changed to the lawn before the Duke's palace. Lord Bidborough bade Jean observe the scenery and dresses. "You see how simple it is, and vivid, rather like Noah's Ark scenery? And the dresses are a revolt against the stuffy tradition that made Rosalind a sort of principal boy . . . Those dresses are all copied from old missals . . . I rather like it. Do you approve?"

Jean was not in a position to judge, but she approved with all her heart.

Rosalind and Celia were saying the words she knew so well. Touchstone had come in — that witty knave; Monsieur le Beau, with his mouth full of news; and again, the young Orlando o'erthrowing more than his enemies.

And now Rosalind and Celia are planning their flight . . . It is the Forest of Arden. Again Orlando and Adam speak together, and Adam, with all his years brave upon him, assures his master, "My age is as a lusty winter, frosty but kindly."

The words came to Jean with a new significance. How Shakespeare *knew* . . . why should she mourn because Age must come? Age was beautiful and calm, for the seas are quiet when the winds give o'er. Age is done with passions and discontents and strivings. Probably those women behind her who had sighed comfortably because nobody in their road could run, whom she pitied, wouldn't change with her tonight. They had had their life. It wasn't sad to be old, Jean told herself, for as the physical sight dims, the soul sees more clearly, and the light from the world to come illumines the last dark bit of the way . . .

They went out between the acts and walked by the river in the moonlight and talked of the play.

Jock and Mhor were loud in their approval, only regretting that Touchstone couldn't be all the time on the stage. Lord Bidborough asked Jean if it came up to her expectations.

"I don't know what I expected . . . I never imagined any play could be so vivid and gay and alive . . . I've always loved Rosalind, and I didn't think any actress could be quite my idea of her, but this girl is. I thought at first she wasn't nearly pretty enough, but she has the kind of face that becomes more intelligent the more you look at it, and she is so graceful and witty and impertinent."

"And Rabelaisian," added her companion. "It really is a very good show. There is a sort of youthful freshness about the acting that is very engaging. And every part is so competently filled. Jacques is astonishingly good, don't you think? I never heard the 'seven ages' speech so well said."

"It sounded," Jean said, "as if he were saying the words for the first time, thinking them as he went along."

"I know what you mean. When the great lines come on it's a temptation to the actor to draw himself together and clear his throat, and rather address them to the audience. This fellow leaned against a tree and, as you say, seemed to be thinking them as he went along. He's an uncommonly good actor . . . I don't know when I enjoyed a show so much."

The play wore on to its merry conclusion; all too short the Jardines found it.

Jock's wrath at the love-sick shepherd knew no bounds, but he highly approved of Rosalind because, he said, she had such an impudent face.

"Who did you like best, Richard Plantagenet?" Mhor asked as they came down the steps.

"Well, on consideration, I think perhaps the most worthy character was 'the old religious man' who converted so opportunely the Duke Frederick."

"Yes," Jean laughed. "I like that way of getting rid of an objectionable character and enriching a deserving one. But Jaques went off to throw in his lot with the converted Duke. I rather grudged that happening."

"Tomorrow," said Mhor, who was skipping along, very wide awake and happy in After-Ten-O'clock Land — "tomorrow I'm going to take Peter to the river and let him snowk after water-rats. I think he's feeling lonely — a Scots dog among so many English people."

"Stark's lonely too," said Jock. "He says the other chauffeurs have an awful queer accent and it's all he can do to understand what they say."

"Oh, poor Stark!" said Jean. "I don't

suppose he would care much to see the plays."

"He told me," Jock went on, "that one of the other chauffeurs had asked him to go with him to a concert called *Macbeth*. When I told him what it was he said he'd had an escape. He says he sees enough of Shakespeare in this place without going to hear him. He's at the pictures tonight, and there's a circus coming — "

"And oh, Jean, cried Mhor, "it's the *very one* that came to Priorsford!"

"Take a start, Mhor," said Jock, "and I'll race you back to the hotel."

Lord Bidborough and Jean walked on in silence.

At the garden where once had stood New Place — that "pretty house in brick and timber" — the shadow of the Norman Church lay black on the white street and beyond it was the velvet darkness of the old trees.

"This," Jean said softly, "must be almost exactly as it was in Shakespeare's time. He must have seen the shadow of the tower falling like that, and the trees, and his garden. Perhaps it was on an April night like this that he wrote:

> *'On such a night*
> *Stood Dido with a willow in her hand*
> *Upon the wild sea banks and waft her lover*
> *To come again to Carthage.'* "

They had both stopped, and Jean, after a glance at her companion's face, edged away. He caught her hands and held her there in the shadow.

"The last time we were together, Jean, it was December, dripping rain and mud, and you would have none of me. Tonight — in such a night, Jean I come again to you. I love you. Will you marry me ?"

"Yes," said Jean — "for I am yours."

For a minute they stood caught up to the seventh heaven, knowing nothing except that they were together, hearing nothing but the beating of their own hearts.

Jean was the first to come to herself.

"Everyone's gone home. The boys'll think we are lost . . . Oh, Biddy, have I done right ? Are you sure you want me ? Can I make you happy ?"

"*Can you make me happy ?* My blessed child, what a question ! Don't you know that you seem to me almost too dear for my possessing ? You are far too good for me, but I won't give you up now. No, not though all the King's horses and all the King's men come in array against me. My Jean . . . my little Jean."

Jock's comment on hearing of his sister's engagement was that he did think Richard Plantagenet was above that sort of thing. Later on, when he had got more used to the idea, he said that, seeing he had to marry somebody, it was better to be Jean than anybody else.

Mhor, like Gallio, cared for none of these things.

He merely said, "Oh, and will you be married and have a brides-cake? What fun! . . . You might go with Peter and me to the station and see the London trains pass. Jock went yesterday and he says he won't go again for three days. Will you, Jean? Oh, *please* — "

David, at Oxford, sent his sister a letter which she put away among her chiefest treasures. Safely in his room, with a pen in his hand, he would write what he was too shy and awkward to say: he could call down blessings on his sister in a letter, when face to face with her would have been dumb.

Pamela, on hearing the news, rushed down from London to congratulate Jean and her Biddy in person. She was looking what Jean called 'fearfully London", and seemed in high spirits.

"Of course I'm in high spirits," she told Jean. "The very nicest thing in the world has come to pass. I didn't think there was a girl living that I could give Biddy to without a grudge till I saw you, and then it seemed much too good to be true that you should fall in love with each other."

"But," said Jean, "how could you want him to marry me, an ordinary girl in a little provincial town? — he could have married *anybody*."

"Lots of girls would have married Biddy, but I wanted him to have the best, and when I found it for him he had the sense to recognise it. Well, it's rather like a fairy-tale. And I have Lewis! Jean, you can't think how differently life in London seems now — I can enjoy it whole-heartedly, fling myself into it in a way I never could before, not even when I was at my most butterfly stage, because now it isn't my life, it doesn't really matter, I'm only a stranger within the gates. My real life is

Lewis, and the thought of the green glen and the little town beside the Tweed."

"You mean," said Jean, "that you can enjoy all the gaieties tremendously because they are only an episode; if it was your life-work making a success of them you would be bored to death."

"Yes. Before I came to Priorsford they were all I had to live for, and I got to hate them. When are you two babes in the wood going to be married? You haven't talked about it yet? Dear me!"

"You see," Jean said, "there's been such a lot to talk about."

"Philanthropic schemes, I suppose?"

Jean started guiltily.

"I'm afraid not. I'd forgotten about the money."

"Then I'm sorry I reminded you of it. Let all the schemes alone for a little, Jean. Biddy will help you when the time comes. I see the two of you reforming the world, losing all your money, probably, and ending up at Laverlaw with Lewis and me. I don't want to know what you talked about, my dear, but whatever it was it has done you both good. Biddy looks now as he looked before the War, and you have lost your anxious look, and your curls have got more yellow in them, and your eyes aren't like moss-agates now; they are almost quite golden. You are infinitely prettier than you were, Jean girl . . . Now, I'm afraid I must fly back to London. Jock and Mhor will chaperone you two excellently, and we'll all meet at Mintern Abbas in the middle of May."

One sunshine day followed another. Wilfred the Gazelle and the excellent Stark carried the party on exploring expeditions all over the countryside. In one delicious village they wandered, after lunch at the inn, into the little church which stood embowered among the blossoming trees. The old vicar left his garden and offered to show them its beauties, and Jean fell in love with the simplicity and the feeling of homeliness that was about it.

"Biddy," she whispered, "what a delicious church to be married in. You could hardly help being happy ever after if you were married here.

Later in the day, when they were alone, he reminded her of her words.

"Why shouldn't we, Penny-plain? Why shouldn't we? I know you hate a fussy marriage and dread all the letters and presents and meeting crowds of people who are strangers to you. Of course, it's frightfully good of Mrs. Hope to offer to have it at Hopetoun, but that means waiting, and this is the spring-time, the real 'pretty ring-time'. I would rush to London and get a special licence. I don't know how in the world it's done, but I can find out, and Pam would come, and David, and we'd be married in the little church among the blossoms. Let's say the thirtieth. That gives us four days to arrange things . . ."

"Four days," said Jean, "to prepare for one's wedding!"

"But you don't need to prepare. You've got lovely clothes, and we'll go straight to Mintern Abbas, where it doesn't matter what we wear. I tell you what, we'll go to London tomorrow and see lawyers and things — do you realise you haven't even got an engagement ring, you neglected child? And tell Pam — Mad? Of course, it's mad. It's the way they did it in the Golden World. It's Rosalind and Orlando. Be persuaded, Penny-plain."

"Priorsford will be horrified," said Jean. "They aren't used to such indecorous haste, and oh, Biddy, I *couldn't be married* without Mr. Macdonald."

"I was thinking about that. He certainly has the right to be at your wedding. If I wired today, do you think they would come? Mrs. Macdonald's such a sportsman, I believe she would hustle the minister and herself off at once."

"I believe she would," said Jean, "and having them would make all the difference. It would be almost like having my own father and mother . . ."

So it was arranged. They spend a hectic day in London which almost reduced Jean to idiocy, and got back at night to the peace of Stratford. Pamela said she would bring everything that was needed, and would arrive on the evening of the 29th with Lewis and David. The Macdonalds wired that they were coming, and Lord Bidborough interviewed the vicar of the little church among the blossoms and explained everything to him. The vicar was old and wise and tolerant, and he said he would feel honoured if the Scots minister would officiate with him. He would, he said, be pleased to arrange things exactly as Jean and her minister wanted them.

By the 29th they had all assembled.

Pamela arriving with Lewis Elliot and Mawson and a motor full of pasteboard boxes found Jean just home from a picnic at Broadway, flushed with the sun and glowing with health and happiness.

"Well," said Pamela as she kissed her, "this is a new type of bride. Not the nerve-shattered, milliner-ridden creature with writer's cramp in her hand from thanking people for useless presents! You don't look as if you were worrying at all."

"I'm not," said Jean. "Why should I? There will be nobody there to criticise me. There are no preparations to make, so I needn't fuss. Biddy's right. It's the best way to be married."

"I needn't ask if you are happy, my Jean girl?"

Jean flung her arms round Pamela's neck.

"After having Biddy for my own the next best thing is having you for a sister. I owe you more than I can ever repay."

"Ah, my dear," said Pamela, "the debt is all on my side. You set the solitary in families . . ."

Mhor entered at that moment, shouting

that the car was waiting to take them to the station to meet the Macdonalds, and Jean hurried away.

An hour later the whole party met round the dinner-table. Mhor had been allowed to sit up. Other nights he consumed milk and bread and butter and eggs at 5.30, and went to bed an hour later, leaving Jock to change his clothes and descend to dinner and the play, an arrangement that caused a good deal of friction. But tonight all bitterness was forgotten, and Mhor beamed on everyone.

Mrs. Macdonald was in great form. She had come away, she told them, leaving the spring cleaning half done. "All the study chairs in the garden and Agnes rubbing down the walls, and Allan's men beating the carpet . . . In came the telegram, and after I got over the shock — I always expect the worst when I see a telegraph boy — I said to John, 'My best dress is not what it was, but I'm going,' and John was delighted, partly because he was driven out of his study, and he's never happy in any other room, but most of all because it was Jean. English Church or no English Church he'll help to marry Jean.

But," turning to the bride-to-be, "I can hardly believe it, Jean. It's only ten days since you left Priorsford, and tomorrow you're to be married. I think it was the War that taught us such hurried ways . . ." She sighed, and then went on briskly: "I went to see Mrs. M'Cosh before I left. She had had your letter, so I didn't need to break the news to her. She was wonderfully calm about it, and said that when people went away to England you might expect to hear anything. She said I was to tell Mhor that the cat was asking for him. And she is getting on with the cleaning. I think she said she had finished the dining-room and two bedrooms, and she was expecting the sweep today. She said you would like to know that the man had come about the leak in the tank, and it's all right. I saw Bella Bathgate as I was leaving The Rigs. She sent you and Lord Bidborough her kind regards . . . She has a free way of expressing herself, but I don't think she means to be disrespectful."

"Has she got lodgers just now?" Pamela asked.

"Oh, yes, she told me about them. One she dismissed as 'an auldish impident wumman wi' specs'; and the other as 'terrible genteel'. Both of them 'a sair come-down frae Miss Reston.' Now you are gone you are on a pedestal."

"I wasn't always on a pedestal," said Pamela, "but I shall always have a tenderness for Bella Bathgate and her parlour." She smiled to Lewis Elliot as she said it.

Jean, sitting beside Mr. Macdonald, thanked him for coming.

"Happy, Jean?" he asked.

"Utterly happy," said Jean. "So happy that I'm almost afraid. Isn't it odd how one seems to cower down to avoid drawing the attention of the Fates to one's happiness, saying, 'It is naught, it is naught,' in case disaster follows?"

"Don't worry about the Fates, Jean," Mr. Macdonald advised. "Rejoice in your happiness and God grant that the evil days may never come to you . . . What, Jock? Am I going to the play? I never went to a play in my life and I'm too old to begin."

"Oh, but, Mr. Macdonald," Jean broke in eagerly, "it isn't like a real theatre; it's all Shakespeare, and the place is simply black with clergymen, so you wouldn't feel out of place. You know you taught me first to care for Shakespeare, and I'd love to sit beside you and see a play acted."

Mr. Macdonald shook his head at her.

"Are you tempting your old minister, Jean? I've lived for sixty-five years without seeing a play, and I think I can go on to the end. It's not that it's wrong or that I think myself more virtuous than the rest of the world because I stay away. It's prejudice, if you like, intolerance perhaps, narrowness, bigotry — "

"Well, I think you and Mrs. Macdonald are better to rest this evening after your journey," Pamela said.

"Wouldn't you rather we stayed at home with you?" Jean asked. "We're only going to the play for something to do. We thought Davie would like it."

"It's *Romeo and Juliet*," Jock broke in. "A silly love-play, but there's a fine scene at the end where they all get killed. If you're sleeping, Mhor, I'll wake you up for that."

"I would like to stay with you," Jean said to Mrs. Macdonald.

"Never in the world. Off you go to your play and John and I will go early to bed and be fresh for tomorrow. When is the wedding?"

"At twelve o'clock in the church at Little St. Mary's," Lord Bidborough told her. "It's about ten miles from Stratford. I'm staying at the inn there tonight, and I trust you to see that they are all off to-morrow in good time." He turned to Mr. Macdonald. "It's most extraordinarily kind, sir, of you both to come. I knew Jean would never feel herself properly married if you were not there. And we wondered, Mrs. Macdonald, if you and your husband would add to your kindness by staying on here for a few days with the boys? You would see the country round, and then you would motor down with them and join us at Mintern Abbas for another week. D'you think you can spare the time? Jean would like you to see her in her own house, and I needn't say how honoured I would feel."

"Bless me," said Mrs. Macdonald. "That would mean a whole fortnight away from Priorsford. You could arrange about the preaching, John, but what about the spring cleaning? Agnes is a good creature, but I'm never sure that she scrubs behind the shutters; they're the old-fashioned kind, and need a lot of cleaning. However," with a deep sigh, "it's very kind of you to ask us, and at our age we won't have many more opportunities of having a holiday together, so perhaps we should seize this one. Dear me, Jean, I don't understand how you can look so bright so near your wedding. I cried and cried at mine. Have you not a qualm?"

Jean shook her head and laughed, and Mr. Macdonald said:

"Off with you all to your play. It's an odd thing to choose to go to tonight —

'*For never was there such a tale of woe
As this of Juliet and her Romeo.*' "

Mrs. Macdonald shook her head and sighed.

"I can't help thinking it's a poor preparation for a serious thing like marriage. I often don't feel so depressed at a funeral. There at least you know you've come to the end — nothing more can happen." Then her eyes twinkled and they left her laughing.

25

"My lord, you nod: you do not mind the
  play."
"Yes, by Saint Anne, do I . . . Madam
  lady . . . Would 'twere done."
  "THE TAMING OF THE SHREW"

JEAN awoke early on her wedding
morning and lay and thought over the
twenty-three years of her life, and
wondered what she had done to be so
blessed, for, looking back, it seemed one
long succession of sunny days. The dark
spots seemed so inconsiderable looking back
as to be hardly worth thinking about.

Her window faced the east, and the
morning sun shone in, promising yet
another fine day. Through the wall she
could hear Mhor, who always woke early,
busy at some game — possibly wigwams
with the blankets and sheets — already the
chamber-maid had complained of finding
the sheets knotted round the bed-posts. He
was singing a song to himself as he played.
Jean could hear his voice crooning. The

sound filled her with an immense tenderness. Little Mhor with his naughtiness and
his endearing ways! And beloved Jock
with his gruff voice and surprised blue eyes,
so tender-hearted, so easily affronted. And
David — the dear companion of her childhood who had shared with her all the
pleasures and penalties of life under the
iron rule of Great-aunt Alison, who understood as no one else could ever quite
understand, not even Biddy . . . But as she
thought of Biddy, she sprang out of bed,
and leaning out of the window she turned
her face to Little St. Mary's where her love
was, and where presently she would join
him.

Five hours later she would stand with
him in the church among the blossoms, and
they would be made man and wife, joined
together till death did them part. Jean
folded her hands on the window-sill. She
felt solemn and quiet and very happy. She
had not had much time for thinking in the
last few days, and she was glad of this
quiet hour. It was good on her wedding
morning to tell over in her mind, like
beads on a rosary, the excellent qualities of
her dear love. Could there be another

such in the wide world? Pamela was happy
with Lewis Elliot, and Lewis was kind and
good and in every way delightful, but
compared with Richard Plantagenet — In
this pedestrian world her Biddy had something of the old cavalier grace. Also, he had
more than a streak of Ariel. Would he be
content always to be settled at home? He
thought so now, but — Anyway, she
wouldn't try to bind him down, to keep
him to domesticity, making an eagle into a
barn-door fowl; she would go with him
where she could go, and where she would
be a burden she would send him alone
and keep a high heart till she could welcome
him home.

But it was high time that she had her
bath and dressed. It would be a morning
of dressing, for about 10.30 she would have
to dress again for her wedding. The
obvious course was to breakfast in bed, but
Jean had rejected the idea as "stuffy". To
waste the last morning of April in bed
with crumbs of toast and a tray was unthinkable, and by 9.30 Jean was at the
station giving Mhor an hour with his
beloved locomotives.

"You will like to come to Mintern

Abbas, won't you, Mhor?" she said.

Mhor considered.

"I would have liked it better," he confessed, "if there had been a railway line quite near. It was silly of whoever built it to put it so far away."

"When Mintern Abbas was built, railways hadn't been invented."

"I'm glad I wasn't invented before railways," said Mhor. "I would have been very dull."

"You'll have a pony to ride at Mintern Abbas. Won't that be nice?"

"Yes. Oh! there's the signal down at last. That'll be the express to London. I can hear the roar of it already."

Pamela's idea of a wedding garment for Jean was a soft, white, cloth coat and skirt, and a close-fitting hat with Mercury wings. Everything was simple, but everything was exquisitely fresh and dainty.

Pamela dressed her, Mrs. Macdonald looking on, and Mawson fluttering about, admiring but incompetent.

> " 'Something old and something new,
>   Something borrowed and something
>   blue,' "

Mrs. Macdonald quoted. "Have you got them all, Jean?"

"I think so. I've got a lace handkerchief that was my mother's — that's old. And blue ribbon in my under-things. And I've borrowed Pamela's prayer-book, for I haven't one of my own. And all the rest of me's new."

"And the sun is shining," said Pamela, "so you're fortified against ill-luck."

"I hope so," said Jean, gravely. "I must see if Mhor has washed his face this morning. I didn't notice at breakfast, and he's such an odd child, he'll wash every bit of himself and neglect his face. Perhaps you'll remember to look, Mrs. Macdonald, when you are with him here."

Mrs. Macdonald smiled at Jean's maternal tone, which persisted even on this, her day of glory.

"I've brought up four boys," she said, "so I ought to know something of their ways. It will be like old times to have Jock and Mhor to look after."

Mhor went in the car with Jean and Pamela and Mrs. Macdonald. The others had gone on in Lord Bidborough's car, as Mr. Macdonald wanted to see the vicar before the service to ensure that everything would go smoothly. The vicar had asked Jean about the music, saying that the village school-mistress, who was also the organist, was willing to play. "I don't much like 'The Voice that breathed o'er Eden,'" Jean told him: "but anything else would be very nice. It is so very kind of her to play."

Mhor mourned all the way to church about Peter being left behind. "There's poor Peter who is so fond of marriages — he goes to them all in Priorsford — tied up in the yard; and he knows how to behave in a church."

"It's a good deal more than you do," Mrs. Macdonald told him. "You're never still for one moment. I know of at least one person who has had to change his seat because of you. He said he got no benefit from the sermon watching you fidgeting about like an eel."

"It's because I don't care about sermons," Mhor replied, and relapsed into dignified silence — a silence sweetened by a large chocolate poked at him by Jean.

They walked through the churchyard,

with its quiet sleepers, into the cool church where David was waiting to give his sister away. Some of the village women, with little girls in clean pinafores clinging to their skirts, came shyly in after them and sat down at the door. Lord Bidborough, waiting for his bride, saw her come through the doorway, winged like Mercury, smiling back at the children following . . . then her eyes met his.

The first thing that Jean became aware of was that Mr. Macdonald was reading her own chapter.

"The wilderness and the solitary place shall be glad for them: and the desert shall rejoice and blossom as the rose . . .

"And an highway shall be there, and a way, and it shall be called The Way of Holiness: the unclean shall not pass over it: but it shall be for those: the wayfaring men, though fools, shall not err therein . . .

"No lion shall be there, nor any ravenous beast shall go up thereon, it shall not be found there, but the redeemed shall walk there.

"And the ransomed of the Lord shall return and come to Zion with songs and

485

everlasting joy upon their heads: they shall obtain joy and gladness, and sorrow and sighing shall flee away."

The school-mistress had played the wedding march from *Lohengrin*, and was prepared to play Mendelssohn as the party emerged from the vestry after signing the register; but when these formalities were completed Mrs. Macdonald whispered fiercely in Jean's ear, "You *can't* be married without 'O God of Bethel'," and ousting the school-mistress from her place at the organ she struck the opening notes.

They knew it by heart — Jean and Davie and Jock and Mhor and Lewis Elliot — and they sang it with the unction with which one sings the songs of Zion by Babylon's streams.

"Through each perplexing path of life
Our wandering footsteps guide,
Give us each day our daily bread
And raiment fit provide.

O spread Thy covering wings around
Till all our wanderings cease,
And at our Father's loved abode
Our souls arrive in peace."

Out in the sunshine, among the blossoms, Jean stood with her husband, and was kissed and blessed.

"Jean, Lady Bidborough," said Pamela.

"Gosh, Maggie!" said Jock, "I quite forgot Jean would be Lady Bidborough. What a joke!"

"She doesn't look any different," Mhor complained.

"Surely you don't want her different," Mrs. Macdonald said.

"Not *very* different," said Mhor, "but she's pretty small for a Lady — not nearly as tall as Richard Plantagenet."

"As high as my heart," said Lord Bidborough. "The correct height, Mhor."

The vicar lunched with them at the inn. There were no speeches, and no one tried to be funny.

Jock rebuked Jean for eating too much. "It's not manners for a bride to have more than one help."

"It's odd," said Jean, "but the last time I was married the same thing happened. D'you remember, Davie? You were the minister and I was the bride, and I had my pinafore buttoned down the front to look grown up, and Tommy Sprott was the bridegroom. And Great-aunt Alison let us have a cake and some shortbread, and we made strawberry wine ourselves. And at the wedding-feast Tommy Sprott suddenly pointed to me and said, 'Put that girl out: she's eating all the shortbread.' Me — his new-made bride!"

The whole village turned out to see the newly-married couple leave, including the blacksmith and three dogs. It hurt Mhor afresh to see the dogs barking happily, while Peter, who would so have enjoyed a fight with them, was spending a boring day in the stable-yard, but Jean comforted him with the thought of Peter's delight at Mintern Abbas.

"Will Richard Plantagenet mind if he chases rabbits?"

"You won't, will you, Biddy?" Jean said.

"Not a bit. If you'll stand between me and the wrath of the keepers, Peter may do any mortal thing he likes."

As they drove away through the golden afternoon Jean said: "I've always wondered what people talked about when they went away on their wedding journey?"

"They don't talk: they just look into each other's eyes in a sort of ecstasy, saying, 'Is it I? Is it thou?'"

"That would be pretty silly," said Jean. "We shan't do that, anyway."

Her husband laughed.

"You are really very like Jock, my Jean . . . D'you remember what your admired Dr. Johnson said? 'If I had no duties I would spend my life in driving briskly in a post-chaise with a pretty woman, but she should be one who could understand me and would add something to the conversation.' Wise old man! Tell me, Pennyplain, you're not fretting about leaving the boys? You'll see them again in a few days. Are you dreading having me undiluted?"

"My dear, you don't suppose the boys come first now, do you? I love them as dearly as ever I did, but compared with you — it's so different, absolutely different — I can't explain. I don't love you like people in books, all on fire and saying wonderful things all the time. But to be with you fills me with utter content. I told you that night in Hopetoun that the boys filled my life. And then you went away, and

I found that though I had the boys my life and my heart were empty. You are my life, Biddy."

"My blessed child."

About four o'clock they came home.

An upland country of pastures and shallow dales fell quietly to the river levels, and on a low spur that was its last outpost stood Mintern Abbas, a thing half of the hills and half of the broad valleys. At its back, beyond the home-woods, was a remote land of sheep walks and forgotten hamlets; at its feet the young Thames in lazy reaches wound through water-meadows. Down the slopes of old pasture fell cascades of daffodils, and in the fringes of the coppices lay the blue haze of wild hyacinths. The house was so wholly in tune with the landscape that the eye did not at once detect it, for its gables might have been part of wood or hillside. It was of stone, and built in many periods and in many styles which time had subtly blended so that it seemed a perfect thing without beginning, as long descended as the folds of downs which sheltered it. The austere Tudor front, the Restoration wing, the offices built under Queen Anne, the library added in the days of the Georges, had by some alchemy become one. Peace and long memories were in every line of it, and that air of a home which belongs only to places that have been loved for generations. It breathed ease and comfort, but yet had a tonic vigour in it, for while it stood knee-deep in the green valley its head was fanned by moorland winds.

Jean held her breath as she saw it. It seemed to her the most perfect thing that could be imagined.

She walked in shyly, winged like Mercury, to be greeted respectfully by a row of servants. Jean shook hands with each one, smiling at them with her "doggy" eyes, wishing all the time for Mrs. M'Cosh, who was not specially respectful, but always homely and humorous.

Tea was ready in a small panelled room, with a view of the lawns and the river.

"I asked them to put it here," Lord Bidborough said. "I thought you might like to have this for your own sitting-room. It's just a little like the room at The Rigs."

"Oh, Biddy, it is. I saw it when I came in. May I really have it for my own? It feels as if people had been happy in it. It has a welcoming air. And what a gorgeous tea!" She sat down at the table and pulled off her gloves. "Isn't life frightfully well arranged? Every day is so full of so many different things, and meals are such a comfort. No, I'm not greedy, but what I mean is that it would be just a little 'stawsome' if you had nothing to do but *love* all the time."

"I'm Scots, partly, but I'm not so Scots as all that. What does 'stawsome' mean exactly?"

"It means," Jean began, and hesitated — "I'm afraid it means — sickening."

Her husband laughed as he sat down beside her.

"I'm willing to believe that you mean to be more complimentary than you sound. I'm very certain you would never let love-making become 'stawsome'. . . . There are hot things in that dish — or would you rather have a sandwich? This is the first time we've ever had tea alone, Jean."

"I know. Isn't it heavenly to think that we shall be together now all the rest of our lives? Biddy, I was thinking . . . If — if ever we have a son I should like to call him Peter Reid. Would you mind?"

"My darling!"

"It wouldn't go very well with the Quintins and the Reginalds and all the other names, but it would be a sort of Thank you to the poor rich man who was so kind to me."

"All the same, I sometimes wish he hadn't left you all that money. I would rather have given you everything myself."

"Like King Cophetua. I've no doubt it was all right for him, but it can't have been much fun for the beggar maid. No matter how kind and generous a man is, to be dependent on him for every penny can't be nice. It's different, I think, when the man is poor. Then they both work, the man earning, the woman saving and contriving. . . . But what's the good of talking about money? Money only matters when you haven't got any."

"O wise young Judge!"

"No; it's really quite a wise statement when you think of it . . . Let's go outside. I want to see the river near." She turned while going out to the door and looked with great satisfaction on the room that was to be her own.

"I *am* glad of this room, Biddy. It has such a kind feeling. The other rooms are lovely, but they are meant for crowds of people. This says tea, and a fire and a book and a friend — the four nicest things in the world."

They walked slowly down to the river.

"Swans!" said Jean, "and a boat!"

"In Shelley's dreams of Heaven there are always a river and a boat — I read that somewhere. . . . Well, what do you think of Mintern Abbas? Did I over-praise?"

Jean shook her head.

"That wouldn't be easy. It's the most wonderful place . . . like a dream. Look at it now in the afternoon light, pale gold like honey. And the odd thing is, it's in the very heart of England, and yet it might almost be Scotland."

"I thought that would appeal to you. Will you learn to love it, do you think?"

"I shan't have to learn. I love it already."

"And feel at home?"

"Yes . . . but, Biddy, there's just one

thing. I shall love our home with all my heart and be absolutely content here if you promise me one thing — that when I die I'll be taken to Priorsford . . . I know it's nonsense. I know it doesn't matter where the fickle dust that was me lies, but I don't think I could be quite happy if I didn't know that one day I should lie within sound of Tweed . . . You're laughing, Biddy."

"My darling, like you I've sometimes wondered what people talked about on their honeymoon, but never in my wildest imaginings did I dream that they talked of where they would like to be buried."

Jean hid an abashed face for a moment against her husband's sleeve; then she looked up at him and laughed.

"It sounds mad — but I mean it," she said.

"It's all the fault of your Great-aunt Alison. Tell me, Jean girl — no, I'm not laughing — how will this day look from your death-bed ?"

Jean looked at the river, then she looked into her husband's eyes, and put both her hands into his.

"Ah, my dear love," she said softly, "if

495

that day leaves me any remembrance of what I feel today, I'll be so glad to have lived that I'll go out of the world cheering."

THE END